EVERYMAN,

I WILL GO WITH THEE,

AND BE THY GUIDE,

IN THY MOST NEED

TO GO BY THY SIDE

EVERYMAN'S POCKET CLASSICS

BERLIN STORIES

EDITED BY PHILIP HENSHER

EVERYMAN'S POCKET CLASSICS
Alfred A. Knopf New York London Toronto

THIS IS A BORZOI BOOK
PUBLISHED BY ALFRED A. KNOPF

This selection by Philip Hensher first published in
Everyman's Library 2019
Copyright © 2019 by Everyman's Library

All rights reserved. Published in the United States by Alfred A. Knopf,
a division of Penguin Random House LLC, New York, and in
Canada by Penguin Random House Canada Limited, Toronto.
Distributed by Penguin Random House LLC, New York. Published
in the United Kingdom by Everyman's Library, 50 Albemarle Street,
London W1S 4BD and distributed by Penguin Random House UK,
20 Vauxhall Bridge Road, London SW1V 2SA.

www.randomhouse.com/everymans
www.everymanslibrary.co.uk

ISBN 978-1-101-90817-4 (US)
978-1-84159-626-6 (UK)

A CIP catalogue reference for this book is available from the
British Library

Typography by Peter B. Willberg

Typeset in the UK by Input Data Services Ltd, Isle Abbotts, Somerset

Printed and bound in Germany by GGP Media GmbH, Pössneck

BERLIN STORIES

Contents

FOREWORD

COMPARED TO PARIS, London or Rome, Berlin has a short history. There are no signs of habitation before the twelfth century, and it remained a relatively insignificant place until the eighteenth century. At the end of the seventeenth century, Berlin's population was around 10,000, when Paris and London both had over half a million inhabitants. After that, the city grew explosively. It is substantially a creation of the nineteenth century, with all that era's addiction to modernity, technology and novelty. Its most celebrated contribution to urban architecture, the Wall, was only erected in the early 1960s. That was demolished thirty years ago in any case. It has always been a city of desperate modernity.

The physical substance is reflected in its characteristic ways of behaving and interacting. It has been a city dedicated to discovering new ways of living. In most decades of the twentieth century, Berlin has produced whole classes of people very conscious that they are living lives that nobody has ever attempted before. It is an arena of the possible, where the imagination carves out cities of the future. The first social housing projects are here. Gay men and lesbians started to live their lives openly in large numbers in the 1920s. The postwar division of the city and the Wall, too, created multiple possibilities, few foreseen, some explosive. In the aftermath of unification, the city was cheap and run-down; it quickly became a hub for creative artists. The sense of making it up as you go along is never far away in Berlin.

The fiction of Berlin exemplifies much of this excitement. Unlike most capital cities, it imposes no obligation on writers to come to terms with it. There are very many great German and German-language writers with absolutely nothing to say about Berlin. Those who do write about it, I suspect, are those who were drawn to it. Such writers may be of a particular type. Despite the different settings, and the totally different nature of each new experience described, a mood recurs. It is a mood of wonder and astonishment, lightly veiled in an affectation of chic boredom. We have seen all this before, suggests each writer, uncovering scenes that have never been dreamt of until this moment. A layer of period nostalgia has settled over Fontane, but in his time, he was an artist of the present moment, even of modernity. Erich Kästner's Fabian, behaving according to his most animal instincts and finding no resistance in those around him, is another example of this languid joy in the unprecedented. Another might be Irmgard Keun's heroine, making her way in the big city with what resources she has, or Ernst Haffner's gang of juvenile derelicts.

These innovations don't always come from outcasts and drop-outs. Sometimes lives of unanticipated modernity are conducted in accordance with the central apparatuses of control and orthodoxy. Thomas Brussig's Stasi officers conduct their meaningless lives of surveillance like realist novelists determined to leave nothing out of the narrative. The Wall imposes its obligation to try to understand – Peter Schneider's wall jumper and Uwe Timm's wanderer in a post-Wall landscape both seem like naïfs, so colossal and impregnable are the things they are trying to understand. Their behaviour is predicted and constrained by the Wall and its sudden absence. For Wladimir Kaminer or Kevin Barry, the newest arrivals in the city are literally making things up as they go along, finding out what the rules of engagement might be. For outsiders like Thomas Wolfe or Christopher Isherwood, it just doesn't seem possible to guess what might happen next; other outsiders, like Chloe Aridjis, place their trust in solitary wandering through the challenges of the city, old and new. Only at the moment of the shattering of the Wall, in Günter Grass's prophetic and historic phantasmagoria, does it seem urgent to gaze backwards, to Fontane and beyond; his characters appear to be given a long vista by the sudden appearance of gaps in the long-standing barrier. Otherwise Berlin lives in the moment. When everything hangs on a thread, there is little appetite for nostalgia or reflection. In dread or excitement, the fiction looks forward.

I first went to Berlin in the 1980s, when the division between east and west seemed permanent, and the general mood was not exactly despairing, but resigned to the fact that nothing much mattered. You could do anything you liked. Nobody would care. I spent much more time there in the mid 1990s. The past made itself apparent – the bullet holes on Wilhelmine façades, the remaining stretches of the Wall. Or just finding that the kitchen cupboard in the flat in Prenzlauer Berg I was borrowing was still half full of dried soups and dessert powders from the DDR. But in this city, you could not look back; you had to decide what you were going to do now, today, this minute.

It was a time of extraordinary possibilities and mad improvisations. People would open illegal bars in abandoned buildings or their own apartments. Some enterprises were undertaken according to anarchist principles. Entertainment could take surprising forms; an omni-sexual tango evening of alarming accomplishment in a Kreuzberg club, or a competition between half a dozen drag queens to determine who made the best goulash (the whole bar had a taste). Once I turned up at a regular bar of mine which occupied a boat on the canal, only to find that it had sunk the night before. Some friends of mine idly bought an entire apartment block in Schöneberg for almost nothing. It was incredibly cheap to live there. I was startled to discover that I could pay six weeks' rent for a flat in Prenzlauer Berg by writing one book review. In such an atmosphere, people have the time to sit around and talk. To listen, as well. I heard a lot of stories, and came to think of the city as a hatcher of stories, many of which had simply never been told before.

The city has changed a good deal in the twenty years since then. The underground experience I remembered has been packaged up and delivered to the entranced young of Europe by hardnosed corporations. The last time I went to the bar that held the great drag-queen goulash competition, the barman had no time or inclination to talk; my neighbour at the bar was keen to explain how much profit he had made from property. It is, unimaginably, now expensive to live in Prenzlauer Berg, or Kreuzberg, or anywhere in Berlin.

For the moment, Berlin is in an unexpected imperial phase of expansion and wealth, its pleasures organized and costed up for the prosperous bourgeoisie and their children. Whether it is currently a fruitful subject for the investigation of the imagination is, I think, a question worth debating. The best Berlin fiction of recent years is concerned with outsiders and with the past. Jean-Philippe Toussaint's novel *Television*, which I extract here, is largely devoted to trying to keep Berlin out of the temporary resident's existence; its idiosyncrasies have a knack of creeping in. Other observers, like Chloe Aridjis, explore the new arrival's necessary and lonely wandering. Finally, one of the most admired of recent German novels, Jenny Erpenbeck's *Go, Went, Gone*, sets an encounter between German high culture and new arrivals in the always provisional arena of Kreuzberg, in a temporary city of tents and squatting. History is here, but also some sense of the future metropolis, and the obligations of the present day. Right now, in 2019, the overwhelming confidence of the capital city is balanced by a creative uncertainty in its fiction. Nobody could say what new forms of existence, and imagination, are going to arise from the new Berlin, in the process of being created, of *becoming*. But that has always been the case.

Philip Hensher

THEODOR FONTANE

From

EFFI BRIEST

Translated by Mike Mitchell

CHAPTER 23

FRIEDRICHSTRASSE STATION WAS crowded, but despite that Effi spotted her Mama, with Cousin Dagobert beside her, from the window of her compartment. Great was their joy at seeing each other again, the wait in the luggage-hall didn't make too great a demand on their patience, and in less than five minutes the cab was driving along Dorotheen-strasse, beside the track of the horse-drawn tram, towards Schadowstrasse, on the first corner of which the pension was. Roswitha was delighted, and enjoyed the way Annie stretched out her little hands to the lights.

Now they were there, and Effi was given her two rooms. They were not, as expected, next to Frau von Briest's, but still in the same corridor, and once everything was in place and Annie settled in a cot, Effi went back to her mother's room, a little parlour with a fireplace in which a fire was burning – a small fire, because the weather was mild, almost warm. Places for three had been set at the round table with the green-shaded lamp, and the tea things were on a little side-table.

'You've got a delightful room, Mama,' Effi said as she sat down opposite the sofa, only to get up immediately to busy herself with the tea. 'May I play the tea-lady again, Mama?'

'Of course, Effi dear. But only for Dagobert and yourself. I'm afraid I have to refrain, which I find almost too hard to bear.'

'I understand, because of your eyes. But tell me now,

Mama, what's the situation with them? In the cab, clattering away as it was, we only talked about Innstetten and our great career, much too much, and it can't go on like that. Believe me, your eyes are more important to me, and in one respect I can see that they are quite unchanged, thank God, and still give me the same friendly look as always.' And she rushed over to her Mama and kissed her hand.

'You're so impetuous. Still the same old Effi.'

'Oh no, Mama. Not the same old Effi. I only wish I were. You change once you're married.'

Her cousin laughed. 'I can't see much of that, Cousin; you're even prettier, that's all. And I suspect the impetuosity's not gone either.'

'There speaks the cousin,' her Mama said, but Effi would have none of it and said, 'Dagobert, you're everything – apart from a judge of character. It's strange. You officers are never good judges of character, certainly not you young ones. You only have eyes for yourselves and your recruits, and those in the cavalry have their horses as well. They know absolutely nothing at all.'

'Whence all this wisdom, Cousin? You don't know any officers. Kessin, I read, has declined the hussars intended for it, a case unique in the annals of the world, by the way. Or are you harking back to the old days? You were still half a child when the hussars from Rathenow went over to Hohen-Cremmen.'

'To that I could say that children are the best observers, but I won't. That's all just idle chat. I want to know how Mama's eyes are.'

Frau von Briest told them that the eye specialist had said it was blood pressure on the brain. That caused the flickering. It had to be dealt with by dieting – beer, coffee, tea, all off the menu – and an occasional removal of some blood, then it would soon improve. 'He was talking about a fortnight. But I know doctors' estimates; a fortnight means six weeks, and I'll still be here when Innstetten comes and you move into your new apartment. I won't deny that that's the best thing about the whole business and reconciles me to the long treatment. Just find something really nice. I thought of Landgrafenstrasse or Keithstrasse, elegant and not over-expensive. For you'll have to tighten your belts. Innstetten's position is a great honour, but it won't bring in much. And Briest's complaining as well. Prices are dropping, and he tells me every day that if they don't introduce protective duties he'll be reduced to beggary and have to give up Hohen-Cremmen. You know how he likes to exaggerate. But now help yourself, Dagobert, and tell us something amusing, if you can. Reports on illnesses are always boring, and your nearest and dearest only listen because they have to. I'm sure Effi would like to hear something, perhaps a story from *Die Fliegenden Blätter* or *Kladderadatsch*, though that's said not to be very good any more.'

'Oh, it's just as good as it used to be. They've still got Strudelwitz and Prudelwitz, and stories about them write themselves.'

'My favourites are Karlchen Miessnick and Wippchen von Bernau.'

'Yes, they're the best. Though forgive me for saying so, my fair cousin, but Wippchen isn't from *Kladderadatsch* and he hasn't anything to do at the moment, since there are no wars for him to write his comic reports on. We'd like to have our turn and finally get rid of this terrible emptiness.' As he said that, he drew his fingers across his chest from the buttonhole to his arm.

'Oh, that's all mere vanity. Tell me something interesting instead. What's in vogue?'

'Well, it's strange, Cousin. It's not to everyone's taste. At the moment we have Bible jokes.'

'Bible jokes? What can they be? . . . The Bible and jokes don't go together.'

'That's what I said, they're not to everyone's taste. But acceptable or not, they're very popular. It's just a fashion, like plover's eggs.'

'Well, if it's not too outrageous, give us an example. Can you?'

'Of course I can. It starts with a question – all these jokes start in that way, this one with a very simple question: Who was the first house-guest? Come on, can you work it out?'

'The first house-guest? I've no idea. Who was it?'

'The first house-guest was sorrow. It says in the Book of Job, "No longer shalt thou be visited by sorrow".'

Effi repeated the sentence, shaking her head. She was very much one of those fortunate people who have no appreciation of that kind of play on words, and her cousin got into more and more of a tangle as he tried to explain the joke.

'Oh, I see. I'm sorry, Dagobert, but I think that really is *too* stupid.'

'Yes, it is stupid,' Dagobert said, abashed.

'Stupid and unseemly; it's enough to spoil Berlin for me. I put Kessin behind me to have a social life again, and the first thing I hear is a Bible joke. Mama's kept silent too, and that says enough. But I'll help you get out of this awkward predicament . . .'

'Please do, Cousin . . .'

'. . . get you out of this awkward predicament by taking it seriously as a good omen that the first thing said to me here by my cousin Dagobert was, "No longer shalt thou be visited by sorrow." It's odd, my cousin, but however weak it is as a joke, I'm still grateful for it.'

22

Hardly was he out of the noose of his own making than Dagobert was trying to poke fun at Effi's earnest tone, but gave up as soon as he saw that she wasn't amused by it.

He left soon after ten, promising to come the next day to see how they were.

As soon as he had gone, Effi also withdrew to her room.

The next day the weather was fine, and mother and daughter set out early. They first went to the eye clinic, where Effi stayed in the waiting-room and leafed through a magazine, then headed for the Tiergarten area, as far as the zoo, to see if they could find an apartment. And they did actually find something suitable in Keithstrasse, which was what they had been hoping for from the very first; the only problem was that it was a new building, not yet finished, and damp. 'It's not possible, Effi,' Frau von Briest said. 'It's out of the question for reasons of health. And then, a Geheimrat isn't the kind of person who takes a cheap tenancy while the apartment dries out.'

Even though she liked the apartment very much, Effi was more than happy to accept these considerations because she wasn't bothered about settling the matter quickly, on the contrary, 'more time, more choice', and putting off a decision was what suited her best. 'But we'll still keep an eye on that apartment, Mama, it's in such a lovely situation and is basically what I had in mind.' Then the two of them drove back to the city centre, dined in a restaurant that had been recommended to them, and went to the opera in the evening, to which the doctor had given his consent on condition that Frau von Briest went to hear more than to see.

The next few days were passed in a similar way; they were genuinely happy to be together again and to enjoy a good long chat with each other. More than once Effi, who, when she felt well, was not only a good raconteur and listener but also had a ready tongue when it came to scandal-mongering, was her old high-spirited self, and her Mama wrote home saying how happy she was to see the 'child' so cheerful and full of laughter again; it took them back to the days almost two years ago when they had bought her trousseau. Cousin Briest was the same as ever too. And that was indeed the case, though with the one difference: his appearances were less frequent, and when asked why he replied, apparently seriously, 'You're too dangerous for me, Cousin.' At that mother and daughter burst out laughing, and Effi said, 'You're still quite young, of course, Dagobert, but no longer young enough for that kind of flirtation.'

Almost a fortnight passed in this way. Innstetten's letters were more and more pressing and becoming rather caustic, almost towards his mother-in-law as well, so that Effi saw it wasn't possible to put off a decision any longer and she really had to take an apartment. But what about after that? There were still three weeks to go before the move to Berlin, and Innstetten was insisting she return soon. There was only one way out: she must put on an act again and pretend to be ill.

She didn't find that easy, and for more than one reason. But it had to be, and once she had decided that, she had also decided how the role was to be played, right down to the very last detail.

'Mama, as you can see, Innstetten's getting rather touchy about my continued absence. I think we'll have to give in and take an apartment today. Then I'll go home tomorrow. But, oh, it will be so hard for me to leave you.'

Frau von Briest agreed. 'And which apartment will you choose?'

'The first one, the one in Keithstrasse, of course. I liked

24

it so well, right from the start, and so did you. It won't be entirely dried out yet, but it is the summer, which is a help. And if the damp is too bad and I get a bit of rheumatism, I've always got Hohen-Cremmen.'

'Don't tempt fate, child; sometimes you can get a touch of rheumatism and you've no idea why.'

These words suited Effi very well. She took the apartment that morning and wrote a card to Innstetten, telling him she'd be returning the next day. The cases were then immediately packed and all preparations made.

But the next morning Effi called her Mama to her bedside and said, 'I can't go, Mama. I've got such aches and pains, I feel sore right across my back. I almost think it must be rheumatism. I'd never have thought it was so painful.'

'You see? Now what did I tell you? You shouldn't tempt fate. Yesterday you were dismissive about it and today here it is. When I see Schweigger, I'll ask him what you should do.'

'No, not Schweigger. He's a specialist, and it's not on to consult him on something else, he might even take it amiss. I think the best thing is just to wait and see. It might pass. I'll live on tea and soda-water for the whole day, and if that makes me sweat, I may get over it.'

Frau von Briest agreed to that course of action, but insisted she must feed herself properly. To starve oneself, as used to be the fashion, she said, was quite wrong and simply weakened one; in that respect she was completely on the side of the new school: take in plenty of food.

All this was of no little comfort to Effi. She sent a telegram to Innstetten in which she spoke of the tiresome occurrence, causing an annoying, though only temporary, delay to her return; then she said to Roswitha, 'You'll have to fetch me some books now, Roswitha; it won't be difficult, I want some old ones, very old ones.'

'Of course, Madam. The lending-library's only just round the corner. What should I get?'

'I'll write them down, a selection, sometimes they haven't got the one you happen to want.' Roswitha brought pencil and paper and Effi wrote down: Walter Scott, *Ivanhoe* or *Quentin Durward*; Fenimore Cooper, *The Spy*; Dickens, *David Copperfield*; Willibald Alexis, *Herr von Bredow's Trousers*.

Roswitha read through the list and cut off the last line in the other room; she would find it embarrassing, both for herself and for her mistress, to hand over the note in its original form.

The day passed without anything special happening. The next morning she was no better, nor on the third day.

'This can't go on, Effi. If something like that gets established, it's difficult to get rid of it again. It's these protracted illnesses doctors warn you about most strongly, and rightly so.'

Effi sighed. 'Yes, Mama, but whom should we consult? Not a young doctor; I don't know why, but I'd feel embarrassed.'

'A young doctor's always embarrassing, and it's all the worse if he isn't. But you can be reassured; I'll bring a very old one who treated me when I was still a boarder at Hecker's school, that was some twenty years ago. At that time he was close on fifty and had lovely grey hair, very curly. He was a ladies' man, but kept it within limits. Doctors who forget that never succeed, and quite right too; our women, at least society women, still have a sound core.'

'You think so? I'm always happy when I hear something good like that. For now and then you hear something different. And it must often be difficult. So what is the name of this Geheimrat? I assume your doctor has that title.'

'Geheimrat Rummschüttel.'

Effi laughed out loud. 'Rummschüttel – Dr Shake-it-all-about! And that a doctor for someone who can't move.'

'You do say some strange things, Effi. You can't be in all that great pain.'

'No, not at the moment. It's changing all the time.'

Geheimrat Rummschüttel appeared next morning. Frau von Briest welcomed him, and when he saw Effi, his first words were, 'Just like your Mama!'

Her mother tried to reject the comparison, saying that twenty years and more were a long time, but Rummschüttel stuck to his opinion, assuring them that while not every face imprinted itself on his mind, once the impression was there it stayed for good. 'And now, my dear Frau von Innstetten, what's the problem, how can we help you?'

'Oh, Herr Geheimrat, I find it difficult to tell you what it is. It's constantly changing. Just at the moment it seems to have disappeared. At first I was thinking of rheumatism, but I could almost believe it's neuralgia, pains down my back, and then I can't sit up. My Papa suffers from neuralgia, so I could observe what it's like when I still lived at home. Perhaps it's hereditary.'

'Very probably,' Rummschüttel said, after having felt her pulse and given his patient a brief but sharp scrutiny. 'Very probably, Frau Baronin.' However, what he was thinking to himself was, 'Acting sick to get off school, a virtuoso performance. A coquette *comme il faut*.' He didn't allow any of this to be seen, instead he said, as earnestly as any patient could desire, 'Rest and warmth is the best I can advise. Some medicine, nothing nasty, will do the rest.'

And he stood up to write the prescription: oil of bitter almonds, half an ounce; oil of neroli, two ounces. 'I would ask you to take half a teaspoon of this every two hours, my dear Frau Baronin. It will calm your nerves. And one more thing I must insist on: no mental exertion, no visits, no reading.' As he said that, he pointed to the book beside her.

'It's Scott.'

'Oh, there's no objection to that. Best of all is travel-writing. I'll call round again tomorrow.'

Effi had kept to her role wonderfully well, but despite that, once she was alone – her Mama was seeing the doctor out – she felt herself go bright red; she had very clearly seen that he had responded to her play-acting with some play-acting of his own. He was clearly a gentleman with great experience of life, who could see everything clearly, but didn't want to see everything, perhaps because he knew that such things sometimes had to be respected. But if there were pretences that shouldn't be respected, was not the one she was acting out of that kind?

Soon afterwards her Mama came back, and mother and daughter were full of praise for the refined old man who, despite the fact that he was nearly seventy, had something youthful about him. 'Send Roswitha out to the pharmacy right away . . . but you're only to take a dose every three hours, he said to me outside. That's the way he was when I knew him before, he didn't often prescribe medicines and never a lot; but it was always invigorating and helped straight away.'

Rummschüttel came two days later, then just every third day, because he could see how embarrassed the young woman was at his visits. This endeared her to him, and after this third visit he had come to a firm opinion: 'There's something here compelling this woman to behave as she is doing.' He had long since stopped feeling irritated by such things.

At his fourth visit Rummschüttel found that Effi was up,

sitting in a rocking-chair, a book in her hand and Annie beside her.

'Ah, my dear Frau Baronin. I'm delighted. I don't ascribe it to my medicine; this fine weather, these bright March days, illness just melts away. My congratulations. And your Frau Mama?'

'She's gone out, Herr Geheimrat, to Keithstrasse where we've rented an apartment. My husband will be here in a few days' time, and I very much hope to be able to introduce you to him once the apartment's in order. For I assume I can look forward to you taking care of me in future.'

He bowed.

'Our new apartment', she went on, 'has just been built, and I'm worried about it. Do you think, Herr Geheimrat, that the damp walls . . .'

'Not in the least, my dear Frau Baronin. Heat the place thoroughly for three or four days, keeping the doors and windows open, and you can risk it, I assure you. And as far as your neuralgia was concerned, it wasn't anything to be very concerned about, but I'm delighted your caution gave me the opportunity to renew an old acquaintance and make a new one.' He repeated his bow, gave Annie a friendly look, and left, giving his regards to her mother.

Hardly had he gone than Effi was at her desk writing a letter.

'DEAR INNSTETTEN,

Rummschüttel was here just now and has pronounced me recovered. I am now well enough to travel, tomorrow for example; but it's the 24th already and you're coming here on the 28th. And, anyway, I'm still suffering from the after-effects. I assume you'll understand if I give up the whole idea of making the journey. Our things are already on the way, and if I came we'd have to stay in Hoppensack's Hotel, like visitors. We must think about the cost as well, our expenses are going to pile up; amongst other things we'll have Rummschüttel's retainer to consider, if he's to remain our doctor. He's a delightful old gentleman. In medical matters he's not quite considered top-drawer, a "ladies' doctor" his jealous colleagues say. But that expression also contains praise, not everyone knows how to deal with us. The fact that I can't say farewell to the Kessiners personally doesn't really matter. I went to see Gieshübler. Frau Crampas always remained distant from me, distant to the point of rudeness; that only leaves the Pastor and Dr Hannemann and Crampas. Give my best wishes to the latter. I will be sending cards to the families out in the country; the Güldenklees, you tell me, are in Italy (I can't imagine what they're doing there), so that just leaves the three others. Make my excuses for me as best you can. You're the man who knows the proprieties, how to find the right word. I'll perhaps write a note to Frau von Padden – I really thought her delightful on New Year's Eve – expressing my regret. Send me a telegram to say whether you're in agreement with all that.

As ever,
your Effi.'

Effi posted the letter herself, as if by that she could make the answer arrive sooner, and the next morning the telegram she had requested from Innstetten arrived: 'In agreement with everything.' Her heart leapt with joy, and she hurried down the stairs to the nearest cab-rank. 'Keithstrasse 1c.' And the cab flew down Unter den Linden, then along Tiergartenstrasse, and stopped outside their new apartment.

Upstairs the things that had arrived the previous day were still lying around higgledy-piggledy, but that didn't bother

her, and when she stepped out on to the wide balcony the Tiergarten Park lay there before her, on the other side of the canal bridge, all its trees already showing a shimmer of green. Above it the sun was shining brightly in a clear blue sky.

She quivered with excitement and took a deep breath. Then she stepped back into the room from the balcony, put her hands together, and looked up.

'And now, with God's aid, a new life. Things are going to be different.'

ROBERT WALSER

THE LITTLE BERLINER

Translated by Harriet Watts

PAPA BOXED MY ears today, in a most fond and fatherly manner, of course. I had used the expression: 'Father, you must be nuts.' It was indeed a bit careless of me. 'Ladies should employ exquisite language,' our German teacher says. She's horrible. But Papa won't allow me to ridicule her, and perhaps he's right. After all, one does go to school to exhibit a certain zeal for learning and a certain respect. Besides, it is cheap and vulgar to discover funny things in a fellow human being and then to laugh at them. Young ladies should accustom themselves to the fine and the noble – I quite see that. No one desires any work from me, no one will ever demand it of me; but everyone will expect to find that I am refined in my ways. Shall I enter some profession in later life? Of course not! I'll be an elegant young wife; I shall get married. It is possible that I'll torment my husband. But that would be terrible. One always despises oneself whenever one feels the need to despise someone else. I am twelve years old. I must be very precocious – otherwise, I would never think of such things. Shall I have children? And how will that come about? If my future husband isn't a despicable human being, then, yes, then I'm sure of it, I shall have a child. Then I shall bring up this child. But I still have to be brought up myself. What silly thoughts one can have!

Berlin is the most beautiful, the most cultivated city in the world. I would be detestable if I weren't unshakably convinced of this. Doesn't the Kaiser live here? Would he need to live here if he didn't like it here best of all? The other day I saw the royal children in an open car. They are enchanting. The crown prince looks like a high-spirited young god, and how beautiful seemed the noble lady at his side. She was completely hidden in fragrant furs. It seemed that blossoms rained down upon the pair out of the blue sky. The Tiergarten is marvelous. I go walking there almost every day with our young lady, the governess. One can go for hours under the green trees, on straight or winding paths. Even Father, who doesn't really need to be enthusiastic about anything, is enthusiastic about the Tiergarten. Father is a cultivated man. I'm convinced he loves me madly. It would be horrible if he read this, but I shall tear up what I have written. Actually, it is not at all fitting to be still so silly and immature and, at the same time, already want to keep a diary. But, from time to time, one becomes somewhat bored, and then one easily gives way to what is not quite right. The governess is very nice. Well, I mean, in general. She is devoted and she loves me. In addition, she has real respect for Papa – that is the most important thing. She is slender of figure. Our previous governess was fat as a frog. She always seemed to be about to burst. She was English. She's still English today, of course, but from the moment she allowed herself liberties, she was no longer our concern. Father kicked her out.

The two of us, Papa and I, are soon to take a trip. It is that time of the year now when respectable people simply have to take a trip. Isn't it a suspicious sort of person who doesn't take a trip at such a time of blossoming and blooming? Papa goes to the seashore and apparently lies there day after day and lets himself be baked dark brown by the summer sun. He always looks healthiest in September. The paleness of exhaustion is not becoming to his face. Incidentally, I myself love the suntanned look in a man's face. It is as if he had just come home from war. Isn't that just like a child's nonsense? Well, I'm still a child, of course. As far as I'm concerned, I'm taking a trip to the south. First of all, a little while to Munich and then to Venice, where a person who is unspeakably close to me lives – Mama. For reasons whose depths I cannot understand and consequently cannot evaluate, my parents live apart. Most of the time I live with Father. But naturally Mother also has the right to possess me at least for a while. I can scarcely wait for the approaching trip. I like to travel, and I think that almost all people must like to travel. One boards the train, it departs, and off it goes into the distance. One sits and is carried into the remote unknown. How well-off I am, really! What do I know of need, of poverty? Nothing at all. I also don't find it the least bit necessary that I should experience anything so base. But I do feel sorry for the poor children. I would jump out the window under such conditions.

Papa and I reside in the most elegant quarter of the city. Quarters which are quiet, scrupulously clean, and fairly old, are elegant. The brand-new? I wouldn't like to live in a brand-new house. In new things there is always something which isn't quite in order. One sees hardly any poor people – for example, workers – in our neighborhood, where the houses have their own gardens. The people who live in our vicinity are factory owners, bankers, and wealthy people whose profession is wealth. So Papa must be, at the very least, quite well-to-do. The poor and the poorish people simply can't live around here because the apartments are much too expensive. Papa says that the class ruled by misery lives in the north of the city. What a city! What is it – the north? I know Moscow better than I know the north of our city. I have been sent numerous postcards from Moscow, Petersburg, Vladivostok, and Yokohama. I know the beaches of Belgium and

Holland; I know the Engadine with its sky-high mountains and its green meadows, but my own city? Perhaps to many, many people who inhabit it, Berlin remains a mystery. Papa supports art and the artists. What he engages in is business. Well, lords often engage in business, too, and then Papa's dealings are of absolute refinement. He buys and sells paintings. We have very beautiful paintings in our house. The point of Father's business, I think, is this: the artists, as a rule, understand nothing about business, or, for some reason or other, they aren't allowed to understand anything about it. Or it is this: the world is big and coldhearted. The world never thinks about the existence of artists. That's where my father comes in, worldly-wise, with all sorts of important connections, and in suitable and clever fashion, he draws the attention of this world, which has perhaps no need at all for art, to art and to artists who are starving. Father often looks down upon his buyers. But he often looks down upon the artists, too. It all depends.

No, I wouldn't want to live permanently anywhere but in Berlin. Do the children in small towns, towns that are old and decayed, live any better? Of course, there are some things there that we don't have. Romantic things? I believe I'm not mistaken when I look upon something that is scarcely half alive as romantic. The defective, the crumbled, the diseased; e.g., an ancient city wall. Whatever is useless yet mysteriously beautiful – that is romantic. I love to dream about such things, and, as I see it, dreaming about them is enough. Ultimately, the most romantic thing is the heart, and every sensitive person carries in himself old cities enclosed by ancient walls. Our Berlin will soon burst at the seams with newness. Father says that everything historically notable here will vanish; no one knows the old Berlin anymore. Father knows everything, or at least, almost everything.

And naturally his daughter profits in that respect. Yes, little towns laid out in the middle of the countryside may well be nice. There would be charming, secret hiding spots to play in, caves to crawl in, meadows, fields, and, only a few steps away, the forest. Such villages seem to be wreathed in green; but Berlin has an Ice Palace where people ice-skate on the hottest summer day. Berlin is simply one step ahead of all other German cities, in every respect. It is the cleanest, most modern city in the world. Who says this? Well, Papa, of course. How good he is, really! I have much to learn from him. Our Berlin streets have overcome all dirt and all bumps. They are as smooth as ice and they glisten like scrupulously polished floors. Nowadays one sees a few people roller-skating. Who knows, perhaps I'll be doing it someday, too, if it hasn't already gone out of fashion. There are fashions here that scarcely have time to come in properly. Last year all the children, and also many grown-ups, played Diabolo. Now this game is out of fashion, no one wants to play it. That's how everything changes. Berlin always sets the fashion. No one is obliged to imitate, and yet Madam Imitation is the great and exalted ruler of this life. Everyone imitates.

Papa can be charming, actually, he is always nice, but at times he becomes angry about something – one never knows – and then he is ugly. I can see in him how secret anger, just like discontent, makes people ugly. If Papa isn't in a good mood, I feel as cowed as a whipped dog, and therefore Papa should avoid displaying his indisposition and his discontent to his associates, even if they should consist of only one daughter. There, yes, precisely there, fathers commit sins. I sense it vividly. But who doesn't have weaknesses – not even one, not some tiny fault? Who is without sin? Parents who don't consider it necessary to withhold their personal storms from their children degrade them to slaves in no time. A father should overcome his bad moods in private – but how difficult that is! – or he should take them to strangers. A daughter is a young lady, and in every cultivated sire should dwell a cavalier. I say explicitly: living with Father is like Paradise, and if I discover a flaw in him, doubtless it is one transferred from him to me; thus it is his, not my, discretion that observes him closely. But Papa may, of course, conveniently take out his anger on people who are dependent on him in certain respects. There are enough such people fluttering about him.

I have my own room, my furniture, my luxury, my books, etc. God, I'm actually very well provided for. Am I thankful to Papa for all this? What a tasteless question! I am obedient to him, and then I am also his possession, and, in the last analysis, he can well be proud of me. I cause him worries, I am his financial concern, he may snap at me, and I always find it a kind of delicate obligation to laugh at him when he snaps at me. Papa likes to snap; he has a sense of humor and is, at the same time, spirited. At Christmas he overwhelms me with presents. Incidentally, my furniture was designed by an artist who is scarcely unknown. Father deals almost exclusively with people who have some sort of name. He deals with names. If hidden in such a name there is also a man, so much the better. How horrible it must be to know that one is famous and to feel that one doesn't deserve it at all. I can imagine many such famous people. Isn't such a fame like an incurable sickness? Goodness, the way I express myself! My furniture is lacquered white and is painted with flowers and fruits by the hands of a connoisseur. They are charming and the artist who painted them is a remarkable person, highly esteemed by Father. And whomever Father esteems should indeed be flattered. I mean, it is worth something if

Papa is well-disposed toward someone, and those who don't find it so and act as if they didn't give a hoot, they're only hurting themselves. They don't see the world clearly enough. I consider my father to be a thoroughly remarkable man, that he wields influence in the world is obvious. – Many of my books bore me. But then they are simply not the right books, like, for example, so-called children's books. Such books are an affront. One dares give children books to read that don't go beyond their horizons? One should not speak in a childlike manner to children; it is childish. I, who am still a child myself, hate childishness.

When shall I cease to amuse myself with toys? No, toys are sweet, and I shall be playing with my doll for a long time yet; but I play consciously. I know that it's silly, but how beautiful silly and useless things are. Artistic natures, I think, must feel the same way. Different young artists often come to us, that is to say, to Papa, for dinner. Well, they are invited and then they appear. Often I write the invitations, often the governess, and a grand, entertaining liveliness reigns at our table, which, without boasting or willfully showing off, looks like the well-provided table of a fine house. Papa apparently enjoys going around with young people, with people who are younger than he, and yet he is always the gayest and the youngest. One hears him talking most of the time, the others listen, or they allow themselves little remarks, which is often quite droll. Father over-towers them all in learning and verve and understanding of the world, and all these people learn from him – that I plainly see. Often I have to laugh at the table; then I receive a gentle or not-so-gentle admonition. Yes, and then after dinner we take it easy. Papa stretches out on the leather sofa and begins to snore, which actually is in rather poor taste. But I'm in love with Papa's behavior. Even his candid snoring pleases me. Does one want to, could one ever, make conversation all the time?

Father apparently spends a lot of money. He has receipts and expenses, he lives, he strives after gains, he lets live. He even leans a bit toward extravagance and waste. He's constantly in motion. 'Clearly he's one of those people who find it a pleasure and, yes, even a necessity, to constantly take risks.' At our house there is much said about success and failure. Whoever eats with us and associates with us has attained some form of smaller or greater success in the world. What is the world? A rumor, a topic of conversation? In any case, my father stands in the very middle of this topic of conversation. Perhaps he even directs it, within certain bounds. Papa's aim, at all events, is to wield power. He attempts to develop, to assert both himself and those people in whom he has an interest. His principle is: He in whom I have no interest damages himself. As a result of this view, Father is always permeated with a healthy sense of his human worth and can step forth, firm and certain, as is fitting. Whoever grants himself no importance feels no qualms about perpetrating bad deeds. What am I talking about? Did I hear Father say that?

Have I the benefit of a good upbringing? I refuse even to doubt it. I have been brought up as a metropolitan lady should be brought up, with familiarity and, at the same time, with a certain measured severity, which permits and, at the same time, commands me to accustom myself to tact. The man who is to marry me must be rich, or he must have substantial prospects of an assured prosperity. Poor? I couldn't be poor.

It is impossible for me and for creatures like me to suffer pecuniary need. That would be stupid. In other respects, I shall be certain to give simplicity preference in my mode of living. I do not like outward display. Simplicity must be a luxury.

It must shimmer with propriety in every respect, and such refinements of life, brought to perfection, cost money. The amenities are expensive. How energetically I'm talking now! Isn't it a bit imprudent? Shall I love? What is love? What sorts of strange and wonderful things must yet await me if I find myself so unknowing about things that I'm still too young to understand. What experiences shall I have?

ALFRED DÖBLIN

From

BERLIN ALEXANDERPLATZ

Translated by Michael Hofmann

PUBLICATION OF A PLAN for the property An der Spandauer Brücke, 10.

The design for an ornamental rosette on the front wall of the property defined in perpetuity as An der Spandauer Brücke, 10, in the borough of Berlin-Mitte, is now open to public inspection. Concerned parties, with relevant supporting documents, are entitled to make objections. The borough planning officer is similarly entitled to raise objections. Any and all such objections to be made in person, or addressed to the council offices of Berlin-Mitte, Room 76, Klosterstrasse 68, Berlin C-2.

– With the agreement of the Chief of Police I gave the lessee, Herr Bottich, a provisional permit to shoot wild rabbits and other pests in the Fauler Seepark on the following days of 1928: said shooting to take place in summer, from 1 April to 30 September and to be concluded by 7 p.m., and in winter from 1 October to 31 March by 8 p.m. During these hours, the public are under advisement not to enter said terrain.

(*Signed*) The Oberbürgermeister, in my capacity of Controller of Hunting Licenses.

– Master furrier Albert Pangel, at the end of almost thirty years' service, has laid down his title, in consequence of advancing years and removal from the district. For an unbroken period of years he served as welfare official, resp. head of welfare. The council has expressed its thanks in writing to Herr Pangel.

Rosenthaler Platz is abuzz.

Weather changeable, bright, just below zero. An anti-cyclone over Germany continues to determine the outlook. An area of low pressure is moving slowly south over a broad front. Daytime temperatures will be a little colder than recently. Now the prospects for Berlin and surroundings.

Tram 68 via Rosenthaler Platz: Wittenau, Nordbahnhof, Heilanstalt, Weddingplatz, Stettiner Bahnhof, Rosen-thaler Platz, Alexanderplatz, Strausberger Platz, Bahnhof Frankfurter Allee, Lichtenberg, Herzberge Asylum. The three Berlin mass-transport firms, tram, rail (under- and overground) and omnibuses, form a single fare grouping. Standard adult fare is 20 pfennigs, half fare 10, children receive a reduction until the end of their fourteenth year, as do full-time students, trainees, war invalids, handicapped men and women with a permit from the local benefit office. Get to know your network. During the winter months, no ingress or egress through the front doors, 39 seats, 5918, to stop the conveyance pull the cord in a timely fashion, no conversation with the driver, getting on and off the moving vehicle is hazardous.

In the middle of Rosenthaler Platz a man with a couple of yellow parcels jumps off the 41 and is almost run over by a taxicab, the traffic policeman watches him scamper away, a ticket inspector turns up, inspector and policeman shake hands: that fellow and his parcels had a bit of a lucky break.

Fruit liqueurs at wholesale prices, Dr Bergell, solicitor and notary, Lukutate, the Indian specific for the rejuvenation of elephants, Fromms Akt, the best rubber sponge, what do people need so many rubber sponges for.

The principal thoroughfare leading away from the

square on the north side is Brunnenstrasse, the premises of AEG are on the left, just before Humboldthain. AEG is a colossal enterprise which, according to the 1928 telephone book, comprises: Electrical Light and Power Plants, Central Administration, NW 40, Friedrich Karl Ufer 2–4, Local Network North 4488, General Management, Janitors and Maintenance, Electrical Bank Ltd, Division of Lighting, Russian Division, Oberspree Metallurgy, Machine Works Treptow, Brunnenstrasse Plant, Hennigsdorf Plant, Insulation Factory, Rheinstrasse Factory, Cable Works Oberspree, Transformer Factory Wilhelminenhofstrasse, Rummelsburger Chaussee, Turbine Factory NW 87, Huttenstrasse 12–16. The Invalidenstrasse winds away to the left, in the direction of the Stettiner Bahnhof, where trains from the Baltic come in: you're all covered in soot – yes, it's dirty all right. – Hello, goodbye. – Does sir have something to wear, 50 pfennigs. – You look refreshed. – Oh, the tan will wear off in no time. – Wonder where people get money to go on holiday from. – In a little hotel in a poky little side street a couple was found shot, a married woman and a waiter from Dresden, they'd signed in under assumed names.

From the south, it's Rosenthaler Strasse that enters the square of the same name. There, Aschinger's Entertainment and Victualling Business provides people with food and beer. Fish is nutritious, some people like to eat fish, others get the heebie-jeebies, eat fish, stay slender, hearty and hale. Ladies' stockings, real artificial silk, here's a fountain pen with an excellent gold nib.

On Elsasser Strasse they've fenced off the entire thoroughfare, with the exception of one lane. Behind the building fence a locomobile is puffing away. Becker-Fiebig Ltd, Construction, Berlin W 35. There's a constant din, dump-trucks are backed up as far as the bank on the corner, a branch of the Commerz- und Privatbank, safe deposits, securities, savings accounts. Five men are kneeling in front of the bank, tapping little stones into the ground. Pavours.

At the stop on Lothringer Strasse four people have just boarded a No. 4, two elderly women, a worried-looking working man and a boy with a cap and ear-flaps. The two women are together, they are Frau Plück and Frau Hoppe. They are buying a girdle for Frau Hoppe, the elder of the two, because she has a tendency to umbilical rupture. They are on their way to the trussmaker on Brunnenstrasse, then they are meeting their husbands for lunch. The man is a coachman, Hasebruck, who is having trouble with a second-hand electric iron he picked up cheap for his boss. He was given a defective one, his boss tried it out for a couple of days, then it no longer got hot, he tried to exchange it, but the vendor refused, he's going back for the third time today, with a little extra money. The lad, Max Rüst, will one day become a plumber, the father of seven little Rüsts, will work for Hallis & Co., installers and roofers. Grünau, at the age of fifty-two he will win a quarter-share of the Prussian State Lottery jackpot and retire, and then, in the midst of a case he is bringing against Hallis & Co., he will die at the age of fifty-five. His obituary will read: On 25 September, suddenly, from heart disease, my dearly beloved husband, our dear father, son, brother, brother-in-law and uncle Max Rüst, in his fifty-sixth year. This announcement is placed by the grieving widow, Marie Rüst, on behalf of all with deep grief. The rendering of thanks will go as follows: Being unable to acknowledge individually the many tokens of sympathy we have received, we extend thanks to all our relatives, friends and fellow-tenants in Kleiststrasse 4 and our wider acquaintances. Especial thanks to Pastor Deinen for his words of comfort. – At present this Max Rüst is fourteen and on his way home from school, via the advice centre for those hard of hearing, with impaired vision, experiencing difficulties of speech, dyspraxia and problems with concentration, where he has been a few times already, about his stammer, which seems to be getting better.

Little bar on Rosenthaler Platz.

At the front there's a pool table, in a back corner two men are drinking tea and smoking. One has sagging features and grey hair, he's still got his coat on: 'OK, fire away. But sit still, and stop fidgeting.'

'You won't catch me playing pool today. My hands are shaking.'

He's chewing at a dry roll, doesn't touch his tea.

'Why should you. We're fine where we are.'

'It's always the same. Well, this time I did it.'

'You did?'

The other man, young, fair hair, taut features, taut body: 'Yeah. You think it's always the others? Now it's all out in the open.'

'In other words, you're out of a job.'

'I spoke to the boss in words of one syllable, and he shouted at me. That night I got my notice effective on the first of the month.'

'There are situations where you should never speak in words of one syllable. If you'd spoken to him in words of two syllables, you'd still be there.'

'What are you talking about, I am still there. I've just clarified my position. They think I'm going to make life easy for them. Now every day, at two in the afternoon, I'm going to turn up and make life hell for them: you see if I don't.'

'Oh, Lord, Lord. I thought you were married and all.'

He props his head on his hand: 'That's the bind, I haven't told her yet, I can't tell her.'

'Maybe it'll sort itself out.'

'She's expecting.'

'Your second?'

'Yeah.'

The man in the coat pulls it closer to him, smiles sardonically, nods and says: 'Well, that's all right then. Children give you courage. You could use some.'

The other shifts: 'Oh, come on. It's the last thing I need. I've got debts up to here. All those instalment payments. I can't tell her. And then to get sacked just like that. I'm used to a bit of organization, and this is a wretched outfit from top to bottom. The boss has his furniture factory, what does he care if I bring in orders for shoes? I'm superfluous. That's all there is to it. Standing round the office, asking: have the specials gone out? What specials? I told them six times, why should I keep chasing the customers. I'm just making a fool of myself. Either he lets the business go bust, or he doesn't.'

'Drink your tea. It seems for the moment he's letting *you* go bust.'

A man in shirt-sleeves wanders over from the pool table, taps the young man on the shoulder: 'Fancy a game?'

The other answers on his behalf: 'He's just had some bad news.'

'Pool helps.' He slopes off. The one in the coat sips at his tea: it's good to drink hot tea with sugar and a shot of rum, and listen to someone else's troubles. It feels cosy in here. 'So I guess you won't be going home tonight, Georg?'

'I don't dare. What am I going to tell her. I can't look her in the eye.'

'Just turn up and look her in the eye.'

'Oh, what do you know about it.'

He slumps across the table, pulling his coat tails over him. 'Listen, Georg, have a drink, or eat something, and stop belly-aching. I know all about it. I wrote the book. When you were yea-high. I'd been all over.'

'I'd like someone to put themselves in my situation. It could have been a half-decent job, and they ballsed it up for me.'

'I used to be a schoolmaster. Before the War. When the War started, I was already the way I am now. This bar was like it is now. They didn't enrol me. They've got no use for people like me, addicts. Or rather: they did enrol me, and I thought, fuck, I've had it. They took my needle away, and the morphine as well. And I joined up. I stuck it out for two days, that's how long my reserves lasted, and then so long, Prussia, and it was the loony bin for me. Then they let me go. Well, what was I saying, then the school fired me, morphine, sometimes you get a bit fuddled first off, it doesn't happen any more. Unfortunately. And my wife? And kid? Well, bye-bye Fatherland. My God, Georg, I could tell you some stories.' The grizzled man drinks, hands cupped round his glass, drinks slowly, deeply, stares at his tea: 'A woman and a kid. It feels like the whole world. I wasn't sorry, I don't feel guilty; you have to find a level for things, and for yourself as well. Don't make a cult of destiny. I'm not a believer in fate. I live in Berlin, not ancient Greece. Why are you letting your tea go cold? Here, take some rum in it.' The young fellow puts his hand over his glass, but the other pushes it away, and pours him a slug from a little metal flask he takes out of his pocket. 'I've gotta go. Thanks all the same. Walk off my nerves.' 'Oh, stay here, Georg, have a drink, play some pool. No disorder, no panic. That's the beginning of the end. When I found my wife and kid not at home, just a note, gone to Mum in West Prussia and so on, botched life, failed husband, the humiliation and all, I cut myself, here in my arm, it looked like an attempted suicide. Take every opportunity to learn, Georg; I'd studied Provençal, but this was anatomy. – I mistook the sinew for the pulse. I still don't really know any better, but I wouldn't make the same mistake again. You know, all that pain and remorse, it was so much bullshit, I was alive, my wife was alive, the kid was alive, she even went on to have a couple more, in West Prussia, I like to think it was remote control. Anyway, we're all alive. This place here makes me happy, the cop on the corner makes me happy, pool makes me happy. I'd like to hear someone say his life was better, and that I didn't know anything about women.'

The fair-haired man looks at him with distaste: 'You're a wreck, Krause, you know that. You're no sort of example to anyone. You're bad luck. Didn't you tell me yourself about starving on what you made from tutoring. I don't want to be buried like that.' The iron-haired man has drained his glass, sits back in his coat on the iron chair, blinks aggressively at the younger man, then he barks, cackles: 'No, no sort of example, you're right about that. Never said I was. No sort of example. Take the fly. The fly sits under a microscope and thinks it's a horse. Who do you think you are, Master Georg? Introduce yourself to me, why don't you: rep. for Smith & Co.'s, shoes. Stop kidding around, telling me about your misery: M for martyr, I for Idiot, S for stupid. You're barking up the wrong tree, mate, barking up the wrong tree.'

A girl gets out of the 99, Mariendorf, Lichtenrader Chaussee, Tempelhof, Hallesches Tor, Hedwigskirche, Rosenthaler Platz, Badstrasse, Seestrasse/Togostrasse, weekend service between Uferstrasse and Tempelhof, Friedrich-Karl-Strasse at fifteen-minute intervals. It's eight in the evening, she is carrying a music case under her arm, her collar is pushed up in her face, she is walking up and down on the corner of Brunnenstrasse and Weinbergsweg. A man in a fur coat accosts her, she jumps, and crosses over to the other side of the street. She stands under a tall lamp-post, observing the corner where she stood before. A compact, elderly gentleman in horn-rims appears, she runs across to him, walks giggling at his side. They go up Brunnenstrasse together.

'I mustn't be so late back tonight, I really mustn't. I shouldn't have come at all. But I'm not allowed to ring you.' 'No, only in an emergency. They listen in the office. It's for your own protection, child.' 'Yes, I'm worried, but I don't think it will get out, you won't tell a soul.' 'That's right.' 'My God, if Papa should hear, or Mama.' The elderly gentleman takes her affectionately by the arm. 'Nothing will get out. I won't say a word to a soul. What did you do in your lesson?' 'Chopin. I'm playing the nocturnes. Are you musical?' 'Yes, at a pinch.' 'I wish I could play for you sometime. But I'm so nervous of you.' 'Oh, come.' 'It's true, I've always been nervous of you, not very, just a little. Not very. But I don't need to be nervous of you, do I.' 'Not a bit. Honestly. You've known me now for three months.' 'It's Papa I'm afraid of, I suppose. If word got out.' 'Oh, come, surely to goodness you can step out with a friend every now and again. You're not a baby any more.' 'That's what I kept saying to Mama too. And I go out.' 'We'll go wherever we please, ducks.' 'Don't call me that. I only told you, so – well, never mind. Where shall we go today. I need to be home by nine.' 'In here. We're already there. Flat of a friend of mine. We can go upstairs without worrying.' 'I feel scared. Are you sure no one's seen us? Will you go on ahead. I'll come up after.'

Upstairs they exchange smiles. She is standing in the corner. He has taken off his hat and coat, she allows him to relieve her of her music and hat. Then she runs across to the door and switches off the light: 'But be quick about it. I haven't got much time, I have to go home, I'll keep my clothes on. Don't hurt me.'

VLADIMIR NABOKOV

From

KING, QUEEN, KNAVE

Translated by Dmitri Nabokov in collaboration with
Vladimir Nabokov

CHAPTER 2

GOLDEN HAZE, PUFFY BEDQUILT. Another awakening, but perhaps not yet the final one. This occurs not infrequently: You come to, and see yourself, say, sitting in an elegant second-class compartment with a couple of elegant strangers; actually, though, this is a false awakening, being merely the next layer of your dream, as if you were rising up from stratum to stratum but never reaching the surface, never emerging into reality. Your spellbound thought, however, mistakes every new layer of the dream for the door of reality. You believe in it, and holding your breath leave the railway station you have been brought to in immemorial fantasies and cross the station square. You discern next to nothing, for the night is blurred by rain, your spectacles are foggy, and you want as quickly as possible to reach the ghostly hotel across the square so as to wash your face, change your shirt cuffs and then go wandering along dazzling streets. Something happens, however – an absurd mishap – and what seemed reality abruptly loses the tingle and tang of reality. Your consciousness was deceived: you are still fast asleep. Incoherent slumber dulls your mind. Then comes a new moment of specious awareness: this golden haze and your room in the hotel, whose name is 'The Montevideo.' A shopkeeper you knew at home, a nostalgic Berliner, had jotted it down on a slip of paper for you. Yet who knows? Is this reality, *the* final reality, or just a new deceptive dream?

Lying on his back Franz peered with myopic agonizingly

narrowed eyes at the blue mist of a ceiling, and then sideways at a radiant blur which no doubt was a window. And in order to free himself from this gold-tinted vagueness still so strongly reminiscent of a dream, he reached toward the night table and groped for his glasses.

And only when he had touched them, or more precisely the handkerchief in which they were wrapped as in a winding sheet, only then did Franz remember that absurd mishap in a lower layer of dream. When he had first come into this room, looked around, and opened the window (only to reveal a dark backyard and a dark noisy tree) he had, first of all, torn off his soiled collar that had been oppressing his neck and had hurriedly begun washing his face. Like an imbecile, he had placed his glasses on the edge of the washstand, beside the basin. As he lifted the heavy thing in order to empty it into the pail, he not only knocked the glasses off the edge of the stand, but sidestepping in awkward rhythm with the sloshing basin he held, had heard an ominous crunch under his heel.

In the process of reconstructing this event in his mind, Franz grimaced and groaned. All the festive lights of Friedrichstrasse had been stamped out by his boot. He would have to take the glasses to be repaired: only one lens was still in place and that was cracked. He palpated rather than re-examined the cripple. Mentally he had already gone out of doors in search of the proper shop. First that, and then the important, rather frightening visit. And, remembering how his mother had insisted that he make the call on the very first morning after his arrival ('it will be just the day when you can find a businessman at home'), Franz also remembered that it was Sunday.

He clucked his tongue and lay still.

Complicated but familiar poverty (that cannot afford

spare sets of expensive articles) now resulted in primitive panic. Without his glasses he was as good as blind, yet he must set out on a perilous journey across a strange city. He imagined the predatory specters that last night had been crowding near the station, their motors running and their doors slamming, when still safely bespectacled but with his vision dimmed by the rainy night he had started to cross the dark square. Then he had gone to bed after the mishap without taking the walk he had been looking forward to, without getting his first taste of Berlin at the very hour of its voluptuous glitter and swarming. Instead, in miserable self-compensation, he had succumbed again, that first night, to the solitary practice he had sworn to give up before his departure.

But to pass the entire day in that hostile hotel room amid vague hostile objects, to wait with nothing to do until Monday, when a shop with a sign (for the seeing!) in the shape of a giant blue pince-nez would open – such a prospect was unthinkable. Franz threw back the quilt and, barefoot, padded warily to the window.

A light-blue, delicate, marvelously sunny morning welcomed him. Most of the yard was taken up by the sable velvet of what seemed to be a spreading tree shadow above which he was just able to distinguish the blurry orange-red hue of what looked like rich foliage. Booming city, indeed! Out there all was as quiet as in the remote serenity of a luminous rural autumn.

Aha, it was the room that was noisy! Its hubbub comprised the hollow hum of irksome human thoughts, the clatter of a moved chair, under which a much needed sock had long been hiding from the purblind, the plash of water, the tinkle of small coins that had foolishly fallen out of an elusive waistcoat, the scrape of his suitcase as it was dragged to a far corner where there would be no danger of one's tripping over it again; and there was an additional background noise – the room's own groan and din like the voice of a magnified seashell, in contrast with that sunny startling miraculous stillness preserved like a costly wine in the cool depths of the yard.

At last Franz overcame all the blotches and banks of fog, located his hat, recoiled from the embrace of the clowning mirror and made for the door. Only his face remained bare. Having negotiated the stairs, where an angel was singing as she polished the banisters, he showed the desk clerk the address on the priceless card and was told what bus to take and where to wait for it. He hesitated for a moment, tempted by the magic and majestic possibility of a taxi. He rejected it not only because of the cost but because his potential employer might take him for a spendthrift if he arrived in state.

Once in the street he was engulfed in streaming radiance. Outlines did not exist, colors had no substance. Like a woman's wispy dress that has slipped off its hanger, the city shimmered and fell in fantastic folds, not held up by anything, a discarnate iridescence limply suspended in the azure autumnal air. Beyond the nacrine desert of the square, across which a car sped now and then with a new metropolitan trumpeting, great pink edifices loomed, and suddenly a sunbeam, a gleam of glass, would stab him painfully in the pupil.

Franz reached a plausible street corner. After much fussing and squinting he discovered the red blur of the bus stop which rippled and wavered like the supports of a bathhouse when you dive under it. Almost directly the yellow mirage of a bus came into being. Stepping on somebody's foot, which at once dissolved under him as everything else was dissolving, Franz seized the handrail and a voice – evidently the conductor's – barked in his ear: 'Up!' It was the first time he had ascended this kind of spiral staircase (only a few old trams served his hometown), and when the bus jerked into motion he caught a frightening glimpse of the asphalt rising like a silvery wall, grabbed someone's shoulder, and carried along by the force of an inexorable curve, during which the whole bus seemed to heel over, zoomed up the last steps and found himself on top. He sat down and looked around with helpless indignation. He was floating very high above the city. On the street below people slithered like jellyfish whenever the traffic froze. Then the bus started again, and the houses, shade-blue on one side of the sweet, sun-hazy on the other, rode by like clouds blending imperceptibly with the tender sky. This is how Franz first saw the city – fantasmally tinted, ethereal, impregnated with swimming colors, in no way resembling his crude provincial dream.

Was he on the right bus? Yes, said the ticket dispenser.

The clean air whistled in his ears, and the horns called to each other in celestial voices. He caught a whiff of dry leaves and a branch nearly brushed against him. He asked a neighbor where he should get off. It turned out to be a long way yet. He began counting the stops so as not to have to ask again, and tried in vain to distinguish cross streets. The speed, the airiness, the odor of autumn, the dizzy mirror-like quality of the world all merged into so extraordinary a feeling of disembodiment that Franz deliberately moved his neck in order to feel the hard head of his collar stud, which seemed to him the only proof of his existence.

At last his stop came. He clambered down the steep stairs and cautiously stepped onto the sidewalk. From receding heights a faceless traveler shouted to him: 'On your right! First street on your—' Franz, vibrating responsively, reached the corner and turned right. Stillness, solitude, a sunny mist. He felt he was losing his way, melting in this mist, and most important, he could not distinguish the house numbers. He felt weak and sweaty. Finally, spying a cloudy passer-by, he accosted him and asked where number five was. The pedestrian stood very near him, and the shadow of foliage played so strangely over his face that for an instant Franz thought he recognized the man from whom he had fled the day before. One could maintain with almost complete certainty that this was a dappled whim of sun and shade; and yet it gave Franz such a shock that he averted his eyes. 'Right across the street, where you see that white fence,' the man said jauntily, and went on his way.

Franz did not see any fence but found a wicket, groped for the button and pressed it. The gate emitted an odd buzzing sound. He waited a little and pressed again. Again the wicket buzzed. No one came to open it. Beyond lay the greenish haze of a garden with a house floating there like an indistinct reflection. He tried to open the gate himself, but found it unyielding. Biting his lips he rang once more and held his finger on the button for a long time. The same monotonous buzzing. He suddenly realized what the trick was: leaned against the gate as he rang, and it opened so angrily that he nearly fell. Someone called to him: 'Whom do you want?' He turned toward the voice and distinguished a woman in a light-colored dress standing on the gravel path that led to the house.

'My husband is not home yet,' the voice said after a little pause when Franz had replied.

Slitting his eyes he made out the flash of earrings and dark smooth hair. She was neither a fearful nor fanciful woman but in his clumsy eagerness to see better he had come up so close that for a ridiculous moment she thought this impetuous intruder was about to take her head between his hands.

'It's very important,' said Franz. 'You see, I'm a relative of his.' Stopping in front of her he produced his wallet and began to rummage in it for the famous card.

She wondered where she had seen him before. His ears were of a translucent red in the sun, and tiny drops of sweat gemmed his innocent forehead right at the roots of his short dark hair. A sudden recollection, like a conjuror, put eye-glasses on the inclined face and immediately removed them again. Martha smiled. At the same time Franz found the card and raised his head.

'Here,' he said. 'I was told to come. On a Sunday.'

She looked at the card and smiled again.

'Your uncle has gone to play tennis. He will be back for lunch. But we've already met, you know.'

'*Bitte?*' said Franz, straining his eyes.

Later, when he remembered this meeting, the mirage of the garden, that sun-melting dress, he marveled at the length of time it had taken him to recognize her. At three paces he was able to make out a person's features at least as clearly as a normal human eye would through a gauze veil. Rather naively he told himself that he had never seen her hatless before, and had not expected her to wear her hair with a parting in the middle and a chignon behind (the only particular in which Martha did not follow the fashion); still it was not so simple to explain how it could have happened that, even in that dim perception of the phantom form, there had not worked again and at once the same tremor, the same magic that had fascinated him the day before. It seemed to him afterwards that on that morning he had been plunged in a vague irreproducible world existing for one brief Sunday, a world where everything was delicate and weightless, radiant and unstable. In this dream anything could happen: so it did turn out after all that Franz had not awakened in his hotel bed that morning but had merely passed into the next stratum of sleep. In the unsubstantial radiance of his myopia, Martha bore no resemblance at all to the lady in the train who had glowed like a picture and yawned like a tigress. Her madonna-like beauty that he had glimpsed and then lost now appeared in full as if this were her true essence now blooming before him without any admixture, without flaw or frame. He could not have said with certitude if he found this blurry lady attractive. Nearsightedness is chaste. And besides, she was the wife of the man on whom depended his whole future, out of whom he had been ordered to squeeze everything he possibly could, and this fact made her seem at the very moment of acquaintance more distant, more unattainable than the glamorous stranger of the preceding day. As he followed Martha up the path to the house he gesticulated, kept apologizing for his infirmity, broken glasses, closed shops, and extolling the marvels of coincidence, so intoxicating was his desire to dispose her favorably toward him as quickly as possible.

On the lawn near the porch stood a very tall beach umbrella and under it a small table and several wicker armchairs. Martha sat down, and Franz, grinning and blinking, sat down beside her. She decided that she had stunned him completely with the sight of her small but expensive garden which contained among other things five beds of dahlias, three larches, two weeping willows, and one magnolia, and did not bother to ascertain if those poor wild eyes could distinguish a beach umbrella from an ornamental tree. She enjoyed receiving him so elegantly *auf englische Weise*, dazzling him with undreamt-of wealth, and was looking forward to showing him the villa, the miniatures in the parlor, and the satinwood in the bedroom, and hearing this rather handsome boy's moans of respectful admiration. And, since generally her visitors were people from her own circle whom she had long since grown tired of dazzling, she felt tenderly grateful to this provincial with his starched collar and narrow trousers for giving her an opportunity to renew the pride she had known in her first months of marriage.

'It's so quiet here,' said Franz. 'I thought Berlin would be so noisy.'

'Oh, but we live almost in the country,' she answered, and feeling herself seven years younger, added: 'the next villa over there belongs to a count. A very nice old man, we see a lot of him.'

'Very pleasant – this quiet simple atmosphere,' said Franz, steadily developing the theme and already foreseeing a blind alley.

She looked at his pale pink-knuckled hand with a nice long index lying flat on the table. The thin fingers were trembling slightly.

'I have often tried to decide,' she said, 'whom does one know better – somebody one has been in the same room with for five hours or somebody one has seen for ten minutes every day during a whole month.'

'*Bitte?*' said Franz.

'I suppose,' she went on, 'the real factor here is not the amount of time but that of communication – the exchange of ideas on life and living conditions. Tell me, how are you related to my husband exactly? Second cousin, isn't it? You're going to work here, that's nice, boys like you should be made to work a lot. His business is enormous – I mean, my husband's firm. But then I'm sure you've already heard about his celebrated emporium. Perhaps emporium is too strong a word, it carries men's things only, but there is everything,

67

everything – neckties, hats, sporting goods. Then there's his office in another part of the town and various banking operations.'

'It will be hard to begin,' said Franz, drumming with his fingers. 'I'm a little scared. But I know your husband is a wonderful man, a very kind good man. My mother worships him.'

At this moment there appeared from somewhere, as if in token of sympathy, the specter of a dog which turned out upon closer examination to be an Alsatian. Lowering its head, the dog placed something at Franz's feet. Then it retreated a little, dissolved momentarily, and waited expectantly.

'That's Tom,' said Martha. 'Tom won a prize at the show. Didn't you, Tom' (she spoke to Tom only in the presence of guests).

Out of respect for his hostess, Franz picked up the object the dog was offering him. It proved to be a wet wooden ball covered with tangible tooth marks. As soon as he took up the ball, raising it up to his face, the specter of the dog emerged with a bound from the sunny haze, becoming alive, warm, active, and nearly knocking him off his chair. He quickly got rid of the ball. Tom vanished.

The ball landed right among the dahlias but of course Franz did not see this.

'Fine animal,' he observed with revulsion as he wiped his wet hand against the chintzed chair arm. Martha was looking away, worried by the storm in the flowerbed which Tom was trampling in frantic search of his plaything. She clapped her hands. Franz politely clapped too, mistaking admonishment for applause. Fortunately at that moment a boy rode by on a bicycle, and Tom, instantly forgetting the ball, lunged headlong toward the garden fence and dashed along its entire length barking furiously. Then he immediately calmed down, trotted back and lay down by the porch steps under Martha's cold eye, lolling his tongue and folding back one front paw like a lion.

As Franz listened to what Martha was telling him, in the vibrant petulant tones he was getting used to, about the Tyrol, he felt that the dog had not gone too far away, and might bring back any moment that slimy object. Nostalgically he remembered a nasty old lady's nasty old pug (a relative and great enemy of his mother's pet) that he had managed to kick smartly on several occasions.

'But somehow, you know,' Martha was saying, 'one felt hemmed in. One imagined those mountains might crash down on the hotel, in the middle of the night, right on our bed, burying me under them and my husband, killing everybody. We were thinking of going on to Italy but somehow I lost the lust. He's pretty stupid, our Tom. Dogs that play with balls are always stupid. A strange gentleman arrives but for him it's a brand-new member of the family. This is your first visit, isn't it, to our great city? How do you like it here?'

Franz indicated his eyes with a polite pinkie: 'I'm quite blind,' he said. 'Until I get some new glasses, I cannot appreciate anything. All I see are just colors, which after all is not very interesting. But in general I like it. And it's so quiet here, under this yellow tree.'

For some reason the thought crossed his mind – a streak of fugitive fancy – that at that very moment his mother was returning from church with Frau Kamelspinner, the taxidermist's wife. And meanwhile – wonder of wonders – he was having a difficult but delicious conversation with this misty lady in this radiant mist. It was all very dangerous; every word she said might trip him.

Martha noticed his slight stammer and the nervous way he had of sniffing now and then. 'Dazzled and embarrassed, and so very young,' she reflected with a mixture of contempt and tenderness, 'warm, healthy young wax that one can manipulate and mold till its shape suits your pleasure. He should have shaved, though, before coming.' And she said by way of experiment, just to see how he would react:

'If you plan to work at a smart store, my good sir, you must cultivate a more confident manner and get rid of that black down on your manly jaws.'

As she had expected, Franz lost what composure he had.

'I shall get new spectacles, I mean respectacles,' he expostulated, or so his flustered lisp sounded.

She allowed his confusion to spin itself out, telling herself that it was very good for him. Franz really did feel most uncomfortable for an instant but not quite in the way she imagined. What put him off was not the remonstrance but the sudden coarseness of her tone, a kind of throaty 'hep!,' as if, to set the example, she were jerking back her shoulders at the word 'confident.' This was not in keeping with his misty image of her.

The jarring interpolation passed quickly: Martha melted back into the glamorous haze of the world surrounding him and resumed her elegant conversation.

'Autumn is chillier around here than in your native orchards. I love luscious fruit but I also like a crisp cold day. There is something about the texture and temperature of my skin that simply thrills in response to a breeze or a keen frost. Alas, I have to pay for it.'

'Back home there is still bathing,' observed Franz. He was all set to tell her about the celebrated limpid lyrical river running through his native town under arched bridges, and then between cornfields and vineyards; about how nice it was to go swimming there in the buff, diving right off the little 'nicker raft' you could hire for a few coppers; but at that instant a car honked and drew up at the gate, and Martha said: 'Here is my husband.'

She fixed her eyes on Dreyer, wondering if his aspect would impress the young cousin, and forgetting that Franz had seen him before and could hardly see him now. Dreyer came at his fast bouncy walk. He wore an ample white overcoat with a white scarf. Three rackets, each in a differently colored cloth case – maroon, blue, and mulberry – protruded from under his arm; his face with its tawny mustache glowed like an autumn leaf. She was less vexed by his exotic attire than that the conversation had been interrupted, that she was no longer alone with Franz, that it was no longer exclusively she who engrossed and amazed him. Involuntarily her manner toward Franz changed, as if there had been 'something between them,' and now came the husband, causing them to behave with greater reserve. Besides, she certainly did not want to let Dreyer see that the poor relative whom she had criticized before knowing him had not turned out too bad after all. Therefore when Dreyer joined them she wanted to convey to him by means of an inconspicuous bit of pantomime that his arrival would now liberate her at last from a boring guest. Unfortunately Dreyer as he approached did not take his eyes off Franz who, peering at the gradually condensing light part of the mottled mist, got up and was preparing to make a bow. Dreyer, who was observant in his own way and fond of trivial mnemonic tricks (he often played a game with himself, trying to recollect the pictures in a waiting room, that pathetic limbo of pictures), had immediately, from a distance, recognized their recent traveling companion and wondered if perhaps he had brought the unopened letter from a milliner that Martha had mislaid during the journey. But suddenly another, much more amusing, thought dawned upon him. Martha, accustomed to the fireworks of his face, saw his cropped mustache twitch and the rays of wrinkles on the temple side of his eyes multiply and quiver. The next instant he burst out laughing so violently that Tom, who had been jumping around him, could not help barking. Not only the coincidence tickled Dreyer but also the conjecture that Martha had probably said something nasty about his relative while the relative had been sitting right there in the compartment. Just what Martha had said, and whether Franz could have heard it, he would never be able to recall now but something there had surely been, and this itchy uncertainty intensified the humorous aspect of the coincidence. In the no-time of human thought he also recalled – while the dog drowned his cousin's greeting – how an acquaintance once had rung him up while he was taking a tumultuous shower, and Martha had shouted through the bathroom door: 'That stupid old Wasserschluss is calling' – and five paces away the telephone receiver on the table was cupping its ear like an eavesdropper in a farce.

He laughed as he shook Franz's hand, and was still laughing when he dropped into one of the wicker chairs. Tom continued to bark. Suddenly Martha lunged forward and, rings blazing, gave the dog a really hard slap with the back of her hand. It hurt, and with a whimper Tom slunk away.

'Delightful,' said Dreyer (the delight quite gone), wiping his eyes with an ample silk handkerchief. 'So you are Franz – Lina's boy. After such a coincidence we must do away with formalities – please don't call me sir but Uncle, dear Uncle.'

'Avoid vocatives,' thought Franz quickly. Nevertheless, he began to feel at ease. Dreyer, blowing his nose in the haze, was indistinct, absurd, and harmless like those total strangers who impersonate people we know in our dreams and talk to us in phony voices like intimate friends.

'I was in fine form today,' Dreyer said to his wife, 'and you know something, I'm hungry. I imagine young Franz is hungry too.'

'Lunch will be served in a minute,' said Martha. She got up and disappeared.

Franz, feeling even more at ease, said: 'I must apologize – I've broken my glasses and can hardly distinguish anything, so I get mixed up a little.'

'Where are you staying?' asked Dreyer.

'At the Video,' said Franz. 'Near the station. It was recommended to me by an experienced person.'

'Fine. Yes, you are a good dog, Tom. Now first of all you must find a nice room, not too far from us. For forty or fifty marks a month. Do you play tennis?'

'Certainly,' replied Franz, remembering a backyard, a second-hand brown racket purchased for one mark at a bric-a-brac shop from under the bust of Wagner, a black rubber ball, and an uncooperative brick wall with a fatal square hole in which grew one wallflower.

'Fine. So we can play on Sundays. Then you will need a decent suit, shirts, soft collars, ties, all kinds of things. How did you get on with my wife?'

Franz grinned, not knowing the answer.

'Fine,' said Dreyer. 'I suspect lunch is ready. We'll talk about business later. We discuss business over coffee around here.'

His wife had come out on the porch. She gave him a long cold glance, coldly nodded, and went back into the house. 'That hateful, undignified, genial tone he always must take with inferiors,' she reflected as she passed through the ivory-white front hall where the impeccable, hospitable white comb and white-backed brush lay on the doily under the pier glass. The entire villa, from whitewashed terrace to radio antenna, was that way – neat, clean-cut, and on the whole unloved and inane. The master of the house deemed it a joke. As for the lady, neither aesthetic nor emotional considerations ruled her taste; she simply thought that a reasonably wealthy German businessman in the nineteen-twenties, in Berlin-West, ought to have a house exactly of that sort, that is, belonging to the same suburban type as those of his fellows. It had all the conveniences, and the majority of those conveniences went unused. There was, for example, in the bathroom a round, face-sized swivel mirror – a grotesque magnifier, with an electric light attached. Martha had once given it to her husband for shaving but very soon he had grown to detest it: it was unbearable every morning to see one's brightly illuminated chin swollen to about three times its natural volume and studded with rusty bristles that had sprouted overnight. The chairs in the parlor resembled a display in a good store. A writing desk with an unnecessary upper stage, consisting of unnecessary little drawers, supported, in place of a lamp, a bronze knight holding a lantern. There were lots of well dusted but uncaressed porcelain animals with glossy rumps, as well as varicolored cushions, against which no human cheek had ever nestled; and albums – huge arty things with photographs of Copenhagen porcelain and Hagenkopp furniture – which were opened only by the dullest or shyest guest. Everything in the house, including the jars labeled sugar, cloves, chicory, on the shelves of the idyllic kitchen, had been chosen by Martha, to whom, seven years previously, her husband had presented on its green-turfed tray the freshly built little villa, still empty and ready to please. She had acquired paintings and distributed them throughout the rooms under the supervision of an artist who had been very much in fashion that season, and who believed that any picture was acceptable as long as it was ugly and meaningless, with thick blobs of paint, the messier and muddier the better. Following the count's advice, Martha had also bought a few old oils at auctions. Among them was the magnificent portrait of a noble-looking gentleman, with sidewhiskers, wearing a stylish morning coat, who stood leaning on a slender cane, illuminated as if by sheet lightning against a rich brown background. Martha bought this with good reason. Right beside it, on the dining-room wall, she placed a daguerreotype of her grandfather, a long-since-deceased coal merchant who had been suspected of drowning his first wife in a tarn around 1860, but nothing was proved. He also had sidewhiskers, wore a morning coat, and leaned on a cane; and his proximity to the sumptuous oil (signed by Heinrich von Hildenbrand) neatly transformed the latter into a family portrait. 'Grandpa,' Martha would say, indicating the genuine article with a wave of her hand that indolently included in the arc it described the anonymous nobleman to whose portrait the deceived guest's gaze shifted.

Unfortunately, though, Franz was able to make out neither the pictures nor the porcelain no matter how skillfully Martha directed his attention to the room's charms. He perceived a delicate blend of color, felt the freshness of abundant flowers, appreciated the yielding softness of the carpet underfoot, and thus perceived by a freak of fate the very quality that the furnishings of the house lacked but that, in Martha's opinion, ought to have existed, and for which she had paid good money: an aura of luxury, in which, after the second glass of pale golden wine, he began slowly to dissolve. Dreyer refilled his glass, and breakfastless Franz, who had not dared to partake of the enigmatic first course, realized that his lower extremities had by now dissolved completely. He twice mistook the bare forearm of the servant maid for that of Martha but then became aware that she sat far away like a wine-golden ghost. Dreyer, ghostly too, but warm and ruddy, was describing a flight he had made two or three years ago from Munich to Vienna in a bad storm; how the plane had tossed and shaken, and how he had felt like telling the pilot 'Do stop for a moment'; and how his chance traveling companion, an old Englishman, kept calmly solving a crossword puzzle. Meanwhile Franz was experiencing fantastic difficulties with the vol-au-vent and then with the dessert. He had the feeling that in another minute his body would melt completely leaving only his head, which, with its mouth stuffed with a cream puff, would start floating about the room like a balloon. The coffee and the curaçao all but finished him. Dreyer, slowly rotating before him like a flaming wheel with human arms for spokes, began discussing the job awaiting Franz. Noting the state in which the poor fellow was, he did not go into details. He did say, however, that very soon Franz would become an excellent salesman, that the aviator's principal enemy is not wind but fog, and that, as the salary would not be much at first, he would undertake to pay for the room and would be glad if Franz dropped in every evening if he desired, though he would not be surprised if next year air service were established between Europe and America. The merry-go-round in Franz's head never stopped; his armchair traveled around the room in gliding circles. Dreyer considered him with a kindly smile, and, in anticipation of the tongue-lashing Martha would give him for all this jollity, kept mentally pouring out upon Franz's head the contents of an enormous cornucopia, for he had to reward Franz somehow for the exhilarating fun lavished upon him by the imp of coincidence through Franz. He must reward not only him, but cousin Lina too for that wart on her cheek, for her pug, for the rocking chair with its green sausage-shaped nape rest bearing the embroidered legend 'Only one little half hour.' Later, when Franz, exhaling wine and gratitude, bade his uncle good-by, carefully descended the steps to the garden, carefully squeezed through the gate, and, still holding his hat in his hand, disappeared round the corner, Dreyer imagined what a nice nap the poor boy would have back in his hotel room, and then himself felt the blissful weight of drowsiness and went up to the bedroom.

There, in an orange peignoir, her bare legs crossed, her velvety-white neck nicely set off by the black of her low thick chignon – Martha sat at her dressing table polishing her nails. Dreyer saw in the mirror the gloss of her smooth bandeaux, her knit brows, her girlish breasts. A robust but untimely throb dispelled sleepiness. He sighed. It was not the first time he regretted that Martha regarded afternoon lovemaking as a decadent perversion. And since she did not raise her head, he understood she was angry.

He said softly – trying to make matters worse so as to stop regretting: 'Why did you disappear after lunch? You might have waited until he left.'

Without raising her eyes Martha answered: 'You know perfectly well we've been invited today to a very important and very smart tea. It wouldn't hurt if you got cleaned up too.'

'We still have an hour or so,' said Dreyer. 'Actually I thought I'd take a nap.'

Martha remained silent as she worked rapidly with the chamois polisher. He threw off his so-called Norfolk jacket, then sat down on the edge of the couch, and began taking off his red-sand-stained tennis shoes.

Martha bent even lower and abruptly said: 'Amazing how some people have no sense of dignity.'

Dreyer grunted and leisurely got rid of his flannel trousers, then of his white silk socks.

A minute or so later Martha chucked something with a clatter onto the glass surface of her dressing table and said: 'I'd like to know what that young man thinks of you now. No formalities, call me Uncle . . . It's unheard-of.'

Dreyer smiled, wiggling his toes. 'Enough playing on public courts,' he said. 'Next spring I'll join a club.'

Martha abruptly turned toward him and, leaning her elbow on the arm of her chair, dropped her chin on her fist. One leg crossed over the other was swinging slightly. She surveyed her husband, incensed by the look of half-mischief, half-desire in his eyes.

'You've got what you wanted,' she continued. 'You've taken care of your dear nephew. I bet you've made him heaps of promises. And will you please cover your obscene nudity.'

Draping himself in a dressing gown, Dreyer made himself comfortable on the cretonne couch. What would happen, he wondered, if he now said something like this: You too have your peculiarities, my love, and some of them are less pardonable than a husband's obscenity. You travel second-class instead of first because second is just as good and the saving is colossal, amounting to the stupendous sum of twenty-seven marks and sixty pfennigs which would otherwise have disappeared into the pockets of the swindlers who invented first-class. You hit a lovable and loving dog because a dog is not supposed to laugh aloud. All right: let's assume this is all right. But allow me to play a little too – leave me my nephew . . .

'Evidently you do not wish to speak to me,' said Martha. 'Oh, well.' She went back to work on her gem-like nails. Dreyer reflected: If only just once you let yourself go, come,

come on, have some good fun and a good fit of crying. After that surely you'll feel better.

He cleared his throat, preparing the way for words, but as had happened more than once, decided at the last minute not to say anything. There is no knowing if it was from a wish to irritate her with silence or simply the result of contented laziness, or perhaps an unconscious fear of dealing a final blow to something he wanted to preserve. Leaning back against the three-cornered cushion, his hands thrust deep into his dressing-gown pockets, he remained contemplating silent Martha; presently his gaze roamed away to his wife's wide bed under its white blanket cover, batiste trimmed with lace, washable, ninety by ninety inches, and severely separated from his, also lace-covered, by a night table on which sprawled a leggy rag doll with a black face. This doll, and the bedspreads, and the pretentious furniture were both amusing and repelling.

He yawned and rubbed the bridge of his nose. Perhaps it would be wiser to change at once and then read for half an hour on the terrace. Martha threw off her orange peignoir, and as she drew back her elbows to adjust a necklace her angelically lovely bare shoulder blades came together like folding wings. He wondered wistfully how many hours must pass till she let him kiss those shoulders; hesitated, thought better of it, and went to his dressing room across the passage.

As soon as the door had noiselessly closed behind him, Martha sprang up and furiously, with a wrenching twist locked it. This was utterly out of character: a singular impulse she would have been at a loss to explain, and all the more senseless since she would need the maid in a minute, and would have to unlock the door anyway. Much later, when many months had passed, and she was trying to reconstruct that day, it was this door and this key that she recalled most

79

vividly, as if an ordinary door key happened to be the correct key to that not quite ordinary day. However, in wringing the neck of the lock she failed to dispell her anger. It was a confused and turbulent seething that found no release. She was angry that Franz's visit had given her a strange pleasure, and that for this pleasure she had to thank her husband. The upshot was that in their arguments about inviting or not inviting a poor relative she had been wrong, and her way-ward and wacky husband right. Therefore she tried not to acknowledge the pleasure so that her husband might remain in the wrong. The pleasure, she knew, would soon be repeat-ed, and she also knew that had she been absolutely sure her attitude would have caused her husband not to receive Franz again, she might not have said what she had said just now. For the first time in her married life she experienced some-thing that she had never expected, something that did not fit like a legitimate square into the parquet pattern of their life after the dismal surprises of their honeymoon. Thus, out of a trifle, out of a chance stay in a ridiculous provincial town, something had started to grow, joyful and irreparable. And there was no vacuum cleaner in the world that could instantly restore all the rooms of her brain to their former immaculate condition. The vague quality of her sensations, the difficulty of figuring out logically just why she had liked that awkward, eager, provincial boy with tremulous long fingers and pimples between his eyebrows, all this vexed her so much that she was ready to curse the new green dress laid out on the armchair, the plump posterior of Frieda who was rummaging in the lower drawer of the commode, and her own morose reflection in the mirror. She looked at a jewel in which an anniversary was coldly reflected, and remembered that her thirty-fourth birthday had passed the other day, and with a strange impatience began consulting her mirror to detect the threat of a wrinkle, the hint of a sagging fold. Somewhere a door closed softly, and the stairs creaked (they were not supposed to creak!), and her husband's cheerful off-key whistle receded out of earshot. 'He is a poor dancer,' thought Martha. 'He may be good at tennis but he will always be a poor dancer. He does not like dancing. He does not understand how fashionable it is nowadays. Fashionable and indispensable.'

With muted resentment against inefficient Frieda, she thrust her head through the soft, gathered circumference of the dress. Its green shadow flew downward past her eyes. She emerged erect, smoothed her hips, and suddenly felt that her soul was temporarily circumscribed and contained by the emerald texture of that cool frock.

Below, on the square terrace, with its cement floor and the purple and pink asters on its wide balustrade, Dreyer sat in a canvas chair by a garden table, and with his open book resting in his lap gazed into the garden. Beyond the fence, the black car, the expensive Icarus, was already waiting inexorably. The new chauffeur, his elbows placed on the fence from the outside, was chatting with the gardener. A cold late-afternoon lucency penetrated the autumn air; the sharp blue shadows of the young trees stretched along the sunny lawn, all in the same direction as if anxious to see which would be first to reach the garden's white lateral wall. Far off, across the street, the pistachio facades of apartment houses were very distinct, and there, melancholically leaning on a red quilt laid on the window sill, sat a bald little man in shirtsleeves. The gardener had already twice taken hold of his wheelbarrow but each time had turned again to the chauffeur. Then they both lit cigarettes. And the wispy smoke was clearly set off as it floated along the glossy black side of the car. The shadow seemed to have moved just a bit farther but the sun still bore down triumphantly on the right from behind the corner of the count's villa, which stood on higher ground with taller trees. Tom walked indolently along the flowerbed. From a sense of duty and without the least hope of success, he started after a low-flitting sparrow, and then lay down by the wheelbarrow with his nose on his paws. The very word terrace – how spacious, how cool! The pretty ray of a spiderweb stretched obliquely from the corner flower of the balustrade to the table standing beside it. The cloudlets in one part of the pale clean sky had funny curls, and were all alike as on a maritime horizon, all hanging together in a delicate flock. At last having heard all there was to hear and told all there was to tell, the gardener moved off with his wheelbarrow, turning with geometrical precision at the intersections of gravel paths, and Tom, rising lazily, proceeded to walk after him like a clockwork toy, turning when the gardener turned. *Die toten Seelen* by a Russian author, which had long been slipping down Dreyer's knee, slid onto the flags of the floor, and he felt too lazy to pick it up. So pleasant, so spacious . . . The first to finish would be no doubt that apple tree over there. The chauffeur got into his seat. It would be interesting to know just what he was thinking about now. This morning his eyes had oddly twinkled. Could it be that he drinks? Wouldn't that be a scream, a tippling chauffeur. Two men in top hats, diplomats or undertakers, went by; the top hats and black coats floated by along the fence. Out of nowhere came a Red Admirable butterfly, settled on the edge of the table, opened its wings and began to fan them slowly as if breathing. The dark-brown ground was bruised here and there, the scarlet band had faded, the fringes were frayed – but the creature was still so lovely, so festive . . .

ERICH KÄSTNER

From

GOING TO THE DOGS

Translated by Cyrus Brooks

A WAITER AS ORACLE
THE OTHER DECIDES TO GO NOTWITHSTANDING
A CLUB FOR INTELLECTUAL CONTACTS

FABIAN WAS SITTING in a café, by name Spalteholz, reading the headlines of the evening papers: English Airship Disaster near Beauvais, Strychnine Stored with Lentils, Girl of Nine Jumps from Window, Election of Premier – Another Fiasco, Murder in Lainz Zoo, Scandal of Municipal Purchasing Board, Artificial Voice in Waistcoat Pocket, Ruhr Coal-Sales Falling, National Railways – Presentation to Director Neumann, Elephants on Pavement, Coffee Markets Uncertain, Clara Bow Scandal, Expected Strike of 140,000 Metal Workers, Chicago Underworld Drama, Timber Dumping – Negotiations in Moscow, Revolt of Starhemberg Troops. The usual thing. Nothing special.

He took a sip of coffee and shuddered. The stuff tasted sweet. Ten years before, in a students' hostel at the Oranienburg Gate, he had forced himself, three times a week, to swallow macaroni with saccharine; since then he had loathed everything sweet. He hurriedly lit a cigarette and called the waiter.

'Yes, sir?'

'Please answer me a question.'

'Yes, sir.'

'Shall I go or not?'

'Where to, sir?'

'I want you to answer questions, not ask them. Shall I go or not?'

The waiter mentally scratched his head. Then he shifted from one flat foot to the other and said with some embarrassment: 'You'd better not go. Keep on the safe side, sir.'

Fabian nodded. 'Right. I'll go. The bill.'

'But I said, don't go.'

'That's why I'm going. The bill, please.'

'So if I'd said, go, you wouldn't have gone?'

'Oh yes I should. The bill, please.'

'It's beyond me,' declared the waiter, in an irritable tone. 'Why did you ask me at all?'

'I wish I knew,' replied Fabian.

'One cup of coffee, one roll and butter, fifty, thirty, eighty, ninety pfennigs,' recited the waiter.

Fabian placed a mark on the table and left the café. He had no notion where he was. If you board a No. 1 bus at Wittenbergplatz, get out at Potsdam Bridge and take a tram, without knowing its destination, only to leave it twenty minutes later because a woman suddenly gets in who bears a resemblance to Frederick the Great, you cannot be expected to know where you are.

He followed three workmen who were striding along at a good pace, stumbled over planks of wood, passed hoardings and grey, dubious hotels and arrived at Jannowitz Bridge Station. In the train, he found the address which Bertuch, the manager at his office, had written down for him: 23 Schlüterstrasse, Frau Sommer. He got out at the Zoo. In the Joachimsthaler Strasse, a thin-legged young lady, rising and falling on her toes, asked him what about it. He rejected her advances, wagged his finger at her and escaped.

The town was like a fair-ground. The house-fronts were bathed in garish light to shame the stars in the sky.

An aeroplane droned above the roofs. Suddenly there was a shower of aluminium thalers. The passers-by looked up, laughed and bent to pick them up. Fabian fleetingly recalled the story of the little girl who lifted her frock to catch the small change that fell from heaven. Then he took one of the thalers from the stiff brim of a stranger's hat. It bore the words: 'Come to the Exotic Bar, 3 Nollendorfplatz, Beautiful girls, Nude tableaux, Pension Condor in same house.' Suddenly Fabian had the impression that he was up there in the aeroplane, looking down at himself, at that young man in the Joachimsthaler Strasse, who stood in the bustle of the crowd, in the glare of street lamps and shop windows, in the turmoil of the inflamed and feverish night. How small the fellow was, and yet it was himself!

He crossed the Kurfürstendamm. On one of the gables a figure in neon lights, that of a youthful Turk, was rolling its electric eyeballs. Then something struck Fabian violently on the heel. He turned round disapprovingly. It was a tram. The conductor swore.

'Look where you're going,' shouted a policeman.

Fabian raised his hat. 'I'll do my best.'

In Schlüterstrasse the door was opened by a Lilliputian in green livery, who climbed an ornamental ladder, helped the visitor out of his coat, and vanished. Scarcely had he gone when a well-developed woman, undoubtedly Frau Sommer, came rustling through the curtains. 'Will you kindly come to my office?' she said. Fabian followed her.

'Your club was recommended to me by a Herr Bertuch.'

She flicked over the pages of a ledger, and nodded. 'Bertuch, Friedrich Georg, manager, aged forty, medium height, dark, 9 Karlstrasse, fond of music, prefers slim blondes of twenty-five and under.'

'That's him.'

'Herr Bertuch became a member last October and has been here five times since.'

'That speaks well for the place.'

'The entrance fee is twenty marks, and there is a further fee of ten marks for each visit.'

'Here are thirty marks.' Fabian put the money on the desk. The well-developed woman slipped the notes into a drawer, took up a fountain-pen and said: 'Your name and address?'

'Fabian, Jacob, aged thirty-two, profession variable, at present advertising copywriter, 17 Schaperstrasse, weak heart, brown hair. What else do you want to know?'

'Have you any special wishes in the matter of ladies?'

'I would rather not tie myself down. My taste is for blondes, but my experience is against them. I have a preference for tall women. But the attraction is not mutual. Better leave that column blank.'

A gramophone was playing somewhere. The well-developed woman rose and said gravely: 'Before we go in I must make you acquainted with the more important rules. There is no objection to members approaching each other, indeed they are expected to do so. The ladies enjoy the same rights as the men. The existence, address and practices of the club must not be revealed except to trustworthy persons. Despite the idealistic aims of our establishment, refreshments must be paid for on consumption. No couple may claim exemption from interference while on the club premises. Couples are requested to leave the club if they wish to be undisturbed. The establishment serves to initiate acquaintanceships, but does not cater for them once made. Members who give each other temporary opportunities for identification are requested to forget them, as otherwise complications are inevitable. Do you understand, Herr Fabian?'

'Perfectly.'

'Then please follow me.'

There must have been thirty or forty persons present. In the first room they were playing bridge. Next door they were dancing. Frau Sommer led the new member to an unoccupied table, said that he could apply to her at any time in case of need, and took her leave. Fabian sat down, ordered a brandy and soda from the waiter, and looked round him. Was he at a birthday-party?

'They look more innocent than they are,' remarked a small, dark-haired girl, and sat down at his side. Fabian offered her a cigarette.

'I rather like you,' she said. 'You were born in December.'

'In February.'

'Oh, Pisces with a spot or two of Aquarius. Rather cold. You've come here out of curiosity?'

'The supporters of the atomic theory maintain that even the smallest particle of matter consists of charges of electrical energy revolving round each other. Do you regard this merely as a hypothesis or as an actual statement of fact?'

'So you are sensitive too?' cried the young woman. 'But that doesn't matter. Have you come to look for a wife?'

He shrugged his shoulders. 'Is that a formal proposal?'

'Nonsense! I've been married twice, and that's enough to go on with. Marriage does not provide me with the right form of self-expression. I'm much too interested in men. I picture every man I meet, provided I like him, as a husband.'

'In his most salient aspects, I hope.'

She laughed as though she had a hiccup, and placed her hand on his knee. 'Quite so. They say I suffer from an inventive imagination. If, in the course of the evening, you should feel a desire to take me home, my flat and I are small but substantial.'

He removed that restless, alien hand from his knee, and said: 'All things are possible. Now I'm going to take a look round.' That was as far as he got. When he rose and turned away from her, he found a tall woman with a figure that answered the programme standing in front of him. 'They are just going to dance,' she said. She was taller than he and blonde into the bargain. The little black-haired buccaneer observed the regulations and vanished. A waiter started the gramophone. People rose from their tables. They were dancing.

Fabian examined the blonde. She had a pale, infantile face and an air of greater restraint than, to judge by her dancing, she possessed. He said nothing, and felt that in a few minutes they would reach that stage of taciturnity when conversation, especially trivial conversation, becomes impossible. Luckily he trod on her toe. She grew talkative. She pointed out the two ladies who had recently boxed each other's ears and torn the clothes off each other's backs for the sake of a man. She informed him that Frau Sommer was engaged in an intrigue with the green Lilliputian, the details of which she dared not imagine. Finally she asked whether he wanted to stay; she was going. He went with her.

In Kurfürstendamm she signalled to a taxi-cab, gave an address, climbed in and constrained him to take a seat at her side. 'But I've only two marks left,' he objected.

'That doesn't make much difference,' she replied, and ordered the driver to put out the lights. They were in darkness. The car started and drove off. At the first turn in the road she fell upon him and bit his lower lip. He struck his temple against the frame of the window, caught his head in his hands and said: 'Ah-oo! That's a good beginning.'

'Don't be so touchy,' she said, and smothered him with her attentions.

The assault was too sudden for him. He had a pain in his head, and his heart was not in the business.

'I really wanted to write a letter,' he groaned, 'before you throttle me.'

She punched him on the collar-bone, laughed up and down the scale with complete self-possession, and went on strangling him. Evidently his attempts to defend himself against the woman were misinterpreted. Every turn of the road led to new entanglements. He asked the gods to spare them further swerves. But the gods were having a day off.

At last the car stopped. Outside the door of a block of flats the blonde powdered her face, paid the fare and said: 'Your cheeks are covered in red smudges, and you're coming up for a cup of tea.'

He rubbed the traces of lipstick from his face, and replied: 'I'm honoured by the invitation, but I've got to be early at the office tomorrow.'

'Don't make me angry. You're going to stay with me. The maid will wake you.'

'But I shan't get up. No, I must sleep at home. I'm expecting an urgent telegram at seven in the morning. My landlady will come into my room and shake me till I wake.'

'But how do you know about this telegram?'

'I even know what's in it.'

'What?'

'It will say, "Get out of bed. Yours ever, Fabian." My name is Fabian.' He blinked up at the leaves of the trees and noted with delight the yellow gleam of the street lamps. The street was completely empty. A cat ran silently away into the darkness. If only he could go now and saunter along in front of those grey house-fronts!

'But your story about the telegram is not true.'

'No, but that's purely a matter of chance,' he said.

'What makes you come to the club if you don't want to take the consequences?' she said irritably, and unlocked the door.

'Someone gave me the address and I'm very curious.'

'Well, come along,' she said. 'We'll set no limits to your curiosity.' The door slammed to behind them.

ERNST HAFFNER

From

BLOOD BROTHERS

Translated by Michael Hofmann

CHAPTER 12

DURING LUDWIG'S TIME in chokey, lots of things have changed in the gang. All the boys have got new clothes. A few, Fred, Jonny and Hans, have new wardrobes from head to toe, with good suits and even winter coats. There's money sloshing around as well. Jonny straight away organises a collection for Ludwig among the Brothers. 'To help him forget his time inside.' Ludwig is presented with forty-two marks. He is to buy himself a coat with the money, and various bits and pieces he needs. On the evening of the day Ludwig made his successful break for freedom, there is a big pub crawl in his honour. All the boys are really glad to have him back. And the fact that he ran away so fearlessly in an underground station, that lifts him up a peg or two in everyone's eyes. While the geezer who gave Ludwig the stolen luggage chit, he'd better count his bones if they ever catch up with him. The meanness. When he could have just gone up to him and said: 'Hey, this is a stolen ticket. Do you want to pick up the suitcase? We'll go fifty-fifty.' That would have been appropriate, but this . . . He'd better watch it!

Ludwig is worried about showing up at so many bars in one night. It would just take one little raid in one of them and he's in shtook, seeing as he's got no papers. Papers, papers . . . Jonny muses. Then: 'Come with me.' They head over to Grenadierstrasse, Berlin's ghetto, the street of the little illicit businesses and dives. Jonny exchanges a few words with an old Jewess standing by a cellar opening. She calls a boy up out of the cellar and sends him off on an errand. After a few minutes, he returns with a little wrinkled-looking Jew in a greasy kaftan. The old man's beard and hair are a greenish tangle, his small eyes peer restlessly this way and that. The Jew takes Jonny and Ludwig into his shop.

The term 'shop' is a wild exaggeration. You could purchase its entire stock and have change from ten marks. A few venerable biscuits, the inevitable garlic, a few packets of kosher margarine. The shop is just a blind anyway, a mask for other, better lines of business that don't need stock. They go into a dark windowless back room. The Jew sits down between Ludwig and Jonny on an erstwhile sofa. Devout, submissive and innocent, the old fence folds his black-veined hands together. 'What are the gentlemen looking for?' 'My friend here needs papers,' begins Jonny. 'Papers . . . oh . . .' Straight away, the old man becomes suspicious and reserved. False papers are a difficult business. Jonny is offering fifteen marks for a police registration certificate or an unemployment card. The old man's fingers are playing nervously with his kaftan, fear and cupidity are in equipoise. No, he doesn't do papers. He is an honest man. Yes . . . But . . . he knows someone who does do that sort of business. 'What are we waiting for, then? Let's go see him,' Jonny interrupts.

The someone turns out to be an ancient wizened old woman on the fourth floor of a back apartment. First off, the old man has a big powwow with the little lady. A grisly mix of Yiddish, Hebrew, and German. Then the old man explains to Jonny and Ludwig in a lachrymose sing-song that someone had lived here, he was registered with the police and everything was in order. But one day he hadn't come home, and had thus cheated the honest old lady out of her rent money. The only things he had left behind were a soiled shirt and a bunch of papers in a cigar box, including police registration, his tax card and a baptismal certificate. 'Let's see 'em,' says Jonny. The registration is made out for the flat on Grenadierstrasse, and is in the name of August Kaiweit from Königsberg, born in 1908. Now, Ludwig was born in 1912, and as a native of Dortmund he has barely heard of Königsberg, but in general the papers are not bad. 'Where did the man live?' Jonny asks. The old lady takes him to a wretched closet. 'Rent?' 'Five marks a week.' 'And the papers?' Once again, the two old people fall into an endless back-and-forth, incomprehensible to Jonny and Ludwig. Result: ten marks for the papers, and five marks commission for the old Jew.

Done. Jonny gives the old lady ten marks for the papers, and five marks' rent down on the first week; the Jew is paid his commission. Ludwig has got himself a new name and new digs, in one fell swoop. Now, August Kaiweit need have no fear of police raids. Admittedly, the papers wouldn't work at police HQ, where they've got Ludwig's prints and photographs on file. Moreover, it's not impossible that the real August Kaiweit has a police record and is on some wanted list somewhere. Perhaps he's even a crook; in view of these dodgy Grenadierstrasse digs, that's even quite likely. But there it is: if Ludwig was risk averse, then he might as well hand himself over to the police. A life outside the law is not the same as shelter in the bosom of Abraham . . .

He takes the front-door key from the old lady, and leaves with Jonny. On Münzstrasse there is the parting of ways. Ludwig to look for an old coat from a dealer, and Jonny . . . Jonny has something to go to that involves Fred. Them and their secrets, thinks Ludwig. Rendezvous: eight o'clock at the Rehkeller on Prenzlauer Strasse, just up from Alexanderplatz.

Alexanderplatz! The focal point of Berlin's underworld.

Familiar – who hasn't seen the movies? The aristocratic gangsters, who won't do a job except in top and tails. Those sinisterly beautiful evil-doers, for whom murder is a perverse hobby. And the beautifully realistic criminal cellars with Apache dancers, Brylcreemed villains, classy two-mark whores with fire-red mops of curls. The discreet champagne lounges in the basements, and the trapdoors. All provided by the glib and deficient imaginations of directors and other second-raters. The amusement industry clamours for the like. It wants cheap thrills for its expensive balcony seats. So the criminal underworld's the thing. And because the social misery of the actual underworld is not the kind of thing Kurfürstendamm pays money to see, Berlin is given a fictitious one instead, one which, as above, lives in the lap of luxury. The superficial observer of this falsified milieu would find Berlin's actual criminal underworld deathly dull. Nothing of interest there, nothing. Blood is a precious liquid, here as there, and Berlin's villains go to admire the demonic super-criminal in the same place as everyone else – the cinema. It needs closer study to get through to those people who, between brief spans at large, measure out their lives in long prison sentences, in constant flight from the law, and – after a few days of joy, vegetate in ever-deeper deprivation.

Their own choice? Not always, by no means! A youth spent in welfare, more or less apprenticed to crime, that isn't a self-chosen destiny. And then: prior convictions? Untold numbers fail at the difficult glass-hard wall of bourgeois prejudice and desire for retribution. Untold numbers who might have liked to try a law-abiding life for a change.

First: the realisation that the criminal basements as they are shown to us in scores of films no longer exist in Berlin today. All those basements on Linienstrasse, Marienstrasse,

Auguststrasse, Joachimstrasse, Borsigstrasse and so on, they were forced out of business after the inflation. And the big beer joints with their lively oom-pah-pah music from early morning on, they are just waiting rooms for armies of pimps, unemployed and casual criminals. But a clientele like that isn't enough to keep a place in business. What keeps these places going is prostitution. It alone keeps them going. It gets the johns in, and drives them to big bar-tabs. Unattached prostitutes aren't great consumers of anything, they wander from table to table offering themselves, or cadging a drink from a guest who's there for a thrill. And when there *is* something really happening in those places, then you may take it for granted that it's all a set-up, so that the voyeurs order another round, and tell their friends about this amazing underworld bar.

The stage set took up the underworld theme, dished up a hundred per cent tall tales, and now the underworld itself is turning into the stage set, so as not to prove too much of a disappointment. It even advertises in the commercial section of the press. Between ads for feudal eateries and worldly *palais de danse*, you see the shout: '*Interested in experiencing the Berlin underworld? Try Europe's best-known restaurant on Alexanderplatz!*' Does it matter that the best-known restaurant in Europe is just a pick-up joint? The underworld is in quotation marks. So much the better for the metropolis, if that was the full extent of its underworld. Alas, it's too good to be true.

Alexanderplatz in the hours between 9 p.m. and midnight. Where to start in the confusion of humanity? Prostitution in every form. From the fifteen-year-old girl, just slipped out of welfare, to the sixty-year-old dreadnought, everyone is feverishly on the make. Male prostitutes, flocks of them, outside the toilets, in bus and tram stops, outside the big bars. Homeless of both sexes sniff around. Loiter, move off. Aimlessly. Sit on a pile of planks for the new underground station. 'Move along now!' Police patrol. Move along, sure, where to? It's almost tempting, the looming bulk of the police HQ on Alexanderplatz. There you can get something to eat and drink and a bed for the night. But only if the desperate fellow has hurled a brick through a shop window.

Pimping, with its specific grimness, is everywhere. Hundreds on Alexanderplatz alone. They own the street, and they certainly own the working girls. They stick to the punters like glue; yes, they animate flagging interest by talking up the girls. Human beings are touted and appraised like lame nags in a horse market.

A swarm of rowdy fun-seekers spills out of an underground beer joint next to the UFA cinema. Straight away, the traffic is brought to a standstill. The crowd is milling around, growing all the time. At the core of the disturbance are a prostitute and her pimp. He is laying into the woman with both fists. She is standing doubled over, her hands protectively in front of her face. She looks like a beast in a slaughterhouse. From the crowd come enthusiastic shouts: 'That's right, Fritz, give it to her!' And Fritz doesn't stint, he gives it to her all right. Not a finger, not a voice is raised on behalf of the woman. Surely, he is among friends here. If the woman gets a beating, she will have deserved it. Finally, the police turn up, clear a way through the surly wall. What happens? Nothing. The pimp has his papers on him, the victim is his wife. And the wife, when invited to by the police, declines to bring charges. She doesn't want to be beaten to a pulp later on by her pimp husband's close friends. 'It looks worse than it is,' is all she says, the blood streaming from her nose.

The huddle of people breaks up. No more trouble.

Interest is gone. The prostitute stands at a bus stop, sobbing and dabbing at her nose. 'Now, that's enough of that, Edith.' The pimp, perfectly amiable. And Edith tries desperately to shut up, but the occasional sob still shakes her. She pulls out lipstick and powder, to try and restore order to her teary face. Then they go, arm in arm, to the nearby Rehkeller.

It's the only one of the so-called cellars to deserve the ascription of criminal dive. But even here everything is lite. Underworld is a style. A low arched room with dim-coloured lights. The ancient oft-painted walls give off an appalling reek of mould. A pianist makes despairing efforts to bang out a coherent sequence of notes from a tangle of wire in front of him. Clientele: the usual Alex mob, admittedly with very few tourists. Doesn't promise much from the outside, the Rehkeller.

The Blood Brothers are sitting at a table in the deepest darkest corner of the bar. Sitting with them is a girl of seventeen or eighteen. Anneliese, the new sweetheart of the Brothers. Anneliese has come into the gang ever since, in some way still unknown to Ludwig, they have come into money. Ludwig shows up in his new coat. Anneliese welcomes him with a great smacking kiss. They have never met before, and Jonny explains to Ludwig that Anneliese is part of the gang. The other Brothers greet Ludwig with a facetious, 'Evening, Herr Kaiweit.' Ludwig is flavour of the month. Anneliese sits on the lap of the 'poor lad who was innocent and did time in Moabit', and comforts him at any opportunity with kisses and petting. The first round of schnapps is brought, and they all solemnly intone: 'Here's to you, Ludwig.' Then he has to tell them all about it. How he was nabbed, the interrogation, his time in the Alex, the juvenile court hearing, the moment he spotted Auntie Elsie's secret message to him on the inside of the sugar bag.

What the food was like inside, how they treated him, and in minute detail, how he did his bunk in Friedrichstadt station. The escort seemed to be a decent enough fellow, but freedom is freedom. The gang are ever so proud of their Ludwig when he tells them about picking up the discarded copy of the *B. Z.* on the train, and how that helped him get the money to make a call. My God, what a sharp lad! 'Cheers! August Kaiweit!' And Jonny adds: 'And here's to us collaring the evil-doer who tricked you in the first place.'

The pianist announces a rumba, and knocks out something that might equally well be a tango or a black bottom. The girls go looking for a few feet of space to dance with their sweethearts, and Anneliese grabs hold of Ludwig, who now has to go and rumba. This time yesterday he was still lying on a pallet in police detention, with the evening's flour soup glugging in his belly, and the guards' hobnailed boots clanking about in the corridor. 'Kiss me, Anneliese,' he manages to whisper.

The bill is paid. The Blood Brothers move off. Where to now? What about the Mexiko? 'Not there again,' replies Fred, grinning. The Alexander Quelle on Münzstrasse is an unappetising place, but always packed. The din of the brass music is enough to blow the head off your pints, and the mass-produced tobacco smoke keeps the paper chains in a constant spin. Gang members of all ages, abjectest prostitution, layabouts, male and female beggars. They are, all of them, responsible for polishing the pate of the landlord, who can no longer stand to breathe the fug of his joint and stands outside the door. It is unbelievably full. The newest latecomer has to squeeze inside the door and yell for his beer or schnapps or whatever he wants. The gang barge their way through; of course there's no space anywhere. Right at the back, in front of the upstairs toilets, they manage to huddle round a couple of already-occupied tables. They don't mind being squashed together.

Ludwig, Anneliese, Jonny and Fred are sitting between skeletal-looking dossers, come to try and forget the chicken ladder of their lives with a *Koks* or a *Korn* with a dot (*Koks*: rum with a piece of sugar; *Korn* with a dot: kummel with a drop of raspberry). Jonny orders a round of *Koks*. The dossers included, of course. An old geezer with a long white beard is finishing his supper. In his left hand he has a half-wrapped sausage end, from which he slices piece after piece with the paring knife in his right, and pops them into his mouth with bread. The ancient face with the sprouting white hair looks like a throwback to those bygone films where the good child by the garden fence throws a coin into the nice old man's hat. 'Well, Grandpa, aren't you going home yet?' asks Fred. 'Home?' The oldster looks up quickly, before returning to his end of sausage. Then: 'The manager's going to throw me out, I already owe him for four nights. I've reached my limit, so he says.'

Calm, objective, quite convinced that the manager is well within his rights, the words come out interrupted by the gummy chewing of his food. The heat in the bar is such that sweat is pouring down the creases of his face. Still the old man won't be induced to take off his coat. Probably he doesn't have a jacket on underneath. He takes his hat off. His snow-white hair curls over his collar and ears. The coppery face has the eyes of a beaten dog. A second schnapps and a cigar give the beggar a little self-confidence. 'Where you from, old man?' He's been out west, around Wittenbergplatz, begging. Up and down backstairs. Since nine o'clock this morning. And all the fine gentry in that area, their contribution to his welfare totalled seventy-two pfennigs, a couple of crusts of bread, and – the old man shows them off proudly – a pair of glacé gloves that are too much of a pair: in fact, they are two right hands.

As he tells his story, a trace of something resembling indignation comes into his voice: 'Four flights up, I'm knocking on the kitchen door. A servant is about to give me a few pfennigs, when along comes the lady of the house. Why are folks always being given money without doing a scrap of work for it, she says. This man is still pretty fit, why shouldn't he beat the bedroom carpet for it. Well, I lost it. All right, I say, give me your mangy old rug. So your crooked Gustav goes down four flights of stairs, beats the carpet, and back up. Then what does the old bird say? There, my dear chap, now you've earned your five pfennigs . . . And that's a lady!' In the hostel on Gollnowstrasse, the old man now owes for four nights, and unless he can pay for at least two of them, the manager will throw him out.

'How old are you, Grandpa?' 'Seventy-four . . . no, eighty-. . . no, seventy-two.' He's not sure any more. He was born in Posen. He doesn't know if he's German or Polish, and he doesn't really care. When he was a young man, he was the best and most honest milker – he stresses that – on the whole estate. And then the owner threw him out, because a cow had lashed out at him, and he had kicked her in the stomach. But that didn't matter. He had to go into the army anyways. Then there were his years as a hobo. Germany, Austria, Switzerland, Italy, France, and Spain, all on shanks's pony. Years, decades. Till shortly before the Great War, when he found himself back in Germany again as an old man. During the war he worked in some munitions factory, and then a gentleman of the road again. More years.

Till he wound up in Berlin, and the four-million-strong city became his highway because he didn't have enough puff any more. He doesn't know where his parents died, nor where his five brothers and sisters are, if they're even still alive. He has never been inside a cinema. As far as he's concerned, a book is something with stories in it, and the prime function of newspapers is wrapping things up.

But one thing he's learned in his long years of experience, be it in Berlin or Italy or some burg in Silesia: rich people don't do charity. They'd rather turn their dogs loose on beggars or slam doors in their faces. Giving, with a deep reflexive understanding of hunger and misery, is something that only poor people do. The Silesian mineworker, the Italian labourer, the unemployed geezer in Berlin. Tomorrow the old man is headed for proletarian Wedding. He knows and likes the area. 'Coppers, only coppers. But at least they add up,' he says, and pensively puts his hat back on. It feels better to be sitting with his hat on.

In a fit of magnanimity, Fred takes a collection from the gang members, to get together money for the old man's kip. Grand total: two marks, eighty-five pfennigs. The beggar is sceptical when he is given the handful of coppers. They've got to be pulling his leg. But then, when the money's stashed in his pocket, he's in a hurry to leave. Keep what you got. You never know: maybe the boys will drink up their money, and then want it back. It's better to scarper. The manager won't chase him away, he'll get his money . . .

Ludwig keeps noticing more ways in which the gang has changed. Fred seems to have become treasurer, and each member is called upon to pay a mark a week into the common exchequer. Johnny, Hans, Fred and Konrad have got a regular kip – with Anneliese – at an invalid jailbird's place on Badstrasse. Heinz, Erwin, Walter and Georg seem to have somewhere as well, two of them at a time. Wonder where all this money comes from, thinks Ludwig. He doesn't trust himself to ask.

The boys break up. It's not possible to have a conversation in this crowd. They decide to ride to Schlesischer Bahnhof, and go to Café Messerstich. Why the Messerstich is called a café, and not a bar, is just as obscure as why it's called the Messerstich* in the first place. The clientele is made up of organ-grinders, buskers, ragmen (also known as naturalists), and mainly handicapped male and female beggars. The only thing they like to stab is a piece of roast or at the very least a sausage. The local speciality here are the extraordinary prodigious pigs' feet in jelly. The gang order, and have a slap-up dinner. Gnawed bones are stacked high on the table, the landlord has to send over the road for more rolls. They all eat like combine harvesters.

A disabled organ-grinder is propping up the bar. His left sleeve hangs down, loose and empty. His single hand is clutching a large glass of schnapps and raising it to his lips. A sip. The schnapps-wet lips purse themselves in a piercing whistle. As on command, two white rats appear from his two jacket pockets. Clamber nimbly up to his shoulders and perch there on their hind legs, begging. Laughter and applause from the other guests. The disabled rat-tamer feels flattered, takes his half-full glass, and holds it under the noses of both his pets. Each head leans in and sips a tiny amount of the sweet schnapps. Another whistle. The rats scuttle back into their pockets. Contentedly, the man finishes his drink. The animals go with him on his tour. Stand up and beg when they hear the music, disappear up his trouser leg and reappear at his open collar. Ratty Paul is a celebrity in his profession and is reputed to be doing quite well, thanks to his little friends.

* Messerstich: a stab with a knife. Maybe a jocular debasement of 'Metternich'?

The Blood Brothers are sitting replete and idle over their beer. Anneliese is jiggling about on her chair. Casts fearful glances at a table by the stove. A young lad is sitting there, staring aggressively at the Brothers. And if his eyes happen to meet Anneliese's, then she gets even more restless and anxious. Suddenly the boy is standing at the gang's table: 'Can I talk to you, Anneliese.' It sounds brutal and menacing. Anneliese is cravenly on the point of obeying when Jonny leaps up: 'What do you want with her?' 'None of your business, you monkey!' is the ungentle reply. With Jonny's characteristic speed, he lands the fellow an almighty slap. Before the lad knows what's happened to him, he's been hit a second time, and finds himself deposited out on the street. Doesn't dare go back in. 'Who was that, Anneliese?' asks Jonny. Anneliese is crying. 'Oh, you know . . . someone from Friedel Peters's gang.'

Only last week Anneliese was the sweetheart of another gang, namely that of Friedel Peters. But life at Friedel's side no longer suited Anneliese. No one had any money, and one day Friedel had even said to her: 'Anneliese, it's time you went and earned for us.' And so she had gone over to Jonny's mob, because they were flush. Really, Anneliese wasn't behaving any differently than the mistress of some industrialist, who won't hesitate to transfer her affections to a bank executive if heavy industry should fall on hard times and can no longer guarantee her pin money.

'Seems we might get a dust-up later tonight,' says Konrad pensively. 'You could be right,' replies Jonny. 'Franz, ten double Koks!' Fred orders. The prospect of a dust-up requires drink. Jonny owns two knuckle-dusters. He gives one to Konrad, who starts furiously hitting the jagged steel against the table. 'Ten schnapps!' Jonny orders. The drinks in quick succession have the effect of making the boys tense and aggressive. But no one comes to claim Anneliese. Anneliese, who only a moment ago was gibbering with nerves and dread, is now flattered to be the bone of contention between two gangs. For the moment, though, everything in the bar is quiet.

A young man, new to the area, walks into the bar, and enters negotiations with the landlord. An unemployed circus performer of some kind, an acrobat or tumbler. Even though the bar is full to bursting, he gets permission to do some of his stunts. There's an audience for that kind of thing here. A couple of chairs, which the fellow needs as props, are willingly vacated. The guests are aware that something is about to happen, and they mill around the artiste like a great family, full of expectation. A handstand on one hand on the top of the chair-back. The drunken one-armed Ratty Paul grouses from the back: 'Thass nothing, you should see wot I . . .' The artiste does a rubber man, twisting and contorting his body till he is puce in the face. That creates an impression. Everyone is fascinated by the artiste's tricks. Even the landlord is watching now, and the waiter leaves the beers on his tray to go flat.

Now here comes the show-stopper. The artiste picks up one chair between his teeth, and sets the second on top of it. That's the high point of the evening's entertainment. That stunt with the teeth wows them. Not least because they can see the incredible strain in the artiste's face. It's contorted, bright red, the eyes are bulging out of their sockets, his whole body is trembling. The spectators are beside themselves. Ideal moment for the performer to pass the hat around. Result: one mark eighty. Even in penurious circles people pay generously for first-class performance. Ratty Paul buys the artiste a drink. He discreetly wipes the blood off his mouth. His barbarous stunt has left him with bleeding gums.

The performer's feat of strength has done nothing to cool the flickering pugnacity of the Brothers. If only Friedel Peters and his boys would come looking for Anneliese. Boy oh boy, the beer glasses would fly, and the broken chair legs would go whizzing through the air. But there's nothing doing. If they're such cowards that they leave their fellow member's beating unavenged, then too bad. Let's go, we've waited long enough. Where to? How about Auntie Minnie's on Warschauer Brücke. There might be dancing. Jonny pays the bill. Thirty marks. Where do they get the money from, Ludwig thinks again.

The street outside is quiet, no sign of any enemy gang members hanging around. Past Schlesischer Bahnhof, the Blood Brothers turn down on to the deserted Mühlenstrasse. A hundred yards ahead of them, someone scampers across the street, and disappears in the shadow of the house fronts. The gang walks in two lines of four, with the gibbering Anneliese and their youngest, Walter, in the middle of the back. Once again, someone runs across the street. This time they are able to recognise the fellow Jonny slapped around. 'Have you got your knuckle-duster, Konrad?' asks Jonny. 'You bet!' Konrad replies. They have walked the hundred yards. Mühlenstrasse widens out into Rummelsburger Platz.

'Go!' comes a shout in the immediate vicinity of the gang. Either side of the Blood Brothers, ten or twelve enemies dart out of dark doorways. The front line of Brothers, with Jonny, and the back line, with Konrad, are prepared. Walter hustles Anneliese to the far side of the road, but he can't stand inaction, and he leaves her in the lurch wailing and jumps right into the knots of tangling boys. Jonny and Konrad's knuckle-dusters are smashing enemy chins, thumping enemy biceps, slamming down on hard enemy skulls. The fight proceeds in near silence. Both sides know that if there's any noise, a squad car will be there in no time at all, and they'd rather tribal warfare go on without police intervention.

If only there was a bit more light. Blood Brother squares up to Blood Brother, and the same thing is happening with the other mob. Things are already looking critical for the assailants, their skulls are no match for the knuckle-dusters. Then a shot rings out. Bang! Like a whiplash. Walter wobbles into the gutter, clasping his left arm. 'Oo . . . oo . . . ow!' The shot, the cry of the wounded boy, are signs that the Peters gang has had enough. They flee. The Blood Brothers have won the day, and they stand there panting and tending to Walter, who is still screaming his 'Ooo . . . oow!' into the silence.

Windows are already being thrown open. Bed jackets and string vests shiver and shout 'Murder!' and 'Police!' and 'Help!' 'Let's go!' orders Jonny. They run off in the direction of Schlesischer Bahnhof. Jonny and Konrad support Walter. Ludwig and Georg have taken charge of the whimpering Anneliese. On Fruchtstrasse, Jonny and Konrad manage to stop a cab, push Walter inside, and jump in after him. Jonny calls out of the window: 'Come after . . . Badstrasse!' And then the scene is over. The gang breaks up into twos. They take a fleet of taxis to Badstrasse.

Gotthelf, ex-jailbird, now responsible gang-godfather, is not especially surprised when his charges turn up with the injured Walter. 'That's Berlin for you,' he says, and examines the wounded boy. Luckily, it's just a flesh wound. Konrad arrives with some bandages bought from a twenty-four-hour pharmacy. In dribs and drabs the other Brothers arrive. Walter's wound is washed and bandaged up. Should he see a doctor tomorrow? A risk. The doctor will ask questions. But Gotthelf has a solution. There's this tame apothecary he knows, who's taken to drink. He'll treat Walter. Walter is feeling rather perky. He likes this role, he likes the attention, and his wound isn't especially painful. He needs to get some sleep. First he knocks back a hefty schnapps. 'Schnapps is always good!' proclaims the wise Gotthelf.

It's three in the morning. Konrad and Jonny, Hans and Fred are at home. Jonny will share Hans's bed, so that Walter gets an uninterrupted night. Those boys who aren't staying at Gotthelf's take their leave. Anneliese is with Ludwig for tonight, and she walks back with him to his new pad on Grenadierstrasse.

IRMGARD KEUN

From

THE ARTIFICIAL SILK GIRL

Translated by Kathie von Ankum

From LATE FALL AND THE BIG CITY

I'M IN BERLIN. Since a few days ago. After an all-night train ride and with 90 marks left. That's what I have to live on until I come into some money. What I have since experienced is just incredible. Berlin descended on me like a comforter with a flaming floral design. The Westside is very elegant with bright lights – like fabulous stones, really expensive and in an ornate setting. We have enormous neon advertising around here. Sparkling lights surround me. And then there's me and my fur coat. And elegant men like white-slave traders, without exactly trafficking in women at the moment, those no longer exist – but they look like it, because they would be doing it if there was money in it. A lot of shining black hair and deepset night eyes. Exciting. There are many women on the Kurfürstendamm. They simply walk. They have the same faces and a lot of moleskin fur – not exactly first class, in other words, but still chic – with arrogant legs and a great waft of perfume about them. There is a subway: it's like an illuminated coffin on skis – under the ground and musty, and one is squashed. That is what I ride on. It's interesting and it travels fast.

So I'm staying with Tilli Scherer in Münzstrasse, that's near Alexanderplatz. There are unemployed people here who don't even own a shirt, and so many of them. But we have two rooms and Tilli's hair is dyed golden and her husband is away, putting down tram tracks near Essen. And she films. But she's not getting any parts, and the agency is handling things unfairly. Tilli is soft and round like a down pillow and her eyes are like polished blue marbles. Sometimes she cries, because she likes to be comforted. So do I. Without her, I wouldn't have a roof over my head. I'm grateful to her and we're on the same wavelength and don't give each other any trouble. When I see her face when she's asleep, I have good thoughts about her. And that's what's important: how you react to someone while they're sleeping and not exerting any influence over you. There are buses too, very high ones like observation towers that are moving. Sometimes I go on them. At home, we had lots of streets too, but they were familiar with each other. Here, there are so many more streets that they can't possibly all know each other. It's a fabulous city.

Later on, I'll be going to a jockey bar with a white-slave trader type that I don't care about otherwise. But this way, I'll get introduced to the kind of environment that will open up some opportunities for me. Tilli also thinks that I should go. Right now I'm on Tauentzien at Zunztz, which is a café but without music, but cheap – and with lots of hectic people like swirling dust, so you can tell that something's going on in the world. I'm wearing my fur and am having an effect. Across the street is the Memorial Church that nobody can get into, because of the cars all around it, but it's an important monument, but Tilli says it's just holding up traffic.

Tonight I'm going to write everything down in order in my book, because there's so much material that's accumulated in me. So Therese helped me skip town that night. I was trembling all over and full of fear and expectation and joy, because everything would be new now and full of excitement and adventure. And she also went to my mother to fill her in and told her that I would pay back both her and Therese handsomely, if it all worked out. And I know that my mother can keep a secret, which is amazing because she's over 50, but hasn't forgotten what it used to be like for her. But they can't send me any clothes. That would be too dangerous – and so I've got nothing except for one shirt which I wash in the morning and then I stay in bed until it's dry. And I need shoes and many many other things. But it'll come. I also can't write to Therese because of the police who are undoubtedly looking for me – because I know the Ellmanns, how tenacious she is and how she enjoys making criminals out of people.

I don't care if she's in trouble because of me, because she was the one who cooked and ate Rosalie, which was our cat – a sweet creature with a silky purr and fur like white velvet clouds with ink spots. She used to lie on my feet at night and keep them warm – now I have to cry – I ordered a piece of cake for myself, Dutch kirsch, and now I can't eat it because I'm full of grief at the thought of Rosalie. But I took a doggy bag. And she had disappeared all of a sudden, without coming back, which she never did, because she was used to me. And I was standing at the window calling: 'Rosalie' at night and into the gutters. I felt so sad that she was gone, not only because she kept me warm, not only my feet. And for something that's so small and so soft and helpless that you can pick it up with your two hands, you have to be full of love for that. And the next Sunday, I go upstairs to the Ellmanns to retrieve the celery slicer that she had borrowed from us, the bitch, because she won't ever buy anything that she can borrow from someone else. They were just sitting down for dinner – that unkempt Herr Ellmann, who looks like a missionary with those hypocritical eyes, sitting on an island unshaven and eating poor black people in order to convert them. His yellow teeth were sticking out of his mouth, that's how greedy he looked. And there was a platter on the table with fried meat on it – and I recognized the shape of Rosalie's body. Also, I could tell because of Frau Ellmann's behavior and her beady eyes. So I told her straight out, and she's lying in a way that I know; I'm telling the truth. And I break into tears in all my grief and smash the celery chopper into her face so her nose starts to bleed and her eye gets all black and blue. Which wasn't nearly enough, because Ellmann has work and they had enough to eat and didn't go hungry and so they didn't need Rosalie. My mother has been worse off many times, but we never would have dreamed of frying Rosalie, because she was a pet with human instincts – and that you shouldn't eat. And that's one reason I'm keeping the fur. Now I'm all worked up from those memories.

And I was on the road all night. One man gave me three oranges and he had an uncle who owned a leather factory in Bielefeld. He looked like it too. But since I had Berlin ahead of me – why should I have bothered with a guy who travels third class and has second-class airs, just because of leather uncles. That never makes a good impression. Plus he had oily hair, full of dust and grease. And smoker's fingers. And only an hour later, I knew of all the girls he'd had. Wild stuff, of course, and superwomen. And he broke their hearts, when he left them – and they'd throw themselves off church steeples, while taking poison and strangling themselves – so they would be dead for sure, and all that because of the leather guy. You know what men will tell you, if they're trying to convince you that they're not as miserable as they are. I, for one, don't say anything anymore, and pretend to believe it all. If you want to strike it lucky with men, you have to let them think you're stupid.

So I arrived at Friedrichstrasse Station, where there's an incredible hustle-bustle. And I found out that some great

Frenchmen had arrived just before I did, and Berlin's masses were there to greet them. They're called Laval and Briand – and being a woman who frequently spends time waiting in restaurants, I've seen their picture in magazines. I was swept along Friedrichstrasse in a crowd of people, which was full of life and colorful and somehow it had a checkered feeling. There was so much excitement! So I immediately realized that this was an exception, because even the nerves of an enormous city like Berlin can't stand such incredible tension every day. But I was swooning and I continued to be swept along – the air was full of excitement. And some people pulled me along, and so we came to stand in front of an elegant hotel that is called Adlon – and everything was covered with people and cops that were pushing and shoving. And then the politicians arrived on the balcony like soft black spots. And everything turned into a scream and the masses swept me over the cops onto the sidewalk and they wanted those politicians to throw peace down to them from the balcony. And I was shouting with them, because so many voices pierced through my body that they came back out of my mouth. And I had this idiotic crying fit, because I was so moved. And so I immediately belonged to Berlin, being right in the middle of it – that pleased me enormously. And the politicians lowered their heads in a statesmanly fashion, and so, in a way, they were greeting me too.

And we were all shouting for peace – I thought to myself that that was good and you have to do it, because otherwise there's going to be a war – and Arthur Grönland once explained to me that the next war would be fought with stinky gas which makes you turn green and all puffed up. And I certainly don't want that. So I too was shouting to the politicians up there.

Then people were starting to disperse and I felt the strong

urge to find out about politics and what those officials wanted and so on. Because I find newspapers boring and I don't really understand them. I needed someone who would explain things to me, and as part of the overall deflation of enthusiasm luck swept a man over to my side of the street. And there was still something of a bell jar of fraternization covering us and we decided to go to a café. He was pale and wearing a navy blue suit and was looking like New Year's Eve – as if he had just handed out his last cent to the mailman and the chimneysweep. But that was not the case. He was working for the city and was married. I had coffee and three pieces of hazelnut torte – one with whipped cream, because I was starving – and I was filled with a desire for political knowledge. So I asked the navy-blue married man what the politicians had come here for. And in turn he told me that his wife was five years older than him. I asked why people were shouting for peace, since we have peace or at least no war. Him: 'You have eyes like boysenberries.' I hope he means ripe ones. And so I was beginning to become afraid of my own stupidity and asked carefully why it was that those French politicians on that balcony had moved us so much and if this means that everyone agrees, when there's so much enthusiasm, and whether there will never be another war. So the navy-blue married man tells me that he's from Northern Germany and that's why he's so introverted. But in my experi-ence those who tell you immediately: 'You know, I'm such an introvert,' are anything but, and you can rest assured that they're going to tell you everything that's on their mind. And I noticed that that bell jar of fraternization was starting to lift off and float away. I made one more attempt, asking him if Frenchmen and Jews were one and the same thing, and why they were called a race and how come the nationalists didn't like them because of their blood – and whether it was risky to talk about that since this could be the beginning of my political assassination. So he tells me that he gave his mother a carpet for Christmas and that he's terribly good-natured, and that he was telling his wife that it was unfair of her to criticize him for having bought himself a new silk umbrella instead of having the big easy chair reupholstered – which makes her too embarrassed to invite her lady friends over, one of whom is a professor – and that he had told his boss straight to his face that he didn't know anything – and that I had feelings in me, which is what he needed, and he was a lonely man and always had to tell the truth. And I know for a fact that those who 'always have to tell the truth' are definitely lying. I lost interest in the navy-blue married man, since I was heavy-hearted and excited and didn't have the patience to flirt with a city official. So I said, 'Just a minute,' and secretly disappeared through the back door. And I was sad about not having gotten any political education. But I did have three pieces of hazelnut torte – which took care of my lunch, which couldn't be said about a lesson in politics.

I was negotiating with a traffic cop about how to get to Friedenau, which is where I needed to go, to Therese's old friend Margretchen Weissbach. I found her in a one-bedroom apartment where she was living with her unemployed husband. She was no Margretchen, but a real Margrete with a face that doesn't take life easily. And she was about to have her first baby. We said hello and immediately said 'du,' since we knew without exchanging a word that what had happened to one of us could just as easily have happened to the other. She's over thirty, but giving birth was easy nonetheless.

I had to call the midwife, since all her husband was capable of was smoking cigarettes at three pfennig apiece. I gave the midwife ten marks and told her to hurry up and that she should come to me for the rest of the money. And so I've been in Berlin for less than three hours and I already owe money to a midwife, which hopefully is not a bad omen. I sat next to Margrete while she was in labor. That's when you're ashamed not to be in pain yourself.

It was a girl. We called her Doris, because I was the only one there – besides the midwife of course, but her name was Eusebia. I spent one night on a mattress in case she needed someone after all. Next to me was the baby in a wooden box that she had filled with cushions and soft blankets with pink roses embroidered on them. On the other side of the baby slept her husband. His breath was hollow with happiness, because Margrete was okay – you could tell, even though he was all hard and grumpy. Margrete was asleep and he was saying things like: what were they going to do with a child, that already they didn't know what to do, and it would be better if the child had never been born. But during the night, I saw him bend over the wooden box, kissing the embroidered pink roses. I turned white with fear, because if he had known that I had seen him, he probably would have killed me. There are men like that. And Margrete thinks she can get another job at the office, now that it's all over.

In the morning, the baby was screaming like an alarm clock and we all woke up. The air felt like a round dumpling and you couldn't swallow it. The baby weighs eight pounds and is healthy. Margrete is breastfeeding, and she's well. Her husband was making coffee and milk. I made the beds. The man was black and angry. He was too ashamed to say nice things to Margrete, but we could tell that they were in him. Then he went out to look for work, but without any hope.

Margrete says that when he comes back, he will get mad at her and reproach her, and that's because he doesn't believe in what they call God. Because what a man like him really needs is a God whom he can blame and whom he can get mad at when things go wrong. This way he's got nobody who can be the target of his anger and hatred and that's why he blames his wife, but she minds – and the one who is called God doesn't mind – and that's why he should have a religion, or he should get political, because then he could also make a ruckus.

So I said goodbye to her, since I really couldn't stay there. Margrete gave me Tilli Scherer's address, a former colleague of hers who is also married, but her husband is frequently out of town. So I bought three diapers and I plan to have a green branch embroidered in the corner for good luck. And I will have them sent to the Weissbachs, since the child has been named after me.

And then I went to Tilli Scherer. She agreed to take me in. She too wants to become a star. And she won't take money from me. But every other morning, I will loan her my fur coat to wear at the film agency. I don't like to do that – not because I'm stingy, but because I don't like it to smell from anybody else. I've also tried film, but there's not much opportunity there.

Things are looking up. I have five undershirts made of Bemberg silk with hand-sewn seams, a handbag made of cowhide with some crocodile appliqué, a small gray felt hat, and a pair of shoes with lizard toes. But my red dress that I'm wearing day and night is starting to tear under the arms. But I've started to make contacts with a textile firm, which, however, isn't doing so well at the moment.

Overall, I can't complain. It all started on Kurfürsten-damm. I was standing in front of a shoe store, where I saw such adorable shoes, when I had an idea. I went in with the assertiveness of a grand lady – helped by my fur coat – and tore off one of my heels and started to limp into the shop. And I handed my broken heel to the salesman.

And he calls me 'Madam.'

I say: 'What a pity. I wanted to go dancing and I don't have time to go home and don't have enough money on me.'

Needless to say, I left the store with lizard toes and that night I went to a cabaret with the salesman. I told him I was one of Reinhardt's new actresses. We both lied to each other tremendously and believed each other just to be nice. He's not stupid and he's a gentleman. He has a stiff knee and falls in love with women because he feels self-conscious about it.

At the Jockey Bar I met the Red Moon – his wife is on vacation, because times are bad and seaside resorts are cheaper in October than in July. He happened to be at the Jockey Bar by coincidence, as he's traditional and he's disgusted by the new times because of their lax morals and politics. He wants the Kaiser back and is writing novels and is well-known from the past. He also says that he has esprit. And his principle is: men can, women cannot. So I'm asking myself: How can men do it without women? What an idiot!

So he says to me: 'Little woman' – and puffs himself up because he feels so superior to me. When he was 50, all the newspapers were in awe of him. And he had readers. He also has a degree and a cultural foundation. And he counts for something. He comes to the Jockey Bar to study. He's studying me too. He's written many novels for the German people, and now those little Jews are writing their decadent stuff. He's not going to play along with that.

So the Red Moon has written a novel, *Meadow in May*, that has been reissued hundreds of times, and he just keeps on writing and right now he's writing *The Blonde Officer*. And he invited me too. He has a beautiful apartment – full of books and so forth and a provocative chaise longue. I was drinking coffee and liqueur and eating a lot. The Red Moon was sweating and started to get heart palpitations, because we weren't drinking decaf. I didn't like it – the coffee or the Red Moon. But we had *Danziger Goldwasser*, which glitters in the small glass like a pond full of tiny gold pieces – they are swimming in it and you can't catch them, and it's highly uneducated to even try, and if you *do* try, then you scratch holes into your fingers and you still won't find anything – so what's the point of behaving in an uneducated way in the first place. But it's nice to know that you're drinking gold that tastes sweet and makes you drunk – it's like a violin and tango in a glass. I love you, my brown madonna . . . wouldn't it be wonderful to be with someone you like. Like, like, like. And he should have a voice as shiny as his hair – and his hands should be shaped so they could fit around my face and his mouth should be waiting for me. I wonder if there are men who can wait until you want to. There's always that moment when you want to – but they want to just a minute too soon, and that ruins everything.

Me – and my fur coat who is with me – my skin gets all tense with the desire that someone find me attractive in my fur, and I find him attractive as well. I'm in a café – violins are playing, sending a waft of weepy clouds into my head – something's crying in me – I want to bury my face in my hands to make it less sad. It has to work so hard, because I'm trying to become a star. And there are women all over the place, whose faces are also trying hard.

But it's a good thing that I'm unhappy, because if you're happy you don't get ahead. I learned that from Lorchen Grünlich, who married the accountant at Grobwind Brothers and is happy with him and her shabby tweed coat and one bedroom apartment and flower pots with cuttings and *Gugelhupf* on Sundays and stamped paper which is all the accountant allows her to use, just to sleep with him at night and have a ring.

And there is ermine and women with Parisian scents and cars and shops with nightgowns that cost more than 100 marks and theaters with velvet, and they sit in them – and everything bows down to them, and crowns come out of their mouths when they exhale. Salespeople fall all over themselves when they come into the store and still don't buy anything. And they smile when they mispronounce foreign words, if they do mispronounce them. And with their georgette adorned bosoms and their cleavage they sway in such a way that they don't need to know anything. Waiters let their napkins trail on the floor when they leave a restaurant. And they can leave expensive rump steaks and à la Meyers with asparagus on their plates without feeling bad and wishing that they could pack them up and take them home. And they hand the bathroom attendant thirty pfennigs without looking at her face to find out if her way makes you want to give her more than necessary. And they are their own entourage and turn themselves on like light bulbs. No one can get near them because of the rays they're sending out. When they sleep with a man, they breathe on pillows with genuine orchids, which are phenomenal flowers. And foreign diplomats admire them and they kiss their manicured feet in fur slippers and don't really concentrate, but no one cares. And so many chauffeurs with brass buttons take their cars to garages – it's an elegant world – and then you take the train to the Riviera in a bed to go on vacation and you speak French and you have pig leather suitcases with stickers on them, and the Adlon bows down to you – and rooms with a full bath, which are called a suite.

I want it, I want it so badly – and only if you're unhappy do you get ahead. That's why I'm glad that I'm unhappy.

CHRISTOPHER ISHERWOOD

A BERLIN DIARY:
WINTER 1932–3

From

GOODBYE TO BERLIN

TONIGHT, FOR THE first time this winter, it is very cold. The dead cold grips the town in utter silence, like the silence of intense midday summer heat. In the cold the town seems actually to contract, to dwindle to a small black dot, scarcely larger than hundreds of other dots, isolated and hard to find, on the enormous European map. Outside, in the night, beyond the last new-built blocks of concrete flats, where the streets end in frozen allotment gardens, are the Prussian plains. You can feel them all round you, tonight, creeping in upon the city, like an immense waste of unhomely ocean – sprinkled with leafless copses and ice-lakes and tiny villages which are remembered only as the outlandish names of battlefields in half-forgotten wars. Berlin is a skeleton which aches in the cold: it is my own skeleton aching. I feel in my bones the sharp ache of the frost in the girders of the overhead railway, in the ironwork of balconies, in bridges, tramlines, lamp-standards, latrines. The iron throbs and shrinks, the stone and the bricks ache dully, the plaster is numb.

Berlin is a city with two centres – the cluster of expensive hotels, bars, cinemas, shops round the Memorial Church, a sparkling nucleus of light, like a sham diamond, in the shabby twilight of the town; and the self-conscious civic centre of buildings round the Unter den Linden, carefully arranged. In grand international styles, copies of copies, they assert our dignity as a capital city – a parliament, a couple of museums, a State bank, a cathedral, an opera, a dozen embassies, a triumphal arch; nothing has been forgotten. And they are all so pompous, so very correct – all except the cathedral, which betrays in its architecture, a flash of that hysteria which flickers always behind every grave, grey Prussian façade. Extinguished by its absurd dome, it is, at first sight, so startlingly funny that one searches for a name suitably preposterous – the Church of the Immaculate Consumption.

But the real heart of Berlin is a small damp black wood – the Tiergarten. At this time of the year, the cold begins to drive the peasant boys out of their tiny unprotected villages into the city, to look for food, and work. But the city, which glowed so brightly and invitingly in the night sky above the plains, is cold and cruel and dead. Its warmth is an illusion, a mirage of the winter desert. It will not receive these boys. It has nothing to give. The cold drives them out of its streets, into the wood which is its cruel heart. And there they cower on benches, to starve and freeze, and dream of their far-away cottage stoves.

Frl. Schroeder hates the cold. Huddled in her furlined velvet jacket, she sits in the corner with her stockinged feet on the stove. Sometimes she smokes a cigarette, sometimes she sips a glass of tea, but mostly she just sits, staring dully at the stove tiles in a kind of hibernation-doze. She is lonely, nowadays. Frl. Mayr is away in Holland, on a cabaret-tour. So Frl. Schroeder has nobody to talk to, except Bobby and myself.

Bobby, anyhow, is in deep disgrace. Not only is he out of work and three months behind with the rent, but Frl. Schroeder has reason to suspect him of stealing money from her bag. 'You know, Herr Issyvoo,' she tells me, 'I shouldn't wonder at all if he didn't pinch those fifty marks from Frl.

Kost . . . He's quite capable of it, the pig! To think I could
ever have been so mistaken in him! Will you believe it, Herr
Issyvoo, I treated him as if he were my own son – and this
is the thanks I get! He says he'll pay me every pfennig if he
gets this job as barman at the Lady Windermere . . . if, *if* . . .'
Frl. Schroeder sniffs with intense scorn: 'I dare say! If my
grandmother had wheels, she'd be an omnibus!'

Bobby has been turned out of his old room and banished
to the 'Swedish Pavilion'. It must be terribly draughty, up
there. Sometimes poor Bobby looks quite blue with cold.
He has changed very much during the last year – his hair is
thinner, his clothes are shabbier, his cheekiness has become
defiant and rather pathetic. People like Bobby *are* their jobs
– take the job away and they partially cease to exist. Sometimes, he sneaks into the living-room, unshaven, his hands
in his pockets, and lounges about uneasily defiant, whistling
to himself – the dance tunes he whistles are no longer quite
new. Frl. Schroeder throws him a word, now and then, like a
grudging scrap of bread, but she won't look at him or make
any room for him by the stove. Perhaps she has never really
forgiven him for his affair with Frl. Kost. The tickling and
bottom-slapping days are over.

Yesterday we had a visit from Frl. Kost herself. I was out
at the time: when I got back I found Frl. Schroeder quite
excited. 'Only think, Herr Issyvoo – I wouldn't have known
her! She's quite the lady now! Her Japanese friend has
bought her a fur coat – real fur, I shouldn't like to think
what he must have paid for it! And her shoes – genuine
snakeskin! Well, well, I bet she earned them! That's the one
kind of business that still goes well, nowadays . . . I think
I shall have to take to the line myself!' But however much
Frl. Schroeder might affect sarcasm at Frl. Kost's expense,

I could see that she'd been greatly and not unfavourably impressed. And it wasn't so much the fur coat or the shoes which had impressed her: Frl. Kost had achieved something higher – the hall-mark of respectability in Frl. Schroeder's world – she had had an operation in a private nursing home. 'Oh, not what you think, Herr Issyvoo! It was something to do with her throat. Her friend paid for that, too, of course . . . Only imagine – the doctors cut something out of the back of her nose; and now she can fill her mouth with water and squirt it out through her nostrils, just like a syringe! I wouldn't believe it at first – but she did it to show me! My word of honour, Herr Issyvoo, she could squirt it right across the kitchen! There's no denying, she's very much improved, since the time when she used to live here . . . I shouldn't be surprised if she married a bank director one of these days. Oh, yes, you mark my words, that girl will go far . . .'

Herr Krampf, a young engineer, one of my pupils, describes his childhood during the days of the War and the Inflation. During the last years of the War, the straps disappeared from the windows of railway carriages: people had cut them off in order to sell the leather. You even saw men and women going about in clothes made from carriage upholstery. A party of Krampf's school friends broke into a factory one night and stole all the leather driving-belts. Everybody stole. Everybody sold what they had to sell – themselves included. A boy of fourteen, from Krampf's class, peddled cocaine between school hours, in the streets.

Farmers and butchers were omnipotent. Their slightest whim had to be gratified, if you wanted vegetables or meat. The Krampf family knew of a butcher in a little village outside Berlin who always had meat to sell. But the butcher had a peculiar sexual perversion. His greatest erotic pleasure was to pinch and slap the cheeks of a sensitive, well-bred girl or woman. The possibility of thus humiliating a lady like Frau Krampf excited him enormously: unless he was allowed to realize his fantasy, he refused, absolutely, to do business. So, every Sunday, Krampf's mother would travel out to the village with her children, and patiently offer her cheeks to be slapped and pinched, in exchange for some cutlets or a steak.

At the far end of the Potsdamerstrasse, there is a fair-ground, with merry-go-rounds, swings, and peep-shows. One of the chief attractions of the fair-grounds is a tent where boxing and wrestling matches are held. You pay your money and go in, the wrestlers fight three or four rounds, and the referee then announces that, if you want to see any more, you must pay an extra ten pfennigs. One of the wrestlers is a bald man with a very large stomach: he wears a pair of canvas trousers rolled up at the bottoms, as though he were going paddling. His opponent wears black tights, and leather kneelets which look as if they had come off an old cab-horse. The wrestlers throw each other about as much as possible, turning somersaults in the air to amuse the audience. The fat man who plays the part of loser pretends to get very angry when he is beaten, and threatens to fight the referee.

One of the boxers is a Negro. He invariably wins. The boxers hit each other with the open glove, making a tremendous amount of noise. The other boxer, a tall, well-built young man, about twenty years younger and obviously much stronger than the Negro, is 'knocked out' with absurd ease. He writhes in great agony on the floor, nearly manages to struggle to his feet at the count of ten, then collapses again, groaning. After this fight, the referee collects ten more pfennigs and calls for a challenger from the audience. Before any bona fide challenger can reply, another young man, who has been quite openly chatting and joking with the wrestlers, jumps hastily into the ring and strips off his clothes, revealing himself already dressed in shorts and boxer's boots. The referee announces a purse of five marks; and, this time, the Negro is 'knocked out'.

The audience took the fights dead seriously, shouting encouragement to the fighters, and even quarrelling and betting amongst themselves on the results. Yet nearly all of them had been in the tent as long as I had, and stayed on after I had left. The political moral is certainly depressing: these people could be made to believe in anybody or anything.

Walking this evening along the Kleiststrasse, I saw a little crowd gathered round a private car. In the car were two girls: on the pavement stood two young Jews, engaged in a violent argument with a large blond man who was obviously rather drunk. The Jews, it seemed, had been driving slowly along the street, on the look-out for a pick-up, and had offered these girls a ride. The two girls had accepted and got into the car. At this moment, however, the blond man had intervened. He was a Nazi, he told us, and as such felt it his mission to defend the honour of all German women against the obscene anti-Nordic menace. The two Jews didn't seem in the least intimidated; they told the Nazi energetically to mind his own business. Meanwhile, the girls, taking advantage of the row, slipped out of the car and ran off down the street. The Nazi then tried to drag one of the Jews with him to find a policeman, and the Jew whose arm he had seized gave him an uppercut which laid him sprawling on his back. Before the Nazi could get to his feet, both young men had jumped into their car and driven away. The crowd dispersed slowly, arguing. Very few of them sided openly with the Nazi: several supported the Jews; but the majority confined themselves to shaking their heads dubiously and murmuring: '*Allerhand!*'

When, three hours later, I passed the same spot, the Nazi was still patrolling up and down, looking hungrily for more German womanhood to rescue.

We have just got a letter from Frl. Mayr: Frl. Schroeder called me in to listen to it. Frl. Mayr doesn't like Holland. She has been obliged to sing in a lot of second-rate cafés in third-rate towns, and her bedroom is often badly heated. The Dutch, she writes, have no culture; she has only met one truly refined and superior gentleman, a widower. The widower tells her that she is a really womanly woman – he has no use for young chits of girls. He has shown his admiration for her art by presenting her with a complete new set of underclothes.

Frl. Mayr has also had trouble with her colleagues. At one town, a rival actress, jealous of Frl. Mayr's vocal powers, tried to stab her in the eye with a hatpin. I can't help admiring that actress's courage. When Frl. Mayr had finished with her, she was so badly injured that she couldn't appear on the stage again for a week.

Last night, Fritz Wendel proposed a tour of the 'dives'. It was to be in the nature of a farewell visit, for the Police have begun to take a great interest in these places. They are frequently raided, and the names of their clients are written down. There is even talk of a general Berlin clean-up.

I rather upset him by insisting on visiting the Salomé, which I had never seen. Fritz, as a connoisseur of nightlife, was most contemptuous. It wasn't even genuine, he told me. The management run it entirely for the benefit of provincial sightseers.

The Salomé turned out to be very expensive and even more depressing than I had imagined. A few stage lesbians and some young men with plucked eyebrows lounged at the bar, uttering occasional raucous guffaws or treble hoots – supposed, apparently, to represent the laughter of the damned. The whole premises are painted gold and inferno-red – crimson plush inches thick, and vast gilded mirrors. It was pretty full. The audience consisted chiefly of respectable middle-aged tradesmen and their families, exclaiming in good-humoured amazement: 'Do they really?' and 'Well, I never!' We went out half-way through the cabaret per-formance, after a young man in a spangled crinoline and jewelled breast-caps had painfully but successfully executed three splits.

At the entrance we met a party of American youths, very drunk, wondering whether to go in. Their leader was a small stocky young man in pince-nez, with an annoyingly prominent jaw.

'Say,' he asked Fritz, 'what's on here?'

'Men dressed as women,' Fritz grinned.

The little American simply couldn't believe it. 'Men dressed as *women*? As *women*, hey? Do you mean they're *queer*?'

'Eventually we're all queer,' drawled Fritz solemnly, in lugubrious tones. The young man looked us over slowly. He had been running and was still out of breath. The others grouped themselves awkwardly behind him, ready for anything – though their callow, open-mouthed faces in the greenish lamp-light looked a bit scared.

'You *queer*, too, hey?' demanded the little American, turning suddenly on me.

'Yes,' I said, 'very queer indeed.'

He stood there before me a moment, panting, thrusting

out his jaw, uncertain, it seemed, whether he ought not to hit me in the face. Then he turned, uttered some kind of wild college battle-cry, and, followed by the others, rushed headlong into the building.

'Ever been to that communist dive near the Zoo?' Fritz asked me, as we were walking away from the Salomé. 'Eventually we should cast an eye in there . . . In six months, maybe, we'll all be wearing red shirts . . .'

I agreed. I was curious to know what Fritz's idea of a 'communist dive' would be like.

It was, in fact, a small whitewashed cellar. You sat on long wooden benches at big bare tables; a dozen people together – like a school dining-hall. On the walls were scribbled expressionist drawings involving actual newspaper clippings, real playing-cards, nailed-on-beer-mats, match-boxes, cigarette cartons, and heads cut out of photographs. The café was full of students, dressed mostly with aggressive political untidiness – the men in sailor's sweaters and stained baggy trousers, the girls in ill-fitting jumpers, skirts held visibly together with safety-pins and carelessly knotted gaudy gipsy scarves. The proprietress was smoking a cigar. The boy who acted as a waiter lounged about with a cigarette between his lips and slapped customers on the back when taking their orders.

It was all thoroughly sham and gay and jolly: you couldn't help feeling at home, immediately. Fritz, as usual, recognized plenty of friends. He introduced me to three of them – a man called Martin, an art student named Werner, and Inge, his girl. Inge was broad and lively – she wore a little hat with a feather in it which gave her a kind of farcical resemblance to Henry the Eighth. While Werner and Inge chattered, Martin sat silent: he was thin and dark and hatchet-faced with the sardonically superior smile of the conscious conspirator. Later in the evening, when Fritz and Werner and Inge had moved down the table to join another party, Martin began to talk about the coming civil war. When the war breaks out, Martin explained, the communists, who have very few machine-guns, will get command of the roof-tops. They will then keep the Police at bay with hand-grenades. It will only be necessary to hold out for three days, because the Soviet fleet will make an immediate dash for Swinemünde and begin to land troops. 'I spend most of my time now making bombs,' Martin added. I nodded and grinned, very much embarrassed – uncertain whether he was making fun of me, or deliberately committing some appalling indiscretion. He certainly wasn't drunk, and he didn't strike me as merely insane.

Presently, a strikingly handsome boy of sixteen or seventeen came into the café. His name was Rudi. He was dressed in a Russian blouse, leather shorts and despatch-rider's boots, and he strode up to our table with all the heroic mannerisms of a messenger who returns successful from a desperate mission. He had, however, no message of any kind to deliver. After his whirlwind entry, and a succession of curt, martial handshakes, he sat down quite quietly beside us and ordered a glass of tea.

This evening, I visited the 'communist' café again. It is really a fascinating little world of intrigue and counter-intrigue. Its Napoleon is the sinister bomb-making Martin; Werner is its Danton; Rudi its Joan of Arc. Everybody suspects everybody else. Already Martin has warned me against Werner: he is 'politically unreliable' – last summer he stole the entire funds of a communist youth organization. And Werner has warned me against Martin: he is either a Nazi agent, or a police spy, or in the pay of the French Government. In addition to this, both Martin and Werner earnestly advise me to have nothing to do with Rudi – they absolutely refuse to say why.

But there was no question of having nothing to do with Rudi. He planted himself down beside me and began talking at once – a hurricane of enthusiasm. His favourite word is 'knorke': 'Oh, *ripping*!' He is a pathfinder. He wanted to know what the boy scouts were like in England. Had they got the spirit of adventure? 'All German boys are adventurous. Adventure is ripping. Our Scoutmaster is a ripping man. Last year he went to Lapland and lived in a hut, all through the summer, alone . . . Are you a communist?'

'No. Are you?'

Rudi was pained.

'Of course! We all are, here . . . I'll lend you some books, if you like . . . You ought to come and see our clubhouse. It's ripping . . . We sing the Red Flag, and all the forbidden songs . . . Will you teach me English? I want to learn all languages.'

I asked if there were any girls in his pathfinder group. Rudi was as shocked as if I'd said something really indecent.

'Women are no good,' he told me bitterly. 'They spoil everything. They haven't got the spirit of adventure. Men understand each other much better when they're alone together. Uncle Peter (that's our Scoutmaster) says women should stay at home and mend socks. That's all they're fit for!'

'Is Uncle Peter a communist, too?'

'Of course!' Rudi looked at me suspiciously. 'Why do you ask that?'

'Oh, no special reason,' I replied hastily. 'I think perhaps I was mixing him up with somebody else . . .'

* * *

This afternoon I travelled out to the reformatory to visit one of my pupils, Herr Brink, who is a master there. He is a small, broad-shouldered man, with the chin, dead-looking fair hair, mild eyes, and bulging, over-heavy forehead of the German vegetarian intellectual. He wears sandals and an open-necked shirt. I found him in the gymnasium, giving physical instruction to a class of mentally deficient children – for the reformatory houses mental deficients as well as juvenile delinquents. With a certain melancholy pride, he pointed out the various cases: one little boy was suffering from hereditary syphilis – he had a fearful squint; another, the child of elderly drunkards, couldn't stop laughing. They clambered about the wall-bars like monkeys, laughing and chattering, seemingly quite happy.

Then we went up to the workshop, where older boys in blue overalls – all convicted criminals – were making boots. Most of the boys looked up and grinned when Brink came in, only a few were sullen. But I couldn't look them in the eyes. I felt horribly guilty and ashamed: I seemed, at that moment, to have become the sole representative of their gaolers, of Capitalist Society. I wondered if any of them had actually been arrested in the Alexander Casino, and, if so, whether they recognized me.

We had lunch in the matron's room. Herr Brink apologized for giving me the same food as the boys themselves ate – potato soup with two sausages, and a dish of apples and stewed prunes. I protested – as, no doubt, I was intended to protest – that it was very good. And yet the thought of the boys having to eat it, or any other kind of meal, in that building made each spoonful stick in my throat. Institution food has an indescribable, perhaps purely imaginary, taste. (One of the most vivid and sickening memories of my own school life is the smell of ordinary white bread.)

'You don't have any bars or locked gates here,' I said. 'I thought all reformatories had them ... Don't your boys often run away?'

'Hardly ever,' said Brink, and the admission seemed to make him positively unhappy; he sank his head wearily in his hands. 'Where shall they run to? Here it is bad. At home it is worse. The majority of them know that.'

'But isn't there a kind of natural instinct for freedom?'

'Yes, you are right. But the boys soon lose it. The system helps them to lose it. I think perhaps that, in Germans, this instinct is never very strong.'

'You don't have much trouble here, then?'

'Oh, yes. Sometimes ... Three months ago, a terrible thing happened. One boy stole another boy's overcoat. He asked for permission to go into the town – that is allowed – and possibly he meant to sell it. But the owner of the overcoat followed him, and they had a fight. The boy to whom the overcoat belonged took up a big stone and flung it at the other boy; and this boy, feeling himself hurt, deliberately smeared dirt into the wound, hoping to make it worse and so escape punishment. The wound did get worse. In three days the boy died of blood-poisoning. And when the other boy heard of this he killed himself with a kitchen knife...' Brink sighed deeply: 'Sometimes I almost despair,' he added. 'It seems as if there were a kind of badness, a disease, infecting the world today.'

'But what can you really do for these boys?' I asked.

'Very little. We teach them a trade. Later, we try to find them work – which is almost impossible. If they have work in the neighbourhood, they can still sleep here at nights ... The Principal believes that their lives can be changed through the teachings of the Christian religion. I'm afraid I cannot feel this. The problem is not so simple. I'm afraid that most of them, if they cannot get work, will take to crime. After all, people cannot be ordered to starve.'

'Isn't there any alternative?'

Brink rose and led me to the window.

'You see those two buildings? One is the engineering-works, the other is the prison. For the boys of this district there used to be two alternatives . . . But now the works are bankrupt. Next week they will close down.'

This morning I went to see Rudi's clubhouse, which is also the office of a pathfinder's magazine. The editor and scoutmaster, Uncle Peter, is a haggard, youngish man, with a parchment-coloured face and deeply sunken eyes, dressed in corduroy jacket and shorts. He is evidently Rudi's idol. The only time Rudi will stop talking is when Uncle Peter has something to say. They showed me dozens of photographs of boys, all taken with the camera tilted upwards, from beneath, so that they look like epic giants, in profile against enormous clouds. The magazine itself has articles on hunting, tracking, and preparing food – all written in super-enthusiastic style, with a curious underlying note of hysteria, as though the actions described were part of a religious or erotic ritual. There were half-a-dozen boys in the room with us: all of them in a state of heroic semi-nudity, wearing the shortest of shorts and the thinnest of shirts or singlets, although the weather is so cold.

When I had finished looking at the photographs, Rudi took me into the club-meeting room. Long coloured banners hung down the walls, embroidered with initials and mysterious totem devices. At one end of the room was a low table covered with a crimson embroidered cloth – a kind of altar. On the table were candles in brass candlesticks.

'We light them on Thursdays,' Rudi explained, 'when we

have our camp-fire palaver. Then we sit round in a ring on the floor, and sing songs and tell stories.'

Above the table with the candlesticks was a sort of icon – the framed drawing of a young pathfinder of unearthly beauty, gazing sternly into the far distance, a banner in his hand. The whole place made me feel profoundly uncomfortable. I excused myself and got away as soon as I could.

Overheard in a café: a young Nazi is sitting with his girl; they are discussing the future of the Party. The Nazi is drunk.

'Oh, I know we shall win, all right,' he exclaims impatiently, 'but that's not enough!' He thumps the table with his fist: 'Blood must flow!'

The girl strokes his arm reassuringly. She is trying to get him to come home. 'But, *of course*, it's going to flow, darling,' she coos soothingly, 'the Leader's promised that in our programme.'

Today is 'Silver Sunday'. The streets are crowded with shoppers. All along the Tauentzienstrasse, men, women, and boys are hawking postcards, flowers, song-books, hair-oil, bracelets. Christmas-trees are stacked for sale along the central path between the tram-lines. Uniformed S.A. men rattle their collecting-boxes. In the side-streets, lorry-loads of police are waiting; for any large crowd, nowadays, is capable of turning into a political riot. The Salvation Army have a big illuminated tree on the Wittenbergplatz, with a blue electric star. A group of students were standing round it, making sarcastic remarks. Among them I recognized Werner, from the 'communist' café.

'This time next year,' said Werner, 'that star will have changed its colour!' He laughed violently – he was in an excited, slightly hysterical mood. Yesterday, he told me, he'd had a great adventure: 'You see, three other comrades and myself decided to make a demonstration at the Labour Exchange in Neukölln. I had to speak, and the others were to see I wasn't interrupted. We went round there at about half past ten, when the bureau's most crowded. Of course, we'd planned it all beforehand – each of the comrades had to hold one of the doors, so that none of the clerks in the office could get out. There they were, cooped up like rabbits . . . Of course, we couldn't prevent their telephoning for the Police, we knew that. We reckoned we'd got about six or seven minutes . . . Well, as soon as the doors were fixed, I jumped on to a table. I just yelled out whatever came into my head – I don't know what I said. They liked it, anyhow . . . In half a minute I had them so excited I got quite scared. I was afraid they'd break into the office and lynch somebody. There was a fine old shindy, I can tell you! But just when things were beginning to look properly lively, a comrade came up from below to tell us the Police were there already – just getting out of their car. So we had to make a dash for it . . . I think they'd have got us, only the crowd was on our side, and wouldn't let them through until we were out by the other door, into the street . . .' Werner finished breathlessly. 'I tell you, Christopher,' he added, 'the capitalist system can't possibly last much longer now. The workers are on the move.'

Early this evening I was in the Bülowstrasse. There had been a big Nazi meeting at the Sportpalast, and groups of men and boys were just coming away from it, in their brown or black uniforms. Walking along the pavement ahead of me were three S.A. men. They all carried Nazi banners on their shoulders, like rifles, rolled tight around the staves – the banner-staves had sharp metal points, shaped into arrow-heads.

All at once, the three S.A. men came face to face with a youth of seventeen or eighteen, dressed in civilian clothes, who was hurrying along in the opposite direction. I heard one of the Nazis shout: 'That's him!' and immediately all three of them flung themselves upon the young man. He uttered a scream, and tried to dodge, but they were too quick for him. In a moment they had jostled him into the shadow of a house entrance, and were standing over him, kicking him and stabbing at him with the sharp metal points of their banners. All this happened with such incredible speed that I could hardly believe my eyes – already, the three S.A. men had left their victim, and were barging their way through the crowd; they made for the stairs which led up to the station of the Overhead Railway.

Another passer-by and myself were the first to reach the doorway where the young man was lying. He lay huddled crookedly in the corner, like an abandoned sack. As they picked him up, I got a sickening glimpse of his face – his left eye was poked half out, and blood poured from the wound. He wasn't dead. Somebody volunteered to take him to the hospital in a taxi.

By this time, dozens of people were looking on. They seemed surprised, but not particularly shocked – this sort of thing happened too often, nowadays. '*Allerhand . . .*' they murmured. Twenty yards away, at the Potsdamerstrasse corner, stood a group of heavily armed policemen. With their chests out, and their hands on their revolver belts, they magnificently disregarded the whole affair.

Werner has become a hero. His photograph was in the *Rote Fahne* a few days ago, captioned: 'Another victim of the Police blood-bath.' Yesterday, which was New Year's Day, I went to visit him in hospital.

Just after Christmas, it seems, there was a streetfight near the Stettiner Bahnhof. Werner was on the edge of the crowd, not knowing what the fight was about. On the off-chance that it might be something political, he began yelling: 'Red Front!' A policeman tried to arrest him. Werner kicked the policeman in the stomach. The policeman drew his revolver and shot Werner three times through the leg. When he had finished shooting, he called another policeman, and together they carried Werner into a taxi. On the way to the police-station, the policemen hit him on the head with their truncheons, until he fainted. When he has sufficiently recovered, he will, most probably, be prosecuted.

He told me all this with the greatest satisfaction, sitting up in bed surrounded by his admiring friends, including Rudi and Inge, in her Henry the Eighth hat. Around him, on the blanket, lay his press-cuttings. Somebody had carefully underlined each mention of Werner's name with a red pencil.

Today, January 22nd, the Nazis held a demonstration on the Bülowplatz, in front of the Karl Liebknecht House. For the last week the communists have been trying to get the demonstration forbidden: they say it is simply intended as a provocation – as, of course, it was. I went along to watch it with Frank, the newspaper correspondent.

As Frank himself said afterwards, this wasn't really a Nazi demonstration at all, but a Police demonstration – there were at least two policemen to every Nazi present. Perhaps General Schleicher only allowed the march to take place in order to show who are the real masters of Berlin. Everybody says he's going to proclaim a military dictatorship.

But the real masters of Berlin are not the Police, or the Army, and certainly not the Nazis. The masters of Berlin are the workers – despite all the propaganda I've heard and read, all the demonstrations I've attended, I only realized this for the first time today. Comparatively few of the hundreds of people in the streets round the Bülowplatz can have been organized communists, yet you had the feeling that every single one of them was united against this march. Somebody began to sing the 'International', and, in a moment, everyone had joined in – even the women with their babies, watching from top-storey windows. The Nazis slunk past, marching as fast as they knew how, between their double rows of protectors. Most of them kept their eyes on the ground, or glared glassily ahead: a few attempted sickly, furtive grins. When the procession had passed, an elderly fat little S.A. man, who had somehow got left behind, came panting along at the double, desperately scared of finding himself alone, and trying vainly to catch up with the rest. The whole crowd roared with laughter.

During the demonstration nobody was allowed on the Bülowplatz itself. So the crowd surged uneasily about, and things began to look nasty. The police, brandishing their rifles, ordered us back; some of the less experienced ones, getting rattled, made as if to shoot. Then an armoured car appeared, and started to turn its machine-gun slowly in our direction. There was a stampede into house doorways and cafés; but no sooner had the car moved on, than everybody rushed out into the street again, shouting and singing. It was too much like a naughty schoolboy's game to be seriously alarming. Frank enjoyed himself enormously, grinning from ear to ear, and hopping about, in his flapping overcoat and huge owlish spectacles, like a mocking, ungainly bird.

Only a week since I wrote the above. Schleicher has resigned. The monocles did their stuff. Hitler has formed a cabinet with Hugenberg. Nobody thinks it can last till the spring.

147

The newspapers are becoming more and more like copies of a school magazine. There is nothing in them but new rules, new punishments, and lists of people who have been 'kept in'. This morning, Göring has invented three fresh varieties of high treason.

Every evening, I sit in the big half-empty artists' café by the Memorial Church, where the Jews and left-wing intellectuals bend their heads together over the marble tables, speaking in low, scared voices. Many of them know that they will certainly be arrested – if not today, then tomorrow or next week. So they are polite and mild with each other, and raise their hats and inquire after their colleagues' families. Notorious literary tiffs of several years' standing are forgotten.

Almost every evening, the S.A. men come into the café. Sometimes they are only collecting money; everybody is compelled to give something. Sometimes they have come to make an arrest. One evening a Jewish writer, who was present, ran into the telephone-box to ring up the Police. The Nazis dragged him out, and he was taken away. Nobody moved a finger. You could have heard a pin drop, till they were gone.

The foreign newspaper correspondents dine every night at the same little Italian restaurant, at a big round table, in the corner. Everybody else in the restaurant is watching them and trying to overhear what they are saying. If you have a piece of news to bring them – the details of an arrest, or the address of a victim whose relatives might be interviewed – then one of the journalists leaves the table and walks up and down with you outside, in the street.

A young communist I know was arrested by the S.A. men, taken to a Nazi barracks, and badly knocked about.

After three or four days, he was released and went home. Next morning there was a knock at the door. The communist hobbled over to open it, his arm in a sling – and there stood a Nazi with a collecting-box. At the sight of him the communist completely lost his temper. 'Isn't it enough,' he yelled, 'that you beat me up? And you dare to come and ask me for money?'

But the Nazi only grinned. 'Now, now, comrade! No political squabbling! Remember, we're living in the Third Reich! We're all brothers! You must try and drive that silly political hatred from your heart!'

This evening I went into the Russian tea-shop in the Kleist-strasse, and there was D. For a moment I really thought I must be dreaming. He greeted me quite as usual, beaming all over his face.

'Good God!' I whispered. 'What on earth are you doing here?'

D. beamed. 'You thought I might have gone abroad?'

'Well, naturally . . .'

'But the situation nowadays is so interesting . . .'

I laughed. 'That's one way of looking at it, certainly . . . But isn't it awfully dangerous for you?'

D. merely smiled. Then he turned to the girl he was sitting with and said, 'This is Mr Isherwood . . . You can speak quite openly to him. He hates the Nazis as much as we do. Oh, yes! Mr Isherwood is a confirmed anti-fascist!'

He laughed very heartily and slapped me on the back. Several people who were sitting near us overheard him. Their reactions were curious. Either they simply couldn't believe their ears, or they were so scared that they pretended to hear nothing, and went on sipping their tea in a state of deaf horror. I have seldom felt so uncomfortable in my whole life.

(D.'s technique appears to have had its points, all the same. He was never arrested. Two months later, he successfully crossed the frontier into Holland.)

This morning, as I was walking down the Bülowstrasse, the Nazis were raiding the house of a small liberal pacifist publisher. They had brought a lorry and were piling it with the publisher's books. The driver of the lorry mockingly read out the titles of the books to the crowd:

'*Nie Wieder Krieg*!' he shouted, holding up one of them by the corner of the cover, disgustedly, as though it were a nasty kind of reptile. Everybody roared with laughter.

'"No More War!"' echoed a fat, well-dressed woman, with a scornful, savage laugh. 'What an idea!'

At present, one of my regular pupils is Herr N., a police chief under the Weimar régime. He comes to me every day. He wants to brush up his English, for he is leaving very soon to take up a job in the United States. The curious thing about these lessons is that they are all given while we are driving about the streets in Herr N.'s enormous closed car. Herr N. himself never comes into our house: he sends up his chauffeur to fetch me, and the car moves off at once. Sometimes we stop for a few minutes at the edge of the Tiergarten, and stroll up and down the paths – the chauffeur always following us at a respectful distance.

Herr N. talks to me chiefly about his family. He is worried about his son, who is very delicate, and whom he is obliged to leave behind, to undergo an operation. His wife is delicate, too. He hopes the journey won't tire her. He describes her symptoms, and the kind of medicine she is taking. He tells me stories about his son as a little boy. In a tactful, impersonal way we have become quite intimate. Herr N. is always charmingly polite, and listens gravely and carefully to my explanations of grammatical points. Behind everything he says I am aware of an immense sadness.

We never discuss politics; but I know that Herr N. must be an enemy of the Nazis, and, perhaps, even in hourly danger of arrest. One morning, when we were driving along the Unter den Linden, we passed a group of self-important S.A. men, chatting to each other and blocking the whole pavement. Passers-by were obliged to walk in the gutter. Herr N. smiled faintly and sadly: 'One sees some queer sights in the streets nowadays.' That was his only comment.

Sometimes he will bend forward to the window and regard a building or a square with a mournful fixity, as if to impress its image upon his memory and to bid it goodbye.

Tomorrow I am going to England. In a few weeks I shall return, but only to pick up my things, before leaving Berlin altogether.

Poor Frl. Schroeder is inconsolable: 'I shall never find another gentleman like you, Herr Issyvoo – always so punctual with the rent . . . I'm sure I don't know what makes you want to leave Berlin, all of a sudden, like this . . .'

It's no use trying to explain to her, or talking politics. Already she is adapting herself, as she will adapt herself to every new régime. This morning I even heard her talking reverently about 'Der Führer' to the porter's wife. If anybody were to remind her that, at the elections last November, she voted communist, she would probably deny it hotly, and in perfect good faith. She is merely acclimatizing herself, in accordance with a natural law, like an animal which changes its coat for the winter. Thousands of people like Frl. Schroeder are acclimatizing themselves. After all, whatever government is in power, they are doomed to live in this town.

* * *

Today the sun is brilliantly shining; it is quite mild and warm.
I go out for my last morning walk, without an overcoat or
hat. The sun shines, and Hitler is master of this city. The sun
shines, and dozens of my friends – my pupils at the Workers'
School, the men and women I met at the I.A.H. – are in
prison, possibly dead. But it isn't of them I am thinking – the
clear-headed ones, the purposeful, the heroic; they recognized and accepted the risks. I am thinking of poor Rudi, in
his absurd Russian blouse. Rudi's make-believe, story-book
game has become earnest; the Nazis will play it with him.
The Nazis won't laugh at him; they'll take him on trust for
what he pretended to be. Perhaps at this very moment Rudi
is being tortured to death.

I catch sight of my face in the mirror of a shop, and am
horrified to see that I am smiling. You can't help smiling, in
such beautiful weather. The trams are going up and down
the Kleiststrasse, just as usual. They, and the people on the
pavement, and the tea-cosy dome of the Nollendorfplatz
station have an air of curious familiarity, of striking resemblance to something one remembers as normal and pleasant
in the past – like a very good photograph.

No. Even now I can't altogether believe that any of this
has really happened . . .

THOMAS WOLFE

THE DARK MESSIAH

From

YOU CAN'T GO
HOME AGAIN

GEORGE HAD NOT been in Germany since 1928 and the early months of 1929, when he had had to spend weeks of slow convalescence in a Munich hospital after a fight in a beer hall. Before that foolish episode, he had stayed for a while in a little town in the Black Forest, and he remembered that there had been great excitement because an election was being held. The state of politics was chaotic, with a bewildering number of parties, and the Communists polled a surprisingly large vote. People were disturbed and anxious, and there seemed to be a sense of impending calamity in the air.

This time, things were different. Germany had changed.

Ever since 1933, when the change occurred, George had read, first with amazement, shock, and doubt, then with despair and a leaden sinking of the heart, all the newspaper accounts of what was going on in Germany. He found it hard to believe some of the reports. Of course, there were irresponsible extremists in Germany as elsewhere, and in times of crisis no doubt they got out of hand, but he thought he knew Germany and the German people, and on the whole he was inclined to feel that the true state of affairs had been exaggerated and that things simply could not be as bad as they were pictured.

And now, on the train from Paris, where he had stopped off for five weeks, he met some Germans who gave him reassurance. They said there was no longer any confusion or chaos in politics and government, and no longer any fear among the people, because everyone was so happy. This was what George wanted desperately to believe, and he was prepared to be happy, too. For no man ever went to a foreign land under more propitious conditions than those which attended his arrival in Germany early in May, 1936.

It is said that Byron awoke one morning at the age of twenty-four to find himself famous. George Webber had to wait eleven years longer. He was thirty-five when he reached Berlin, but it was magic just the same. Perhaps he was not really very famous, but that didn't matter, because for the first and last time in his life he felt as if he were. Just before he left Paris a letter had reached him from Fox Edwards, telling him that his new book was having a great success in America. Then, too, his first book had been translated and published in Germany the year before. The German critics had said tremendous things about it, it had had a very good sale, and his name was known. When he got to Berlin the people were waiting for him.

The month of May is wonderful everywhere. It was particularly wonderful in Berlin that year. Along the streets, in the Tiergarten, in all the great gardens, and along the Spree Canal the horse chestnut trees were in full bloom. The crowds sauntered underneath the trees on the Kurfürsten-damm, the terraces of the cafés were jammed with people, and always, through the golden sparkle of the days, there was a sound of music in the air. George saw the chains of endlessly lovely lakes around Berlin, and for the first time he knew the wonderful golden bronze upon the tall poles of the kiefern trees. Before, he had visited only the south of Germany, the Rhinelands and Bavaria; now the north seemed even more enchanting.

He planned to stay all summer, and one summer seemed

too short a time to encompass all the beauty, magic, and almost intolerable joy which his life had suddenly become, and which he felt would never fade or tarnish if only he could remain in Germany forever. For, to cap it all, his second book was translated and brought out within a short time of his arrival, and its reception exceeded anything he had ever dared to hope for. Perhaps his being there at the time may have had something to do with it. The German critics outdid each other in singing his praises. If one called him 'the great American epic writer,' the next seemed to feel he had to improve on that, and called him 'the American Homer.' So now everywhere he went there were people who knew his work. His name flashed and shone. He was a famous man.

Fame shed a portion of her loveliness on everything about him. Life took on an added radiance. The look, feel, taste, smell, and sound of everything had gained a tremendous and exciting enhancement, and all because Fame was at his side. He saw the world with a sharper relish of perception than he had ever known before. All the confusion, fatigue, dark doubt, and bitter hopelessness that had afflicted him in times past had gone, and no shadow of any kind remained. It seemed to him that he had won a final and utterly triumphant victory over all the million forms of life. His spirit was no longer tormented, exhausted, and weighted down with the ceaseless effort of his former struggles with Amount and Number. He was wonderfully aware of everything, alive in every pore.

Fame even gave a tongue to silence, a language to unuttered speech. Fame was with him almost all the time, but even when he was alone without her, in places where he was not known and his name meant nothing, the aura which Fame had shed still clung to him and he was able to meet each new situation with a sense of power and confidence, of warmth, friendliness, and good fellowship. He had become the lord of life. There had been a time in his youth when he felt that people were always laughing at him, and he had been ill at ease with strangers and had gone to every new encounter with a chip on his shoulder. But now he was life's strong and light-hearted master, and everyone he met and talked to – waiters, taxi drivers, porters in hotels, elevator boys, casual acquaintances in trams and trains and on the street – felt at once the flood of happy and affectionate power within him, and responded to him eagerly, instinctively, with instant natural liking, as men respond to the clean and shining light of the young sun.

And when Fame was with him, all this magic was increased. He could see the wonder, interest, respect, and friendly envy in the eyes of men, and the frank adoration in the eyes of women. The women seemed to worship at the shrine of Fame. George began to get letters and telephone calls from them, with invitations to functions of every sort. The girls were after him. But he had been through all of that before and he was wary now, for he knew that the lion hunters were the same the whole world over. Knowing them now for what they were, he found no disillusion in his encounters with them. Indeed, it added greatly to his pleasure and sense of power to turn the tactics of designing females on themselves: he would indulge in little gallantries to lead them on, and then, just at the point where they thought they had him, he would wriggle innocently off the hook and leave them wondering.

And then he met Else. Else von Kohler was not a lion hunter. George met her at one of the parties which his German publisher, Karl Lewald, gave for him. Lewald liked to give parties; he just couldn't do enough for George, and was always trumping up an excuse for another party. Else did not know Lewald, and took an instinctive dislike to the man as soon as she saw him, but just the same she had come to his party, brought there uninvited by another man whom George had met. At first sight, George fell instantly in love with her, and she with him.

Else was a young widow of thirty who looked and was a perfect type of the Norse Valkyrie. She had a mass of lustrous yellow hair braided about her head, and her cheeks were two ruddy apples. She was extremely tall for a woman, with the long, rangy legs of a runner, and her shoulders were as broad and wide as a man's. Yet she had a stunning figure, and there was no suggestion of an ugly masculinity about her. She was as completely and as passionately feminine as a woman could be. Her somewhat stern and lonely face was relieved by its spiritual depth and feeling, and when it was lighted by a smile it had a sudden, poignant radiance, a quality of illumination which in its intensity and purity was different from any other smile George had ever seen.

At the moment of their first meeting, George and Else had been drawn to each other. From then on, without the need of any period of transition, their lives flowed in a single channel. They spent many wonderful days together. Many, too, were the nights which they filled with the mysterious enchantments of a strong and mutually shared passion. The girl became for George the ultimate reality underlying everything he thought and felt and was during that glorious and intoxicating period of his life.

And now all the blind and furious Brooklyn years, all the years of work, all the memories of men who prowled in garbage cans, all the years of wandering and exile, seemed very far away. In some strange fashion, the image of his own success and this joyous release after so much toil and desperation became connected in George's mind with Else, with the kiefern trees, with the great crowds thronging the Kurfürstendamm, with all the golden singing in the air – and somehow with a feeling that for everyone grim weather was behind and that happy days were here again.

It was the season of the great Olympic games, and almost every day George and Else went to the stadium in Berlin. George observed that the organizing genius of the German people, which has been used so often to such noble purpose, was now more thrillingly displayed than he had ever seen it before. The sheer pageantry of the occasion was overwhelming, so much so that he began to feel oppressed by it. There seemed to be something ominous in it. One sensed a stupendous concentration of effort, a tremendous drawing together and ordering in the vast collective power of the whole land. And the thing that made it seem ominous was that it so evidently went beyond what the games themselves demanded. The games were overshadowed, and were no longer merely sporting competitions to which other nations had sent their chosen teams. They became, day after day, an orderly and overwhelming demonstration in which the whole of Germany had been schooled and disciplined. It was as if the games had been chosen as a symbol of the new collective might, a means of showing to the world in concrete terms what this new power had come to be.

With no past experience in such affairs, the Germans had constructed a mighty stadium which was the most beautiful and most perfect in its design that had ever been built. And all the accessories of this monstrous plant – the swimming pools, the enormous halls, the lesser stadia – had been laid out and designed with this same cohesion of beauty and of use. The organization was superb. Not only were the events themselves, down to the minutest detail of each competition, staged and run off like clockwork, but the crowds – such crowds as no other great city has ever had to cope with, and the like of which would certainly have snarled and maddened the traffic of New York beyond hope of untangling – were handled with a quietness, order, and speed that was astounding.

The daily spectacle was breath-taking in its beauty and magnificence. The stadium was a tournament of color that caught the throat; the massed splendor of the banners made the gaudy decorations of America's great parades, presidential inaugurations, and World's Fairs seem like shoddy carnivals in comparison. And for the duration of the Olympics, Berlin itself was transformed into a kind of annex to the stadium. From one end of the city to the other, from the Lustgarten to the Brandenburger Tor, along the whole broad sweep of Unter den Linden, through the vast avenues of the faëry Tiergarten, and out through the western part of Berlin to the very portals of the stadium, the whole town was a thrilling pageantry of royal banners – not merely endless miles of looped-up bunting, but banners fifty feet in height, such as might have graced the battle tent of some great emperor.

And all through the day, from morning on, Berlin became a mighty Ear, attuned, attentive, focused on the stadium. Everywhere the air was filled with a single voice. The green trees along the Kurfürstendamm began to talk: from loud-speakers concealed in their branches an announcer in the stadium spoke to the whole city – and for George Webber it was a strange experience to hear the familiar terms of track and field translated into the tongue that Goethe used. He would be informed now that the *Vorlauf* was about to be run – and then the *Zwischenlauf* and at length the *Endlauf* – and the winner:

'Owens – Oo Ess Ah!'

Meanwhile, through those tremendous banner-laden ways, the crowds thronged ceaselessly all day long. The wide promenade of Unter den Linden was solid with patient, tramping German feet. Fathers, mothers, children, young folks, old – the whole material of the nation was there, from every corner of the land. From morn to night they trudged, wide-eyed, full of wonder, past the marvel of those banner-laden ways. And among them one saw the bright stabs of color of Olympic jackets and the glint of foreign faces: the dark features of Frenchmen and Italians, the ivory grimace of the Japanese, the straw hair and blue eyes of the Swedes, and the big Americans, natty in straw hats, white flannels, and blue coats crested with the Olympic seal.

And there were great displays of marching men, some-times ungunned but rhythmic as regiments of brown shirts went swinging through the streets. By noon each day all the main approaches to the games, the embannered streets and avenues of the route which the Leader would take to the stadium, miles away, were walled in by the troops. They stood at ease, young men, laughing and talking with each other – the Leader's bodyguards, the Schutz Staffel units, the Storm Troopers, all the ranks and divisions in their different uniforms – and they stretched in two unbroken lines from the Wilhelm-strasse up to the arches of the Brandenburger Tor. Then, suddenly, the sharp command, and instantly there would be the solid smack of ten thousand leather boots as they came together with the sound of war.

It seemed as if everything had been planned for this moment, shaped to this triumphant purpose. But the people – they had not been planned. Day after day, behind the unbroken wall of soldiers, they stood and waited in a dense and patient throng. These were the masses of the nation, the poor ones of the earth, the humble ones of life, the workers and the wives, the mothers and the children – and day after day they came and stood and waited. They were there because they did not have money enough to buy the little cardboard squares that would have given them places within the magic ring. From noon till night they waited for just two brief and golden moments of the day: the moment when the Leader went out to the stadium, and the moment when he returned.

At last he came – and something like a wind across a field of grass was shaken through that crowd, and from afar the tide rolled up with him, and in it was the voice, the hope, the prayer of the land. The Leader came by slowly in a shining car, a little dark man with a comic-opera mustache, erect and standing, moveless and unsmiling, with his hand upraised, palm outward, not in Nazi-wise salute, but straight up, in a gesture of blessing such as the Buddha or Messiahs use.

From the beginning of their relationship, and straight through to the end, Else refused to discuss with George anything even remotely connected with the Nazi regime. That was a closed subject between them. But others were not so discreet. The first weeks passed, and George began to hear some ugly things. From time to time, at parties, dinners, and the like, when George would speak of his enthusiasm for Germany and the German people, various friends that he had made would, if they had had enough to drink, take him aside afterwards and, after looking around cautiously, lean toward him with an air of great secrecy and whisper:

'But have you heard . . . ? And have you heard . . . ?'

He did not see any of the ugly things they whispered about. He did not see anyone beaten. He did not see anyone imprisoned, or put to death. He did not see any men in concentration camps. He did not see openly anywhere the physical manifestations of a brutal and compulsive force.

True, there were men in brown uniforms everywhere, and men in black uniforms, and men in uniforms of olive green, and everywhere in the streets there was the solid smack of booted feet, the blare of brass, the tootling of fifes, and the poignant sight of young faces shaded under iron helmets, with folded arms and ramrod backs, precisely seated in great army lorries. But all of this had become so mixed in with his joy over his own success, his feeling for Else, and the genial temper of the people making holiday, as he had seen and known it so many pleasant times before, that even if it did not now seem good, it did not seem sinister or bad.

Then something happened. It didn't happen suddenly. It just happened as a cloud gathers, as fog settles, as rain begins to fall.

A man George had met was planning to give a party for him and asked him if he wanted to ask any of his friends. George mentioned one. His host was silent for a moment; he looked embarrassed; then he said that the person George had named had formerly been the editorial head of a publication that had been suppressed, and that one of the people who had been instrumental in its suppression had been invited to the party, so would George mind—?

George named another, an old friend named Franz Heilig whom he had first met in Munich years before, and who now lived in Berlin, and of whom he was very fond. Again the anxious pause, the embarrassment, the halting objections. This person was – was – well, George's host said he knew about this person and knew he did not go to parties – he would not come if he were invited – so would George mind—?

George next spoke the name of Else von Kohler, and the

response to this suggestion was of the same kind. How long had he known this woman? Where, and under what circumstances, had he met her? George tried to reassure his host on all these scores. He told the man he need have no fear of any sort about Else. His host was instant, swift, in his apologies: oh, by no means – he was sure the lady was eminently all right – only nowadays – with a mixed gathering – he had tried to pick a group of people whom George had met and who all knew one another – he had thought it would be much more pleasant that way – strangers at a party were often shy, constrained, and formal – Frau von Kohler would not know anybody there – so would George mind—?

Not long after this baffling experience a friend came to see him. 'In a few days,' his friend said, 'you will receive a phone call from a certain person. He will try to meet you, to talk to you. Have nothing to do with this man.'

George laughed. His friend was a sober-minded German, rather on the dull and heavy side, and his face was so absurdly serious as he spoke that George thought he was trying to play some lumbering joke upon him. He wanted to know who this mysterious personage might be who was so anxious to make his acquaintance.

To George's amazement and incredulity, his friend named a high official in the government.

But why, George asked, should this man want to meet him? And why, if he did, should he be afraid of him?

At first his friend would not answer. Finally he muttered circumspectly:

'Listen to me. Stay away from this man. I tell you for your own good.' He paused, not knowing how to say it; then: 'You have heard of Captain Roehm? You know about him? You know what happened to him?' George nodded. 'Well,' his friend went on in a troubled voice, 'there were others

165

who were not shot in the purge. This man I speak of is one of the bad ones. We have a name for him – it is "The Prince of Darkness."'

George did not know what to make of all this. He tried to puzzle it out but could not, so at last he dismissed it from his mind. But within a few days the official whom his friend had named did telephone, and did ask to meet him. George offered some excuse and avoided seeing the man, but the episode was most peculiar and unsettling.

Both of these baffling experiences contained elements of comedy and melodrama, but those were the superficial aspects. George began to realize now the tragedy that lay behind such things. There was nothing political in any of it. The roots of it were much more sinister and deep and evil than politics or even racial prejudice could ever be. For the first time in his life he had come upon something full of horror that he had never known before – something that made all the swift violence and passion of America, the gangster compacts, the sudden killings, the harshness and corruption that infested portions of American business and public life, seem innocent beside it. What George began to see was a picture of a great people who had been psychically wounded and were now desperately ill with some dread malady of the soul. Here was an entire nation, he now realized, that was infested with the contagion of an ever-present fear. It was a kind of creeping paralysis which twisted and blighted all human relations. The pressures of a constant and infamous compulsion had silenced this whole people into a sweltering and malignant secrecy until they had become spiritually septic with the distillations of their own self-poisons, for which now there was no medicine or release.

As he began to see and understand the true state of affairs, George wondered if anyone could be so base as to exult at this great tragedy, or to feel hatred for the once-mighty people who were the victims of it. Culturally, from the eighteenth century on, the German was the first citizen of Europe. In Goethe there was made sublimely articulate a world spirit which knew no boundary lines of nationality, politics, race, or religion, which rejoiced in the inheritance of all mankind, and which wanted no domination or conquest of that inheritance save that of participating in it and contributing to it. This German spirit in art, literature, music, science, and philosophy continued in an unbroken line right down to 1933, and it seemed to George that there was not a man or woman alive in the world who was not, in one way or another, the richer for it.

When he first visited Germany, in 1925, the evidence of that spirit was manifest everywhere in the most simple and unmistakable ways. For example, one could not pass the crowded window of a bookshop in any town without instantly observing in it a reflection of the intellectual and cultural enthusiasm of the German people. The contents of the shop revealed a breadth of vision and of interest that would have made the contents of a French bookshop, with its lingual and geographic constrictions, seem paltry and provincial. The best writers of every country were as well known in Germany as in their own land. Among the Americans, Theodore Dreiser, Sinclair Lewis, Upton Sinclair, and Jack London had particularly large followings; their books were sold and read everywhere. And the work of America's younger writers was eagerly sought out and published.

Even in 1936 this noble enthusiasm, although it had been submerged and mutilated by the regime of Adolph Hitler, was still apparent in the most touching way. George had heard it said that good books could no longer be published and read in Germany. This, he found, was not true, as some of the other things he had heard about Germany were not true. And about Hitler's Germany he felt that one must be very true. And the reason one needed to be very true was that the thing in it which every decent person must be against was false. You could not turn the other cheek to wrong, but also, it seemed to him, you could not be wrong about wrong. You had to be right about it. You could not meet lies and trickery with lies and trickery, although there were some people who argued that you should.

So it was not true that good books could no longer be published and read in Germany. And because it was not true, the tragedy of the great German spirit was more movingly evident, in the devious and distorted ways in which it now manifested itself, than it would have been if it were true. Good books were still published if their substance did not, either openly or by implication, criticize the Hitler regime or contravert its dogmas. And it would simply be stupid to assert that any book must criticize Hitler and contravert his doctrines in order to be good.

For these reasons, the eagerness, curiosity, and enthusiasm of the Germans for such good books as they were still allowed to read had been greatly intensified. They wanted desperately to find out what was going on in the world, and the only way they had left was to read whatever books they could get that had been written outside of Germany. This seemed to be one basic explanation of their continued interest in American writing, and that they *were* interested was a fact as overwhelming as it was pathetic. Under these conditions, the last remnants of the German spirit managed to survive only as drowning men survive – by clutching desperately at any spar that floated free from the wreckage of their ship.

So the weeks, the months, the summer passed, and

everywhere about him George saw the evidences of this dissolution, this shipwreck of a great spirit. The poisonous emanations of suppression, persecution, and fear permeated the air like miasmic and pestilential vapors, tainting, sickening, and blighting the lives of everyone he met. It was a plague of the spirit – invisible, but as unmistakable as death. Little by little it sank in on him through all the golden singing of that summer, until at last he felt it, breathed it, lived it, and knew it for the thing it was.

HANS FALLADA

From

ALONE IN BERLIN

Translated by Michael Hofmann

VICTORY DANCE AT THE ELYSIUM

THE FLOOR OF THE Elysium, the great dance hall in the north of Berlin, that Friday night presented the kind of spectacle that must gladden the heart of any true German: it was jam-packed with uniforms.

While the Wehrmacht with its greys and greens supplied the background to this colourful composition, what made the scene so vibrant were the uniforms of the Party and its various bodies, going from tan, golden brown, brown, and dark brown to black. There, next to the brown shirts of the SA you saw the much lighter brown of the Hitler Youth; the Organization Todt was as well represented as the Reichsarbeitsdienst; you saw the yellow uniforms of Sonderführer, dubbed golden pheasants; political leaders stood next to air-raid wardens. And it wasn't just the men who were so delightfully accoutred; there were also many girls in uniform; the Bund Deutscher Mädel, the Arbeitsdienst, the Organization Todt – all seemed to have sent their leaders and deputies and rank and file to this place.

The few civilians present were lost in this swarm. They were insignificant and boring among so many uniforms, just as the civilian population out in the streets and factories never amounted to anything compared to the Party. The Party was everything, and the people nothing.

Thus, the table at the edge of the dance floor occupied by a girl and three young men received very little attention.

None of the four wore a uniform; there wasn't so much as a party badge on display.

A couple, the girl and a young man, had been the first to arrive. Then another young man had asked for permission to join them, and later on a fourth civilian had come forward with a similar request. The couple had made one attempt to dance in the seething mass. While they were away, the other two men had started a conversation in which the returning couple, looking hot and crushed, participated from time to time.

One of the men, a fellow in his early thirties with thin, receding hair, leaned way back in his chair and silently contemplated the crowd on the dance floor and at the other tables. Then, barely looking at his companions, he said, 'A poor choice of venue. We're almost the only civilian table in the whole place. We stick out a mile.'

The girl's partner smiled at her and said – but his words were meant for the balding man – 'Not at all, Grigoleit, we're practically invisible here, and if they do see us, at the most they despise us. The only thing on the minds of these people is that the so-called victory over France has secured them dancing rights for a couple of weeks.'

'No names! You know the rules!' the balding man said sharply.

For a while no one spoke. The girl doodled something on the table and didn't look up, though she could feel they were all looking at her.

'Anyway, Trudel,' said the third man, who had an innocent baby face, 'it's time for whatever you wanted to tell us. What's new? The next-door tables are almost all empty, everyone's dancing. Come on!'

The silence of the other two could only indicate agreement. Haltingly, not looking up, Trudel Baumann said: 'I think I've made a mistake. At any rate, I've broken my word. In my eyes, admittedly, it's not really a mistake . . .'

'Oh, come on!' exclaimed the balding man angrily. 'Are you going to start gabbling like a silly goose? Tell us what it is, straight out!'

The girl looked up. She looked at the three men one after the other, all of them, it seemed to her, eyeing her coldly. There were tears in her eyes. She wanted to speak, but couldn't. She looked for her handkerchief . . .

The man with the receding hairline leaned back. He let out a long, soft whistle. 'I tell her she's not supposed to blab. I'm afraid she already has. Look at her.'

The cavalier at Trudel's side retorted quickly, 'Not possible. Trudel is a good girl. Tell them you haven't blabbed, Trudel!' And he squeezed her hand encouragingly. The Babyface directed his round, very blue eyes expressionlessly at the girl. The tall man with the receding hairline smiled contemptuously. He put his cigarette in the ashtray and said mockingly, 'Well, Fräulein?'

Trudel had got herself under control, and bravely she whispered, 'He's right. I talked out of turn. My father-in-law brought me news of my Otto's death. That somehow knocked me off balance. I told him I was in a cell.'

'Did you name names?' No one would have guessed that the Babyface could ask questions so sharply.

'Of course not. That's all I said, too. And my father-in-law is an old workingman, he'll never say a word.'

'Your father-in-law's the next chapter, you're the first! You say you didn't give any names . . .'

'I'll thank you for believing me, Grigoleit! I'm not lying. I'm freely confessing.'

'You just used a name again, Fräulein Baumann!'

The Babyface said, 'Don't you see it's completely

immaterial whether she named a name or not? She said she was involved in a cell, and that means she's blabbed, and will blab again. If the men in black lay hands on her, knock her about a bit, she'll talk, never mind how much or how little she's said so far.'

'I will never talk to them, even if I have to die!' cried Trudel with flaming cheeks.

'Pah!' said the balding man. 'Dying's the easy bit, Fräulein Baumann, sometimes they do rather unpleasant things to you before that!'

'You're unkind,' the girl said. 'Yes, I've done something wrong, but . . .'

'I agree,' said the fellow on the sofa next to her. 'We'll go and see her father-in-law, and if he's a reliable sort . . .'

'Under the torturer's hand there are no reliable sorts,' said Grigoleit.

'Trudel,' said the Babyface with a gentle smile, 'Trudel, you just told us you haven't told anyone any names?'

'And that's the truth, I haven't!'

'And you claimed you would rather die than give us away?'

'Yes, yes, yes!' she exclaimed passionately.

'Well then, Trudel,' said the Babyface, and smiled charmingly, 'what if you were to die tonight, before you blabbed any more? That would give us a certain measure of security, and save us a lot of trouble . . .'

A deathly hush descended on the four of them. The girl went white. The boy next to her said 'No,' and laid his hand over hers. But then he took it away again.

The dancers returned to their various tables and for a while made it impossible to continue the conversation.

The balding man lit another cigarette, and the Babyface smiled subtly when he saw how the other's hands were shaking. Then he said to the dark-haired boy next to the pale, silent girl, 'You say no? But why do you say no? It's an almost entirely satisfactory solution to the problem, and as I understand it, was suggested by your neighbour herself.'

'It's not a satisfactory solution,' said the dark-haired boy slowly. 'You'll remember that sentence when the People's Court has you and me and her . . .'

'Quiet!' said the Babyface. 'Go away and dance for a few minutes. It seems like a nice tune. You can discuss things between yourselves there, and we will here.'

Reluctantly, the dark-haired boy got up and bowed lightly to the lady. Reluctantly, she laid her hand on his arm, and the two pale figures headed, with a whole stream of others, to the dance floor. They danced earnestly, in silence, and he had the sense he was dancing with a corpse. He shuddered. The uniforms on all sides of them, the dangling swastikas, the blood-red banners on the walls with the repulsive emblem, the portrait of the Führer tricked out in green: swingtime for Hitler. 'Don't do it, Trudel,' he said. 'He's crazy to ask for something like that. Promise me . . .'

They were almost dancing in place in the ever thickening mass of bodies. Perhaps because there were continual collisions with other couples, she didn't speak.

'Trudel!' he said again. 'Please promise me! You can go to a different company, work there, stay away from them. Promise . . .'

He tried to force her to look at him, but she kept her eyes obstinately directed at a point behind his shoulder.

'You're the best of us,' he said suddenly. 'You're humanity. He's just dogma. You must go on living, don't give in to him!'

She shook her head, whether it was yes or no was unclear. 'I want to go back,' she said. 'I don't feel like dancing any more.'

'Trudel,' said Karl Hergesell hastily as they made their way back through the dancing couples, 'your Otto died yesterday, or at least yesterday you got news of his death. It's too soon. But you know it anyway: I've always loved you. I've never expected anything from you, but now I expect at least that you stay alive. Not for my sake, nothing like that, but, please, just stay alive!'

Once again she moved her head slightly, and it was unclear what she thought of either his love or his wish that she at least remain alive. Then they were back at their table with the others. 'Well?' asked Grigoleit with the receding hair. 'What's the feeling on the dance floor? A bit packed, eh?'

The girl hadn't sat down. She said, 'I'm going now. All the best. I would have liked to work with you . . .'

She turned to leave.

But now the plump, innocent-looking Babyface got up and took her by the wrist, and said, 'One moment, please!' He said it with due politeness, but there was menace in his expression.

They returned to the table and sat down again. The Baby-face asked, 'Do I understand correctly what you meant by your goodbye just now?'

'You understood me,' she said, looking back at him with unyielding eyes.

'Then I would like permission to accompany you for the rest of the evening.'

She made a motion of appalled resistance.

He said very politely, 'I don't want to force myself upon you, but I would like you to consider that further mistakes can be made in the execution of such a plan.' He whispered threateningly, 'I don't want to have some idiot fishing you out of a canal, or have you coming round from an attempted overdose in hospital tomorrow morning. I want to be there!'

'That's right!' said the balding one. 'I agree. That's our only insurance . . .'

The dark-haired boy said emphatically, 'I will remain at her side today and tomorrow and every following day. I will do everything I can to foil the execution of such a plan. I will even go to the police for help, if you force me to!'

The balding man whistled again, low, long, and maliciously.

The Babyface said, 'Aha, it seems we have a second blabber among us. In love, eh? I always suspected it. Come on, Grigoleit, this cell is wound up. There is no cell any more. And that's what you call discipline, you women!'

'No, no!' cried the girl. 'Don't listen to him. It's true, he does love me. But I don't love him. And I want to go with you tonight . . .'

'Forget it!' said the Babyface, now furious. 'Can't you see that we're in no position to do anything any more, now that you . . .'

He tipped his head in the direction of the dark-haired boy. 'Ach, who cares!' He then said, 'It's over. Come on, Grigoleit!'

The balding one was already on his feet. Together, they walked toward the exit. Suddenly a hand was laid on the Babyface's arm. He looked into a smooth, slightly puffy face in a brown uniform.

'One moment, please! What was that you just said about a cell being wound up? I would be very interested to know . . .'

The Babyface pulled his arm away. 'You leave me alone!' he said, very loudly. 'If you want to know what we were talking about, ask the young lady over there! Yesterday her fiancé fell, and today she's got the hots for someone else! Bloody women!'

He kept pushing toward the exit, which Grigoleit had already reached. Then he, too, left the premises. The fat man watched him go for a moment. Then he turned back to the table, where the girl and the dark-haired fellow were still sitting, both looking rather pale. That relieved him. Perhaps I didn't make a mistake in letting him go. He took me by surprise. But . . .

Politely he asked, 'Would you mind very much if I sat with you for a few minutes and asked you some questions?'

Trudel Baumann replied, 'I can't tell you any more than what the gentleman just said to you. I received news of the death of my fiancé yesterday, and today this gentleman here has asked me to become engaged to him.'

Her voice sounded firm and unwavering. Now that there was danger seated at the table, her fear and unrest were gone.

'Would you mind telling me the name and rank of your fallen fiancé? And his regiment?' She told him. 'And your own name? Address? Place of work? Do you have other documentation on you? Thank you! And now you, sir.'

'I work in the same factory. My name is Karl Hergesell. Here's my pay stub.'

'And the two other gentlemen?'

'Never met them before. They sat down at our table and got involved in our argument.'

'And what were you arguing about?'

'I don't love him.'

'Why was the other gentleman so indignant about you, then, if you don't love him?'

'How do I know? Maybe he didn't believe me. He was annoyed that I agreed to dance with him.'

'I see!' said the chubby face, snapping his notebook shut and looking from one to the other. They really did seem more like a quarrelsome pair of lovebirds than conspirators caught red-handed. Even the way they shyly avoided looking at each other . . . And yet their hands were almost touching on the tabletop. 'I see! Of course we'll have your answers checked, but it seems to me . . . anyway, I wish you a more congenial end to your evening . . .'

'I don't!' said the girl. 'I don't!' She got up simultaneously with the brownshirt. 'I'm going home.'

'I'll take you.'

'No, thanks, I'd rather go alone.'

'Trudel!' the boy begged. 'Just let me say two more words to you!'

The brownshirt smiled from one to the other. They clearly were lovers. A superficial check would do.

Suddenly she made up her mind: 'All right, but only two minutes!'

They walked out. At last they were away from this appalling hall and its atmosphere of concerted hatred. They looked about them.

'They've gone.'

'We will never see them again.'

'And you can live. No, Trudel, you must live! An unconsidered step on your part would plunge the others into danger, many others – always remember, Trudel!'

'Yes,' she said, 'now I must live.' And with a swift decision, 'Goodbye, Karl.'

For an instant she pressed herself against his chest and her lips brushed his. Before he knew what was happening, she was running across the carriageway to a waiting tram. The driver moved off.

He made as if to take off after her. Then he thought better of it.

I will see her in the factory from time to time, he told

himself. A whole life lies ahead of us. And I know now that she loves me.

SATURDAY: DISCORD AT THE QUANGELS'

The Quangels didn't speak to each other all of Friday either – that meant three days of silence between them, not even giving each other the time of day. This had never happened in the entire course of their marriage. However laconic Quangel might be, he had managed a sentence from time to time, something about someone at work or at least the weather or that his dinner had tasted particularly good. But none of that now!

The longer it lasted, the more keenly Anna Quangel felt it. Her deep grief for her son was being sidetracked by disquiet about the change in her husband. She wanted to think only of her boy, but she couldn't when she saw Otto in front of her, her husband of so many years, to whom she had given the greater and better part of her life. What had got into the man? What was up with him? What had changed him so?

By midday on Friday Anna Quangel had lost all her rage and reproach against Otto. If she had thought it might accomplish anything, she would have asked him to forgive her for blurting out that sentence about 'You and your Führer'. But it was plain to see that Otto was no longer thinking about that reproach; he didn't even seem to be thinking about her. He seemed to look past her, if not right through her, standing by the window, his hands in the pockets of his work tunic, whistling slowly and reflectively, with long intervals between, which was something he'd never done before.

What was the man thinking about? What was going on inside him? She set down the soup on the table, and he started spooning it down. For a moment she observed him from the kitchen. His sharp bird face was bent low over the bowl, he lifted his spoon mechanically to his mouth, his dark eyes looked at something that wasn't there.

She went back into the kitchen, to heat up an end of cabbage. He liked reheated cabbage. She had decided she would say something to him when she returned with his cabbage. He could answer as sharply as he pleased: she had to break this unholy silence.

But when she came back into the dining room with the warmed-up cabbage, Otto was gone, and his half-eaten dinner was still on the table. Either Quangel had sensed her intention and crept away like a child intent on remaining stubborn, or he had simply forgotten to carry on eating because of whatever it was that was so consuming him. Anyway, he was gone, and she would have to wait till night-time for him to come back.

But on Friday night, Otto returned from work so late that for all her good intentions she was already asleep when he came to bed. It was only later that he woke her with his coughing. Softly, she asked, 'Otto, are you asleep?'

His coughing stopped; he lay there perfectly still. Again she asked, 'Otto, are you asleep already?'

Nothing, no reply. The two of them lay there in silence a very long time. Each knew that the other was not sleeping. They didn't dare move in bed, so as not to give themselves away. Finally, they both fell asleep.

Saturday got off to an even worse start. Otto Quangel had got up unusually early. Before she could put his watery coffee substitute out on the table, he had already set off on one of those rushed, mysterious errands that he had never undertaken before. He came back, and from the kitchen she could hear him pacing around the parlour. When she came in with the coffee, he carefully folded away a large white sheet of paper he had been reading by the window and put it in his pocket.

Anna was sure it wasn't a newspaper. There was too much white on the paper, and the writing was bigger than in a newspaper. What could her husband have been reading?

She got cross with him again, with his secrecy, with these changes that brought with them so much disturbance, and so many fresh anxieties in addition to all the old ones, which had surely been enough. All the same, she said, 'Coffee, Otto!'

At the sound of her voice, he turned and looked at her, as though surprised that he was not alone in the apartment, surprised that he had been spoken to by her. He looked at her, and yet he didn't: it wasn't his spouse, Anna Quangel, he was looking at, so much as someone he had once known and now had to struggle to remember. There was a smile on his face, in his eyes, spreading over the whole expanse of his face in a way she had never seen before. She was on the point of crying out: Otto, oh Otto, don't you leave me too!

But before she had made up her mind, he had walked past her and out of the flat. Once more no coffee, once again she had to take it back to the kitchen to warm it up. She sobbed gently. Oh, that man! Was she going to be left with no one? After the son, was she going to lose the father?

In the meantime, Quangel was walking briskly in the direction of Prenzlauer Allee. It had occurred to him that it was a good idea to look at a building like that properly, to see if his impression of it was at all accurate. Otherwise, he would have to think of something else entirely.

On Prenzlauer Allee, he slowed down; his eye scanned

the nameplates on the housefronts as though looking for something specific. On a corner house he saw signs for two lawyers and a doctor, in addition to many other business plates.

He pushed against the door. It was open. Right: no porters in houses with so many visitors. Slowly, his hand on the banister, he climbed the steps, once a grand staircase with oak flooring, which through heavy use and years of war had lost all trace of grandeur. Now it looked merely dingy and worn, and the carpets were long since gone, probably taken in at the beginning of the war.

Otto Quangel passed a lawyer's sign on the first floor, nodded, and slowly walked on up. It wasn't as though he was all alone on the stairway, not at all. People kept passing him – either from behind, or coming down the other way. He kept hearing bells going off, doors slamming, phones ringing, typewriters clattering, people talking.

But in between there was a moment when Otto Quangel was all alone on the stairs, or at least had his part of the stairs all to himself, when all of life seemed to have withdrawn into the offices. That was the moment to do it. In fact, everything was exactly the way he had imagined it. People in a hurry, not looking each other in the face, dirty windowpanes letting in only a murky grey light, no porter, no one anywhere to take an interest in anyone.

When Otto Quangel had seen the plate of the second lawyer on the first floor, and an arrow pointing visitors up another flight of steps to the doctor's office, he nodded in agreement. He turned around: he had just been to see a lawyer, and now he was leaving the building. No point in looking further: it was exactly the sort of building he needed, and there were thousands upon thousands of them in Berlin.

Foreman Otto Quangel is standing in the street again. A dark-haired young man with a very pale face walks up to him.

'You're Herr Quangel, aren't you?' he asks. 'Herr Otto Quangel, from Jablonski Strasse?'

Quangel utters a stalling 'Mhm?' – a sound that can indicate agreement as much as dissent.

The young man takes it for agreement. 'I am to ask you on behalf of Trudel Baumann,' he says, 'to forget her completely. Also tell your wife not to visit Trudel any more. Herr Quangel, there's no need for you to . . .'

'You tell her,' says Otto Quangel, 'that I don't know any Trudel Baumann, and I don't like to be approached by strangers on the street . . .'

His fist catches the young man on the point of the chin, and he crumples like a wet rag. Quangel strides casually through the crowd of people gathering, straight past a policeman, toward a tram stop. The tram comes, he climbs in, and rides two stops. Then he rides back the other way, this time on the front platform of the second car. As he thought: most of the people have gone on their way; ten or a dozen onlookers are still standing in front of a café where the man was probably carried.

He is already conscious again. For the second time in the space of two hours, Karl Hergesell is called upon to identify himself to an official.

'It's really nothing, officer,' he assures him. 'I must have trodden on his toe, and he bopped me one. I've no idea who he was, I'd hardly started apologizing when he caught me.'

Once again, Karl Hergesell is allowed to leave unchallenged, with no suspicion against him. But he realizes that he shouldn't push his luck. The only reason he went to see Trudel's ex-father-in-law was to gauge her safety. Well, where

Otto Quangel is concerned, he can set his mind at ease. A tough bird, and a wicked right. And certainly not a chatter-box, in spite of the big beak on him. The way he lit into him!

And for fear that such a man might blab, Trudel had almost been sent to her death. He would never blab – not even to them! And he wouldn't mind about Trudel either, he seemed not to want to know her any more. All the things a sock on the jaw can teach you!

Karl Hergesell now goes to work completely at ease, and when he learns there, by asking discreetly around, that Grigoleit and the Babyface have quit, he draws a deep breath. They're safe now. There is no more cell, but he's not even all that sorry. At least it means that Trudel can live!

In truth, he was never that interested in this political work, but all the more in Trudel!

Quangel takes the tram back in the direction of his home, but he goes past his own stop. Better safe than sorry, and if he still has someone tailing him, he wants to confront him alone and not drag him back home. Anna is in no condition to cope with a disagreeable surprise. He needs to talk to her first. Of course he will do that: Anna has a big part to play in the thing that he is planning. But he has other business to take care of first. Tomorrow is Sunday, and everything has to be ready.

He changes trams again and heads off into the city. No, the young man he silenced with a punch just now doesn't strike Quangel as a great threat. He's not convinced he has any further pursuers, and he's pretty sure the boy was sent by Trudel. She did suggest, after all, that she would have to confess to breaking a sort of vow. Thereupon they will have banned her from seeing him at all, and she sent the young fellow to him as a sort of envoy. All pretty harmless. Childish games for people who have let themselves in for something they don't understand. He, Otto Quangel, understands a little more. He at least knows what he's letting himself in for. And he won't approach this game like a child. He will think about each card before he plays it.

He sees Trudel in front of him again, pressed against the poster of the People's Court in that corridor – clueless. Once again, he has the disturbing feeling he had when the girl's head was crowned by the line, 'in the name of the German people': he can see their names up there instead of those of the strangers – no, no, this is a task for him alone. And for Anna, of course for Anna too. He'll show her who his 'Führer' is!

When he gets to the city centre, Quangel makes a few purchases. He spends only pennies at a time, a couple of postcards, a pen, a couple of engraving nibs, a small bottle of ink. And he distributes his custom among a department store, a Woolworths, and a stationery shop. Finally, after long thought, he buys a pair of thin, worsted gloves, which he gets without a receipt.

Then he sits in one of those big beer halls on the Alexanderplatz, drinks a glass of beer, and has a bite to eat, without using his ration cards. It's 1940, the looting of the invaded nations has begun, the German people are suffering no very great hardship. You can still find most things in the shops, and they're not even all that expensive.

As far as the war itself is concerned, it's being fought in foreign countries a long way from Berlin. Yes, from time to time British planes appear over the city. They drop a few bombs, and the next day the populace treks out to view the damage. Most of them laugh at what they see, and say, 'Well, if that's the best they can do, they'll be busy for another hundred years, and meanwhile we'll have removed their cities from the face of the earth!'

That's the way people have been talking, and since France sued for peace, the number of people talking like that has grown considerably. Most people are impressed by success. A man like Otto Quangel, who during a prosperous period quits the ranks, is a rarity.

He sits there. He still has time, he doesn't have to go to the factory yet. But now the stress of the last few days falls away. Now that he's visited that corner building, now that he's made those few small purchases, everything is decided in his mind. He doesn't even need to think about what he still has to do. It'll do itself, the way is open before him. He only needs to follow it. The decisive first few steps have already been taken.

When it's time, he pays and heads out to the factory. Although it's a long way from the Alexanderplatz, he walks. He's spent enough money today, on transport, on little purchases, on food. Enough? Too much! Even though Quangel has decided on a whole new life, he won't change his old habits. He will remain frugal, and will keep people away from him.

And then he's back at work, alert and awake, laconic and unapproachable as ever. There's no visible sign of the change in him.

HEINZ REIN

BERLIN, APRIL 1945

From

BERLIN FINALE

Translated by Shaun Whiteside

LISBON, SAN FRANCISCO and Tokyo were destroyed by earthquakes in a matter of minutes; it took several days for the fires of Rome, Chicago and London to be extinguished. The fires and earthquakes that raged upon the spot on the earth's surface marked by the geographical intersection of 52 degrees 30 minutes northern latitude and 13 degrees 24 minutes eastern longitude lasted almost two years. They began on the clear, dark night of 23 August 1943 and ended in the rainy grey of 2 May 1945.

It was at this spot, thirty-two metres above sea level, that the city of Berlin lay nestled in an Ice Age dune until that night when destruction began its baleful course. It had risen from a fishing village to a fortress town, to the seat of the margraves and prince-electors of Brandenburg, to the residence of the kings of Prussia and the capital of the imperial and republican German Reich. It had come into being with the advance of colonizing German tribes into the settlement zones of the Wends and Slavs, and had lain for centuries far from the tribal territories of German culture. It had become a bulwark in the German colonial nation, an outlier of the old German West and an outpost of the new German East, and was late in entering the Reich and still later in becoming the centre of German history. It consists of a multiplicity of small, middle-sized and large towns, of villages, settlements, farms and barbicans that lay scattered between the Havel and the lake-land to the east of the Marches, and merged together towards the old fortress towns of Berlin and Kölln. The scourge of history worked very sparingly here, there were few traces of its rise and its transformations, but they refined an ambiguous appearance with certain noble features that were firmly engraved upon the city's core. There are innumerable traces of the city's downfall, which began as soon as it was elevated to the capital of the Greater German Reich. Devastating conflagrations, storms of steel and carpet-bombing have transformed the city's lively face into the grimace of a death's head.

On August 23 1943 the city was dealt its first wound when 1,200 British Air Force planes launched their first great strike. The southern suburbs of Lankwitz, Südende and Lichterfelde were rendered into a smoke-blackened island of death in the middle of the sea of life. But this time it was not sea engulfing the island, it was the island ousting the sea, because soon it was no longer alone. Everywhere, in Moabit and Friedrichstadt, around Ostkreuz and in Charlottenburg, at Moritzplatz and around the Lustgarten, islands of death appeared, their shores advancing further and further and amalgamating, until at last the whole city became a land of death with a few patches of water that still contained a trace of life. Each attack broke a piece from the structure of the city, destroyed property and lowered living conditions.

Whole districts were turned to barren rubble. Large factory sites, flanked by unused chimneys, became a wilderness of shattered hangars and rusting machinery, pipes, metal bars, wires and joists. Many streets were still lined with the façades of buildings that looked like living houses but were now nothing but cynical backdrops. Mutilation has left other districts so disfigured as to be unrecognizable, filling them with wheezing, struggling life. The stumps of their mutilated buildings rise naked and ugly among the heaps of rubble, they loom like islands from the sea of destruction, torn and shredded, the spars of roofs which have been blown away like ribs stripped of skin, the windows as blind as eyes with permanently lowered lids, occasionally blinking glassily, the walls bare, having shed their plaster, looking like ageing women whose faces have been ruthlessly wiped of foundation and rouge.

In other parts of the city the destruction is less complete, but in those rows of houses the war's claws have torn great gaps, often revealing a surprising view of the inner courtyards of buildings. Having escaped the airstrikes, they are visible from the streets for the first time, and so can no longer hide their ugly countenances behind the shoddy flamboyance of their external façades; in a sense, the hurricane of explosions has raised the curtain on them. These streets hold all degrees and varieties of destruction, from total annihilation to shelters cobbled together from cardboard and cellulose. There are houses whose roofs have burned away, and others consumed by flames up to the first floor, and some that have been emptied by the blasts, their window frames, shutters and doors ripped from their bodies, the dry skeletons of the roof beams protruding like bones from corpses. There are flats that hang like swallows' nests above the exploded façades because the bombs fell at an angle, and basements that have survived the pressure of the collapsing houses. Only smoking stove-pipes among the piles of rubble suggest that people are vegetating in there as if in a fox's den. The anatomy of the houses presents itself unadorned, the stairs and the partition walls, the lift shafts and chimneys are like bones, the gas and water pipes like arteries, the radiators and bathtubs like entrails. The remains of life are wasting away amidst the jungle of ruins, and nature alone begins to clothe the naked destruction, covering the piles of debris with greenery.

The wide network of the public transport system, woven from the many tram and bus lines, the overground and the underground, the Stadtbahn and the Ringbahn, the local and suburban trains, has been torn to pieces, provisionally repaired with the most makeshift of patches. The timetables change from one day to the next because the destruction of platforms, overhead wires, tunnels, viaducts, bridges and stations has led to restricted services, cancellations and diversions.

The typical features of the city, those classically bourgeois buildings clustered around the island on the Spree and the swiftly flowing axis of Unter den Linden, which once lent it its characteristic features, created by the masterly hands of Schinkel, Schlüter and Eosander, Rauch, Knobelsdorff and Langhans, have been erased even before Speer's drawing-board architecture could supplant it. Its landmarks now are high-rise bunkers, accumulators of anxiety, inhalers of flight, olive-drab lumps of concrete with anti-aircraft guns which, heavy as gigantic mammoths, stamp down the grass of the Friedrichshain, the Humboldthain and the Zoological Garden, no conciliatory feature mitigating the brutal functionality of their architecture. To these are added the many bunkers, both below and above ground, in the squares and by the stations of the city centre, in the estates and leafy colonies of the periphery, and their most primitive variety, the slit trenches, carved into parks, patches of forest and the embankments of the suburban railways.

At the beginning of the war the city had 4,330,000 inhabitants, but in April 1945 there are only 2,850,000. The men have been conscripted to military service, they have been recruited to the Todt Organization, to the Volkssturm territorial army, they have been sent elsewhere with their factories. The women have fled to areas supposedly safe from air attacks, the old and the sick have been evacuated, the young called up for work duty, the schoolchildren lodged in rural evacuation camps, and the Jews removed. The decline in population is in fact far greater than that, because among the 2,850,000 inhabitants of the city 700,000 are foreign forced labourers from conquered and subject countries, Ukrainians, Polish, Romanians, Greeks, Yugoslavians, Czechs, Italians, French, Belgians, Dutch, Norwegians, Danish, Hungarians and those Jews and inmates saved from the death camps in the east because they were fit for work. They are crammed in barracks on the desolate stretches between the city and the suburbs, in sites cleared of bomb damage, usually along the railway lines, hastily thrown up and surrounded by barbed wire fences. They bear a striking similarity to the emergency settlements that stand grey and bleak between patches of woodland and allotments, except that here (as everywhere else) the barbed wire is replaced by the invisible network of a system of surveillance and control, calculated down to the tiniest detail.

The ministries have left Berlin, they have been 'transferred', or moved to 'temporary quarters', the offices on Wilhelmstrasse are being dismantled, freight trains are being loaded night and day with files, cabinets and boxes, but also with furniture, household effects and suitcases. Senior ministry and Party officials have fled, leaving only the so-called 'intelligence centres', but there are plans for them too, and the extensive 'Thusnelda transport operation' is already in progress, with the special trains 'Adler' and 'Dohle' in Lichterfelde West and Michendorf, and numerous private cars.

Beneath the roar of the air-raid sirens, the muses fall silent. In the brief intervals between power cuts and air-raid warnings, all that emerges from microphones and cinema soundtracks are the voices of the illegitimate sisters of those muses, although the heroic bass of Mars is drowned out by a hysterical descant of compulsory frivolity; the little troop that consists of *Comrades, Kolberg, Hallgarten Reconnaissance Unit, Johanna the Black Hunter* and *The Great King* stand lonely among the interminable armies of *Young Hearts, A Happy House, My Colleague Will Be Right With You, The Ideal Husband, All Around Love, The Woman of My Dreams, It Started So Well, Long Live Love, The Honeymoon Hotel, The Greatest Love, The Man Who Was Sherlock Holmes, Women Make Better Diplomats, A Man for My Wife, Fritze Bollmann Wanted to Go Fishing, Love Letters, Easy Blood, Nights of Madness, Don't Talk to Me About Love.* The flagging thrust of *Fridericus Rex* and the *Horst Wessel Song* mix with the *Königswalzer*, the music of the weekly newscasts, the tormented laughter and the wailing sounds of the sirens mingle into a horrible cacophony.

In this city of ruins, whose body is burnt and broken, whose entrails are shredded and torn, people live pressed closely together, they lead a life more terrible and difficult than the lives of soldiers, devoted entirely to battle and danger. Beneath the constant threat – and it is no less of a threat – from explosions and fire, asphyxiation and entombment, the people of this city still lead a kind of private life, and carry the pitiful ballast of civilization around with them. They need to look after themselves and their families, they need to work and at every second they expect that they will have to interrupt whatever activities they happen to be engaged in, whether it be sleeping or making love, drilling or calculating, cooking or shaving, and devoting themselves to a fate that gives them no chance of escape. They lead a nomadic, troglodytic life, they allow the seed of a neurosis that may well be incurable to grow within their children, and surrender them to illiteracy. They watch the substance of youth being consumed in labour camps and anti-aircraft batteries, and the sense of a meaningful, orderly life dying away while their children are raised as warlike nomads. They have already moved so far from their origins, they have allowed their humanity to wither and atrophy to such an extent that at last they are merely machines which react willingly to the gentlest pressure of a finger or a phrase. It is the phlegmatic quality of people who have become fatalistic, who have rid themselves entirely of their own will and stubbornly continue along the path on which they have embarked, impassively accepting orders and special assignments, and praising as heroism their inner and outer indifference, and as perseverance their readiness to suffer; they ceased long ago to be the 'reckless race' described by Goethe. Beneath the ashes of their numbed souls there still smoulders the hope of divine providence announced by the mouth of the Antichrist, that famous covenant with God to which Hitler and Goebbels, Fritzsche and Dittmar are now so keen to refer. They know that fate, as unstoppable as a flood from the Volga and the Atlantic Ocean, will not halt at the gates of their city, but no spark of revolutionary zeal comes alive within them, no unleashed rage bursts the chains of duty, no cry of despair stirs the pangs of conscience. The disasters that the British and American Air Forces are delivering so masterfully in the airspace above the city absorb all capacity for thought, they send their victims off in search of refuge, food and clothing, ration coupons, food cards and bomb-damage certificates. They leave those who have been spared busy with repairs, safeguarding their belongings and struggling to reach their workplaces. The forms of civilized life are shattered, apartments have turned into dark caves since the protecting shell surrounding the sensitive cortices of the city, the telephone and electric cables, the gas and water pipes and the sewerage system, is torn and frayed. The people of the city have returned to the pump, the stove and the tallow candle.

There is something frantic about their movements, about their language, any unusual sound that springs suddenly from the flowing monotony makes them flinch and listen excitedly. They have only one single topic of conversation: the situation in the air, whether the Reich is free of enemies, whether any bomber units have flown in, where they are headed, whether they are flying away again. Everyone who leaves his apartment says goodbye to his family like someone undertaking a long and difficult journey into the uncertainty of an unknown and dangerous country, everyone carries with him a suitcase, a rucksack, a full briefcase or a shoulderbag, since the alarms often take them by surprise and force them to seek refuge somewhere far from home.

But it is not only the danger of war from the air that weighs down on the people, another menace has added to the weight of that burden: the front lines. Since the crossings of the Rhine in Remagen and Oppenheim, the Western Allies have reached the Elbe in a surprise incursion across western and central Germany, the Soviet armies have advanced as far as the Oder from the bridgeheads of Puławy, Warka and Baranów, through Poland and eastern Germany, but even though the western front is constantly shifting, Berlin has turned its face to the east, where the Soviet armies wait menacingly beyond the Oder.

It is the unease before the storm that lies over the city, an unease caused by the uncanny peace that spreads behind this last barrier in the east of the city, it is a restless peace, in which the railway trains and columns of motor cars from the Russian hinterland, from Chelyabinsk, from Sverdlovsk, from Gorky, from Magnitogorsk, from the collective farms of the Urals and Kuznetsk, advance towards the Oder. There is no one in the city who doesn't know that each day the lull before the big storm is being used to put new gunners in the firing position, to drive new tanks into place, new aeroplanes are preparing to launch, new divisions are reaching their combat zones. Those far-off worlds, the Soviet Union and the United States, have come frighteningly close, the distance between the Stars and Stripes and the Red Flag has shortened to the distance between Frankfurt an der Oder and Magdeburg, and in the middle lies the besieged city which – once protected by the waters of the Volga and the English Channel – seemed an unattainable hinterland, the stump that is Berlin. The enemy armies are still beyond the big rivers that form the final obstacle, but they are already bringing in their fleets of planes and severing their last thin threads of life. They are preparing for the final onslaught, which could break out at any moment, across the Oder and the Elbe, rolling towards the city with the force of an avalanche.

The city's stump has been turned into a makeshift fortress which is preparing to defend itself. Anti-tank ditches have been carved deep into the areas on the outskirts, communication trenches run diagonally across fields and allotments, one-man trenches have been dug into railway embankments, hillocks and patches of woodland, gun emplacements and anti-tank barriers block all access routes, immobilized tanks are buried at crossroads, flak artillery has been adapted to fire at ground-level targets, factories have downed tools, electricity, coal and fuel are now unavailable; the clerical and manual workers stay busy on the city's edge, digging yet more trenches and lining up barricade after barricade. In the streets, in the restaurants and cinemas, in shelters and railway waiting rooms, patrols of the Wehrmacht, the SS, the Todt Organization, the Gestapo and the police go in search of those unwilling to work and deserters: once again the Party has mobilized all means within its power to force each individual to do his part.

And to the east and west of the city the fronts rise up like a dark curtain of clouds. They seem like storms in the distance, no rumble of thunder can yet be heard, lightning still lurks behind the wall of clouds, but a whirling wind heralds the approaching storm, an oppressive, sulphurous yellow brightness spreads, a stormy closeness weighs upon the city. A fearful sense of expectation has taken hold of the city's inhabitants, they oscillate between hope of a miracle that has been repeatedly promised and presented as imminent by the Party leadership, and the paralysing horror of a terrible end. While exploding and incendiary bombs fall on the city, just as pitch and sulphur once rained on Sodom and Gomorrah, the little groups of the resistance movement wait with painful longing for liberation, because they cannot free themselves by their own power.

PETER SCHNEIDER

From

THE WALL JUMPER

Translated by Leigh Hafrey

CHAPTER 1

IN BERLIN, THE prevailing winds are from the west. Consequently a traveler coming in by plane has plenty of time to observe the city from above. In order to land against the wind, a plane from the west must cross the city and the wall dividing it three times: initially heading east, the plane enters West Berlin airspace, banks left in a wide arc across the eastern part of the city, and then, coming back from the east, takes the barrier a third time on the approach to Tegel landing strip. Seen from the air, the city appears perfectly homogeneous. Nothing suggests to the stranger that he is nearing a region where two political continents collide.

The overriding impression is of a linear order, one which derives from the rectangle and rules out any bending. In the center of the city, the apartment buildings are massed like fortresses. For the most part they are built in squares enclosing an inner courtyard, each with a chestnut tree in the middle. When the top of one of these chestnuts begins to move gently, residents can assume that a force six to eight gale is sweeping along the streets outside. Berliners commonly call these apartment houses apartment barracks, an expression which accurately conveys the architects' inspiration. And from above, their jagged chimneys awaken memories of the broken glass cemented into backyard walls for protection against the neighbors' cats and children.

The new houses on the edge of the city do not seem to be built from the bottom up. They resemble cement blocks dropped from an American or Soviet military helicopter; even as the plane begins its descent, the stranger still can't distinguish the two parts of the city. While the Eastern countryside was recognizable by the uniform color of the crops and the absence of artificial boundaries between fields, the cityscape offers hardly any guide to political affiliation. At most, the duplication of public landmarks – television tower, convention hall, zoo, city hall, and sports stadium – prefigures a city in which the same taste has brought forth the same things twice.

Among all these rectangles, the wall in its fantastic zigzag course seems to be the figment of some anarchic imagination. Lit up in the afternoon by the setting sun and lavishly illuminated by floodlights after dark, the wall seems more a civic monument than a border.

On a clear day the traveler can watch the plane's shadow skimming back and forth across the city. He can track the plane closing in on its shadow until it touches down right on top of it. Only when he disembarks does he notice that in this city, the recovered shadow signifies a loss. After the fact, he realizes that only the plane's shadow was free to move between the two parts of the city; and suddenly the plane seems to him a vehicle like those Einstein dreamed of, from which laughably young and unsuspecting travelers emerge to tour a city where, since yesterday, a thousand years have passed.

I've lived in this Siamese city for twenty years. Like most of those drawn away from the West German provinces, I came here because I wanted to move to a bigger town, because a girlfriend lives here, because survival in this outpost counts as a kind of alternative service and saves one the years in West German barracks. Like most, I stayed on initially from one year to the next; but the truth is too that after only a short stay in Berlin, all the cities in West Germany struck me as artificial.

I like Berlin, really, for the ways in which it differs from Hamburg, Frankfurt, and Munich: the leftover ruins in which man-high birches and shrubs have struck root; the bullet holes in the sand-gray, blistered facades; the faded ads, painted on fire walls, which bear witness to cigarette brands and types of schnapps that have long ceased to exist. Sometimes in the afternoon, the face of a person appears over two elbows propped on a cushion in the only window of those walls. It is a face framed by twenty thousand bricks – a Berlin portrait. Berlin traffic lights are smaller, the rooms higher, the elevators older than in West Germany; there are always new cracks in the asphalt, and out of them the past grows luxuriantly. I like Berlin best in August, when the shutters have been rolled down and handwritten signs hang in the shop windows announcing a now hardly plausible return; when the 90,000 dogs are on holiday and the windshield wipers of the few remaining cars clasp sheaves of leaflets for some Live Entertainment; when the chairs stand empty inside open barroom doors, and the two solitary customers no longer raise their heads even if a third one enters.

Only occasionally, when the natives invite me for a Sunday stroll around Grünewaldsee, do I recognize from my unease that I associate these excursions with exercise period in a prison yard. From time to time when a West German visitor remarks on it, I remember something I had almost forgotten, namely that Berliners drive like murderers. They seem in the center of the city to be seized by the need for movement that West German drivers work out on their highways and turnpikes. That same need, it would appear, gives bartenders the steady and apparently limitless growth that their trade alone shows. Now and again, when I see them, I feel irritated by the training crags on the mountain – the only one – constructed from the ruins of the city: a cement block twelve feet high, donated by the German Alpine Association, with every degree of climbing difficulty built into it. Once, when I stopped to watch a rope team outfitted in climbing boots, anoraks, and goggles begin their bold ascent, and then saw the leader at the summit shade his eyes with his hand as he reported the view to the anchor man below, I felt for a moment that I had adapted too well.

But then, when I go on vacation to the Black Forest and a southern German asks me whether I live in East or West Berlin, the price of having all those real mountains seems too high. I've noticed the same ignorance in Dresden or Leipzig; the further you are from the border, the more casually each half-people imagines itself whole. In response to the question of what it is like to live in a city surrounded by concrete and barbed wire, I've long since come to answer like most Berliners: living here is no different from living in any other city. I really don't see the Wall anymore, even if it is the only structure on earth, apart from the Great Wall of China, that can be seen from the moon with the naked eye.

A winter night at Schönefeld Airport; it's snowing. Vehicles glide over the field, cast yellow circles of light across the white surface, storm the snow. A tractor digs and shovels, another loads up and carries away, and a third machine, spouting fountains of snow, blows a path free. The field looks like a frozen lake set in a landscape of the future. Only a few automatons have survived here, and are preparing for the arrival of extraterrestrial beings.

An icy wind buffets the arrivals on the gangway; even on the bus it works its way under skirts and up pants legs. For an eternity the driver keeps the doors open in expectation of a passenger lost in the to-and-fro of walkie-talkies. The people waiting come from another part of the globe and another season. Duty-free goods drag at their frozen fingers, their straw hats and kerchiefs offer shelter only from the sun. On the bus there is swearing in Spanish and Russian, silence in German – German lips don't curse the driver. Only when the doors close do Saxon and Berlin accents express relief. But the unity on the bus, certified by a common language, barely lasts for the short run from the plane to the terminal. A gap appears even before the Germans take up positions in front of the two doors marking entry into two different states. A magnetic force emanating from the groups of letters over the doors separates those who, a moment before, stood and walked together; they collect like iron filings around opposite poles. Leather coats part company with vinyl ones, Levis with imitation jeans, natural with synthetic fiber, gaudy with gray. But it's not just the clothes; faces and body motions reveal tribal characteristics, too. Those who group themselves beneath the letters BRD* move carefully and seem to anticipate getting caught in some mistake. In their almost whispered exchanges, High German has won out over the dialect. Their gaze seems to turn inward, and the wrinkles around their eyes mark the fatigue of a people whose wishes have come true too soon. The group seeking admission through the other door seems younger, cruder in

* Bundesrepublik Deutschland (BRD) – German Federal Republic as opposed to Deutsche Demokratische Republik (DDR) – German Democratic Republic. Schönefeld Airport is on the outskirts of East Berlin; Tegel and Tempelhof – mentioned later – are in West Berlin.

its gestures, indifferent to strange bystanders. Saxon, Mecklenburg, Berlin dialects clash. Speech demands gesture, and carries hands and shoulders with it.

The two groups conclusively separate as they halt before the two doors: Western faces stare into Eastern faces like men studying apes.

As soon as the rows have formed, all eyes look forward; fingers grip papers, a last token of identity. Elevator quiet spreads among those waiting, and although there is no shortage of air, everyone limits himself to slow and shallow breaths. It is as though they had all reached a doorman who took nothing other than citizenship into account. There is no sound but the buzz of the door opener and then the sliding of the door as it opens and shuts.

With the door closed behind me, I stand blocking the stream of cleared passengers, whose paths now diverge once and for all. Some go right to the Westbound bus, the others left to the parking lot and taxi stand for points East. The terminal is only half-lit, the video monitors no longer show arrivals and departures, the post office is closed, the Siemens pay phone won't take my West German coins. Everyone I ask for change seems to feel he's being watched, and wants nothing to do with my currency. For a long time I walk down the corridors of the terminal building, hoping to find an open exchange bureau, till in the end I hear only the echo of my own footsteps. A man presses his face against a shop window, his profile silhouetted in the glow of a cigarette lighter held up to the glass.

The man turns to me. 'You know where Schönhauser Allee?' His accent comes from no language I can designate, except by means of a compass.

'You no Berliner?' he asks.

'Me West Berlin, other side.' My native's habit of

answering foreigners in pidgin doesn't help us understand each other.

The Pole/Bulgarian/Russian wants to share a cab with me to Schönhauser Allee.

I say, 'Me apartment West Berlin, no taxi!' I seize the hand with the lighter and guide it in a westerly direction over the city map hanging in the shop window.

'You there, me here,' I say.

To my surprise, the lighter shines on total emptiness. The place I want to call home has no streets, no squares, no subway stations. There are only vacant yellow spaces, relieved by a couple of green oases.

'You living there?' the Pole/Russian/Bulgarian asks, and laughs. 'No streets, no houses, everything yellow! Desert!'

'That West Berlin! Berlin: Capitalist, Marlboro, Coca Cola, Mercedes – understand?'

'Ah, you capitalist?'

'No capitalist; I just live there.'

'Why no capitalist?' He offers me a cigarette from a pack with a label I've never seen, and takes one of mine.

I notice the big hand on the face of the clock jump across my departure time.

'Me there, you here,' I yell, and run toward the exit. But the Pole/ Russian/ Bulgarian sticks to my heels. Together we stand outside and watch the taillights of my bus disappear in the dark.

'Bus gone, taxi gone, hitchhike,' he says.

I nod and point in the two directions at issue. But the man from the East doesn't want to go into the built-up area without me, and he doesn't want to leave me in the desert. After a few steps on the road, he stops.

'Where you go?'

'To Berlin.'

'Me too! We taxi together!'

And so we part, stopping over and over again to put down our suitcases and shake our heads, each of us pointing in the other's direction.

The Wall is hard to find on a city map in West Berlin. Only a dotted band, delicate pink, divides the city. On a city map in East Berlin, the world ends at the Wall. Beyond the black-bordered, finger-thick dividing line identified in the key as the state border, untenanted geography sets in. That is how the Brandenburg lowlands must have looked at the time of the barbarian invasions. The only reference to the existence of a wall comes under the rubric 'Sights': the tourist's attention is drawn to the remains of Berlin's historic city wall, near the old Klosterkirche.

When I moved to Berlin, the new Wall had just gone up. Once the initial panic died, the massive structure faded increasingly to a metaphor in the West German consciousness. What on the far side meant an end to freedom of movement, on the near side came to symbolize a detested social order. The view East shrank to a view of the border complex and finally to a group-therapy absorption with the self: for Germans in the West, the Wall became a mirror that told them, day by day, who was the fairest one of all. Whether there was life beyond the death strip soon mattered only to pigeons and cats.

My first forays into the city on the other side awoke no great curiosity. I went to the Berliner Ensemble, paid visits to second and third cousins, had a conversation in a bar in Prenzlauer Berg. Of these first visits I recall little more than a smell, one that I later recognized immediately when I stood on a West German balcony facing the east wind: a smell of fuel mix, disinfectants, hot railroad tracks, mixed vegetables, and railroad terminal.

A friend later took me with him to hear the singer Wolf Biermann. It was during these visits that I first learned of a choice which for me and most of my peers seemed to have been made by birth and our parents' place of residence. Singing his nostalgic and plaintive songs in the apartment on Chausseestrasse was someone who of his own free will had gone to the 'better Germany'; and he stood by that address even after no one but his guards and West German visitors were still allowed to listen to him. All his arguments for staying on there referred to a distant past; he himself seemed constantly to reject hopes for the future; and concerning the present, he had nothing but horrors to report. I couldn't figure out what he still liked about the Germany of his choice. In any case, I failed in my attempt to turn his sung and spoken monologues into a conversation. I raised questions and objections with myself in his stairwell, because I hadn't got them out in his kitchen; I rehearsed them for the next visit, which proved just as much a monologue; and finally the unspoken phrases piled up on the steps and blocked my way to him.

On later trips, though, I was amazed by East Berlin. Two conflicting feelings reinforced each other: The half-city beyond the Wall struck me from the start as thoroughly familiar. Not only the garbage cans, the stairwells, the door handles, the radiators, the lampshades, the wallpaper, but even the muted, distrustful life-style over there seemed to me boringly familiar. This was the shadow city, the afterbirth, the emergency edition of West Berlin. Yet, the tendency to recognition was contradicted by the impression of having abruptly landed on another planet. Life there didn't differ simply in outward organization; it obeyed another law. To

213

attribute this to a different social order and pace of development was to label it too hastily. I could orient myself better in New York than in the half-city just a little over three miles from my apartment.

But the inhabitants of the half-city were no longer aware of this other law within a similar life. It remained in force even among those whose 'Petition for Release from Citizenship in the DDR' had been answered years ago. In exchanges of political opinion, the difference made itself only slightly felt. It came through more in half-sentences, in a gesture which left something unsaid, a laugh where none was expected, a manner of looking around. Not just ways of talking, but even certain facial lines could be linked to compass points in Germany.

Such impressions were quickly forgotten; yet over the years they accumulated to form a puzzle. It was surprising enough that two antagonistic social systems could have been set up in a span of thirty years and among a people whose spirit was once supposed to 'heal the world.' That this external antagonism had permeated the behavior and reflexes of each individual in the two systems was even more so.

So long as the puzzle was limited to the Germans on the other side of the Wall, it was only one of many reasons for my visits. But the suspicion that individuals in Germany are in a frightening way interchangeable cannot be discarded at the border. An awareness of individual plasticity in this country doesn't stop at the Wall; and sooner or later, one approaches it in the first person: What would I have become, how would I think, how would I look, *if*?

I live on the ground floor of an apartment house that was built around the turn of the century. In those days the part which faced the street, the front part, served as living space for people called gentry; the same was true of the wings. The back part, called the garden house, was designed for the servants, who could tell by a Hammacher & Pätzold Ltd. bell whether they were to wait on the dining-, the living-, or the bedroom. After the second of the Great Wars, democracy, in the form of a dividing wall, took over the apartment houses: the doors between the front and the back apartments were walled up. From then on, income rather than birth and class decided who used the front and who used the back entrance.

The plaster on the building has the sandy gray color that sets the general tone in Berlin; it hasn't been redone in decades. No one can say whether the bullet holes in the back of the building date from World War II or from the street fighting of the twenties. The windows of my rear apartment look onto a small, rectangular garden, which is separated by a six-foot wall from the garden of the neighboring residential fortress. In a chimney-like recess between windowless fire walls stands a maple; it bears leaves only from the fifth floor up, where it catches the sunlight a few hours a day. Flower beds have been marked out with stones along the rear wall of the building. Surprisingly, they sometimes produce flowers and strange bushes whose names no one knows. As a rule, though, the steadily eroding plaster discourages everything except weeds and bushy sumac, whose thin leaves never turn yellow but simply drop just before the first snow. The sumac takes root all over and seems indestructible; in its simple organic structure, maybe even in geologic age, it is the cockroach of the vegetable kingdom.

In both the first and the second inner courtyards, the walls stand so close together that tenants of the lower apartments have to stick their heads out the window to determine the state of the weather. On the other hand, these rear apartments offer a peace and quiet in the midst of the city not to be found anyplace else in the world, not even in the country. This stillness probably ties in with the Germans' habit of hearing their own noise through their neighbors' ears – a consideration which even three-year-olds are taught to show.

Both of the front ground-floor apartments, together with the wings, are leased to bars. One proprietor caters in his cooking and his prices to a public that rides up on bicycles and mopeds; the other to a clientele that has come to expect culinary rather than political excitement from Bolivia. I differentiate the two sets of customers by the marks they leave on my Citroën. The lovers of Latin American cooking put dents in my fenders; the friends of French fries and Schnitzel smash in the side window and rip off my stereo.

The bars haven't changed their cassettes in a decade. I hear the same music whenever I cross the courtyard: on the left, the hollow blowing of a bamboo flute; on the right, the bass guitars of the Rolling Stones. Since I have to skirt the garbage of both establishments on my way to the street, I've never entered either. The difference between German and Latin American cooking becomes trivial when you see the garbage cans. Both cooks fill them with the same tomato cans, moldy green peppers, sprouting potatoes, worm- and maggot-covered cutlets, and yellow and red sauces, which spill out across the courtyard from bursting blue plastic bags.

Once when I found a garbage can filled to the brim with empty cans of cat food, I had hopes of doing in one of the proprietors. There isn't a single cat in the building – the only conclusion to be drawn was that either German meatballs or Bolivian stew had been stretched with cat food. But my attempt to lay a path from the garbage can to one of the kitchens failed: both cooks use the same condiments, and the dill pickle jars and catsup bottles among the cat food cans didn't provide sufficient evidence.

The tenants of my building seldom meet; I know them mostly by their noises. Some of them are so regular I can set my watch by them. Every morning in the apartment overhead, the German hit parade blasts out like a gas oven exploding; then I hear thudding, and the radio is turned down. It took me a while to associate a face with the noise; anyway, I didn't want to meet someone who woke to that crash and started the day with a sprint to the radio alarm. Then one day a baby carriage appeared in the hall, and I hoped the radio alarm might now become superfluous.

Until recently, I could tell it was almost ten by the violin notes wafting across from a window on the upper floors. At first I thought someone shared my preference for certain recordings: Bach's E-flat Partita, Corelli's La Folia, Czerny's Etudes, the slow movement of the Mendelssohn violin concerto. Then I saw a small, very thin man, much too old to be a symphony player, darting between the garbage cans with a black violin case. I saw him maybe four times, and then no more. One day I began to miss his practicing; by the time I asked after the man with the violin case, a hearse had long since taken him away. Since then I've missed that sound among the others – the blaring hit parade in the morning, the moaning of the pigeons, and the pounding of cutlets in the German kitchen that begins punctually at seven in the evening.

The only person in the building who really stands out is a man about seventy who lives directly behind the garbage cans of the Latin American kitchen. His windows give onto the dark inner courtyard; to judge by their number, his apartment consists of a kitchen, one room, and a bathroom. Of all the shadows young and old who pass among the garbage cans, this man cuts by far the brightest figure. I've never seen him other than smartly dressed: he wears a silk scarf over a starched shirt; his face is tanned the year round; and when I say hello, he stops and smiles at me, as though something ought to follow my greeting. Holding himself very erect and not wrinkling his nose, he strides past the garbage cans and ascends the two steps – covered with pigeon droppings – to his door, all with the dignity of someone whose two servants are waiting inside to take his coat and draw him a bath. Once, with his key in the lock, he turned his head and nodded to me as if I were an accomplice in his kindness. I thought I should follow him: behind his door there had to be some secret, a guide to serenity, to a carefree life.

It is just a few steps from my apartment to Robert's. Sometimes we meet for breakfast at a café, sometimes for a cup of coffee at his apartment in the afternoon, pretty definitely at Charlie's in the evening. The pinball machine at Charlie's doesn't chirp electronically yet, and when the ball comes toward the flippers, we throw all our weight against the table. The machine reacts as slowly as if it worked by pulleys.

I met Robert in East Berlin, and I knew right away that I wanted him for a friend. I like his quick, strangely persistent gaze and the way he pulls his shoulders up to his ears when he's explaining something. Robert won't talk to just anybody, but when he does speak to you, no one else in the room exists for him. Although he isn't short, he always manages to look at you from below. Occasionally something flares up in his eyes; the grains in his iris shoot apart like fireworks, then regroup around the pupil like a rain of splinters after an explosion.

There aren't any pinball machines in the DDR. At Charlie's, just a couple of months after arriving in the West, Robert showed me the spot on the flipper where you have to catch the ball in order to shoot it off on the most profitable trajectory. He showed me how you catch and slowly let it roll along the flipper to the spot from which the bumpers can be hit. He had figured out how much shoving the machine would take before it penalized the player by flashing TILT. We play either for the next round of drinks or for the next game; the difference is that I play with my hands and Robert with his body, and I usually lose. There are other games, ball games, that I play better, but Robert doesn't like them.

At Charlie's I tell Robert I've begun collecting stories about the divided city.

'Does that really interest you?' he asks. 'Who cares about partition besides a few politicians? And they only pretend to, because they want to be elected by people who expect the politicians, at least, to take an interest in the German question.'

Robert and I usually talk to each other in the singular. But situations arise in which one or the other lapses into the you-we vein. Robert didn't say 'your' German question, but that's how I hear it. The expression 'German question' doesn't exist in the DDR, either in official or in daily speech. If Robert uses it, the reason is that he associates my plan with the kind of politicians in the West whom he already didn't trust in the East. His question does, as it happens, give shape to my own doubts. I'm not sure of my purpose in collecting these stories. It isn't the sense of an unbearable situation that has pushed me to the project; rather, my uneasiness at the absence of that sense. The crazy thing is, though, that for all his denial that 'the German question' exists, Robert is much more visibly marked by the effects of partition than I am.

After emigrating to the West, he was bombarded with so many questions on the subject that he finally decided not to answer them. It was easy to see that people were interested in him not as a poet who could no longer publish in the

DDR, but as a political phenomenon. And Robert had no desire to provide the cheap ego-boost that the West German media try to extract from every emigrant. Since queries about his impressions of the West were usually tied to the hope that he would pledge allegiance to a Western life-style, he preferred instead to hunt for a no-man's-land between the borders. 'If it's either Erna or Rita,' he would say, 'I won't take either; I'd rather jerk off.' On the other hand, nothing makes him madder than West Germans' ignorance about their brothers and sisters in the East. Once West German television broadcast an American show on the Holocaust, and the West German chancellor recommended to the chairman of the DDR's state council that East Germany also broadcast the show as a way of atoning for the past. Robert slammed his hand on the table so hard that it bled. 'Imagine an ex-Wehrmacht officer,' he said, 'giving that advice to a veteran of the resistance who spent ten years in a Nazi prison!'

I knew those facts about both politicians, but it wouldn't have occurred to me to link them to the present. I understood Robert's anger; but it was his anger, not mine. Obviously the historical events had different weights in our minds.

Still, Robert rejects any allusion to those differences between us. Nothing else I say can make him quite so mad as the comment that something about him is typically DDR. Probably he knows from experience that the observation of difference often conceals nothing but a mild contempt. Robert counters my readiness to see traces of another social mold in him by stressing the similarities between us. The passage from East to West Berlin probably caused him less strain, he says, than my move from the south German provinces to the Prussian metropolis. After all, he knew the streets, the cry of the newsboy, the haze in the beer hall, the super's glance.

The fact is that after three months in West Berlin, he knew his way around better than I did after three years. He had barely moved into his apartment before he came up with a bar where he could drink on credit. A little later he took me along to a book dealer who gave him discounts; a few months after that, he referred me to his tax expert. He phoned me once from the United States and persuaded me to stop looking at my watch during our conversation: in two days he had gotten the hang of calling toll-free anywhere in the world from America.

All this shows only that we're trapped: I by my tendency to pin Robert to his origins in the DDR; he by his irritated rejection of any allusion to those origins.

In conversations with Robert, it has become clearer what I'm looking for: the story of a man who loses himself and starts turning into nobody. By a chain of circumstances still unknown to me, he becomes a boundary-walker between the two German states. Casually at first, he begins making comparisons; as he does so, he imperceptibly contracts a sickness from which inhabitants with a fixed place of residence are shielded by the Wall. In his own person and as though at split-second speed, he lives through the partition process and comes to believe that he has to make a decision, one he had previously been spared by birth and socialization. But the more he crosses from one half of the city to the other, the more absurd the choice seems. Having come to distrust the hastily adopted identity that both states offer him, he feels at home only on the border. And if the philosopher is right when he says a joke is always an epitaph for a feeling that has died, the boundary-walker's story must turn out to be a comedy.

*　　*　　*

One possible name for this man would be Gerhard Schalter, the name of my first landlord in Berlin, whom I lost track of years ago. Until the evening when I visited his apartment, he had struck me only by his Swabian accent ringing out in the stairwell and by a smile which seemed ready for whatever happened. An expectant pleasure always lit up his face, and when I asked him how he was doing, he would look at me as though testing whether I could stand a serious answer.

'You know,' he said once, 'things are fantastic! Take this morning: I woke up at six and could hardly wait for the day to start. I do exactly the kind of work I like, I get along fine with my bosses, I've got the most amazing people for friends and, as if that weren't enough, I've just found the woman I've been looking for all my life. Every day brings a new, pleasant surprise; and when I go to bed, I can hardly wait until the alarm goes off again. Too bad we have to sleep at all, don't you think?'

The rear exit from Schalter's apartment lay next to the door of my apartment. One evening Schalter rang my bell and asked whether I had had dinner yet. I accepted the invitation and followed him down an endless white corridor to the Berliner parlor. I was struck by the fact that such a small man would live in such a huge apartment. Schalter had rented not only the front apartment, but one whole wing of the building as well. The walls and doors had been freshly painted, new wiring had been installed but not yet fully connected, hooks for pictures had been hammered in, and the smell of varnish still hung in the room. In the parlor stood a drafting table covered with a white tablecloth; the setting for two and the candlelight promised a festive and elaborate dinner.

I took the chair Schalter offered, and while he hurried back down the hall to the kitchen, I sat feeling like a traveler in a railroad station waiting to meet a wedding party. The air vibrated with hope; only a loudspeaker was missing to announce the party's arrival. Schalter came back with snails and popped the cork on the champagne. As he brought his glass up to mine, I toasted the guest I was clearly replacing. Schalter didn't waver. That triumphant smile immediately shaped his mouth, and if there was a doubt to be read in his eyes, it again merely addressed the question of whether I could stand the radiance of his answer.

'Do you know what it's like to look into someone's face and have your life change completely?' he asked.

In the course of our conversation – more a monologue, really – it turned out that Schalter had just returned from Schönefeld Airport. The plane Schalter expected had landed, but the face he sought wasn't among the passengers. It was a complicated story. Schalter was expecting a woman married to a German TV correspondent based in Africa. The agreement was that she would leave her husband in Africa and move into Schalter's apartment with her child. But time and again her departure was postponed. The husband apparently had connections at the highest levels; just one call would make customs officials and airline companies his co-conspirators. Whatever the case, he could prevent his wife's escape; Schalter was convinced that her husband was keeping her caged like an animal, by force and by extortion. Schalter would probably have to go there himself, in order to set his beloved free.

After that dinner I saw Schalter at increasingly distant intervals. Though he still had the inner gleam in his eyes, I no longer asked so carelessly how he was doing. His appearance changed. It wasn't just that he grew a beard or stopped shaving regularly; he didn't seem to care if the sole of his shoe came loose or his shirt split a seam. The pores in his face grew larger, and so did the checks on his shirts.

In general, his shirts and shoes made me think that he was digging up the clothes of a relative who had died in the fifties. Wherever he was going during the day, it wasn't the hotel where he worked as an interior decorator – more likely it was Schönefeld Airport.

His trips to East Berlin, which at first had the airport as their goal, evidently drifted from their purpose. His visits to friends he had gradually acquired over there grew more frequent, if only because it was cheaper at the black market rate to call Africa from an Eastern connection. Then he made the discovery that the beer and the food were also more reasonably priced. His visits became overnight ones, and sometimes I wondered, when I didn't see him for awhile, whether he had just stayed in the East. The lower cost of living there made it easier for him to maintain his expensive West Berlin apartment. Almost as a matter of course, Schalter came to see the advantages of the social system in the other part of town. He complained more and more often about the cutthroat competition in the West, about the loss of a sense of solidarity and willing sacrifice. He extolled the DDR's untouched lakes and villages, which reminded him of his childhood in southern Germany, and the women there seemed to him more trustworthy. He spoke with increasingly detailed knowledge about the unbroken power of ex-Nazi officials in the West. My sense grew that Schalter was shifting his exterior and, ultimately, his interior life to the other part of the city. It seemed he came to West Berlin just to get his mail and buy a few presents for his friends in the East.

He appeared bound to the Schöneberg apartment only by a defiant hope, which must have come gradually to seem as hollow to him as the glow of the lights along Kurfürstendamm.

One day a moving van came and took away his things.

*　*　*

As long as I've lived in West Berlin, I have treated the structure that is considered a state border over there and a tourist attraction over here as simply an inconvenience. For the first time now, I decide to visit the Wall. I see a tour group climb out of a bus and then take the stairs to a lookout tower. Up top, a few of them put binoculars to their eyes and begin waving. What they see is a tour group on the other side of the Wall just climbing out of a bus run by the same travel agency. They wave back, and people in both groups now train their sights on the watchtower standing between them. What they see there, once they've focused their glasses, are glasses just being focused. Other travelers meanwhile have readied their cameras for shooting. Looking into their viewfinders, they follow the tour leader's finger as he points to an Eastern housefront. There a woman is cleaning windows, a little boy is playing on a balcony, and on another balcony an old man is taking his midday nap. The cameras click. When the woman notices she is being watched, she pauses and stares over from her side. Curious about what she can see from her window, I turn around. I see a man in a grey-green jacket holding a plastic bag in his hand. He wants to cross the street and is waiting until a red Opel has driven by. A woman is waiting on the other side of the street, but not for the man. She is holding a leash in her hand and watching a gray mongrel on the end of it, crouched on its hind legs and straining. Before the man reaches the other side of the street, he stops. I get the impression that he is looking toward the lookout tower from which I'm watching him. I turn back around and follow the tour leader's finger, pointing now at a barely noticeable, grayish-brown rise in the ground. This rise, which hardly deserves to be called a hill, lies in the middle of the prohibited zone and is inaccessible to residents on both sides of the Wall. The leader describes the spot in three foreign tongues, in each of which a German word recurs: *Führerbunker*. The travelers' whispered repetition of the word, the clicking of the camera shutters, the watchtowers all endow the hill with the power of a hallowed place. For a moment the image forms of an armed host to the left and right of their general's command post, sunk in sleep but still waiting for an order.

In the evening the television newscaster reports a UN resolution condemning the Soviet invasion of Afghanistan as interference in the internal affairs of the country. On the screen, columns of Russian tanks roll through Afghanistan's capital city. The newscaster says that such footage hasn't been shown in the Eastern media for weeks.

Shortly afterward I switch channels. Again there is a newscaster sitting in front of a map of the world and delivering the news. He is wearing the same tie and the same sports jacket; he has the same receding hairline and speaks the same language as the newscaster on the other channel. He cites a Pravda article condemning the UN resolution as interference in the internal affairs of Afghanistan. The footage is of American and Chinese weapons captured from Afghan soldiers. The newscaster notes that these pictures are not being shown in the Western media.

For a split second, as I turn the television off, I see the shadow of his West channel counterpart; then the screen goes gray.

History has taken all the humor out of Karl Marx's ironic phrase, 'A specter haunts Germany – the specter of Communism.' The specter has settled east of the Elbe, and does in fact look frightful. Political exorcists never tire of assuring us that it remains nothing more than a specter, even though it has grown into a state. Still, they too have long since become used to the sight; now they pretend to be alarmed only on holidays.

When it became clear that the specter couldn't be driven out by the use of quotation marks or the reproachful phrase 'so-called' or the pious droning of the Hallstein Doctrine,* the politicians started negotiating with it. The German question has put on weight in thirty years, and you can't claim that Germans west of the Elbe fret over it much. There are people delegated to deal with the question, but they find it increasingly hard to keep their audience alert. It is true that the Constitution mandates resolution of the German question, but the furious parliamentary debates, the struggle over concepts like 're-unification' and 'nation' seem artificial. It's like watching the 1,011th performance of a repertory play in which actors and audience both stifle their yawns. The fact that the drama about the sorrows of a divided Germany is still running in Bonn seems less due to anybody's real concern than to tacit understanding that this play has not been staged for the theatergoers at all, but for others who unfortunately can't make it. And besides, what else is there to put on?

It would be unwise to conclude, from the frequency of official appeals to the will for unity and the survival of the nation, that the corresponding feelings also survive. A more realistic inference is that most Germans west of the Elbe

* Official doctrine articulated in 1955, whereby the West Germans claimed to be the only valid representative of the whole German people. The doctrine was superseded by Willy Brandt's *Ostpolitik* in 1969.

have long since reconciled themselves to partition. In their separation pangs they resemble a lover grieving not so much for his loved one as for the strong emotion he once felt. In Germany, it seems, time doesn't heal wounds; it kills the sensation of pain.

'Your turn,' says Robert, after he's diverted the pinball from its path toward the gutter with a deft blow to the table and played it for another 25,000 points. I can't possibly catch up anymore, and I say to the bartender, for whom it's nothing new: 'This round's on me.'

The only new thing is the drink Robert orders: vodka. Since his arrival in West Berlin, he has tried out several drinks and declared them by turns the only drinkable one. After the whisky period came the sherry era, the sherry era was followed by the cognac season, which after a short and listless gin interlude flowed into the champagne epoch. The champagne epoch seemed definitive. I assumed that vodka, in any case, was completely out.

'Oh, for God's sake, I know what you're thinking again! But it has nothing to do with nostalgia! Vodka is just the all-around best drink. Besides being the healthiest!'

I order a vodka too and tell Robert the story of Gerhard Schalter, my first landlord. Robert listens closely, thinks for a while, orders the next round of vodka and beer, and then asks, without wasting another word on Schalter: 'Do you know the story of Kabe and his fifteen jumps?'

Mr. Kabe, who was in his mid-forties and on welfare, first came to the attention of the police when, with a running start from the West, he jumped the Wall in mid-Berlin, heading East. Right by the Wall he had discovered a lot where abandoned rubble formed a natural staircase. He could climb it so high that he had only to push himself up by the arms in order to swing onto the Wall. Other reports mention a Volkswagen bus, whose roof Kabe allegedly used for a springboard. It is more likely that he got that idea later, after the authorities had ordered a cleanup operation because of him.

Kabe stood on the top for a while in the searchlights of the Western patrol which hurried to the spot. He ignored the calls of officials trying at the last minute to explain to him which was East and which was West, and then jumped off to the East. The guards of the other German state arrested Kabe as a border violator. Yet even under hours of grilling, Kabe displayed neither political aim nor serious desire to stay on. When asked who had sent him, Kabe replied that he had come for his own sake, that he had simply wanted to get to the other side. He wore out his interrogators, who wanted to know why he hadn't used a border crossing, by pointing out again and again that he lived right across the way and had taken the only direct path over the Wall.

The interrogators could think of no better explanation for this extraordinary reversal in direction than that Kabe had several screws loose. They sent him to the psychiatric clinic at Buch, but the doctors could find nothing wrong with him, other than a pathological desire to overcome the Wall. Kabe enjoyed a special position at the clinic as a blockade runner whose jump had defined the points of the compass anew.

Three months later, a well-fed Kabe was turned over to the permanent delegation of the Federal Republic of Germany. They brought him back to West Berlin in a government Mercedes. There, without showing any emotion, he read the newspaper articles about his jump that a neighbor had collected. Then he shut himself up in his Kreuzberg apartment and remained incommunicado.

The Eastern newspapers sized him up alternately as a 'border provocateur' and as 'unemployed and desperate.' A Western tabloid speculated that Kabe had been paid by the Eastern secret police to jump, so that they could point to one escapee who wasn't visible only from behind. This hypothesis drew fresh support from a journalist who claimed to have traced Kabe from Kreuzberg to Paris. Directly after his return to the West, it seemed, Kabe had taken himself to the French metropolis and, in a suspect part of town, had run up bills which could hardly have been covered by welfare checks.

The truth about this story is that, after three months of free care in the psychiatric clinic in the East, Kabe found three months' worth of welfare payments in his West Berlin account. In order to fulfill an old desire, he withdrew this sum and bought a ticket on the sleeper to Paris. However, once he had recuperated in Paris at the expense of the two German states, he returned to West Berlin and jumped again.

Brought back once more three months later, Kabe promptly repeated the offense. The West Berlin authorities failed in their attempts to get at Kabe by legal means. After all, he had illegally crossed a state border which doesn't exist in the eyes of the West German regime. In the language of the constitutional law experts, Kabe had merely been exercising his right to freedom of movement.

West Berlin authorities no longer found this interpretation satisfactory, once the East Berlin clinic had presented bills for Kabe's room and board. The West Berliners decided to incarcerate him in Havelhöhe Hospital for self-destructive tendencies. But the diagnosis didn't hold up under scrutiny: after all, Kabe's jumps had proved that the Wall could be crossed going East without damage to body or soul. What's more, they demonstrated that in town, the border strip behind the Wall was not mined. The doctor in charge found nothing wrong with Kabe other than an irresistible urge to overcome the Wall. Rather than a straitjacket, he recommended that the authorities recognize the Wall as a border. They replied that the Federal Republic of Germany couldn't recognize the Wall of Shame as a state boundary just for Kabe's sake. This didn't prevent the doctor from declaring Kabe competent.

Released from the clinic, Kabe went straight back to the Wall. Altogether he jumped fifteen times and put a serious strain on German–German relations. After one of his last jumps, it occurred to authorities to take him far from Berlin, to quieter areas where he might continue his jumps over old castle walls. He was driven in a government Mercedes to relatives in south Germany, where he behaved very reasonably for two days. On the third day, he bought a train ticket to Berlin and jumped.

Questions about the motives of his jumping drew nothing more from Kabe than this: 'Sometimes it's so quiet in the apartment and so gray and cloudy outside and nothing's happening and I think to myself: Hey, let's go jump the Wall again.'

During the night before the day when I'm to pick up my visa for a longer stay in the DDR, I dream of a boat ride on a mud-brown river whose waters stretch to the horizon. In the stern of the boat, I come upon the vague, somehow blurred figure of a woman. I see her only from behind, but from the contour of her back and the fall of her hair I recognize Lena, with whom I shared the apartment next to Schalter's in Schöneberg. Her presence on the boat seems the fulfillment of an old invitation, too often postponed. I want to speak to her, to express my joy at our taking this voyage of discovery together; but before I can touch the nape of her neck, a wave upsets my balance and I slide overboard. Although the suddenly violent waters keep me level with the stern, my hand can't reach the boat's fender. I swim to shore. Smoke rises among exotic trees, light glows behind windows, human silhouettes become visible; I will not be lost. But I'll have to find my way through the primeval forest unarmed; all my personal belongings – money, papers, clothes – are still on the boat with Lena, sailing off with her.

I wait until morning and call Lena.

If I have something specific in mind, she wants to know, could I please say so right away.

'I want to see you.'

'What for?' she asks.

'Specifically, because I had a dream about you last night.'

'Well, let me tell you how things look here at the moment' – and she is already counting, Point One, Point Two, Point Three, all the things she has to take care of before her imminent departure on a trip. She can find a minute only if it's something definite, unpostponable, really concrete.

'Only if you need my help,' her answer runs in the language of our past. But for the present, there is no urgency and certainly no need of help – at most a troubling desire that has slipped out of a dream and that, before translation into the language of the waking, sounds like this: 'I'd like to spend a day with you, in the land which you were the first to show me. And since, as soon as we speak to each other, we talk ourselves farther and farther apart, I'd like to sleep with you first.'

THOMAS BRUSSIG

From

HEROES LIKE US

Translated by John Brownjohn

From TAPE 5

FEM. PERS. EMRGD. ST. 0834

I CAN TELL you how I saw my situation. I was destined for great things, so there was, of course, a deeper meaning to all that I did. Although that meaning still eluded me, the day would come when it revealed itself. Someone had deliberately banished me to an insignificant outpost and assigned me tasks unworthy of a master spy. Someone endowed with great influence and perspicacity, someone whose desk bore a battery of telephones, someone whose hands held all the reins of power – someone who would make himself known to me when he deemed the time ripe. My part in this game was to stick it out, to fulfill my allotted role and never let on that I was a top-flight secret agent. The master of my fate was simply assuring himself of my patience and commitment, and the harsher and more humiliating the ordeals to which I was subjected, the more important my future mission. Why ask questions? Being the most ill-informed person imaginable, I was used to living in a state of nebulous uncertainty. It was enough that I and *he* (whoever he might be – Minister Mielke himself?) knew of my special status and realized that all my current experiences were merely a prelude. Someone had *plans* for me, and all the things that were happening to me now were pieces of a mosaic that would combine to form a picture and convey a meaning. I felt certain that I only had to do as I was told, and that anything more was beyond my present scope. I was waiting, and nothing I did at this time was the product of deliberate intent on my part. It wasn't *I* that burglarized, abducted, hunted, harassed, and intimidated. *I* merely waited.

At seven one November morning my doorbell rang and Owl excitedly informed me over the intercom that I had been given a new assignment and must come with him at once. That was how I had always pictured my X-Day: a routine, unheralded operation on a gray, rainy morning. Owl hustled me into his car and drove to the center of the city. We didn't speak on the way, but anyone familiar with novels and films of espionage knows that little or nothing is ever said on such occasions. Owl made for the Spittelmarkt and pulled up outside the offices of USIMEX, an export-import agency.

After a minute Raymund emerged and joined us in the car. Yes, Radiant Mouth with a 'y,' the devil-may-care onanist and organizer of moonlight cruises. What was up? What was his game? Why had he got in with us? Was I at liberty to disclose to Owl that we knew each other? Was this a test of my sangfroid? (*How did our most promising recruit react when confronted by an old acquaintance in the presence of a third party?*) At first I merely looked out of the window, feverishly analyzing the situation. I: outwardly calm and casual, inwardly alert and focused. A person of my caliber was simply *bound* to make it someday!

Owl drove off and turned into Leipziger Strasse. We were nearing Checkpoint Charlie. I might have guessed: they would hand me a manila envelope and allow me half an hour in which to memorize its contents. Then I would be given a false passport in a new name and some last-minute verbal instructions. Before passing the barrier I would turn for a moment, see my colleagues bidding me a clenched-fist farewell from a safe distance, and, like Teddy in the prison yard, surreptitiously return the salute. If not, it could be inserted in the film version.

Instead of bearing left for Checkpoint Charlie, however, the car turned right into Friedrichstrasse. I guessed I was being taken to Friedrichstrasse Station, where the East and West Berlin S-Bahn tracks ran parallel to each other. There was rumored to be an agents' 'rathole' somewhere in the vicinity, with an insignificant-looking little door, unguarded but firmly locked, beyond which lay a dusty underground passage that led straight from an S-Bahn station to the street. So it was true, I thought: they were going to 'insert' me by way of that passage. Owl must have the key to the sinister door in his glove compartment, and I would soon be boarding one of the U-Bahn or S-Bahn trains that ran beneath the city and the border guards' killing ground at ten-minute intervals. I would be lying if I said the prospect didn't excite me.

While we're on the subject of Friedrichstrasse, Mr. Kitzelstein, I shall finally reveal how, as an eighteen-year-old youth in sexual torment, I strove to get as close as possible to the forbidden West – how I tried to smell, hear, and touch it. I didn't station myself at the Brandenburg Gate, where the West was still a hundred and twenty meters away – no, I crouched over a subway ventilation shaft, so whenever a train passed beneath it, the West was only four meters from me! I spent *hours* on those subway grates, sexually tormented by my first sight of a Quelle mail order catalogue. A fellow student of mine had thrown a big party to celebrate his eighteenth birthday, and there it was, lying around in his apartment: eight hundred pages of four-color printing on glossy paper. Was *that* the West? Did the West look like a Quelle catalogue, or was there a difference between the two?

The stereos! The bicycles! The cameras! I formed an entirely new picture of the West. They could do anything over there! That socialism was historically superior to the West went without saying, but bicycles with twenty-one gears existed only in the Quelle catalogue!

From then on, I held the West in awe and spoke its name in a whisper; from then on, I was convinced that only *Western* power stations supplied a stable alternating current of precisely 50 Hz; from then on, I failed to see the joke about the man who takes half a roast chicken to the vet and asks if he can save it. Having studied the Quelle catalogue, I felt convinced of a Western vet's ability to restore half a roast chicken to health sufficiently for it to resume clucking and lay lots more Western eggs.

But the bicycles and cameras were nothing, absolutely nothing, compared to what I saw on the lingerie pages. Did Western women really look like that? Were such creatures an everyday sight in the West? Incredible! Those laughing faces, that long, wavy hair, those figures, that skin, those alluring eyes! And the eyelashes! Captivating! Breathtaking! Downright *besotting*! I positively melted. I was infatuated with them, those stupefyingly beautiful Western women. I couldn't tear myself away from the lingerie section through-out the birthday party – in fact I ended by surreptitiously ripping out four double-page spreads (an early indication of my criminosexual proclivities).

But that wasn't enough for me. I wanted to be so *near* those women I could inhale their perfume and hear them nibble on chips. But where in the East was the nearest I could possibly get to women of the West? Where save above a U-Bahn shaft in Friedrichstrasse, at a distance of only four meters! I couldn't see them, admittedly, but I did have my four double-page spreads (carefully preserved in four transparent sheet protectors). I spent hours on those grates, and every time I heard the rumble of a U-Bahn I would cast a languishing glance at the Quelle women on my four ripped-out double-page spreads and know that the train just below me was full of such creatures. I strained my nose and ears. Perhaps the train's slipstream would waft a minuscule whiff of eau de toilette in my direction. Perhaps one of the little transom windows would be open, enabling the scent of a Western woman's skin to penetrate my nostrils or a Western woman's giggle to be heard above the noise of the train. It wasn't just that they resembled the women in my transparent sheet protectors; they probably possessed those legendary G spots as well! Had I already been ruled by the perverted urges that took possession of me only a few years later, I would have raped the grates. At eighteen, however, I still had scruples.

So Owl drove Raymund and me from Leipziger Strasse into Friedrichstrasse and headed in the direction of the S-Bahn station. I felt a trifle sentimental as we passed the places where I'd wallowed in youthful fancies, the mute witnesses of my burgeoning sexuality, but I permitted myself that luxury. I was expecting to be sent through that fateful little door and into the West. Another few minutes, and I would be surrounded by Quelle catalogue beauties, by women who possessed G spots and suffered themselves to be photographed with dicks in their mouths – a poetic prospect indeed!

But we drove straight past Friedrichstrasse Station. What, no spy thriller, no Quelle women? Could we be making for another crossing point? There were two more possibilities, one in Invalidenstrasse and the other in Chausseestrasse, the continuation of Friedrichstrasse.

But no, we turned right into Wilhelm-Pieck-Strasse and

my hopes of an assignment in the Blue World evaporated. After two hundred meters, Owl turned, pulled in to the curb, and switched the ignition off. Having given us each a clipboard, pencil, and paper, he lit a cigarette.

'All right,' he said, expelling a plume of smoke, 'keep your eyes open, both of you.'

Huh? Was something about to happen? What was there to see? What did he mean?

'It all looks pretty normal to me,' I said, at a loss.

'Keep your eyes open just the same,' he said. 'And write everything down.'

We sat there for hours, saying nothing and making notes of all that happened. Nothing did happen, most of the time, but that wasn't the point. I knew it was part of my probation to endure boredom. I'd already renounced a Nobel Prize in order to pursue a career as a historic missionary; now I must show that I could possess my soul in patience, stoically and without complaint. There had to be some reason why we should sit outside this building for weeks on end, an activity – no, *in*activity – that would have tried the patience of a Buddhist monk. Raymund often complained of its tedium and futility, but that I took to be a ploy designed to erode my own perseverance. Being just as smart as 'them,' I refused to be provoked and conscientiously maintained my surveillance while Raymund and Owl got in each other's hair.

'What are we sitting here for? Why does it take three of us to—'

'Observation is important, Raymund. There's a basic rule of detection: the criminal always feels an urge to revisit the scene of his crime.'

'So what?'

'It's a scientifically proven fact. That's why observation is so important.'

'Fair enough, but who's committed a crime and where?'

'Well, imagine if, one day, you had a chance to get at the NATO Secretary-General's microfish.' Owl broke off. 'No, that's a stupid analogy,' he amended swiftly, and produced another, but it was too late: Owl had let the cat out of the bag.

I pricked up my ears. Had he inadvertently divulged some aspect of my *real* assignment? But what did he mean? What were *microfish*? Why didn't I know the word? Was it yet another of the gaps in my knowledge? Were microfish very small fish? So small that one could see them only under a microscope? The microfish of the *NATO Secretary-General* . . . Great heavens! Had *I* been assigned to get hold of them one day? How did 'they' envisage the operation? How was I to purloin a phial of the NATO Secretary-General's microfish, and what did our people want with them? Were microfish replete with DNA, genetic material from which they proposed to clone a second NATO Secretary-General? A doppelgänger to be dispatched to Brussels, where, armed with the authority of his office, he would order NATO's surrender? What a coup! Almost the whole of Europe would turn red overnight, with North America thrown in, and all without bloodshed! Was that why I had to steal the microfish, because no perfect double could be fabricated without them? Was it scientifically feasible? Could I believe it?

Of course I believed that artificial people could be fabricated, Mr. Kitzelstein; what do you expect? After all, I lived in a city traversed by a killing ground – the 'death strip,' as we called it – that ran right across its densely inhabited heart, not even along a river. Would I have believed *that* if I hadn't seen it with my own eyes? Beneath that death strip, day after day, U-Bahn and S-Bahn trains ran strictly according to schedule. Would I have believed *that* if I hadn't heard them myself (and inhaled the breeze of their passing)? How sinister must imaginings become before they cease to be fanciful? Fabricating a human being was a mere bagatelle to *them*. Anyone who could drive a hermetically sealed frontier through the middle of a normally functioning city could do absolutely anything. Fabricating one measly human being would be child's play – provided *I* came up with the requisite microfish. A team of geneticists must even now be waiting for the phial in a secret underground laboratory. The rest was just a matter of days. Not a life would be lost, and I would take the salute at the victory parade up Broadway. Streets would bear my name, newspapers and magazines my likeness . . .

After work, as part of our observers' training, we compared notes. Our target, whom I judged to be in his early forties, was short and wiry and intellectual-looking. We were not told his name, just his code name, which Owl said was AE Harpoon. Why such a grisly code name? Were we keeping watch on a terrorist who wrought havoc with a harpoon? If so, would the Little Trumpeter's modern successor, when laying down his insignificant life, have to let himself be skewered by a *harpoon*? Wasn't that expecting a bit too much? I had no wish to shirk my responsibilities, but I was rather squeamish, and the thought of having my chest transfixed by a weapon that protruded from my back put a damper on my spirit of self-sacrifice. My absolute commitment was not as absolute as it had been. Or was Harpoon a metaphorical code name? Did it have something to do with 'sharpness': for instance, with the official belief that the class struggle was growing steadily more *acute*? Was Harpoon someone who represented a *thorn in the flesh* of the socialist political and social system?

I didn't ask, knowing the kind of outfit I was in, but all became clear the day we were instructed to raid Harpoon's mailbox. Owl still refused to tell us his real name. All he said, between chuckles, was 'See if you can figure it out by yourselves. Our brand of humor is an acquired taste.' Raymund and I ran our eyes over the mailboxes and came across a Fred Armbruster. *Armbruster* equals 'crossbowman' in German, so Fred Armbruster had to be Harpoon. I stood guard while Raymund extracted the mail from the box.

'Well?' said Owl, when we were back in the car.

'Nothing much,' Raymund replied. 'Just a couple of Christmas cards and a letter.'

'A letter? Anything in it?'

Owl tore open the envelope. After half a minute he cast his eyes up to heaven and passed the letter to me. 'Can you read that writing?'

'Well?' Owl asked impatiently. 'Anything in it?'

'Like what?'

'Like something interesting – like where to apply for tickets for concerts and things.'

'No, nothing of that kind.'

'I got into a Mary and Gordy concert once,' Owl said proudly.

'No, there's nothing about tickets.'

'Photograph it all the same. That goes for the postcards, too, back and front.' Owl handed me a camera and I did my duty. 'You've got to try your hand at everything once.' He stuffed the letter back in its torn envelope and told Raymund to return it to the mailbox. A few days later we evaluated the quality of the photographs, discussed their shortcomings, and photographed another batch of mail addressed to Fred Armbruster. Owl timed us with his stopwatch – we were inside the time limit – and the photographs proved satisfactory. We never had to 'collect the mail' again, as Owl put it.

After two weeks' surveillance, Raymund demanded to know why we were watching Harpoon at all.

Owl sighed. 'Look to your right,' he said. 'Where are we?'

'In Wilhelm-Pieck-Strasse.'

'Correct. And what can you see, right on the corner?'

'A children's library.'

'Correct. Now look straight ahead. What do you see about a hundred meters away on the left-hand side of the street?'

'The West German Diplomatic Mission.'

'Wrong. That's two hundred and fifty meters away. What do you see at a hundred meters?'

'The youth club?'

'Correct. And what runs the full length of the left-hand side of the street?'

Silence.

'Well?'

'Apartment houses?'

'Of course! And how long do you think those buildings have been there?'

'They're new. Three or four years at most.'

Then it came. Owl was Eulert, Martin, Lieutenant, once more: 'Although we've done our utmost for our fellow citizens – they've got a children's library, a youth club, brand-new housing – there are, I regret to say, one or two elements in our midst who oppose our system and disrupt our communal life. They're the ones we deal with.'

Owl sounded like the supervisor of a model playground: *We've got such lovely swings and such a lovely jungle gym. All the children play nicely together except Karl, who's naughty sometimes and pushes the others into the sandbox.*

Owl once more, surveying the new apartment houses: 'I can't think why these scum are allowed to live in such nice apartments. They don't know how lucky they are.' The very thought of them put Owl in a really bad mood. Not even the negation of negation could console him. Life was unfair.

'What has Harpoon done?' asked Raymund. 'Or *possibly* done?'

'Not a clue,' said Owl. 'How should I know? It's immaterial, anyway. This is all about you two, not him. You've got to learn to write a surveillance report, and write it – so to speak – in a *new* language. You'll sit here until you've done it.'

I stared at him. 'You mean this is all to do with *language*?'

'Of course,' said Owl. 'What else?'

It had happened on our very first day's surveillance, ten minutes after Owl told us to keep our eyes open: *A woman came out of the building.* My palms began to sweat. What should I put down? What terminology should I use? Woman? Female person? Member of the female sex? She? How did you write down *A woman came out of the building* if you worked for the Stasi? Had she come out of a building or a five-story edifice? Had she emerged from an apartment house or the object under surveillance? Had she come out into Wilhelm-Pieck-Strasse or simply the street? And the time – was that important? How precise should I be? Would 'approx. half-past eight' be good enough, or must I be accurate to the nearest minute? Or less than a minute? Or not at all? Did I have to describe the woman? Detail her appearance, her clothes? Whether she looked as if she'd had a good night's sleep? Whether she could be an ovo-lacto-vegetarian? Or ignore her altogether?

Eventually I wrote down *fem. pers. emrgd. st. 0834.*

When I had stolen the microfish – when the world was as red as I was famous – this entry in my log would be displayed in a showcase at the Museum of German History (or the Klaus Uhltzscht Museum), and tour guides would jocularly point out that everyone has to begin somewhere. All the same, Mr. Kitzelstein, don't you feel that *fem. pers. emrgd. st. 0834* betrayed a certain promise?

Every day's surveillance ended with a comparison of our notes.

'All right, Raymund,' said Owl, 'read yours aloud.'

'Seven-fifteen: Took up position level with No. 204 Wilhelm-Pieck-Strasse.'

'Klaus?'

'Seven-fifteen: Commenced surveillance of Harpoon. Location: parked outside No. 204 Wilhelm-Pieck-Strasse.'

'Very good! "Commenced surveillance of Harpoon" – very precisely worded. Raymund, yours means nothing. "Took up position"? What were you watching, the sunrise?'

'Harpoon.'

'Make a note of it, Raymund, make a note of it! Go on.'

'Ten-forty: Harpoon left building accompanied by woman, thirty-fivish, flat-chested . . .' Raymund dissolved into laughter. His first log entry after three and a half hours' surveillance. He'd been waiting all day to get his little joke out. And the amateurish wording! This wasn't the Stasi, or not the genuine one.

'Stop that coarse laughter and get on with it!'

'. . . flat-chested, blue jeans—'

'Why this obsession with her flat chest? We're not judging a beauty contest. If you think it's so vital to inform higher authority that the person was flat-chested, give her a code name like Salt Flats or Flat Battery. For the last time, Raymund, stop that coarse laughter, this isn't a burlesque show! Unless, of course, you'd like to make an inventory of the contents of Harpoon's garbage can? We'll see who laughs then. You wouldn't be the first cadet I've seen knee-deep in garbage.'

Raymund drew a deep breath. 'All right, woman, mid-thirties, Levi's, umber jacket—'

'We don't say Levi's – this isn't America. We say blue denim trousers. And your colors! They're an absolute disaster! Her jacket wasn't umber, it was ocher.'

'It was umber.'

'This isn't an art college! For service use we have a color guide containing thirty-nine standard shades. *Umber* doesn't exist! The color in question is *ocher*! What you call it for your personal amusement is your affair.' Owl lit a cigarette. 'Confront our comrades with wholly utopian colors, to coin a phrase, and the result would be chaos. Let me illustrate what I mean with an analogy. On that course I attended – conversational psychology, or was it psychological conver-sation? – we were always taught to illustrate our points with an analogy, so here goes: Imagine you've got to describe the appearance of a football team, Bayern Munich, for example, because they're playing an East German team in the Euro-pean Cup. We'd need some soccer strips in our opponents' colors, but that would be impossible unless you'd defined them in advance, exactly according to the color guide. If everyone employed his own definition, our comrades would only get confused.'

'Why would we need some Bayern Munich strips?' asked Raymund.

'Well . . . For substitutes, for example.'

'Substitutes?'

'Yes, substitutes. Send one of our boys onto the field in a Bayern Munich strip and Bayern wouldn't know him from their own.' Owl broke off, floored by his own cock-eyed reasoning. 'Well, maybe that wasn't a good analogy,' he conceded, 'but you know what I'm getting at.'

'Besides,' said Raymund, 'you wouldn't have to keep Bayern under surveillance, you'd only have to watch them on TV.'

'I wouldn't advise it,' I said, seeing a chance to score some more points. 'Everyone knows our adversaries use the electronic media for disinformation purposes.'

'Surely not where soccer strips are concerned?' Raymund protested.

'We must be careful not to underestimate the enemy,' I retorted, giving Owl a look that invited him to arbitrate.

'I already said it wasn't a particularly good analogy,' said Owl, disheartened. Owl wasn't Wunderlich, but if the major got to hear of my remark he would sing my praises again. *A lot of people take twenty years to learn to think like that . . .*

Besides, someone obviously had plans for me. Our present activities couldn't be as pointless as they seemed. Color guides! Soccer strips! Substitutes! Such an absurdity was inconceivable. There had to be some plan behind it all.

Owl would read out his own surveillance log at the end of every day and gaze at us triumphantly when he was through.

'I'll never get the hang of it,' said Raymund.

'Don't worry,' said Owl, 'you will sooner or later.' One could almost see the burden of responsibility weighing him down. 'I mean, that's why you're sitting here.'

It must also have been the burden of responsibility that prompted him to share the fruits of his experience with us. Our return journey in the evenings was almost always held up by the traffic lights near the Friedrichstadtpalast. Owl gestured at the surrounding area. 'I once did a long-term surveillance job here,' he said with a sigh. 'It was hard to leave the place: a shit house nearby, a hot dog stand just across the street, and a big parking lot where the pedestrians-only mall is now. We could position the car so we didn't have to crane our necks. You'll appreciate the value of a spot like this once you've done a couple of weeks' surveillance.'

'We have already,' I said.

'A couple of months, then,' said Owl, yawning. 'Or years.'

LEN DEIGHTON

From

FUNERAL IN BERLIN

CHAPTER 5

When a player offers a piece for exchange or sacrifice
then surely he has in mind a subsequent manœuvre
which will end to his advantage.

Monday, October 7th

BRASSIERES AND BEER; whiskies and worsteds; great
words carved out of coloured electricity and plastered along
the walls of the Ku-damm. This was the theatre-in-the-round
of western prosperity: a great, gobbling, yelling, laughing
stage crowded with fat ladies and dwarfs, marionettes on
strings, fire-eaters, strong men and lots of escapologists.
'Today I joined the cast,' I thought. 'Now they've got an
illusionist.' Beneath me the city lay in huge patches of light
and vast pools of darkness where rubble and grass fought
gently for control of the universe.

Inside my room the phone rang. Vulkan's voice was calm
and unhurried.

'Do you know the Warschau restaurant?'

'Stalin Allee,' I said; it was a well-known bourse for information pedlars.

'They call it Karl Marx Allee now,' said Vulkan sardonically. 'Have your car facing west in the car park across the
Allee. Don't get out of your car, flash your lights. I'll be ready
to go at 9.20. OK?'

'OK,' I said.

* * *

I followed the line of the canal from the Berlin Hilton to Hallesches Tor U-Bahnstation, then turned north on to Friedrichstrasse. The control point is a few blocks north. I flipped a passport to the American soldier and an insurance card to the West German policeman, then in bottom gear I moved across the tram tracks of Zimmerstrasse that bump you into a world where 'communist' is not a dirty word.

It was a warm evening and a couple of dozen transients sat under the blue neon light in the checkpoint hut; stacked neatly on tables were piles of booklets and leaflets with titles like 'Science of the GDR in the service of Peace', 'Art for the People' and 'Historic Task of the GDR and the future of Germany'.

'Herr Dorf.' A very young frontier policeman held my passport and riffed the corners. 'How much money are you carrying?'

I spread the few Westmarks and English pounds on the desk. He counted them and endorsed my papers.

'Cameras or transistor radio?'

At the other end of the corridor a boy in a leather jacket with 'Rhodesia' painted on it shouted, 'How much longer do we have to wait here?'

I heard a Grepo say to him, 'You'll have to take your turn, sir – we didn't send for you, you know.'

'Just the car radio,' I said.

The Grepo nodded.

He said, 'The only thing we don't allow is East German currency.' He gave me my passport,* smiled and saluted. I walked down the long hut. The Rhodesian was saying,

* To catch people with stolen passports, or people who spend nights in the East, the passports are often marked with a tiny pencil spot on some pre-arranged page.

'I know my rights,' and rapping on the counter but everyone else was staring straight ahead.

I walked across to the parking bay. I drove around the concrete blocks, a Vopo gave a perfunctory glance at my passport and a soldier swung the red-and-white striped barrier skywards. I drove forward into East Berlin. There were crowds of people at Friedrichstrasse station. People coming home from work, going to work or just hanging around waiting for something to happen. I turned right at Unter den Linden – where the lime trees had been early victims of Nazidom; the old Bismarck Chancellery was a cobweb of rusty ruins facing the memorial building where two green-clad sentries with white gloves were goose-stepping like Bismarck was expected back. I drove around the white plain of Marx-Engels Platz and, at the large slab-sided department store at Alexanderplatz, took the road that leads to Karl Marx Allee.

I recognized the car park and pulled into it. Karl Marx Allee was still the same as when it had been Stalin Allee. Miles of workers' flats and state shops housed in seven-storey Russian-style architecture, thirty-foot-wide pavements and huge grassy spaces and cycle tracks like the M1.

In the open-air café across the road, lights winked under the trees and a few people danced between the striped parasols while a small combo walked their baby back home with lots of percussion. 'Warschau', the lights spelled out and under them I saw Vulkan get to his feet. He waited patiently until the traffic lights were in his favour before walking towards the car park. A careful man, Johnnie; this was no time to collect a jaywalking ticket. He got into a Wartburg, pulled away eastward down Karl Marx Allee. I followed keeping one or two cars between us.

Johnnie parked outside a large granite house in Köpenick.

I edged past his car and parked under a gas lamp around the corner. It was not a pretty house but it had that mood of comfort and complacency that middle-class owners breathe into the structure of a house along with dinner-gong echoes and cigar smoke. There was a large garden at the back and here near the forests and the waters of Müggelsee the air smelled clean.

There was just one name-plate on the door. It was of neat black plastic: 'Professor Eberhard Lebowitz', engraved in ornate Gothic lettering. Johnnie rang and a maid let us into the hall.

'Herr Stok?' said Johnnie.

He gave her his card and she tiptoed away into the interior.

In the dimly lit hall there stood a vast hallstand with some tricky inlaid ivory, two clothes-brushes and a Soviet officer's peaked hat. The ceiling was a complex pattern of intaglio leaves and the floral wallpaper looked prehensile.

The maid said, 'Will you please come this way?' and led us into Stok's drawing-room. The wallpaper was predominantly gold and silver but there were plenty of things hiding the wallpaper. There were aspidistras, fussy lace curtains, shelves full of antique Meissen and a cocktail cabinet like a small wooden version of the Kremlin. Stok looked up from the 21-inch baroque TV. He was a big-boned man, his hair was cropped to the skull and his complexion was like something the dog had been playing with. When he stood up to greet us his huge hands poked out of a bright red silk smoking-jacket with gold-braid frogging.

Vulkan said, 'Herr Stok; Herr Dorf,' and then he said, 'Herr Dorf; Herr Stok,' and we all nodded at each other, then Vulkan put a paper bag down on the coffee table and Stok drew an eight-ounce tin of Nescafé out of it, nodded, and put it back again.

'What will you drink?' Stok asked. He had a musical basso voice.

'Just before we move into the chat,' I said, 'can I see your identity card?'

Stok pulled his wallet out of a hip pocket, smiled archly at me and then peeled loose the stiff white card with a photo and two rubber stamps that Soviet citizens carry when abroad.

'It says that you are Captain Maylev here,' I protested as I laboriously pronounced the Cyrillic script.

The servant girl brought a tray of tiny glasses and a frosted bottle of vodka. She set the tray down. Stok paused while she withdrew.

'And your passport says that you are Edmond Dorf,' said Stok, 'but we are both victims of circumstance.'

Behind him the East German news commentator was saying in his usual slow voice, '. . . sentenced to three years for assisting in the attempt to move his family to the West.' Stok walked across to the set and clicked the switch to the West Berlin channel where a cast of fifty Teutonic minstrels sang 'See them shuffle along' in German. 'It's never a good night, Thursday,' Stok said apologetically. He switched the set off. We broke the wax on the fruit-flavoured vodka and Stok and Vulkan began discussing whether twenty-four bottles of Scotch whisky were worth a couple of cameras. I sat around and drank vodka until they had ironed out some sort of agreement. Then Stok said, 'Has Dorf got power to negotiate?' – just like I wasn't in the room.

'He's a big shot in London,' said Vulkan. 'Anything he promises will be honoured. I'll guarantee it.'

'I want lieutenant-colonel's pay,' Stok said, turning to me, 'for life.'

'Don't we all?' I said.

Vulkan was looking at the evening paper; he looked up and said, 'No, he means that he'd want the UK Government to pay him that as a salary if he comes over the wire. You could promise that, couldn't you?'

'I don't see why not,' I said. 'We'll say you've been in a few years, that's five pounds four shillings a day basic. Then there's ration allowance, six and eight a day, marriage allowance, one pound three and something a day, qualification pay five shillings a day if you get through Staff College, overseas pay fourteen and three and . . . you *would* want overseas pay?'

'You are not taking me seriously,' Stok said, a big smile across his white moon of a face. Vulkan was shifting about on his seat, tightening his tie against his Adam's apple and cracking his finger joints.

'All systems go,' I said.

'Colonel Stok puts up a very convincing case,' said Vulkan.

'So does the "find the lady" mob in Charing Cross Road,' I said, 'but they never come through with the QED.'

Stok threw back two vodkas in quick succession and stared at me earnestly. He said, 'Look, I don't favour the capitalist system. I don't ask you to believe that I do. In fact I hate your system.'

'Great,' I said. 'And you are in a job where you can really do something about it.'

Stok and Vulkan exchanged glances.

'I wish you would try to understand,' said Stok. 'I am really sincere about giving you my allegiance.'

'Go on,' I said. 'I bet you say that to all the great powers.'

Vulkan said, 'I've spent a lot of time and money in setting this up. If you are so damn clever why did you bother to come to Berlin?'

'OK,' I told them. 'Act out the charade. I'll be thinking of words.'

Stok and Vulkan looked at each other and we drank and then Stok gave me one of his gold-rimmed oval cigarettes and lit it with a nickel-silver sputnik.

'For a long time I have been thinking of moving west,' said Stok. 'It's not a matter of politics. I am just as avid a communist now as I have ever been, but a man gets old. He looks for comfort, for security in possessions.' Stok cupped his big boxing-glove hand and looked down at it. 'A man wants to scoop up a handful of black dirt and know it's his own land, to live on, die on and give to his sons. We peasants are a weak insecure segment of socialism, Mr Dorf.' He smiled with his big brown teeth, trimmed here and there with an edge of gold. 'These comforts that you take for granted will not be a part of life in the East until long after I am dead.'

'Yes,' I said. 'We have decadence now – while we are young enough to enjoy it.'

'Semitsa,' said Stok. He waited to see what effect it would have on me. It had none.

'That's what you are really interested in. Not me. Semitsa.'

'Is he here in Berlin?' I asked.

'Slowly, Mr Dorf,' said Stok. 'Things move very slowly.'

'How do you know he wants to come west?' I asked.

'I know,' said Stok.

Vulkan interrupted, 'I told the colonel that Semitsa would be worth about forty thousand pounds to us.'

'Did you?' I said in as flat a monotone as I could manage.

Stok poured out his fruit vodka all round, downed his own and poured himself a replacement.

'It's been nice talking to you boys,' I said. 'I only wish you had something I could buy.'

'I understand you, Mr Dorf,' said Stok. 'In my country we have a saying, "a man who trades a horse for a promise ends

259

up with tired feet".' He walked across to the eighteenth-century mahogany bureau.

I said, 'I don't want you to deviate from a course of loyalty and integrity to the Soviet Government to which I remain a friend and ally.'

Stok turned and smiled at me.

'You think I have live microphones planted here and that I might attempt to trick you.'

'You might,' I said. 'You are in the business.'

'I hope to persuade you otherwise,' said Stok. 'As to being in the business: when does a chef get ptomaine poisoning?'

'When he eats out,' I said.

Stok's laugh made the antique plates rattle. He groped around inside the big writing-desk and produced a flat metal box, brought a vast bunch of tiny keys from his pocket and from inside the box reached a thick black file. He handed it to me. It was typed in Cyrillic capitals and contained photostats of letters and transcripts of tapped phone calls.

Stok reached for another oval cigarette and tapped it unlit against the white page of typing. 'Mr Semitsa's passport westward,' he said putting a sarcastic emphasis on the 'mister'.

'Yes?' I said doubtfully.

Vulkan leaned forward to me. 'Colonel Stok is in charge of an investigation of the Minsk Biochemical labs.'

'Where Semitsa used to be,' I said. It was coming clear to me. 'This is Semitsa's file, then?'

'Yes,' said Stok, 'and everything that I need to get Semitsa a ten-year sentence.'

'Or have him do anything you say,' I said. Perhaps Stok and Vulkan were serious.

CHRISTA WOLF

From

THEY DIVIDED THE SKY

Translated by Luise von Flotow

CHAPTER 26

THAT JULY THE SUN shone equally on the just and the unjust. *When* it shone. It was a rainy summer.

August started well: hot and dry, with high open skies, though people hardly noticed, except when they looked up at the planes, more numerous than usual, that were flying over the country. 'Let August be over,' people said, 'and a bit of September. Nobody starts a war late in the year.'

Rita thought: you can't even talk about summer or winter without *that* coming up. Later we will wonder how we ever put up with this. There is no getting used to it. You never get used to this kind of pressure.

It is the first Sunday of August. Early morning, and Rita is on the fast train to Berlin. Since yesterday she has had a letter on her that says: 'This is the moment. I expect you any day. Don't ever forget . . .'

Nobody knows where she is going – that is the advantage of living alone and not having to render accounts. And nobody, not even she herself, can predict whether she will return. Though her suitcase is light. She is going to him without any luggage. As though to test out this option, she lets her farewell gaze slip over the chimneys that slide along the horizon, over villages, woods, a single tree, groups of people who are harvesting grain in the fields. A week earlier she was working here, in this very region, with Hänschen and some of the others from the train carriage plant. She knows the harvest will be poor, and that it is difficult to bring in even what little there is. But are those still her worries? Everywhere in the world there are trees and chimneys and grain fields . . .

It would be a hot day. Rita took off her jacket. Unbidden, another passenger reached out to help her. She thanked him, and studied him more carefully. A tall, slender fellow with a pale, long face, glasses, brown hair. Nothing special. His gaze was a little intrusive, or was she imagining that? He averted his eyes when she looked at him. Still, his presence felt oppressive. She got up and went to stand at an open window in the passage. She liked the way one image after another appeared inside the strict frame of the window, colourful and diverse.

Only the sky remained the same for a long time: pale morning blue, lit by the low angle of the sun, a few light grey clouds that dispersed as the day progressed.

So, what else do you want? Hadn't he written in a way that allayed all her doubts? He's waiting for you the way you wait for freedom after a long period of imprisonment, or for food and drink after a long period of hunger and thirst. So, take your little suitcase – it doesn't matter if it's light or heavy – and go to him. A two-hour train ride; it's laughably short. And it's the most natural, most real thing in the world. So what's the matter? This aching feeling that just won't go away? You can't go by that. That's not a measure.

'Are you happy, my child?' Oh, mother, that's not the issue anymore. And besides, isn't that exactly the question, a question you think still makes sense to ask, that separates us from you, the constant worriers, the well-meaning oldies, the ones who understand absolutely nothing.

All of a sudden she knew what had bothered her about the letter. The same words that had always worked to smooth out a misunderstanding or a shadow between them were no longer sufficient. She wished she'd seen it more clearly: he knows exactly what he's asking of me, but he has no choice. The casual way he'd abandoned her, though ('they offered me opportunities here that I couldn't let slip by'), his dependence on brand-new acquaintances that were suddenly classified as friends . . . That's not how you do the things you need to do. That's just drifting along, when you've lost control of the steering and nothing matters.

And can he even fathom what these eleven weeks have done to me? It would be good if he doesn't think everything has been decided when I arrive. He needs to let me ponder this, together with him. Once I recover the consciousness he took with him when he left. I just hope I don't lose it again when he puts his hand on my arm, and these past days and nights run together as though they never happened.

The train made the only stop of the journey. Half of the trip was over. She had to quickly think through the most important points. But when you have something specific and important to consider and want to keep it clear in your head, it rushes by, rendered unrecognizable by its speed, and instead, all kinds of tranquil images that you don't really need crop up at the edges of your consciousness.

Rita returned to her compartment to get rid of those useless thoughts. She accepted a cigarette from the other traveller. She saw the magazine he offered her.

Maybe she should have spoken to Wendland after all, she thought. Yesterday would have been a good moment. It's almost arrogant to rely only on yourself . . .

Last evening, an hour before midnight, she'd been the last person on the late shift to leave the assembly hall. As always, she looked back one more time and counted the cars the early shift would be finishing. She'd found it hard to leave the heavy, dull grey blocks. She'd had Manfred's letter on her since midday, and knew all the details of her journey to him.

When she finally left the plant, she saw Wendland standing on the top step of the entrance to the administrative building, right under the light, less than twenty meters away. He didn't see her because she kept to the shadows. He lit a cigarette and slowly walked toward the factory gate.

She followed, keeping a slight distance. They met no one along the way. There must be some reason why he, the director, was walking through his plant that evening. He walked slowly, heavily almost, but was attentively looking ahead and at the buildings on both sides.

The silence in the place seemed unnatural and sad. Light and dark were differently arranged than in daytime. The darker spots that sunlight never touched were illuminated by floodlights at night. Even the narrow passage between the forge and the shop where the turntables were built, which Wendland now turned into, was lit up. The place he was just walking past was where someone had said to her: Do I have to be the one who destroys what I like best about you?

Rita walked more quickly even though Wendland might discover her. The sharp flames made by the welders hissed out of the shop, and their blue tremors marked her path.

As Wendland passed by the gateman, Rita called his name. He stopped short and walked back toward her. 'Rita!' he said, and repeated what she had once said to him, 'You've come at just the right moment!'

He didn't notice that he'd addressed her informally. He'd been doing so in his thoughts for a long time. He told her that this time *he* had undergone a kind of exam. His knees were still soft. And contrary to her, he hadn't held up very well.

Rita recalled that many unfamiliar cars had been on the grounds that day, a big conference of factory directors. Had they criticized him?

Yes, some, Wendland replied. 'I don't take criticism easily, you know. I can see for myself that we haven't been making much progress in the past weeks. But the way these things go, my critics only had half the story, half the bad and half the good. I didn't really deserve the praise either, so that was no comfort. Later on, they brought out the heavy guns, and I forgot the rest.'

Rita started when he said abruptly, 'We're not building the new car!' What? That was impossible. For weeks they'd been talking of nothing else in the plant: Never mind, just wait till we start building the new car . . . 'No,' Wendland said. 'There are certain metals we need, which we've been buying in the West. Now, they won't sell them to us anymore. They keep finding ways to get at us!'

But we're not giving up, he continued. We have to re-think. We need time.

'What about Meternagel?' Rita asked. 'Will you tell him yourself?'

Wendland nodded. He had two nights and a day to get ready for Monday morning's meeting in the plant offices where he would quietly say: we'll be building the new car later. Here are the new measures we have to develop in order to no longer depend on the metals they're trying to pressure us with.

It was midnight when they turned into Rita's street.

Wendland fell silent. All the disappointment that would flood back tomorrow (or maybe even in a few minutes) had lifted. Here he was, walking next to this girl, finally talking to her as a friend, here they were at her door, and what was he talking about the whole time? 'Remember,' he said, 'this is where I saw you for the first time? We ran into each other in the doorway. I had just been made director.'

They both thought: God, that was a long time ago . . .

'Yes,' Rita said. 'But it wasn't the first time. I was with the Ermisch people in the bar.'

'Right!' he said. 'Did you notice me then?'

She laughed. 'Couldn't miss you! You spoiled everybody's good mood.'

That would have been the moment to talk about the letter that was in my pocket and that I couldn't forget for even a second. He will never understand why I didn't tell him.

They were still standing there. As the silence grew too long, Wendland said brightly, 'That's often what happens to me, I don't say enough. I would be sorry in your case. I hope you know you can count on me.'

Neither one of them said what they really wanted to say – at least not in the right tone. They didn't know how to start over – he, for one, didn't know this might be the last opportunity to speak, and she did. A few more undecided seconds, then Wendland said goodnight and Rita went upstairs. She packed her small suitcase quickly; then she stepped to the window and for the first time in a long time, watched the stars. It'll be a clear day, she thought. She set the alarm and went to bed.

'Well,' said the man seated across from her on the fast train to Berlin, 'I didn't expect you to take such an interest in my modest magazine.'

Rita blushed. She finally looked at the page at which the magazine had lain open for God knows how long. Three black letters: OAS. Below them, the mutilated corpse of a woman. She turned the page: the beaming face of a child. And more black letters: USSR.

'The Medusa of our times,' said her fellow traveller.

'Everybody has their own problems: some have plastic bombs, others toothpaste grins. If you can believe what you read in the magazines.'

What does he want exactly? 'Pretty different problems, don't you think?' Rita asked in surprise.

'Indeed,' he replied politely. 'As you say. So, are you travelling to Berlin for a visit?'

'My fiancé,' she said coolly and with a note of triumph. Strange, it didn't seem to bother him. A beautiful day to visit your fiancé, he said. An exceptionally beautiful day.

What did he mean? It was impossible to tell. It would be best to just dislike him. On the other hand, he was an amusing storyteller. Oh, so he's a teacher! He's not surprised to find a future colleague in her.

'What do you mean? It's hardly something you can see from the outside.'

He laughed winsomely. It was her improving-the-world-look. The typical look of the German teacher, who wore it to make up for the meagre salary they earned . . . She didn't really feel angry at him, even if in some unpleasant way she felt he'd caught her out. And she didn't know what to make of his polite insinuations.

Was he also going to visit relatives?

He laughed, as though she'd again been excessively naïve. Of course, he said. You could call it that.

Rita became tired of the complicated conversation, which he respected. He dug a book out of his pocket and leaned back into the corner.

Rita doesn't remember when the city began or when she first started to feel the icy strength she would need to get through whatever happened.

This was not her first trip to Berlin, but this time she

realized that she didn't know the city at all. They travelled past garden plots, parks, then the first factories. Not a pretty place, she thought. But her face didn't show it.

Her travel companion looked up. 'I hope your fiancé lives in Pankow or Schöneweide?' he said in a friendly tone.

'Why?' Rita asked, trembling.

'You could be asked.'

'Oh,' she said quickly. 'Yes, in Pankow. He lives in Pankow.'

'That's good then.'

Does he want to find out where I'm going? Or warn me? And what do I say if they ask for the street? I'm really not prepared for this . . . Who's going to believe that I actually have to do this?

There was no time left to think. The train stopped. Police came in and demanded to see identity papers. (If they ask me, I won't lie. I'll tell everything, from beginning to end, to the first one who asks.) They leafed through her papers and handed them back. Her hands shook as she put them back in her purse. Not very effective, these controls, she thought, almost disappointed.

The man across from her wiped his forehead with a snow-white handkerchief that had been ironed and folded in sharp creases. 'Hot,' he said.

They spoke nothing more. Rita saw him again at the gate, with a woman who'd arrived on the same train and whom he seemed to know very well.

Then she forgot about him. She had her own worries. In the adjacent hall she located a big city map. She stood in front of it for some time memorizing the names of streets and stations she didn't know. It was clear to her that she would have to manage the day's events all alone.

She stepped up to the ticket window. For the first time she had to say what she was doing.

'To the Zoological Garden,' she said.

A small piece of yellow cardboard was slipped indifferently toward her. 'Twenty,' said the woman behind the glass.

'And if you . . . want to come back?' Rita asked gingerly.

'Forty, then,' the woman said. She took the ticket back and pushed a different one through the wicket. This was what made the city different from all other cities in the world: for the price of forty pfennigs, it offered you two different lives.

Rita looked at the ticket and carefully put it away. I have to keep my head clear for other things.

She was already feeling tired as she let people who were out on their Sunday excursions push her along the tunnel and up the stairs onto the platform. The day was just beginning here. Pretty dresses, crowds, the chatter of children. A normal Sunday in summer. Rita stood by the wide doors that opened and closed silently at every new station. For the first time in her life she wished she were someone else – one of those harmless folks on a Sunday outing – just not herself. This wish was the only sign that she was getting into a situation that went against her grain.

Now there were no more clouds in the sky at all, if you took the trouble to look up from the moving train. Rita couldn't shake the distressing feeling that with every moment she was missing something important. She kept repeating the names of the stations and streets that lay along her way. She had no idea what there might be to the left or the right, and she didn't want to know. A thin, fine line had been sketched out for her through this immense and awesome city. She had to stick to it. Otherwise there would be complications whose end she could not imagine.

In the end, she missed nothing, and arrived. She got off the train punctually, carefully and without haste. She forced herself to take the time to look in a few kiosk windows on the platform (so those are the oranges and chocolates, the cigarettes and the cheap books . . .), and discovered that she had pictured them just like that.

She was among the last to reach the barrier. There she encountered a small group of people who were blocking her way, completely engrossed in their own affairs, and expressing effusive joy or profound pain – it was hard to tell. Maybe both. Suddenly, Rita noticed that her fellow traveller from the fast train was at the centre of this group. The woman with whom he'd passed through the barrier was now hanging from his arm, crying openly along with a few other women who had probably come to meet the couple.

Rita stopped short. At the same moment, the man spotted her and recognized her. He raised his arm in a greeting – he couldn't get out of the circle of women – and gave her a knowing smile.

Rita quickly ran down the steps. It could not have been a worse start, she thought. Why did that person have to cross her path? Am I as marked as he is by a guilty conscience?

CHAPTER 27

She shut her eyes for a moment to have the whole picture in front of her, the way she'd seen it on the big city map, neat and clear.

Turn right first. Cross the wide street, where (and the map does not show this) you have to wait for minutes before the impeccably trained policeman executes the elegant arm movements that stop the stream of cars in both directions and let people cross. Turn into the famous shopping street (that has become the source of legends, reputed to be *so* beautiful, *so* rich, *so* brilliant that it hasn't been able to keep up with its own mythology). Follow this street to the fifth cross street and turn right. Rita entered a quieter area now, still following the thin line she'd drawn on the map and which she saw more clearly than the actual streets. Without once having asked for directions, she was suddenly standing in front of the house where Manfred lived.

She'd been here in her thoughts every day, and now she actually saw it. She suppressed her surprise that this place – an ordinary apartment block in an ordinary city street – could be the object of someone's longing and their refuge. She stepped into the cool entrance and only then noticed how hot it was outside. Slowly she made her way up the worn but polished linoleum-covered stairs. The harder she felt her heart beat, the more she knew: this is not some harmless venture you're engaged in. It is risky, and you should not have undertaken it alone. But it's too late to turn back now.

She was already at the door with the bright nameplate. The doorbell was sounding, a brief, thin tone. Footsteps. The gaunt woman in black who stood before her had to be Manfred's aunt.

The entire building gave off a sour smell, redolent of poverty struggling to appear elegant. It was teetering at the edge of the abyss; workers' housing started one street over. The sour smell and the shiny linoleum in the stairwell had made their way into the dark entrance of the apartment where Rita was now reluctantly ushered in. Bashful, she stepped into a room and in the brighter light got a better view of the woman, who plied her for information.

Yes, this was the sister of the deceased Frau Herrfurth. A

sister whom fate had discriminated against, at least as far as it was possible to say that a dead person has some advantage over a living one. The slightly triumphant look mixed with self-pity and pious grief on this woman's face could well have stemmed from the realization that, finally, she had gained the upper hand over her dead sister.

'Go ahead,' said Frau Herrfurth's sister. For the first time since her nephew had been living with her, she was opening his door to a visitor.

All the tears Rita shed later were set off by what she saw in the few seconds as she entered the room. Manfred was sitting at a table that had been moved directly in front of the window, with his back to the door. He was reading a book, his elbows planted on the table: the narrow back of his head, the short hair that stood up at the cowlick, his youthful curved shoulders. As the door opened and someone came in (his aunt, he thought) he stayed where he was, motionless, but did not continue reading, stiffening in defence. When no one spoke, he slowly turned his head.

His cold, dispassionate gaze told Rita more about his life in this room than he could ever have expressed.

Then he saw her.

He closed his eyes, and opened them again with a completely different expression: disbelief, consternation and foolish hope. He came up to her, raised his arms as though he wanted to rest them on her shoulders, and quietly said her name. The enormous relief on his face pained her. But she smiled and gently stroked his hair.

She'd done the right thing in coming to him. But she already knew every detail of what would come next. It pained her that they would have to go through these steps, say the words, spend this day. He knew too, and so it was easier to bear.

That moment didn't last long, only as long as they looked at each other. Then they forgot what they had known with such lucid certainty. Once again, anything was possible.

'You've changed,' Manfred said as she sat on the only chair there was, the one at the table, and he huddled at the head of the bed.

She just smiled. Once again, they knew exactly why they loved each other. As she had foreseen: nights filled with great torments and days of hard decisions were burned away in a single glance, in the light, perhaps accidental, touch of his hand.

Rita looked around. The woman in the next room, his aunt, had achieved what his mother had failed at for years: the room was painfully tidy. A small, endlessly dreary rectangle. The few dust mites that could survive here were dancing in the long narrow ray of sun that came in for half an hour at this time of day. In a moment, it would slide silently off the edge of the table, and onto Manfred's motionless hands, which would still not move.

How long can you sit there like that?

Rita got up, just as Manfred did too, as though at a sign. They stepped into the aunt's room, 'ante-hell' as Manfred quickly told Rita in a whisper. The woman was sitting at the window, in the light of the same uncanny, silent sunbeam, knitting away at a black scarf for winter. She had nothing else; only the grief for her deceased sister, which would have to last a long time.

When she realized where the young lady was from, she was suddenly willing to make coffee. A little light entered her pale eyes. Who would miss the opportunity to host someone from the East, and interrogate them?

With several polite words they escaped. Outside, as the door closed, they looked at each other openly for a few moments. Is this what you were looking for here? – How can you ask that? No, this isn't it. – What is?

Manfred looked down. He took her hand and pulled her down the stairs behind him. He swung her around the bends. Then they ran through the cool, echoing, stone entrance hall and were finally outside: in the street noise, the heat and the glaring noon light.

'Right,' Manfred said with a grin, 'now take a look around. The free world is at your feet.'

All the church steeples rang out twelve o'clock.

IAN McEWAN

From

THE INNOCENT

CHAPTER 4

THERE WAS ANOTHER man sitting in the front passenger seat of the Beetle when Leonard went down onto the street with Bob Glass. His name was Russell, and he must have been watching their approach in the rear-view mirror for he sprang out of the car as they approached it from behind and gave Leonard's hand a ferocious shake. He worked as an announcer for Voice of America, he said, and wrote bulletins for RIAS, the West Berlin radio service. He wore a gold-buttoned blazer of a shameless Post Office red, and cream coloured trousers with sharp creases, and shoes with tassels and no laces. After the introductions, Russell pulled a lever to fold down his seat and gestured Leonard into the back. Like Glass, Russell wore his shirt open to reveal a high-necked white vest underneath. As they pulled away, Leonard fingered his tie knot in the darkness. He decided against removing the tie in case the two Americans had already noticed him wearing it.

Russell seemed to think it was his responsibility to impart as much information as possible to Leonard. His voice was professionally relaxed, and he spoke without fumbling a syllable or repeating himself or pausing between sentences. He was on the job, naming the streets as they passed down them, pointing out the extent of the bomb damage, or a new office block going up. 'We're crossing the Tiergarten now. You'll need to come by here in daylight. There's hardly a tree to be seen. What the bombs didn't destroy, the Berliners burnt to keep warm in the Airlift. Hitler used to call this the East-West Axis. Now it's Street of June 17, named for the Uprising the year before last. Up ahead is the memorial to the Russian soldiers who took the city, and I'm sure you know the name of this famous edifice . . .'

The car slowed down as they passed West Berlin Police and Customs. Beyond them were half a dozen Vopos. One of them shone a torch at the licence plate and waved the car into the Russian sector. They drove beneath the Brandenburg Gate. Now it was much darker. There was no other traffic. It was difficult to feel excitement, however, because Russell's travelogue continued without modulation, even when the car crashed through a pothole.

'This deserted stretch was once the nerve centre of the city, one of the most famous thoroughfares in Europe. Unter den Linden . . . Over there, the real headquarters of the German Democratic Republic, the Soviet Embassy. It stands on the site of the old Hotel Bristol, once one of the most fashionable . . .'

Glass had been silent all this while. Now he interrupted politely. 'Excuse me Russell. Leonard, we're starting you in the East so you can enjoy the contrasts later. We're going to the Neva Hotel . . .'

Russell was reactivated. 'It used to be the Hotel Nordland, a second-class establishment. Now it has declined further, but it is still the best hotel in East Berlin.'

'Russell,' Glass said, 'you badly need a drink.'

It was so dark they could see light from the Neva lobby slanting across the pavement from the far end of the street. When they got out of the car they saw there was in fact another light, the blue neon sign of a co-operative restaurant opposite the hotel, the H.O. Gastronom. The condensation on the windows was its only outward sign of life. At the Neva reception a man in a brown uniform silently handed them towards a lift just big enough for three. It was a slow descent, and their faces were too close together under a single dim bulb for conversation.

There were thirty or forty people in the bar, silent over their drinks. On a dais in one corner a clarinettist and an accordion player were sorting through sheets of music. The bar was hung with studded, tasselled quilting of well-fingered pink which was also built into the counter. There were grand chandeliers, all unlit, and chipped gilt-framed mirrors. Leonard was heading for the bar, thinking to buy the first round, but Glass guided him towards a table on the edge of a tiny parquet dance floor.

His whisper sounded loud. 'Don't let them see your money in here. East marks only.'

At last a waiter came and Glass ordered a bottle of Russian champagne. As they raised their glasses, the musicians began to play Red Sails in the Sunset. No one was tempted onto the parquet. Russell was scanning the darker corners, and then he was on his feet and making his way between the tables. He returned with a thin woman in a white dress made for someone larger. They watched him move her through an efficient foxtrot.

Glass was shaking his head. 'He mistook her in the bad light. She won't do,' he predicted, and correctly, for at the end Russell made a courtly bow, and, offering the woman his arm, saw her back to her table.

When he joined them he shrugged, 'It's the diet here,' and relapsing for a moment into his wireless propaganda voice, gave them details of average calorie consumption in East and West Berlin. Then he broke off, saying, 'What the hell,' and ordered another bottle.

The champagne was as sweet as lemonade and too gassy. It

hardly seemed a serious drink at all. Glass and Russell were talking about the German question. How long would the refugees flock through Berlin to the West before the Democratic Republic suffered total economic collapse through a shortage of manpower?

Russell was ready with the figures, the hundreds of thousands each year. 'And these are their best people, three-quarters of them are under forty-five. I'll give it another three years. After that the East German state won't be able to function.'

Glass said, 'There'll be a state as long as there's a government, and there'll be a government as long as the Soviets want it. It'll be pretty damn miserable here, but the Party will get by. You see.' Leonard nodded and hummed his agreement, but he did not attempt an opinion. When he raised his hand he was rather surprised that the waiter came over for him just as he had for the others. He ordered another bottle. He had never felt happier. They were deep in the Communist camp, they were drinking Communist champagne, they were men with responsibilities talking over affairs of state. The conversation had moved on to West Germany, the Federal Republic, which was about to be accepted as a full member of NATO.

Russell thought it was all a mistake. 'That's one crappy phoenix rising out of the ashes.'

Glass said, 'You want a free Germany, then you got to have a strong one.'

'The French aren't going to buy it,' Russell said, and turned to Leonard for support. At that moment the champagne arrived.

'I'll take care of it,' Glass said, and when the waiter had gone he said to Leonard, 'You owe me seven West marks.'

Leonard filled the glasses and the thin woman and her

girl friend walked past their table, and the conversation took another turn. Russell said that Berlin girls were the liveliest and most strong-minded in all the world.

Leonard said that as long as you weren't Russian you couldn't go wrong. 'They all remember when the Russians came in '45,' he said with quiet authority, 'they've all got older sisters, or mothers, even grannies, who were raped and kicked around.'

The two Americans did not agree, but they took him seriously. They even laughed on 'grannies'. Leonard took a long drink as he listened to Russell.

'The Russians are with their units, out of the country. The ones in town, the officers, the commissars, they do well enough with the girls.'

Glass agreed. 'There's always some dumb chick who'll fuck a Russian.'

The band was playing How You Gonna Keep Them Down on the Farm? The sweetness of the champagne was cloying. It was a relief when the waiter set down three fresh glasses and a refrigerated bottle of vodka.

They were talking about the Russians again. Russell's wireless announcer's voice had gone. His face was sweaty and bright, reflecting the glow of his blazer. Ten years ago, Russell said, he had been a twenty-two-year-old lieutenant accompanying Colonel Frank Howley's advance party which had set off for Berlin in May 1945 to begin the occupation of the American sector.

'We thought the Russians were regular guys. They'd suffered losses in the millions. They were heroic, they were big, cheerful, vodka-swilling guys. And we'd been sending them mountains of equipment all through the war. So they just had to be our allies. That was before we met up with them. They came out and blocked our road sixty miles west of Berlin.

We got out of the trucks to greet them with open arms. We had gifts ready, we were high on the idea of the meeting.' Russell gripped Leonard's arm. 'But they were cold! Cold, Leonard! We had champagne ready, French champagne, but they wouldn't touch it. It was all we could do to make them shake us by the hand. They wouldn't let our party through unless we reduced it to fifty vehicles. They made us bivouac ten miles out of town. The next morning they let us in under close escort. They didn't trust us, they didn't like us. From day one they had us fingered for the enemy. They tried to stop us setting up our sector.

'And that's how it went on. They never smiled. They never wanted to make things work. They lied, they obstructed, they were cruel. Their language was always too strong, even when they were insisting on a technicality in some agreement. All the time we were saying, What the hell, they've had a crappy war, and they do things differently anyhow. We gave way, we were the innocents. We were talking about the United Nations and a new world order while they were kidnapping and beating up non-Communist politicians all over town. It took us almost a year to get wise to them. And you know what? Every time we met them, these Russian officers, they looked so fucking unhappy. It was like they expected to be shot in the back at any moment. They didn't even enjoy behaving like assholes. That's why I could never really hate them. This was policy. This crap was coming from the top.'

Glass poured more vodka. He said, 'I hate them. It's not a passion with me, I don't go crazy with it like some guys. You could say it's their system you got to hate. But there's no system without people to run it.' When he set his glass down he spilled a little drink. He pushed his forefinger into the puddle. 'What the Commies are selling is miserable, miserable, and inefficient. Now they're exporting it by force. I was in Budapest and Warsaw last year. Boy, have they found a way of minimizing happiness! They know it, but they don't stop. I mean, look at this place! Leonard, we brought you to the classiest joint in their sector. Look at it. Look at the people here. Look at them!' Glass was close to shouting.

Russell put out his hand. 'Take it easy Bob.'

Glass was smiling. 'It's OK. I'm not going to misbehave.'

Leonard looked around. Through the gloom he could see the heads of the customers bowed over their drinks. The barman and the waiter who were standing together at the bar had turned to face the other way. The two musicians were playing a chirpy marching song. This was his last clear impression. The following day he was to have no memory of leaving the Neva.

They must have made their way between the tables, ascended in the cramped lift, walked past the man in the brown uniform. By the car was the dark window of a shopping co-operative and inside, a tower of tinned pilchards, and above it a portrait of Stalin framed in red crêpe paper with a caption in big white letters which Glass and Russell translated in messy unison – *The unshakeable friendship of the Soviet and German peoples is a guarantee of peace and freedom.*

Then they were at the sector crossing. Glass had switched the engine off, torches were shone into the car while their papers were being examined, there were sounds of steel-tipped boots coming and going in the darkness. Then they were driving past a sign which said in four languages, *You are leaving the Democratic Sector of Berlin*, towards another which announced in the same languages, *You are now entering the British Sector.*

'Now we're in Wittenbergplatz,' Russell called from the front seat.

They drifted by a Red Cross nurse seated at the foot of a gigantic model of a candle with a real flame on top.

Russell was attempting to revive his travelogue. 'Collecting for the Spätheimkehrer, the late homecomers, the hundreds of thousands of German soldiers still held by the Russians . . .'

Glass said, 'Ten years! Forget it. They ain't coming back now.'

And the next thing was a table set among scores of others in a vast and clamorous space, and a band up on the stage almost drowning the voices with a jazzed-up version of Over There and a pamphlet attached to the menu, this time in only German and English with clumsy print that swayed and danced. '*Welcome to the Ballhouse of technical wonders, the place of all places of entertainments. One hundred thousand contacts are guaranteeing* . . .' The word was an echo he could not place. '. . . *are guaranteeing you the proper functioning of the Modern Table-Phone-System consisting of two hundred and fifty Table-Phone sets. The Pneumatic-Table-Mail-Service is posting every night thousands of letters or little presents from one visitor to the other – it is unique and amusing for everyone. The famous RESI-Water-Shows are magnificent in their beauty. It is amazing to think, that in a minute eight thousand litres of water are pressed through about nine thousand jets. For the play of these changing light effects there are necessary one hundred thousand coloured lamps.*'

Glass had his fingers in his beard and was smiling hugely. He said something, and had to repeat it at a shout. 'This is better!'

But it was too noisy to begin a conversation about the advantages of the Western sector. Coloured water spouted up in front of the band, and rose and fell and lurched from side to side. Leonard avoided looking at it. They were being sensible by drinking beer. As soon as the waiter had gone a girl appeared with a basket of roses. Russell bought one and presented it to Leonard who snapped off the stem and lodged the flower behind his ear. At the next table something came rattling down the pneumatic tube and two Germans in Bavarian jackets leaned forwards to examine the contents of a canister. A woman in a sequined mermaid suit was kissing the bandleader. There were wolf whistles and cheers. The band started up, the woman was handed a microphone. She took off her glasses and began to sing It's Too Darn Hot with a heavy accent. The Germans were looking disappointed. They stared in the direction of a table some fifty feet away where two giggling girls were collapsing in one another's arms. Beyond them was the packed dance floor. The woman sang Night and Day, Anything Goes, Just One of Those Things, and finally Miss Otis Regrets. Then everyone stood to cheer and stamp their feet and shout encore.

The band took a break and Leonard bought another round of beers. Russell took a good look round and said he was too drunk to pick up girls. They talked about Cole Porter and named their favourite songs. Russell said he knew someone whose father had been working at the hospital when they brought Porter in from his riding accident in '37. For some reason the doctors and nurses had been asked not to talk to the press. This led to a conversation about secrecy. Russell said there was far too much of it in the world. He was laughing. He must have known something about Glass's work.

Glass was serious in a punchy way. His head lolled back and he sighted Russell along his beard. 'You know what the best course I ever took at college was? Biology. We studied evolution. And I learned something important.' Now he included Leonard in his gaze. 'It helped me choose my career. For thousands, no, millions of years we had these huge brains, the neo-cortex, right? But we didn't speak to each other, and we lived like fucking pigs. There was nothing. No language, no culture, nothing. And then, suddenly, wham! It was there. Suddenly it was something we had to have, and there was no turning back. So why did it suddenly happen?'

Russell shrugged. 'Hand of God?'

'Hand of God my ass. I'll tell you why. Back then we all used to hang out together all day long doing the same thing. We lived in packs. So there was no need for language. If there was a leopard coming, there was no point saying, Hey man, what's coming down the track? A leopard! Everyone could see it, everyone was jumping up and down and screaming, trying to scare it off. But what happens when someone goes off on his own for a moment's privacy? When he sees a leopard coming, he knows something the others don't. And he knows they don't know. He has something they don't, he has a *secret*, and this is the beginning of his individuality, of his consciousness. If he wants to share his secret and run down the track to warn the other guys, then he's going to need to invent language. From there grows the possibility of culture. Or he can hang back and hope the leopard will take out the leadership that's been giving him a hard time. A secret plan, that means more individuation, more consciousness.'

The band was starting to play a fast, loud number. Glass had to shout his conclusion, 'Secrecy made us possible,' and Russell raised his beer to salute the theory.

A waiter mistook the gesture and was at his elbow, so a fresh round was ordered, and as the mermaid shimmered to the front of the band and the cheers rang out there was a harsh rattling at their table as a canister shot down the tube and smacked against the brass fixture and lodged there. They stared at it and no one moved.

Then Glass picked it up and unscrewed the top. He took out a folded piece of paper and spread it out on the table. 'My God,' he shouted, 'Leonard, it's for you.'

For one confused moment he thought it might be from his mother. He was owed a letter from England. And it was late, he thought, he hadn't said where he was going to be.

The three of them were leaning over the note. Their heads were blocking out the light. Russell read it aloud. 'An den jungen Mann mit der Blume in Haar.' To the young man with the flower in his hair. 'Mein Schöner, I have been watching you from my table. I would like it if you come and asked me to dance. But if you can't do this, I would be so happy if you would turn and smile in my direction. I am sorry to interfere, yours, table number 89.'

The Americans were on their feet casting around for the table, while Leonard remained seated with the paper in his hands. He read the German words over. The message was hardly a surprise. Now it was before him, it was more a matter of recognition for him, of accepting the inevitable. It had always been certain to start like this. If he was honest with himself, he had to concede that he had always known it really, at some level.

He was being pulled to his feet. They turned him about and forced him across the ballroom. 'Look, she's over there.' Across the heads, through the dense, rising cigarette smoke back-lit by stage lights, he could make out a woman sitting alone. Glass and Russell were pantomiming a fuss over his appearance, dusting down his jacket, straightening his tie, fixing the flower more securely behind his ear. Then they pushed him away, like a boat from a jetty. 'Go on!' they said. 'Atta boy!'

He was drifting towards her, and she was watching his approach. She had her elbow on the table, and she was supporting her chin with her hand. The mermaid was singing, Don't sit under zuh apple tree viz anyone else but me, anyone else but me. He thought, correctly as it turned out, that his life was about to change. When he was ten feet away she smiled. He arrived just as the band finished the song. He stood swaying slightly, with his hand on the back of a chair, waiting for the applause to die, and when it did Maria Eckdorf said in perfect but sweetly inflected English, 'Are we going to dance?' Leonard touched his stomach lightly, apologetically with his fingertips. Three entirely different liquids were sitting in there.

He said, 'Actually, would you mind if I sat down?' And so he did, and they immediately held hands, and many minutes passed before he was able to speak another word.

GÜNTER GRASS

THE DIVING DUCK

From

TOO FAR AFIELD

Translated by Krishna Winston

NO ONE WOULD ever have said 'Comrade Fonty,' even in jest; and because he had never been a card-carrying Party member, he made it a point of honor to be addressed as 'Herr.' Indeed, such boorish greetings as 'Hallo, Fonty, what's up?' would usually elicit the irritable response, 'Herr Wuttke to you, young man.'

His civilian name protected him, and he liked to remind people of the file courier, still working well past retirement age, whose contributions were often cited and in years past had even been highlighted on the bulletin board. Whether at the Cultural Union or in the Ministries Building, Theo Wuttke had the reputation of being an activist. With grumpy glee, he claimed to have been committed from the outset to the Workers' and Peasants' State, a loyal citizen. But to be thought of only as Theo Wuttke was as difficult as it was easy for him to convince us all as Fonty.

He was both. And in this twofold guise he was dangling on the hook. We who saw him wriggling at first merely suspected what later became a certainty: too many open files weighed down his extended existence. And because each file was significant enough to make him the subject, over time, of more or less tight surveillance, all that paper resulted in his being constantly shadowed. There was ample reason for assigning to him a person who, like Theo Wuttke, wasn't born yesterday. Thus two wreaths of immortelles should be awarded – and even a third, for we hardly fared better ourselves; nothing is more immortal than an archive.

As anxiously as we tried to stay out of Hoftaller's way, ducking down did not help; we and Fonty were in the same trap, for, like him, the archival collective went under the name of the Immortal, though for decades we were protected by an official finding that categorized us as secondary, and harmless to boot.

Hoftaller did not take the Archives seriously. He sneered at the gaps in our catalogue, persisted in viewing Fonty as a subject, and probably for that reason refused to cooperate with his own biographer, who wanted to snuff him out after more than a hundred years in the service. If he had responded to the biographical summons – 'Comrades! Come! Help me!' – and carried out his own sentence by placing his head under the guillotine, Fonty would have been better off, and we with him. We would have had more freedom of movement, just a little more. From 13 February 1955 on, the Archives would have been left in peace – by state directive. And along with the case 'Tallhover, Ludwig, b. 23 March 1819, former member of the secret police,' the Fonty case could have been filed away for good.

Or would this death, logical only in a literary sense, have provided no occasion for celebration after all? Might there have been reasons to mourn Tallhover's passing? Could it in fact be Fonty protesting toward the end of the biography, on page 283, demanding that it be continued – in a pinch even by us – because after being the subject of solicitous concern for so long he would have felt lonely, exposed, shadowless, like Peter Schlemihl, without his day-and-night-shadow?

Questions to which the facts have provided an answer. Fonty remained under pressure. He was dangling on the hook. And we, who sat in the Archives as though in house arrest, saw him struggling.

Nonetheless, the file courier Theo Wuttke managed to make little breaks for freedom. Time and again he slipped away from his pacesetter and overseer, the goad and barbed hook in his memory. He thought, at any rate, that after work he was free to take day-and-night-shadowless outings. Before the Wall came down, the Friedrichshain People's Park had offered him an outlet; but now, without having to take a running jump first, he could cross Potsdamer Platz, on whose cleared surface garish speculation was blooming, and not only since spring had broken out. After that he would stroll along the western end of Potsdamer Strasse, from shop window to shop window, as far as the pathetic remnant of Number 134C. There, in spite of the impenetrable traffic, he would hark back to garret-drudgery and the novels it had produced; or, indulging another habit, he would strike out from Potsdamer Platz, pursuing the repeatedly branching paths, punctuated by benches, that the Tiergarten had to offer, either to the goldfish pond or to the Amazon, or to the banks of Rousseau Island. Of course he walked with his stick. He had a youthful stride, as contemporary accounts tell us. And when he sat down, the walking stick lay beside him.

Most of the time Fonty sat there by himself, more furloughed than alone of his own free will. Had specific time limits been set for him? Had he had to wrest these solitary excursions from his day-and-night-shadow? Or is it possible that Hoftaller gave in for pedagogical reasons, granting him unconditional permission for abrupt turnabouts, often in midsentence – 'Company is good, solitude better!' – because this was the only way Fonty could adjust to the new freedom peculiar to the West?

Their temporary partings usually took place right after

work, on street corners – for instance, at the corner of Otto-Grotewohl-Strasse and Leipziger Strasse. Hoftaller intended to go straight, while Fonty was turning left. After a curt good-bye – 'Till tomorrow, then' – he struck out on his own. Hoftaller stood still, confirming, 'Right, till tomorrow.' He gazed after his charge and his billowing scarf for a time, then went on his way; Fonty, meanwhile, was already putting distance between them.

Here we must admit that both of them sometimes succumbed to an urge characteristic of men of their age, and such was the case on this occasion, too, as they took leave of one another. Farting between one step and the next, each went in the direction he considered his own, one with the swinging gait of the eternal youth, assertively bouncing his walking stick on the pavement, the other with small, bustling steps. Even as they drew farther apart, they remained sure of one another. They would be reunited by the next day at the latest, when Hoftaller got onto the paternoster, for they had no lack of shared work. From floor to floor, the file courier Theo Wuttke was in demand in the Ministries Building, and, all the way up to the attic, where the sofa stood, always obliging and accessible: 'You're needed, Fonty – it's urgent. Room 718, Transportation Division, been waiting a long time, and in the Personnel Department some files are piling up, too. . . .'

Only on Tiergarten benches was he alone. Even when a pensioner sat down next to him, and the two of them tallied up the afflictions of old age for one another or maligned their doctors as bunglers, solitude was assured him. Although he amiably countered 'asthma' with 'nervous prostration,' the chatter remained on the surface, and he could keep his background to himself.

Nature, here tamed into an expansive park, helped him

be alone, even in company. Yet that was not the only reason Fonty loved the Tiergarten. We shall see that within this artistically designed landscape he was unmistakable from the very beginning.

When Theo Wuttke had parted from the overseer he jokingly referred to as his 'guardian angel,' and had slipped out of his file-courier identity like a costume, he sallied forth, as he had throughout the month of April, now in splendid May weather. With the exception of a rolled newspaper poking out of his right coat pocket, he resembled, with his hat and walking stick, a caricature of his predecessor that had conveyed the latter's unique features so tellingly that a good twenty years after the Immortal's officially recorded death it could be printed in the satirical journal *Simplicissimus* as the latest thing; in the Archives we have preserved a copy as evidence.

Above the caption – 'Is this how Brandenburg's aristocracy looks these days?' – there he is, in the flesh, striding along with his walking stick in his right hand. The left arm is crooked across his back. Without displaying its plaid, the often cited Scottish scarf is draped casually over one shoulder, falling to either side of the left pocket in his loose-fitting overcoat. His face shadowed by the curved brim of his artist's hat, he gazes into the distance, past his immediate surroundings. The bushy mustache beneath his boldly molded nose is matched by his hair, which hangs in strands past his ears and over the nape of his neck. An image suggestive of the lord of a manor, distantly resembling even Bismarck in the Sachsenwald or Dubslav von Stechlin, who is said to have looked like Bismarck. And that is why a bourgeois couple, descending a flight of stairs only a few steps away, their two rambunctious children dashing on ahead, are posing the obviously parvenu question concerning the current appearance of Brandenburg's aristocracy.

All this the caricaturist T. T. Heine captured on paper, with a sure eye for contours and great economy of detail. He knew what an antiquated figure the Immortal had cut in the Tiergarten, and what amused astonishment he had aroused there. And we know that it is not only in *Stechlin* that the Tiergarten provides a backdrop for walks and coach rides. It also promises peace and quiet to Waldemar von Haldern; the young count, who lives nearby on Zeltenstrasse, goes to the Tiergarten in search of a bench, there to put his indecision to rest, an end to his relationship with Stine, and a bullet to his head: 'A fresh breeze was blowing, tempering the heat, but from the flower beds wafted the delicate scent of mignonette, while across the way, in Kroll's Music Garden, a concert was just commencing. . . .' The Music Garden and the Kroll Opera, built there later, no longer exist. Much has been cleared away, but the Tiergarten manages to renew itself time and again. Fonty was a witness to that.

His image was firmly established from the beginning; only the man-made landscape around him had been altered, either in cautious phases or at one stroke. Until the Wall went up, the Tiergarten was accessible to Fonty, in spite of the city's division into occupation zones. But then for almost three decades the walking paths had remained off limits to all those who, like him, had to make do with the eastern part of Berlin, proclaimed the capital of the Workers' and Peasants' State.

Now he was astonished to see how lushly the postwar plantings had branched and twigged out in both height and width. The fast-growing poplars and alders, the first plantings on the devastated expanse, had in the meantime given way to beech and oak, maple and weeping willow. Here single trees on tree-lined meadows, there grovelike stands of trees, elsewhere actual woods, lakeshore plantings, pruned shrubbery. Of course there was no shortage of the conifers and birches native to Brandenburg's sandy soil. And the entire park, which extended from the Brandenburg Gate to the Landwehr Canal and the Zoo beyond, was, as the urban planner Lenné had originally conceived it, crisscrossed by tree-lined avenues. In the northern part of the park, seven such avenues fanned out from Zeltenplatz, planted with chestnuts, elms, plane trees, and so forth; in the southern part, avenues crossed the Little Star and Great Star or else were shaded by double rows, like the Hofjägerallee, which likewise led to the Great Star. Yet among the traffic-jammed motorways and on both sides of the former Avenue of Victory, later renamed Avenue of the Seventeenth of June, a network of quietly meandering footpaths opened up vistas of meadows, ponds, and lakes. They led to the Rose Garden or over Queen Luise Bridge, and made it possible to stroll from monument to monument, from Goethe to Lessing, from Moltke to Bismarck, and on into the English Garden, which bordered the grounds of Bellevue Palace and the nearby Academy of the Arts, dear to the western half of the city. Until recently the Academy had preserved its peace and quiet, but since the fall of the Wall it had been roused by the spirit of the times and robbed of its smugness; the eastern half of the city likewise harbored an Academy of the Arts, and now that they were condemned to unification, both institutions, which had avoided each other for decades, were looking back, with an embarrassed grimace, to a Prussian institution whose secretary had once been the Immortal, although only for half a year – that was how quickly conditions at the Academy had come to disgust him.

Fonty returned again and again to certain spots. He liked to stroll from the Friedrich Wilhelm III monument to the Lortzing monument and try out various benches to see if he could find an unobstructed view of Rousseau Island. And as we know, there was a favorite bench, half in shade, with an elderberry bush behind its backrest.

Sometimes he walked to Fasanerieallee and the bronze sculptures that represented the rabbit chase and the fox hunt, then on to New Lake, which fed the Landwehr Canal and was alive with rowboats, starting in early May. Here he watched from bankside benches and was filled with thoughts of rowing excursions in which he had participated or which had found their way into literature – the Easter Monday boat trip in Stralau, for instance, or later the boat ride on the Spree at Hankel's Depot – but at the very beginning it was a quiet arm of the Elbe where a twosome went rowing; and always Lene Nimptsch was present, either as premonition or posthumous experience – that Lene whom Frau Dörr affectionately called 'Leneken.'

These were his favorite spots. Fonty seldom crossed Hofjägerallee to see a sculpture called 'Folk Song,' for near it, by the edge of the Tiergarten, he would have been forced to see himself, in the form of a marble statue, gazing out hatless from his round pedestal, with a damaged walking stick and an upright Prussian carriage.

He did not want to encounter himself as a petrified civil servant. Better to take the Great Way time and again to the quiet waters around Rousseau Island. There, after sitting still for a while – with the blooming or ripe elderberry at his back – he could enjoy this special contemplation of changing times; for example, those around 1836, when his apprenticeship in Wilhelm Rose's White Swan Apothecary Shop began. That was shortly after he, still in trade school, first laid eyes on Emilie Rouanet, at the house of his father's brother, Uncle August, that incorrigible money-borrower. Because of her illegitimate birth, she bore the sorrowful last name of Kummer, after her foster father. A child in a becoming poke bonnet, but with an air of wildness about her, whom he must have startled, as indeed the girl startled him at first sight. Even in those days he could have taken the girl by the hand and, if the child were willing, led her along sandy riding paths through the still-unfinished Tiergarten until they came in view of the island, named even that early for a philosopher; just as in the spring of 1846, the year after their engagement, he had searched with Emilie Rouanet-Kummer for a place to sit in the Tiergarten, and had found a bench with a view of the island dedicated to that raving pedagogue and practitioner of enlightenment.

Fonty saw himself in retrospect at the side of the young woman of twenty-one, who no longer resembled a wild, black-eyed goatherd from the Abruzzi but now sized up the world with gray-blue eyes like a normal citizen of Branden-burg and wore her chestnut hair demurely piled on her head: ripe for marriage.

At that time, the layout of the Tiergarten, designed by the landscape architect Lenné, was considered complete. According to his plans, the area around Rousseau Island had achieved its definitive form. Everything was greening on schedule. And the Great Way led past the lake to Great Star Avenue, in the same configuration as forty years later, when daughter Martha, known as Mete, would occasionally accompany her father through the Tiergarten to his favorite spots; but as Fonty rewound to this period and saw himself with Mete in several longer sequences, he could not stop a time shift from zooming in on nine-year-old Martha Wuttke as she dashed across the path, followed by Theo

Wuttke, calling out again and again, 'Come back, Mete!'

That was shortly before the Wall went up. Father and daughter had been visiting her grandfather, Max Wuttke, in his cellar apartment by Rabbits' Run. Then he saw himself again, tearing through the Tiergarten alone, this time in the guise of a distraught Young Turk. That was a few weeks after the funeral staged for those who had died on the barricades in March '48, at which even the king had been forced to doff his hat.

Incidentally, the marriage to Emilie Rouanet-Kummer took place a good two and a half years later, on 16 October 1850, and the reception was held on the edge of the Tiergarten, near Bellevuestrasse, in a restaurant called the Georgian Garden, a place that attracted many guests, both before and after the revolution, with its sheltered location and excellent food. The Tunnel brethren had taken up a collection for the gift. Of his friends from the early years in Leipzig and Dresden, only Wolfsohn was present. Three decades later, when the moment arrived to celebrate the anniversary at 134C Potsdamer Strasse, one of those tell-all letters noted, 'Only a few friends showed any interest in what has become our "Thirty Years' War." . . .'

But from his favorite bench Fonty saw more than family comings and goings. He saw himself with Lepel at his side, saw Storm and Zöllner, bumped into Heyse and Spielhagen, swaggered about with Ludwig Pietsch; later, much later, he shared a bench with Schlenther and Brahm: endless theater gossip.

In changing seasons he saw himself, between and after those three military campaigns soon dubbed the Wars of Unification, weighed down by various manuscripts, each filled with battle and landscape descriptions – representing years of drudgery that earned him nothing but annoyance

– whose hurly-burly of words he nonetheless hauled to the Tiergarten, whence he hauled it home again, rather the worse for the effort, to a succession of residences. Not until he had the Academy rubbish behind him and had finally, to Emilie's dismay, become a freelance writer, did he see himself setting out with cargo of a different sort: novels bursting with deftly captured conversations were the Tiergarten booty the Immortal now carried up to his garret on Potsdamer Strasse, a late bloomer at sixty, then on his way to seventy and beyond.

Before the Storm came to fruition here. During walks, his mind continued to tweak at whatever novellas and novels he had in the hopper: 'I'm in favor of headings, which is to say resting places, and that goes for life as well; I have no use for parks without benches. . . .' But when the family told him, 'Chapter headings are old-fashioned,' he suggested to his publisher that all the chapters in *L'Adultera* have numbers; but the headings remained. And when all the 'ands' in *Grete Minde* and *Ellernklipp* came in for criticism, he replied, '. . . I consider myself a stylist who derives his style from the subject matter, and that explains the many "ands." . . .'

And so on to the very last. *Effi Briest*, appearing in serialization, had hardly met her sad end when he was already out roaming around with old Stechlin: in overcoat and with walking stick and hat, striding purposefully from Number 134C toward the Queen Luise Bridge, conversing all the while with Rex and Czako, keeping an ear out for witticisms, repeatedly pouring on Gundermann's 'grist for the mills of social democracy,' warning time and again of the 'great worldwide conflagration,' and provoking Domina Adelheid in Wutz Cloister with cutting remarks, for which she repaid her brother Dubslav, old Stechlin, in the same coin: 'Keep your French to yourself. It always depresses me.'

And then for a long time nothing more. The silence of the grave. Monuments. The literary estate unloaded by his son for a paltry eight thousand reichmarks. Assiduous professors parsing and paraphrasing. His devastating judgment on such pedants: 'Bone-dry gibberers – they're supposed to support us, and instead just wreck everything. . . .' To some he was too Prussian, to others not Prussian enough. Each hacked out the slice that appealed to him: sometimes he was stylized as the 'rambler through the Mark Brandenburg,' sometimes abbreviated to the 'serenely detached observer,' sometimes celebrated as the balladeer, sometimes rediscovered as a revolutionary or dismissed on partisan grounds. Schools were named after him, even apothecary shops. And further misuse and abuse. Already he was dismissed in schoolbooks, consigned to the dustbin of the ages, threatened with oblivion, when at last this young man in Luftwaffe blue turned up, sat down on this particular bench in the Tiergarten, alone or with a companion, and proceeded to become a mouthpiece, for him, and for him alone, the 'Immortal.'

The name's Wuttke, Theo no less. Hails from Neuruppin and offers his date of birth, the thirtieth of December 1919, as proof of identity. Has tales old and new from France to tell his fiancée, Emmi Hering, who wears her hair combed high, and in her sprigged dress inclines to plumpness. Initially only Gravelotte and Sedan, but then, in quick succession, lightning victories, pincer operations, Guderian's tanks, air supremacy all the way to the Pyrenees, Sedan and Metz falling this time almost without a struggle, crossing the Marne, and on to Paris, Paris! And then the distant view from the Atlantic coast, across the beaches of Normandy and Brittany at low tide to England, the hated cousin. And, dotting the coast of France, the islands, one of which is Oléron, with special significance: many richly atmospheric mood pieces.

Time and again he returns, on leave from the front or on assignment, escorts his betrothed Emmi on his arm through the Rose Garden, past the Lortzing statue, and has already walked with her once around the pond and over bridges, succumbing completely to the pedagogic enchantment of the island: freedom and virtue clash, or give birth to committees of public safety and death by guillotine; Robespierre was Rousseau's most obedient disciple. . . .

Yet the reports the airman gives his fiancée, who is pretty and something of a chatterbox, reports whispered in a style so polished you might think he was reading from a text, are out searching for traces in the crumbling hamlet of Domrémy. There he delivered literary lectures for enlisted men and officers: Where Schiller's 'Virgin of Orléans' was born . . . Why 'La Pucelle' is immortal . . . And how the Immortal, in search of Jeanne d'Arc during the war of '70–'71, with his Red Cross armband and that unfortunate pistol, was nabbed as a Prussian spy and ended up a prisoner of war.

Time and again he returns, with fresh travel impressions, which his fiancée types for him. Accounts from Besançon, Lyon, and finally from the Cévennes, where he tracked down Huguenot hiding places, putting himself in harm's way. Yet he continues to file those reports, confident of victory and devoted to things cultural, even though, before receiving his final marching orders, he found the Tiergarten badly battered, retreat on all the fronts since Stalingrad, his fiancée Emmi pregnant, and Aunt Pinchen nagging them to get married. . . .

The moment came when the airman and war correspondent Theo Wuttke failed to return. Not until all the trees in the Tiergarten had been felled and all the bomb craters had filled with water, not until all the statues had been reduced to

305

torsos, not until the benches, Queen Luise Bridge, and the Kroll Opera were destroyed, not until all the glories around Zeltenplatz lay in ruins, and only the Victory Column remained standing, like some kind of bad joke – not until the war was over did he return, from the French prison camp in Bad Kreuznach, emaciated and shaky in his tattered uniform, searching for his fiancée, whom he found, with his baby son, Georg, under Aunt Pinchen's bomb-damaged roof, and married retroactively in October of 1945.

Immediately after the ceremony, the young couple had to go off to scrounge for firewood, for Aunt Pinchen's coal cellar was bare except for blackish dust. And since all that remained of the Tiergarten, for the Wuttkes and hundreds of thousands of other Berliners, was scraps of firewood, even roots were hacked out; nothing was left.

These and other flashbacks came to him on his favorite bench. Having first seen himself out in search of the last stubs and stumps with ax, handsaw, and rickety pushcart, he was moved almost to tears by a family tableau: Like ten thousand others, he and Emmi were digging up a plot with pick and spade, while baby Georg trotted back and forth between his parents with his toy shovel. They were planting potatoes, sowing turnip seed; from April '46 on, the clear-cut Tiergarten was chopped into allotments all the way from the Brandenburg Gate to the flak bunker by the Zoo.

This was done by official decree – that's how great the need was. And then came the terrible winter of '46–'47. Many died, including Pauline Piontek, née Hering. Only by two years did she outlive her younger brother, Emmi Wuttke's stepfather, who, along with his wife, had most likely met his death in encircled Breslau. Aunt Pinchen was not even sixty when she left her apartment to the Wuttkes: three and a half rooms, plus kitchen and bath, in Berlin's Prenzlauer Berg district, a circumstance that made them both happy for a while.

Only now, after the lean years, did Fonty return from his excursions into the past. With astonishment he observed that the dream of master gardener Peter Josef Lenné, which neither the skinflint king nor the Berliners' destructive frenzy had been able to snuff out, had finally been realized, after numerous stages of planting, plotting paths, channeling water: Round about him everything was clothed in its May finery; thousands of buds were bursting before his eyes; birdsong, so richly blended that even the blackbird had trouble making her cadences heard. Behind him the elderberry was beginning to unfurl its fans of bloom. And because the waters around Rousseau Island were similarly lively, Fonty found himself tempted to continue Lenné's dream in installments, as if nothing had happened, as if there had been neither war nor devastation, as if the park landscape would remain unscathed in its beauty, as indeed it had always been a feast for his eyes and a refuge. But suddenly everything seemed foreign to him: children from another world – two Turkish girls with sternly knotted kerchiefs – stood before him and the Tiergarten bench, where he thought he had been sitting since his earliest years as an apothecary's apprentice.

Both girls wore a solemn expression. They seemed to be ten or twelve. Both the same height and with the same solemnity; they gazed at him without wanting to take in his smile. Since they said nothing, he did not want to risk speaking either. Only birdsong and distant shouts over the water. Far off in the distance, the roar of the city. For a long time foreignness hovered between Fonty and the Turkish girls. The kerchiefs framed dark-skinned oval faces. Four eyes remained fixed on him. Slow blinks. Now even the blackbird was silent. Fonty was about to formulate a friendly question to break the silence when one of the girls said in German, with barely a trace of a Berlin accent: 'Would you be so kind as to betray to us what time it is?'

At once everything seemed less foreign. Fonty fumbled under his coat for his pocket watch, drew it out with a glint of gold, read off the time without having to reach for his glasses, and betrayed it to the girls, who thanked him with a nice little bob, turned, and went on their way. After a few steps they broke into a run, as fast as if they had to get the betrayed time to safety as quickly as possible.

Alone with himself again, Fonty thought he would be able to gaze at Rousseau Island without wandering thoughts, or perhaps without any thoughts at all, and watch the ducks, two swans, and other waterfowl, among them a diving duck; but he wasn't alone for long.

Not that anyone plumped down beside him on the bench and began to talk about the weather. No pensioner, no arthritic grandma, and no wet nurse still in residence from the previous century – 'The women from the Spree Woods all smell of sour milk' – turned up to prey on his nerves. No actual person had to sit down beside him to persuade him to recount anecdotes and pick to pieces entire dinner parties. Even sitting by himself, he was caught up in conversation.

This time the tone was not chatty. Compelled to listen, he had Hoftaller's droning clerk's voice in his ear, not so much stern as dryly calculating the weight of evidence. As Tallhover he picked up where it hurt: with the Herwegh Society. The Leipzig period. And already, without even having to leave Saxony, he was in Dr. Gustav Struve's Salamonis Apothecary Shop, and promptly brought up the initially revolutionary, later romantically inclined gardener's daughter Magdalena

Strehlenow, rowboat excursions on the Elbe – Dresden and the consequences: 'Come now, it wasn't as bad as all that. In a pinch, one could tap Lepel for a loan. One was free, had that year of sentry duty with the Kaiser Franz Guards behind one, likewise the unplanned holiday, that disastrous two-week detour to England. And the apothecary's license was finally in hand, the state boards having been passed with distinction – congratulations! A more or less happy engagement, without, it must be said, the future bride's having been let in on the Dresden secrets. Those boat rides were suppressed out of cowardice, likewise the love-crazed coupling and the squalling of infants. Instead our Forty-eighter brandished a rusty rifle. Being there is everything! Even so, we didn't step in. No matter how some of the Tunnel doggerel and later the conspiratorial Herwegh Society nettled us, nothing happened, not even a reprimand. Well, because we had our hands full, me especially. As superintendent of detectives I'd been assigned to the Georg Herwegh case. He was spawning epigones wherever he went, and that with an arrest warrant out for him that my biographer rightfully describes as "ridiculous." But when the *Dresdner Zeitung* published a series of political dispatches in twenty-nine installments, with the author identified only by a cipher, we found ourselves forced to start a file after all: code word "Fontaine." The pieces were partly overwrought, partly inflammatory, each and every one aimed at Prussia's police state – nothing new there, to be sure, but this flailing about was certainly dangerous. . . .'

Fonty heard all this in his mind's ear. Any passerby who had noticed him on the park bench and paused to listen would have witnessed his head-shaking and grimacing: an old man at odds with himself and others. Now and then he exclaimed, 'Balderdash!' And: 'Autodidacts always exaggerate!' He protested: 'Wrong, Tallhover! Even Pietsch

309

confirmed that I spared neither myself nor others in *Between Twenty and Thirty*. . . .' He offered a detailed response: 'Glad to hear your memory's so colossally faulty. Our first contact occurred not before but soon after my wedding. In the late autumn of '50, shortly before the "Literary Cabinet" was dissolved. We met here in the Tiergarten, specifically at the In den Zelten rowboat-rental stand. You were bound and determined to go out on the water. But I was in no mood for rowing. So we went and sat in the Moritzhof beer garden. The last chestnuts were falling. White beer and falling leaves. And after I'd taken one swallow, my dossier appeared on the table, not thick, but thick enough. . . .'

Even if Fonty fell silent after such explanations, or pretended to be interested only in mallard families and one particularly enterprising diving duck, he did not succeed in being deaf as well as dumb. Someone kept talking at him. If not Hoftaller, then Tallhover. His constant carping could not be switched off: 'It wasn't in late fall, after your latest foolhardy adventure, your failed attempt to play the war hero on the side of Schleswig against the Danes, but rather at the end of August '50 that I had to reel you in. You're right about the Tiergarten rendezvous. What a hot day! At any rate, before the wedding the groom was already assured of our support. From September on, you were on the government payroll as a reviewer for the *Literary Cabinet*. High time you were taken under the wing. In every respect. In your private life, your strict Emmi saw to that, and officially you were supervised by Herr von Merckel, your patron, true, but also our man. The kindest censor imaginable, such as you hardly find anymore in our service. Knew a lot – well-rounded and cultured, a model I could never live up to. He could rhyme army with democracy, but also had other strings to his bow. His solicitous policy of paying sparingly but regularly worked like a charm. At any rate, your young wife was delighted to be able to count on a steady income at last. And just a year later George, the son and heir, was there. . . .'

Meanwhile, out there amidst the mallards the diving duck was demonstrating an alternative. 'Let him blither on,' Fonty may have said to himself. 'After all, my collected poems did get published. And as for Merckel, a friendly and collegial relationship was developing. . . .'

'But of course. Family to family, later with regular exchange of letters. No one cared as lovingly for your poor Theo, neglected by his father, as the Merckels. No wonder, then, with that kind of protection, that a position became available, at the Central Press Office, to be exact, a minimally camouflaged censorship agency to which our botched existence had to adjust – despite all the yammering at home – especially since after Rastatt his last revolutionary cock feathers had been plucked. Hinkeldey was the name of Berlin's police commissioner. . . .'

The tufted duck had dived out of sight, and suddenly resurfaced somewhere else. Fonty let himself be taken by surprise. After every dive he bet against himself – and lost. He would have loved to be similarly unpredictable, out of sight, now here, now there, at his will and pleasure – even if only for minutes at a time: 'All frightfully true, Tallhover! Sold my soul to see a wish fulfilled. To escape from those dry strictures – finally. To London by way of Cologne, Brussels, Ghent, and Ostende, even with ministerial shackles on my ankles. My first real trip to England – the very first one, those two weeks on borrowed money, doesn't count. Even with commissioned reports to file, I had to do better as the bread-winner – gave German lessons! That's how poorly I was paid. That's how wretchedly Prussia rewarded my little betrayal.

What more do you want, Tallhover! You eternal snoop! Why don't you just beat it? We're not on the interrogation couch now. You old regurgitator! Scram, sir! Keep your distance, will you! This is my Tiergarten. This was always my favorite bench, Rousseau Island is mine, mine to feast my eyes on. And that's my diving duck!'

With his left hand Fonty was making shooing motions, as if flies were buzzing around him. With his right hand he was clutching his walking stick so tightly that he trembled. An angry old man flailing in the air.

Turkish families passed in their appointed order: the men first, then the wives and children. A steady stream of Turks with shopping nets and plastic bags. From the women's and girls' head scarves – many of them black or white, some motley – Fonty tried to derive a significance analogous to the Scottish color spectrum.

But after yet another extended Turkish family had passed without a moment's glance at his struggle with his demon, he exclaimed, 'Listen, Tallhover! Besides me, the Tiergarten belongs to those people. The paths, the meadows, the benches, everything. This is indubitably Turkish terrain. Read the paper: After Istanbul and Ankara, Berlin is the third largest Turkish city. And they just keep coming. Even you folks can't impose control on that many. Got it? The Turks are the new Huguenots! They'll create their own order here, they'll set up a system; yours capitulated yesterday, and mine long ago. To be sure, before I was made censorship's handmaiden, I wrote to my friend Friedrich Witte: "I despise this cowardly, stupid, and mean-spirited policy, and three-and sixfold the wretches who lend themselves to defending this swindle, intoning daily: Herr von Manteuffel is a great statesman! You could offer me my previous position again: I don't want it . . ." – but six months later I had no choice but to confess to Lepel: "Sold myself to the reactionaries today for thirty pieces of silver monthly. A decent person simply has no way to survive nowadays. I am making my debut as a hired hack for Adler's paper with a poem in ottava rima – in praise of Manteuffel. Contents: the prime minister crushes the dragon of revolution beneath his heel!" Yet when I was in London, and Ambassador von Bunsen, a liberal of course, wanted to incite me against Manteuffel, I resisted, despite my sympathies, and wrote to my Emilie, who was naturally terrified that I might just jettison all the rubbish, "To live at Manteuffel's expense and write against him would heighten the moral shabbiness. . . ." Then, back in Berlin, the second child died before I had a chance to see him. A wretched business. No longer a drug pusher but a scribbler under surveillance. And that for the duration, whether with the Reich Aviation Ministry or the Cultural Union. You folks always had your hand in, making sure my thoroughly botched existence . . . Even now, with the Wall gone . . . I'm graciously permitted to haul files around, and have to look the other way while you . . . And never alone, not even in the paternoster . . . And if it weren't for the Tiergarten, all these Turks, and the diving duck . . .'

After that Fonty just went on muttering to himself. He cut a fart, then another. Sitting there, his head with its wispy white hair bowed, he propped both hands on his walking stick, his nervously trembling lower lip covered by the upper one. Aged, as if the end were near; no thought seemed to animate him. Only flight – down, down, down into the past.

A person walking slowly past him would have been able to make out single words, even half-sentences; and we archivists would have been in a position to decode the flow of his speech. Much took the form of quotations from the

Immortal's travel narrative 'Beyond the Tweed,' written after his third and longest sojourn in England, when he visited Scotland with his friend Lepel: 'As we strolled down High Street . . . at every corner, sons of the highlands in kilt and plaid . . . presumably recruiters for the Highlanders. . . .'

Then he was no longer pounding the sidewalks of Edinburgh but was living in the days of King James IV. The issue was chivalry and 'Bell-the-Cat.' With a schooled ear, one could make out some of the words: 'At the court of King James was Spens of Kilspindie . . . In Stirling Castle as the sweet wine flowed . . . The House of Douglas's growing might . . . The blow was deadly, it struck to the heart. . . .'

Then he merely watched the diving duck – now you see him, now you don't. The repetition never grew tiresome. Even when he got up, approached the bank, and fed the mallards bread crusts from his coat pocket, he was preoccupied with the tufted duck and its tricks. Nothing could distract him. True, stuck in his other coat pocket was a rolled-up *Tagesspiegel* with the election results from the provinces panting for annexation; but Fonty had taken leave of the Workers' and Peasants' State. Current events that he witnessed as Theo Wuttke – when they thrust themselves upon him – did not count in the Tiergarten; there he was on a journey backward in time; in Scotland again, from Stirling Castle to Loch Katrine . . .

WLADIMIR KAMINER

BUSINESS CAMOUFLAGE

From

RUSSIAN DISCO

Translated by Michael Hulse

ONE DAY, I chanced to venture forth as far as Wilmersdorf. I wanted to show my friend Ilia Kitup, a poet from Moscow, some typical nooks of Berlin.

It was already midnight, we were hungry, and we ended up in a Turkish snack bar. The two men who worked there evidently had nothing to do and were placidly drinking their tea.

The music from the speakers sounded familiar to my friend. He recognised the voice of a famous Bulgarian female singer and sang along with a couple of verses.

'Do the Turks always listen to Bulgarian music at night?' I asked Kitup, who studied anthropology in Moscow and is thoroughly familiar with the ways of these people. He got into a conversation with the two men at the counter.

'They aren't Turks, they're Bulgarians pretending to be Turks,' explained Kitup, who had a little Bulgarian blood in his own veins too. 'It's probably their business camouflage.' 'But why should they do that?' I asked. 'Berlin is already too diverse,' the men told us. 'There's no point in complicating the situation unnecessarily. The consumer is used to being served by Turks at a Turkish snack bar, even if they're really Bulgarians.'

The very next day I went to a Bulgarian restaurant I had recently discovered. I had a notion that the Bulgarians there were really Turks, but they turned out to be the genuine Bulgarian article. The Italians in the Italian restaurant next door, however, proved to be Greek. They had taken over the restaurant and then signed on for evening classes in Italian, they told me. When you go to an Italian restaurant, you at least expect the staff to talk a bit of Italian to you. A little later I went to a Greek restaurant. My instinct was spot on: the staff turned out to be Arabs.

Berlin is a mysterious city. Nothing is as it first appears. In the sushi bar in Oranienburger Strasse there was a girl from the Buryat Republic behind the counter. From her I learned that most sushi bars in Berlin are in the ownership of Jews, who have arrived here not from Japan but from America. This is not unusual in the gastronomic field. Just as cheap tinned carrots from the Aldi supermarket are served up as hand-trimmed Gascony fruits of the earth, the principle remains that nothing is the real thing here, and everyone is at the same time himself and someone else.

I remained on the trail and continued my investigations. Every day I learned more. The Chinese at the snack bar across from my house are Vietnamese. The Indian in Rykestrasse is in reality a Tunisian of conviction, from Carthage. And the man who runs the Afro-American bar with all the voodoo stuff on the walls is – a Belgian.

Even those last bulwarks of authenticity, the Vietnamese cigarette vendors, are little more than a cliché created by television series and police crackdowns. But still, everyone involved maintains the illusion, even though every police-man knows that most of these so-called Vietnamese are from Inner Mongolia.

I was extremely surprised by what my investigations had brought to light, and continued them all around the city, in quest of the last remaining unfaked truth. Above all, I wanted to know who the people known as Germans really are, the ones who run those typical German restaurants that serve knuckle of pork with sauerkraut, those little cosy pubs called Olly's or Scholly's or some such, where the beer always costs half what it costs elsewhere. But there I encountered a wall of silence. My instinct tells me I am on the track of a big story. But I cannot get any further with it on my own. If anyone can really say what lies concealed behind the attractive façade of a 'German' pub, do please get in touch. I'd be grateful for any help.

CHLOE ARIDJIS

From

BOOK OF CLOUDS

AUGUST 11, 1986
BERLIN

I SAW HITLER at a time when the Reichstag was little more than a burnt, skeletal silhouette of its former self and the Brandenburg Gate obstructed passage rather than granted it. It was an evening when the moral remains of the city bobbed up to the surface and floated like driftwood before sinking back down to the seabed to further splinter and rot.

Berlin was the last stop on our European tour – we'd worked our way up from Spain, through France, Belgium and the Netherlands – and soon we would be flying home, back across the Atlantic, to start the new school year. My two brothers, still thrumming with energy, lamented that we had to leave. In every town and city they'd wandered off into the night and not returned until breakfast, answering in cranky monosyllables, between sips of coffee, whenever anyone commented on the amount of money being wasted on hotel rooms. My two sisters, on the other hand, weighed down by stories and souvenirs, were desperate to unload, and my parents too felt weary and ready for home. Not to mention that we'd used up 60 percent of the money we'd just inherited from my grandfather, and the remaining 40 had allegedly been set aside for our ever-expanding deli.

On our final evening, after an early dinner, our parents announced they were taking us to a demonstration against the Berlin Wall to protest twenty-five years of this 'icon of the Cold War.' Wherever you went in Berlin, sooner or later you would run into it, even on the day we visited Hansa Studios where Nick Cave and Depeche Mode used to record, or the secondhand shop that sold clothes by the kilo. No matter where you went – east, west, north, south – before long you hit against the intractable curtain of cement and were able to go no further. That was our impression, anyway, so we figured that we too might as well protest against this seemingly endless structure that limited even *our* movement, though we were just seven tourists visiting the city for the first time.

When we arrived at the demonstration there were already thousands of people gathered on the west side of the Brandenburg Gate, young couples, old couples, scampering children, punks with dogs, Goths, women with buzz cuts, men in blue overalls – a cross section, looking back, of what West Berlin had been in those days. Most people remained standing but there were also large groups spread out on the pavement, singing and chanting and passing around bottles of beer. Two nights before, we'd heard, a human chain had started to form along the Wall with an aim to cover all 155 kilometers.

On the east side, meanwhile, men in grey uniforms and steel helmets were marching up and down Karl-Marx-Allee. I envisioned dramatic clashes between metal and flesh, order and chaos, homogeny and diversity, but I knew that in real life these clashes were far more abstract. My parents had wanted to take us across the border to show us 'a true portrait of Communism' but there had been a mysterious problem with our visas so we'd stayed in the West all week, left to imagine as best we could what life was like on the other side, ever more intrigued by notions of 'this side' and 'beyond.'

People continued to arrive. The singing and chanting grew louder and I could hardly hear when anyone in my family leaned over to say something, as though on that night our language had been put on hold and German was the only means of communication. But there were other ways of having a voice, and before long we had joined the lengthy chain following the Wall and I found myself clasping the hand of a man with a ponytail and a black leather jacket until one of my brothers insisted on changing places with me. I tried to imagine the thousands of people across West Berlin to whom we would be connected through this gesture of solidarity but the thought was dizzying so I focused instead on the punks playing nearby with their dogs, as they threw what looked like battered tennis shoes, which the dogs would race to retrieve. The punks would then throw the bait in another direction, every now and then missing and hitting someone on the head or shoulder, the sight of which triggered boisterous rounds of laughter.

Twilight came on. Some of the organizers walked through the crowd passing out white candles. A number of people declined and flicked on their lighters instead. Against the sea of lights the Reichstag looked even gloomier and more forsaken and the Brandenburg Gate, with its goddess of Victory and twelve Doric columns, doubly silenced by dusk. Not far from us an old punk with a torch jumped onto the Wall and screamed some words into the East, rabid words, though we couldn't understand what he was saying. On the other side, my mother told us, invisible eyes would be following his every movement. There didn't seem to be anyone in the watchtowers across the way yet we imagined men in round caps with cat slit eyes surveying the whole spectacle, ready to pounce should any of us trespass one inch into their territory.

We stayed at the demonstration until the candles burned down and the fuel in the lighters ran out and all the voices grew hoarse, until our watches read midnight and people gathered their things and began to leave. We followed our parents down the street, then down many more, in the direction that everyone seemed to be heading. There was no chance of finding a taxi, we would have to take the U-Bahn, so along with hordes of others we descended into Gleisdreieck station like a screaming eight-hundred-headed monster.

The frenzied crowds made it impossible to get within arm's reach of the ticket machines so when the next train pulled into the station we jumped on without having paid. It was one of those nights, we sensed, when anything was permitted. Hundreds of people were crammed into the carriage, it was impossible to even turn around, and with the heat my sweater began to feel like a straitjacket but there was barely enough room to remove it. After tugging on the zipper and successfully extracting one arm I noticed that my family was standing at the opposite end of the car; swept up in the confusion, we must have boarded through different doors and now dozens of bodies were between us, though it didn't really matter since I knew where to get off, and as if in some bizarre Cubist composition, all I saw were corners and fragments of their angled faces, my mother's lips, my father's nose, my sister's hair, and I remember thinking to myself how this amalgam would have been far more attractive, a composite being, cobbled together from random parts of each, rather than the complex six-person package to which I was bound for life.

The train continued its journey and I began to examine the passengers sitting and standing nearby. There was general mirth in the carriage and I began to feel as if I was in some kind of aviary, though one populated with less exotic species than those we had at home. Groups of large black and grey birds with blond tufts laughed and told jokes while scruffy brown birds with ruffled feathers waved bottles of beer. Solemn birds read the evening paper, others squawked over crossword puzzles and the smallest birds, of which there were only a few, emitted the occasional chirp, as if aware of the hierarchy but uncertain how to participate. And then I noticed one bird, a bird with unusual plumage, which, unlike the others, didn't seem to want to draw attention to itself. Sitting directly in front of me was a very old woman, nearly a century old I would say, wearing a scarf that framed a wide forehead, which peered out like an angry planet. She had dark, deep-set eyes and a square, jowly face that was remarkably masculine. Stiff and erect, the old woman sat in her seat clutching her purse and stared straight ahead.

The jowly face, the sweeping forehead, the deep-set furnacy eyes, everything seemed horribly familiar and I felt as if I had seen this face before, but in black and white. Since I was standing directly in front of her I had the perfect perspective to really study it, and the more I stared the more certain I was . . . Yes, that it was Hitler, Hitler as an old woman, riding westwards. *This is Hitler*, I said to myself, *there is no doubt that this is Hitler*. The old woman had the same-shaped face, the same black eyes and high forehead, and, now that I looked again, even a shadowy square area where the mustache would have been. I stared and then I stared some more, petrified, horrified, amazed by what I saw. All of a sudden the train jerked around a curve. The woman, startled out of her rigid position and thrown back into the present, finally looked up and around and it was then that she caught me staring. I couldn't believe it: I was making eye contact with Hitler. Hitler was making eye contact with me. At least for a few seconds. The woman frowned and turned away, then back to me and smiled faintly, her lips barely moving, probably to ingratiate herself since my staring must have unnerved her.

My heart pounded. The sight in front of me, added to the stifling heat in the carriage, might have been enough to give anyone a heart attack, even me, at age fourteen, yet a heart attack at age fourteen was still more probable than seeing Hitler on the U-Bahn disguised as an old woman. How could it be, I wondered, that forty years after the war I found myself face-to-face with the devil himself, the devil whose very name cast a shadow on nearly every landscape of my young life? I waved to my brother Gabriel, who happened to glance my way, and made an urgent sign for him to join me even if he had to bulldoze his way through the crowd, but he took one glance at all the large Germans standing between us and shrugged. I then pointed at my parents, motioning to him to get their attention, but the fool just shrugged a second time and turned away. My mother, nose deep in a guidebook, was a lost cause, as was my father, busy trying to decipher the signs on the walls of the train. My two sisters were just as useless, huddled together in a conference of whispers, oblivious to everything but each other, and I couldn't even see my other brother, who was eclipsed by at least ten bodies.

My entire family stayed rooted like metal poles on the U-Bahn while I stood one foot away from Hitler with not a witness in sight. To my great surprise, *not a single person* seemed to notice the old woman in the head scarf. All these birds were simply too caught up in their feather ruffling and gregarious squawking to pay much attention to their fellow passengers, especially to those seated below eye level, on a different perch. But how could no one else notice the forehead and the eyes and the shaded patch between nose and mouth, when the combination of these features seemed so glaringly, so obscenely, real and factual and present?

We plowed deeper into the West. The train stopped at Wittenbergplatz and then, a few minutes later, at Zoologischer Garten. Dozens of people stepped out, freeing up the space considerably but my family stayed where they were. Now that the crowd had thinned, although there were still quite a few people between us, I noticed strapping men posted at each of the four doors of the carriage, four buzzards in their sixties or seventies, all wearing the same bulky grey coat. There was no need for these coats in August, coats cut from a cloth so thick it barely dented, and I couldn't help wondering whether they were hiding weapons beneath them.

Their eyes were riveted on the old lady. Every now and then one of them would turn to study the passengers around her, monitoring their movements with narrowed eyes, but most of the time they just watched her. *These are former SS men*, it then occurred to me, *here to guard the incognito hag, aging secret agents who survived the war and have for the past forty years lived in hiding with their Führer*. The old woman raised an arm to rearrange her scarf. Two guards tensed their shoulders, mistaking the gesture, fleetingly, for a command. I couldn't bear it any longer and again tried to wave my parents over, but my mother was glued to her guidebook, my father to the signs on the train, my sisters to their gossip and my brothers to who knows what.

At Sophie-Charlotte-Platz the old woman rose from her seat and brushed past me, her shoulder nudging mine a little harder than necessary. I moved aside. Within seconds all four men left their stations by the doors and closed in to form a tight circle around her. The train came to a halt. Two of the buzzards stepped out, then the old lady, followed by the

329

other two. The grey gang had disembarked. The doors closed and the train, its load considerably lightened, continued on its way.

No one in my family believed me, not even my brother Gabriel, the most adventurous-minded of the lot. They told me it was absurd: Hitler shot himself in his bunker in 1945. It was common knowledge. His skull had been found by the Soviets and was on display in a museum in Moscow. There was more than enough proof. End of story.

Three years later, the Wall fell. And I, in one way or another, grew up.

THE NEW NEIGHBORHOOD was happily free of references, banal or nostalgic, and the apartment satisfied all the usual criteria – fifteen minutes from a park, ten from a landmark, five from a bakery – and the rest was of little consequence. I would adjust. Since returning to Berlin in 2002 I had already lived in Charlottenburg, Kreuzberg and Mitte and now the time had come, perhaps belatedly given how fast things were changing, to try Prenzlauer Berg. After five years I still had the impulse, every ten to twelve months, to find a new home. Spaces became too familiar, too elastic, too accommodating. Boredom and exasperation would set in. And though of course nothing really changed from one roof to another, I liked to harbor the illusion that small variations occurred within, that with each move something was being renewed.

My latest dwelling was blessed with ceilings twice my height, wooden floors, double windows with brass knobs and an aluminum Soviet bathtub from the eighties that still had the factory label attached to the side. All in all, it was a good deal for three hundred euros a month and no doubt a step up from my last home on a sleepless junction in Kreuzberg. Like many old houses, this one had a front section, where I lived, and at the back an interior courtyard, the Hof, enclosed on all three sides by more apartments. Deprived of a street view, the main compensation for these homes at the rear was silence and little balconies. Some families seemed especially proud of their flower arrangements, miniature gardens jutting out of the concrete; for those not given to small-scale floriculture, this bonus section of suspended space was used to cram in any surplus object that didn't fit inside, from plastic tables to desk chairs to bicycles to laundry racks. I could look into these balconies from my kitchen window, which commanded a generous view of the Hof, although I preferred to focus on the old oak that rose in the middle, its thick trunk and changing leaves kindly blocking out the row of garish recycling bins behind.

On the afternoon of the storm, succumbing to the usual restlessness born of too much time between four walls, I slipped on a jacket and double locked the door. Out on the street a mild breeze stirred the smaller branches of the trees but left the larger ones at rest. It was late August and the air was warm, tending towards moist. As I stood outside my building deciding in which direction to walk I noticed a wrinkled face peering at me from behind the lace curtain of a ground-floor window. Two other faces, equally impassive, were stationed right behind. These were my neighbors from below, three ancient women, most likely widows from the war, and so far they were the only neighbors I'd seen. We had yet to exchange a word but I felt certain that my arrival

331

had furnished them with material for discussion during their empty, loveless hours.

As for my own empty, loveless hours, how I spent them varied from day to day, week to week. The money trickling in from home helped supplement what little savings remained from my last employment, as assistant to the assistant editor of a second-rate psychology journal. After six months I no longer wanted to know about the fickle tides of the human brain, far too many to count, nor how to treat the pathologies that rattle every one of us. As a matter of pride, I quit one day before they were planning to annul my flimsy contract. I felt dizzied by the odor of mothballs given off by Herr Schutz, my employer, as he hovered over me while I cleared out my desk drawers and erased all personal files from the computer. I stuffed everything into an Aldi shopping bag while he hung around in a cloud of camphor, checking that I wasn't taking anything that wasn't mine.

On the corner outside my local bakery, one of those places featuring long arrays of berry tarts, cream pies and cupcakes with radioactive pink icing, I watched four boys crowd around a hatted woman as she opened a paper bag. Four pairs of impatient hands clutched at the cinnamon buns that were doled out, one by one. All of a sudden a gust of wind blew the woman's hat off but the children failed to notice. Before the woman could react, a passing deliveryman jumped off his yellow bicycle and ran to fetch it. From inside the shop a baker watched.

The day turned muggier, a column of hot, rising air encircling me as I went down the next street and then on to another and another. I paused outside the cracked windows of the once lively and now deserted Café Titanic, a mass of ivy obscuring half its sign. A few doors down the smell of varnish wafted out from the antiquarian's, where two polished mahogany tables, unsteady on their new bases, wobbled on the pavement.

The restless air was closing in and I decided to head back home. A plastic bag, the discarded ghost of the object it once carried, was blown toward me and clung to my leg for a few seconds before I managed to shake it off. Birds twittered nervously in the trees but were nowhere to be found, not a single beak, claw or feather when I looked up. And then they fell silent. The sky had grown a shade or two darker, a slate grey cumulonimbus blotting the horizon.

The atmosphere was changing fast, the air driven by a new buoyancy. The larger tree branches were swaying now too. Everything was in motion. Fiery strokes lit the sky, followed, a second or two later, by a low, steady rumbling. It was as if a herd of cattle, galvanized by the massive electrical sparks, had been set loose in the streets of Berlin. I quickened my pace.

Drops of rain began to fall. The drops became larger and more frequent. Before long, the streets turned into a vertigo of hurrying shapes. A squat woman, the top half of her body hidden under her umbrella, waddled by like a windup toadstool.

At the entrance to my building I noticed one of the old women at her window, looking for signs like the rest of us, but upon seeing me she quickly retreated behind the lace curtain. Back in my apartment I rushed through the rooms to close any windows that may have remained open – there were indeed two, in the kitchen and the bedroom – but not without difficulty. The mounting pressure fought to enter, a tremendous suction at each point of entry, as if the harbinger winds were seeking refuge from an advancing sovereign. I had to push hard. From the living room I could see treetops bending and awnings flapping, the breath of the storm. Everything was in motion.

Once I'd closed the windows there was nothing left to do but take a seat at the kitchen table and wait for the storm to pass. Seconds later the entire building swayed, just a centimeter I think, perhaps less, responding to the furious vacuum outside. I could feel it trying to suck us into its mobile chaos, into the powerhouse of energy churning within, enough energy to power a village for a year. The rain made a deafening sound, an uneven pour like the decanting of ten thousand aquariums, and I stood at my window, nothing but two panes of glass separating me from the torrent, watching as the rain washed the dirt from car windows, promises from fulfillment, a small bird from its nest.

Yet my building held tight through the wind and the rain and the thunder. Unable to uproot it, the storm finally marched off. It was a classic summer storm, a factory of hot weather. Our actual encounter was brief, a few minutes at most, and once the building finished swaying I walked through the rooms to see what might have changed. Everything was still in place, the objects on tables and shelves unmoved, even the glass of water by my bed showed no signs of having spilled over. The storm had not left anything in its wake, or so it seemed, until I noticed the dirt. Row upon row of dirt, risen from the cracks between the floorboards. Each room, apart from the bathroom with its seamless linoleum, was crossed by long caterpillars of dust. The dirt and dust of decades, I imagined, drawn to the surface by the sheer force of suction. It looked as if an army of termites had been unleashed. I spent twenty minutes sweeping it all up and another twenty wandering from room to room, with a growing hunch that although the storm had moved on, something in the building's very foundation had shifted, ever so slightly, revealing new fault lines.

* * *

334

The day after the storm the sky was empty, uninterrupted blue save for a white plume left by an airplane. When the kitchen clock struck two I decided to go for a walk to see what changes had been wrought. It was Sunday, the ideal day for strolling, even better than Saturday, and I needed to get out of the house.

Ever since arriving in Berlin I'd become a professional in lost time. It was impossible to account for all the hours. The hands on clocks and watches jumped ahead or lagged behind indiscriminately. The city ran on its own chrono-metric scale. Days would draw to a close and I would ask myself what had been accomplished, how to distinguish today from yesterday and the day before. This was especially evident when I was between jobs. But no matter where I was in my life, I always preferred the anticipation of the weekend to the weekend itself. And there was also the fact, I couldn't deny it, that after five years in the city I had yet to find someone with whom to spend my Sundays. There had been the odd companion of a few weeks or months, like the dreamy but muddled student from the Humboldt or the raucous actor from the Volksbühne, never without his tweed cap, but nothing had ever lasted or even left a dent so with every Sunday sun arose the question of how to fill the hours. I had no problem spending Monday through Friday alone, Saturdays were neutral, but each Sunday had to be reckoned with. There's solitude and then there's loneliness. Monday through Saturday were marked by solitude but on Sundays that solitude hardened into something else. I didn't necessarily *want* to spend my Sundays with someone, but on those days I was simply reminded, in the nagging pitch that only Sundays can have, that I was alone.

The day after the storm was one of those Sundays. I put on a jacket and headed towards the Wasserturm, an old water tower surrounded by shops and restaurants. The air had cooled, the city had been stilled, everything was a few keys quieter. I passed Bar Gagarin on the corner and debated whether to go in. From what I remembered, the place served homemade borscht and thick slices of bread. As I stood deciding whether to enter or resume my walk, a black hairless dog appeared out of nowhere. He was a small dog, with dry, taut skin like that of a rhinoceros and a sparse black mohawk that ran from the top of his forehead down the nape of his neck. His tail was set low and tucked in, almost hidden from sight, his genitals as black as the rest of him.

Everyone noticed him at the same time and I watched in amusement as the Germans lunching outside laid down their knives and forks and stared in disbelief, unable, surely, to classify this creature with the shape and gait of a dog but lacking the other distinguishing feature, namely, fur. But I recognized him instantly, this Xoloitzcuintle, Xolo for short, member of the ancient canine breed from Mexico that in Aztec myth would guide human souls through Mictlan, the ninth and lowest circle of the labyrinthine underworld, to their eternal resting place. Only four thousand Xolos were said to exist but here was one, standing on a street corner in Berlin on a cool Sunday in August.

Oblivious, or simply indifferent, to the mural of inquisitive eyes, the dog singled me out and trotted over to where I stood. He lifted his head and gazed into my face. His own eyes were dark and shiny, emanating something unfathomable, almost prehistoric. I bent down to pet him, his skin strangely warm despite the chill in the air, and felt a dark mole on his cheek from which sprouted a tuft of coarse hairs. I asked the waitress for a bowl of water. The dog lapped it up in seconds, his tongue shockingly pink against the black of his body.

'Is that your dog?' the waitress asked.

I shook my head *no* while enormously tempted to nod *yes*.

'Well, who knows where he came from.'

I knelt down and murmured some kind words into the Xolo's ear. Should I bring him home, I wondered, or take him for a walk? But what if his owner was at another café on the square? Yet he didn't seem to belong to anyone. I decided to circle the block and consider the options. I remembered once hearing that the skin of Xolos was especially susceptible to wind and sunshine and that prolonged exposure to the elements could lead to all kinds of cutaneous eruptions. Who looked after this dog in Berlin, and how did he endure the German winters? After centuries of warming souls in life and guiding them in death was this all he got in return? I would take him home.

But when I reached Gagarin eight minutes later, the dog was gone. A young couple kissing at a table stopped kissing to inform me that he had wandered off not long ago, in the direction of Kollwitzplatz. I did not know whether to believe them, they seemed quite distracted, but after not finding him anywhere near the Wasserturm I concluded that he had indeed left, and spent the rest of the afternoon searching every street and square in the vicinity. At one point I thought I saw him but it was only a shadow under a park bench. Once it grew dark I gave up and walked home, aware that he would be camouflaged by night. Over the next week I returned daily to Gagarin only to hear the waitress repeatedly confirm, with growing impatience, that no dog 'of that sort' had been seen again. I left my number just in case.

UWE TIMM

THE REICHSTAG, WRAPPED

From

MIDSUMMER NIGHT

Translated by Peter Tegel

BELOW, THE TAXI was already waiting outside the house; on the balcony above stood Kubin, sou'wester on his head, yelling: 'Mast and bulkheads broken!'

He was leaning far over the balcony railing, alarmingly far. 'Be careful,' I called up to him.

But he sang on into the stormy night: 'Fourteen men on a dead man's chest, yo ho ho, and a bottle of rum.'

The taxi driver asked: 'Is he a skipper?'

'No. Management consultant. But his grandfather was a skipper. I've never seen him like this before. He used to sing Irish folk songs when he was drunk.'

'Where to?'

'The Reichstag.'

'Ah,' said the driver, 'the wrapping, don't get excited, there's not much to see at night. Mind you, it's good for business. Hotels and boarding houses are full, yes, and taxis have been doing good business in the last two days.'

'Is it all that bad otherwise?'

He nodded his bald head and looked in the mirror, but I couldn't see his eyes. Though it was night he was wearing sunglasses, pilot model, thirties style, the frame anodized in gold.

'Since Reunification we've been stuck in traffic jams. Building sites, redirected traffic, one-way streets all over the place, where there was nothing the day before. Now there's even a lake on Potsdamer Platz. A huge excavation with dredges, barges, and two tugs.' The taxi clattered. We were driving over a temporary bridge.

'If there's mutiny on board a barge, maritime law applies. The traffic aggression that's built up here since Reunification, it's unbelievable. I came to Berlin twenty years ago, didn't want to go into the army. Berlin then was the place for dropouts and outsiders. A microcosm, walled in, well guarded. Now it's the boys wanting to make a quick killing that are coming here. I'm thinking of leaving.'

'Where would you go?'

'Cologne or Hamburg.'

Gusts of wind shook the car. A few drops of rain on the windshield. He turned on the windshield wipers.

'What do you do when you're not driving a taxi, I mean as a profession?'

'A lot of people ask that. They think I'm one of those taxi drivers with a Ph.D. I've a driving license, a taxi license, and two years of Romance languages and literature, and that's it. When I'm not driving a taxi I don't do much of anything, except read, go to movies, listen to music. And travel, Africa, the Sahara. I once wrote a little guidebook on the Sahara before it became so fashionable, but it's been out of print a long time. We're already at the barrier,' he said, 'from here you'll have to walk. I can drive round it, it won't make much difference though, except for the higher fare.'

For a moment I wondered whether I shouldn't just ask him to take me to my hotel. But I was curious to see how much of the Reichstag had been wrapped. So I paid and got out.

The wind was cold and a fine rain was falling. I'd believed the weather report on the previous evening and for convenience left my raincoat at home. I now froze pitifully in the thin silk jacket I'd bought in Munich during the heat wave.

The Brandenburg Gate stood there as though lit from within. A few pedestrians were making their way wrapped in raincoats or capes. A car came, drove to the barrier and stopped. A car with an Italian license plate, a Lancia. My damp silk jacket was giving out a peculiar smell, strange, not like wool that smells so soothingly of wet sheep or the straw smell that comes from wet cotton. But the smell exuding from my jacket reminded me of slime, of a glandular secretion, it smelled almost gelatinous. I crossed the Strasse des 17 Juni, named after the 1953 East Berlin uprising. The Lancia turned at the barrier railing and came towards me with headlights on, braked, the driver shouted something out to me. I went to the car and immediately said into the lowered window: 'I'm not from here. Sono straniero.'

'Ahh, Lei parla italiano.'

'Solamente un poco.'

He let fly in Italian. I only understood something about a fair and a night journey. And as he saw that I wasn't really understanding him he switched to German and spoke it well, if with a heavy accent, explaining that he was coming from a trade fair. 'Here in Berlin. Leather goods. Didn't you read about it?'

'No,' I said, 'I just arrived today.'

He told me he had some leftover stock. Two leather jackets. Display models. He had to get to Milan, tonight. Why take the jackets back with him? He opened the door, beckoned me to get in. For a moment I hesitated because I thought of all the stories I'd heard from travelers to Berlin in recent months: strangled hotel managers, ring fingers cut off, mugged tourists, assault, and murder. But the driver gestured at me to get in, and then there was that cheerful Italian laugh: 'Prego, si accomodi,' and so I got in the passenger seat. I'd hardly slammed the door shut before he drove off. The car moved a short distance into the dark area between two street lamps. I was alarmed and thought, this is a mugging after all. I quickly turned around, but there was nobody hiding on the back seat, there was only a black bag, though in the shape of a body. The Italian turned off the engine.

'Is cold?' He pointed to my jacket.

'Yes,' I said. The smell exuding from my wet silk jacket was now really oppressive and I suddenly realized what this silk jacket smelled like – semen. I thought of the marsupial mice and decided that as soon as I got home I'd look in an encyclopedia to see from what orifice silkworms spun their thread.

'Actually it's forbidden,' said the Italian, 'unclean competition.'

'Unfair competition,' I said, and was immediately annoyed at my schoolmasterly correction. 'I'm sorry.'

'Why,' he said, 'it's important. Otherwise you keep making the same stupid mistake.'

'Well,' I said, 'it's that friendly patience of the Italians, that's why they don't correct you when you try to speak Italian.'

'When you speak, no. But they do when you sing.'

'How's that?'

'You know the story about the American singer? The guy was singing for the first time at the opera, in Naples? He sings the first aria. The audience roars da capo. The American sings the aria again. The audience yells, roars da capo, the singer sings it again and again and again. The other singers are getting impatient, they want to sing their arias too. But the audience shouts: da capo. Finally the exhausted American singer asks: How many times am I supposed to sing this aria? Someone in the audience calls out: Until you get it right.' He looked me over: 'What size are you? Forty-two?'

'It depends, in Italian sizes more likely forty-four.'

'Then these jackets will fit you perfectly. Good design, best quality leather, first-class workmanship.' He reached back, pulled one jacket and then another from the black bag, showed me the label: Giorgione, and below it the size, forty-four, in fact. 'I really wanted three-fifty for each jacket, you can have both for four-fifty. The actual price is twelve hundred, each, that is. I couldn't stay any longer at my hotel. You understand,' he looked at me, smiled. I nodded and wondered why the more he spoke the less accent his German had. He must have lived in Germany for quite a while.

'I wanted to sell the jackets tomorrow in a boutique,' he said, 'but no hotel vacant, everything booked, the whole city. They're wrapping the Reichstag. People are going crazy. With us, they come to see weeping madonnas. With you, the Reichstag. This Christo,' he laughed: 'Dio mio, a magician. But I'm a good Catholic. I'm leaving tonight. So, both jackets for four-fifty.'

'No,' I said, 'I don't need two jackets, it's June, these are fall jackets. Though it's raining. But what should I do with two leather jackets?'

'Sell them. You can easily ask two hundred more.'

I shook my head.

'Good, then one. I want to sell both jackets today, this evening. Everyone knows there was a trade fair. I'll be driving all night, straight to Milan.'

'The whole stretch,' I asked.

'Yes,' he said, 'there's no one on the highway at night. I can, how do you say, rave up.'

'No,' I said and had to laugh, 'it's rev up.'

'Good,' he said, 'the one jacket for two-eighty. You're not wearing a coat. With this weather, the jacket. Rain.' He pointed outside. The drizzle had in fact turned into rain, the wind flung it against the windshield.

'Well, leather isn't exactly suitable for rain either,' I tried to show I knew about this. 'And anyway, I don't have that much money on me.'

'A credit card? We could drive to an ATM.'

'I don't have any credit cards with me.' Which was a lie. But if I was going to buy I wanted to bargain a little. I'm not completely clueless, I know Italy and the Italians, and I told him this, said, 'Italy's the country I like traveling to the most and I really like Italians, their language, their fashions, their food. Tutto!'

This clearly pleased him, this tutto; he put his hand on my shoulder, said: 'You speak very good Italian. OK then, two hundred and twenty marks for the jacket. See here, silk lining. Red, lined, elegant.'

I felt the leather, soft, really soft to the touch. The brand name Giorgione reminded me of Giorgione's painting: 'The Storm.' That's a painting I can keep coming back to, and each time I discover new details. For example the white bird on the roof of the house, really tiny, a stork, I think, sitting there while lightning flashes through the black thunder-clouds. The jacket lining was really red, a dark red. I tried to examine the quality of the seams in the dim light, felt them. I said I'd once been a furrier. I had to explain to him what that was. Somebody who deals in fur and leather.

'Oh,' he said, 'an expert,' pulled the jacket away from me and held it up: 'You see, styled after il famoso barone rosse. Richthofen. Elegant cut. Old aviator design. Double-decker. Protects from wind and rain.'

It looked good, especially as there was a triple-decker in the inner lining. At home my father had had a photo of Richthofen, whom he revered, up on the wall, and in this photo Richthofen was wearing a leather jacket that, I was certain, resembled this one.

'How much money have you got?'

I searched through my pockets. And thought, what luck, with this rain, this cold, getting a genuine soft leather jacket this cheap. I showed him my money: one hundred and seventy marks and a few pennies. Of course I didn't tell him that I had another hundred marks in my passport for an emergency. 'One hundred and seventy marks, that's all. And then I can't even take a taxi back.'

'Have you got a bus ticket?'

'No.'

He gave me back four marks. 'A good buy,' he said. 'Now I'm going on the autostrada and rave up.'

'Rev up,' I said.

He laughed: 'German is very complicated: rev up! Yes, rave up! Lots of luck! Arrivederci!'

The Italians, I thought, are wonderful. They do their little deals, their little swindles, but always in such a way that you can still enjoy being cheated, and that's where I pulled a nice fast one on him, I said to myself and waved. That tutto, that softened him. He waved again, shouted addio and thank you, and drove off with tires screeching.

I put on the leather jacket, beautifully warm at last in all this wind and rain, at last. A really good buy, only one hundred sixty-six marks instead of twelve hundred. Almost a lucky number. Almost like that buy at the flea market on Lake Kleinhesseloh a year ago, where lost clothes were being sold and I bought myself a raincoat for a hundred and eighty, a Burberry as good as new, hardly worn, in the lining a label worked in gold from golden Basel: Conrad. High class for men. The previous owner must have had extremely short Swiss arms, because I had to have the sleeves of the coat, which otherwise was just right, let out a good four centimeters. While this jacket was a perfect fit, and it was warm, wonderfully warm.

The Reichstag: massive, heavy, rustling darkly. As in a dream, the hanging strips of cloth billowed in the gusting wind, dark and strange. The middle section was already wrapped, the four corner towers were still uncovered.

I walked along the yellow wire fence intended to keep the curious away from the work of art in progress.

Men in yellow rain capes guarded the fence. A few inquisitive people were walking, mute and muffled, by the fence; a woman struggled with her reversed umbrella, a man pulled a morose, wet, shaggy dog behind him on a lead, a little man in an old motorcyclist's jacket studied a billboard by a pile driver. Construction work I read on the sign.

I went further along the wire fence. My leather jacket was getting heavier in the rain, so heavy that, for the first time in years, I thought of the lead vest I once used during training, sprinting up the path to Richmond Castle, five, six times. The jacket had been light as a feather when I put it on, a typical Italian product. The leather had clearly only been tanned for sunny climes. Meanwhile my solid American leather shoes were also soaked. My feet were cold and wet. The storm rustled in the strips of grey synthetic material. In this lighting the color reminded me of the hideous bomber jackets of the People's Army. A man in a blue mining outfit stood behind the fence, a yellow helmet on his head, around his hips a wide belt with thick snap links. I'd seen the men in the news yesterday, unrolling the massive strips of material like sailors on the yards of sailing boats.

I suddenly understood Kubin's cry: 'Mast and bulkheads broken.' He'll also have seen these pictures. I asked the man if he'd worked too on wrapping the Reichstag.

348

'Veiling,' he instantly corrected me. 'What gets veiled, at some point gets unveiled, at any rate that's what Christo says.' He looked up anxiously at the billowing strips of cloth. 'We had to stop work at noon. Regular gale-force winds. We were rocking up there like monkeys on bush ropes.'

'Are you from Berlin?'

'No, I come from Rostock.'

'Could you climb in the GDR?'

'No, only a little in the mountains along the Elbe. And of course factory chimneys.'

'Factory chimneys?'

'Yes, under socialism we trained on chimneys. There was so little scaffolding. A deficient economy also has its advantages. So we worked with ropes from the top. That was powerful training. I once did repair work on a two-hundred-and-sixty-meter-high chimney. Now I'm independent. I specialize in chimneys, repair work: joining, replacing rungs. The money's good. I used to be a Hero of Labor, good for nothing except sticking in my cap. So,' he said, 'time to hit the sack. Have to get up early, at five.'

I went on walking and suddenly I felt my joints ache with fatigue. I'd gotten up at five o'clock in the morning, raced through the book I was reading, *The Potato and Its Wild Relatives*, then gone to the State Library to look at the statistics for potato and sugar beet cultivation in the 19th century, flown in the afternoon from a warm summery Munich to a stormy cold Berlin, had plenty to eat and drink with Kubin, now I was running around at night in this leaden jacket and I said to myself, enough. I went down Unter den Linden heading for the Friedrichstrasse station, in order to go to Bahnhof Zoo with the four marks the Italian had left me. Meanwhile the jacket had soaked up so much water it hung from my shoulders as if the side pockets were crammed with boulders. I tried to cheer myself up with the thought that the leather could be impregnated with a spray. Then it would be good for the cold but dry October days in Munich. Anyway, it still kept me warm. And I no longer smelled like the gelatinous excretion of silkworms, now I smelled of – what, actually? The smell reminded me of the secondhand dealer on the Eppendorferweg to whom I used to bring paper and cardboard when I was a child, and depending on the weight, get a few pennies for it. It was at the beginning of the fifties, at the time of the Korean War, scrap metal prices had risen sharply, when my father had called me. He was standing in the cellar, his feet wet, his trouser legs wet. He beckoned me to come closer and gave me a couple of slaps around the ear. Why did my father have to go and wash his hands at this basin in the cellar of all places, a washbasin that was normally never used? I'd removed the drain which was lead. Lead fetched the highest price, so I suppose you could say that the slaps were worth it. Exactly! It was this smell of paper from the secondhand dealer's cellar that I was carrying around now.

I was just turning into the Friedrichstrasse when three men came towards me, all three in shiny bomber jackets, their heads not exactly shaved, but close-cropped. A practical haircut, I thought, while my hair hung in strands in my face. Why hadn't I let my wife cut it before I left?

'What you starin' at, you there,' said one of them and came towards me. 'You old bum.' And the other said: 'Dirty aldi.' Then the first one gave me a feeble punch in the stomach. Water squirted out from my jacket as from a sponge. I winced and let out a faint cry although it had been more like a push and hadn't hurt. But the jacket had still torn. The three stared for a moment dazed, then horrified at the hole from which red was oozing. I pressed my hands to the mushy mess. I was stiff with surprise but felt no pain. The three ran, raced away. I slowly recovered from my shock, looked at my hands. They weren't red. The wet red inner lining was hanging out. I pushed it back into the jacket, a piece came off. Perhaps the man who slammed me had had a knife hidden in his hand, or a metal comb, or a key ring which, I'd heard, left terrible face wounds if you struck with it. So perhaps the bloated jacket had saved me from injury. But the rip in the jacket was big. A mended jacket, I tried consoling myself, would show that it was well worn. It would certainly take a lot of mending to patch this hole.

At the train station, finally dried out, I saw myself in the filthy pane of the swinging door that had probably not been cleaned since the Eighth Party Congress.

My dingy reflection also explained the words dirty aldi. The word was albi, and it meant the illegal Albanians sleeping out on the streets. The jacket wasn't just torn in two places, there was also something wrong with the collar. What a mess. My hair hung in strands in my face. I thought, lucky I'm not as dark as my reflection. I looked down at my jacket, it was literally frayed. No, it was in shreds. It was coming apart. I fingered it, pulled something away, a slimy mass like blotting paper. In school we tore blotting paper into pieces, chewed it into lumps and then spat it at the blackboard where it stuck like grey-white cookie mixture. The clump in my hand was black. I could pull off the inner lining in little red lumps. At least, I thought, looking at my fingers, the color doesn't come off, so it hasn't bled into the silk jacket. A young man walked by, gave me a friendly nod, and pressed a cigarette pack into my hand, blue, Gauloises, on it Mercury's helmet. This Italian was an ingenious fellow, I said to myself. I didn't even need to travel without a ticket. And the one hundred and sixty-six marks, they, my mother would have said, are an offering to the gods. Fear their envy. And lately things have gone well for me, even very well. No, I wasn't furious, wasn't bitter. And there were still three cigarettes in the pack. I pressed the pack into the hand of one of the homeless people, took off the disintegrating, dripping jacket, shoved it where it belonged – in a trash can – and ran up the steps to the platform.

KEVIN BARRY

BERLIN ARKONAPLATZ – MY LESBIAN SUMMER

I

SILVIJA TURNED TO me from the studio couch and said:

'Patrick, I am going to teach you everything you need to know about the female genitalia.'

I was at this moment twenty-one years old and coming to terms with the cold hard fact of my genius.

'But I've got a terrible trembling sensation in my hands,' I said. 'I'm not sure now is the ideal time for genitals.'

'Patrick,' she said. 'You are not going to be using your hands.'

She sat on the couch, in her underwear, with a scarred Macbook perched on her strong, thin, walnut-cracker thighs. She smoked as only a Slav can smoke – *devouring* her smoke. She had a flicky fringe and superstar cheekbones. Technically, she was lesbian, but there appeared to be movement on the matter.

'Patrick,' she said. 'Take your clothes off and get out of bed.'

Even in early summer, the studio was cold as the steppe, and I would put extra layers on to sleep. Silvija was born in the teeth of the wind of an actual steppe and she did not feel the cold. She put aside the laptop, and she stood and eyed me derisively as I approached. With a thumb and forefinger she massaged a nipple. She had small tits but enormous nipples.

'If you do okay, I will kiss you,' she said. 'But only once.'

She turned out to be as good as her word on this, and the kiss was not the least of her gifts to me.

By her own reckoning, Silvija was at this time the most brilliant fashion photographer in all of Berlin. This didn't mean that she got paid. The magazines she worked for tended to fold after an issue or two. And *Vogue* wasn't going to come calling anytime soon. Asked to photograph, say, a vampy spike-heeled ankle boot, Silvija would commit to print only the leather of its sole, and that blurrily, as some meth-thinned model, wearing latex knickers and a sneer, aimed a high kick at the camera, down some malevolent alleyway with gemstones of broken glass – Berlin diamonds – scattered to sparkle all around.

'But you don't really see the boot, Silvija?'

'I do not photograph the motherfucking boot, Patrick. I photograph the motherfucking life!'

Money was always tight, and we supplemented the magazine work by shoplifting, breaking and entering, and hiring out to the younger designers as they compiled their portfolios. The designers were routinely troublesome – I remember the schizophrenic Croat with his pioneering cutting technique, the polyamorous Frenchman who weighed about as much as a bag of feathers and was reinventing the frock coat, and the epileptic Tasmanian allegedly wanted in Australia for setting fire to a model during Melbourne Fashion Week.

We descended the eerie stairwell from the studio. We emerged onto Arkonaplatz in the morning. The nicotine burn of her kiss was on my lips still. The sun had come strongly through; already the tables were full outside the cafés. We stopped for tiny smoking thimbles of black coffee at Niko's, and I felt some prose coming on. Silvija shook her head in amusement at my lovelorn state.

'There will be no honeymoon, Patrick,' she said. 'You did fine. And there will be further business between us. There will be instruction. But do you know how much it means to me?'

She snapped her fingers to indicate the sheer nothingness of what had that morning occurred, and I nodded glumly in understanding.

'Got it?'

'Yes.'

Silvija snapped her fingers like this a lot. She allowed weight to nothing. All of life, she implied, was without meaning or lasting import, and in this way, I believe, she was teaching me how I should operate (and how I should think) if I truly intended to be an artist. We left the muddy remains of our coffees, stubbed our Marlboro Lights, and set out for a towerblock in the district of Wedding, there to photograph for the deranged Tasmanian model-burner a double-jointed Turkish neurotic capering with a string of anal beads.

And a Rottweiler.

III

The Berlin designers had until this time mostly lived and worked in Prenzlauer Berg. By 2005, however, the bohemian bourgeoisie from five continents were arriving for the quarter's cut-price lofts and superb childcare facilities, and gentrification was fast spreading through the old tenements and squares.

'Motherfucking breeders,' Silvija called the new arrivals.

The fashion crowd generally was in arch dismay at the intrusion, and had started to venture north from P'berg into the riskier neighbourhoods of Wedding. This was where most of the serious shoots happened that summer. We stopped at a corner shop on the way for some bottles of pils. I uncapped mine with the opener chained to the counter, Silvija hers with her teeth. We drank pils more or less constantly and ate very rarely. We crossed Bremenstrasse, dodging the ironically bearded cyclists on their high-nellies, and breathed in the petrol views. I lugged all the gear; Silvija *strode*. Inclined as always to be artistically late, we lay for a while on the scraggy hilltop in Mauerpark. We slipped in an earpiece each from my headphones and listened religiously to the Nina Simone version of 'Lilac Wine'. We looked out across the city.

'I give it six months,' Silvija said, and spat dramatically.

I was only a few months off the plane from Cork but Silvija had ten years of Berlin under her belt, and she allowed me to share the old-hand snootiness that those years granted; I had learned to affect the same languid woe as all the other old hands. A constant of hip cities is that much of the conversation centres around the fact the city is not as hip as once it was. In Mauerpark that morning, Silvija talked seriously for the first time of leaving Berlin behind, and I felt a terrible spike of nausea.

'Don't worry,' she said. 'Not for a while yet.'

We flung our empty bottles and made for the shoot. She hoicked another of her awful thick green phlegmy spits and I tried not to notice. She was so lean, with a ferocious mouth, and XXX-rated eyelashes. I'd found her through a small ad – a share offered on a studio apartment. The sense memory of the morning's events was still with me. First the mouth, and after a long time my hands had stopped trembling enough to be brought into play. She talked me through the operation. It was delicate stuff. My hands felt so heavy, but then she laid hers on mine to guide, and lifted the weight – everything was suddenly lighter.

IV

Wedding was a raw expanse of towerblocks, tattoo pits, kebab shops. Nogoodniks in mauve-coloured tracksuits decorated every corner. We had a properly respectful air as we passed through. This was how Berlin was supposed to be. We cut down a back way, for a while, to avoid the main drag, because the sight of the kebab gyros was sickening Silvija's stomach, which was troublesome. The rearsides of the towerblocks loomed either side of a dirt pathway itchy with catkins beneath our sandals, and the word 'proletariat' rolled its glamorous syllables over my tongue. Silvija may have been lazy as a feline in her stride but she made as sly and sure-footed a progress. She wore black military fatigues cut off at the knee and a black vest a couple of sizes too small the better to ride sexily high on her waist. Just as we approached the tenement where the shoot would take place, Silvija received a call to say the Tasmanian had 'technically died' that morning but the show would go on.

There were always such complications. The Tasmanian's assistant, a serene Vietnamese, was instead in charge when we reached the old apartment where the shoot would happen. Politely, we asked after the designer.

'At six a.m.?' the Vietnamese grinned. 'Clinical death! Now? Much improve!'

The room was peopled with hipster flunkies, and the Turkish model was in place. She had a pair of recent stab wounds in her side and looked as if she had walked straight off a human rights-type poster about torture. Silvija began to set up – she would not go digital and used commie-era Leicas always. I attempted to calm the model who was mouthing vengeance of death against a two-timing girlfriend. The anal beads and the Rottweiler were introduced. Silvija declared that the dog lacked a sufficiently vicious mien and she smashed a camera lens off the wall. She attempted to goad the dog to promote a viciousness but there was no response, and the shoot, as so often, broke down into a period of tense analysis. Pils was sent for to help smooth the debate. It went not well, even so, with Silvija questioning the talents of the absent Tasmanian.

'Motherfucker calls himself a designer,' she said. 'And his autumn fucking accessory? Anal fucking beads! Once again with the anal fucking beads!'

In my innocence, I did not know the exact purpose of anal beads, and I confided as much to the Turkish model.

'Is sex toy,' she said. 'Lots and lots of glitter beads on a chain. These beads they get bigger in sequence. What you do with these beads . . .'

I put a hand to my empty stomach, and pleaded.

Silvija opened the scarred laptop and mailed the Tasmanian – he was apparently online even in intensive care – and sprayed some heavy snark about his autumn accessories. The Vietnamese clucked contentedly and went to the kitchen zone and stirfried some scallions and chicken gizzards. The flunkies lounged in hipster bliss, and then fizzed madly and loudly for a few moments – looking for knickers or garter belts – and then lounged some more. The Turkish model stroked the inside of my arm and said she was not exclusively homo and had always liked redheads. I was on a roll with ladies who liked ladies. Eventually some photos were taken. The Rottweiler took a dump in the middle of the floor. Silvija said:

'Perfect! We use the shit!'

This was the Berlin fashion scene, in the summer of 2005, in the district of Wedding. There was a lot of heroin and a lot of dog shit. Everybody was thin and gorgeous.

And Jesus, did we smoke.

V

I was finding out how carelessly life might be lived. The people I met through Silvija were all addictions and stylish madness. Every other hour, there was a crack-up, or an arrest, or an abortion, or somebody jumped out a window, or fucked an Austrian heiress, and every deranged turn of events was so gladly met and swirled with. They were attuned to the wild moment, while I was yet nervous, careful, locked to the past. It seemed to me that they had all grown up godless and without foul repressions. They had not grown up sitting on three-piece suites of floral design in the beige suburbs. They had not come to adulthood in rooms laid with unpleasantly diamond-patterned carpets bought off the travellers at the markets of drab Irish towns. How can I begin to explain? Does it suffice to say that the olive oil in my childhood home was kept in the bathroom? It was bought at the chemist shop and drizzled mournfully onto my father's problem scalp. Hair was never good for our people, generally, perhaps on account of the remorseless wind that assaults the sides of west Limerick mountains. It is no exaggeration to say that the male forebears of my clan – my father and his brothers – were scarred by wind. They all had the permanently startled look that comes from working outside in hard gusts, and something of it had been passed on to me, this look; even though I had never myself stood in the teeth of a force six gale wrestling a stuck cow from the boggy sump of a ditch; even though I spent my time writing lurid short stories and (increasingly perceptive and subtle) essays about the emergence of Italian Neo-Realism in the 40s, and the troubled legacy of the Nouvelle Vague.

Silvija, of course, was fanatically well read. She read everything and in six languages. She had informed me quietly that I was a genius. She told me that I was the culmination of Irish literature. (She said it 'litra-chure'.) It had all been leading up to me.

She had such faith.

VI

The shoot broke down into the usual chaos. There were taunts and ultimatums. Silvija and I walked. We decided to go instead and rob some Americans. There was a roost of them in our building. They were on the floor directly beneath the studio. We could hear the insect trilling of their talk down there.

'When the Americans appear,' Silvija said, 'it means that Berlin is officially over. May it rest in peace. Amen.'

Daily, the gauche and Conversed hordes priced out of San Francisco and Brooklyn were arriving, with their positivity, their excellent teeth and their MFAs. They could be spotted a mile off in the clubs – their clothes were wrong, their hair was appalling and their dancing was just terrible.

We rang the bell on their apartment. We listened. It was empty – they must have been out photographing the TV tower or taking rides in the tourist-rental Trabants. We went upstairs to our studio and shinned down from the studio balcony to theirs. We quickly made through the place. We found eight hundred dollars in the drawer of a vanity and two passports – Becky Cobb and Corey Mutz, in chunky retro eyewear both – and we took these also. There was a price to be had for American passports from the Ukrainians who drank at Dieter's. We left the way we had come – Silvija climbed like a jungle cat; I laboured. But we made it, and we went and had us a royal day on the town.

In a vast Old German-type trough, we stuffed ourselves with many potato-based dishes and many enormous sausages. We drank exquisite Burgundy and Bavarian whisky. And pils. We touched each other beneath the tablecloth. What Silvija could do with her toes was extraordinary. She taught me, phonetically, the choruses of some enchanting childhood songs of the steppe.

'But what are these songs about?' I asked.

'Mostly they are about oxen and death,' she said.

We left the restaurant and went to Dieter's. It was a low bar on Schönhauser Allee, and there we had more pils and a rendezvous with the scarred and mysterious Hoods of Kiev. These were among the characters lately populating my stories but I could get them only palely. There was no way to render with a still-callow pen the force of intrigue stored in the black heat of Victor's eyes, nor the sexual languidity in the way that Xcess (as she styled herself) drained her glass, nor the . . . I just couldn't get it down right. We made another two hundred euro from the passports. We left the bar and walked down the street – the plan was to buy some new and impractical shoes. There was the rumble above us of the elevated trains. I complained at the lack of true lustre in my stories. Silvija sighed and stopped up on the pavement and she took hold of my elbow. She gave me one of her statements or manifestos, then, one of her great orations on the Nature of Art:

'When you are worried, that is when you are working. When you are doing nothing, that is when the work is happening. It does not happen in the front section of the brain, Patrick. It happens in back section. Here is the subconscious level. This is the place the story come from. You just have to let it happen. Liberate yourself! If it is going to come, it will come. You just make yourself available and open to it. If it comes good, some day, it comes good. Champagne! But you have no power over it. It is all involving luck. When it feels like nothing is happening, that is when it is all happening. And remember that when you are worried, you are working.'

Still I search for a more succinct explanation of how it all occurs, but I know I will not find one.

VII

It was in odd scraps and rags that Silvija's own story came through to me. Mostly in the small hours, when deep in her cups and whuzzled from the hashpipe, when in that borderland between wakefulness and sleeping, with her eyes half closed, wrapped in blankets against the night chill, this is when she would tell me of the viking-level horrors she had witnessed and been a part of: the rape, the pillage, the evil marauding. War-lands I could not imagine. And Silvija as a scared child among it all – Silvija scared was even harder to imagine. Such a story I had in my selfish way yearned for – maybe I could steal it, and recast it, and it would lend my work the gravitas it lacked; writers are such *maggots*, especially the young ones – but as she fed it to me in these night-time crumbs, I could not even begin to process the detail. I have made myself forget most of it. I know that she had as a kid dispensed blow jobs for soup money. She had been tied up in a facility once and brutalised with a broom handle. She had escaped but only to long broken years trailing madly through the squats of Barcelona (held captive once by a Sudanese in El Born, she had been made to eat catfood) and then there was a period of homelessness in Genoa (she cracked up and became obsessed with reading the words of the streetname signs backwards – Via Garibaldi . . . Idlabirag) and it was Berlin before she recovered, it was Berlin where she found her talents and the balance of her humours and the makings of a hard shell.

Nights at the studio she would go to the bathroom and spit blood in the sink. She would wash it away but I would find on the porcelain smeared traces in the mornings.

VIII

The summer deepened, and our days became toned with sadness, and other, unnameable things. I sat up in bed one morning, smoking. I tapped the ash into an empty pils bottle. Silvija squatted on her heels on the couch, in her underwear, battering the laptop – she had a wide circle of acquaintance, 80 per cent of which she was feuding with at any given time. The light poured in from the climbing sun, and caught her bare, brown muscles. The windfall from the Americans and the passports was long since consumed and we were again in the depths of poverty, but we looked pretty good poor. The Wedding scene was slow, due to the season and the usual inclemence of luck that afflicted the fashion people: the arrests, the random plagues, the near-death experiences. This particular morning, there was something like shyness between us. Briefly, in the night, Silvija's strict no-penetration dictat had been lifted. I knew even at the moment it was a mistake, despite the luxuriousness of the sensation. I could feel the scaredness in her. I knew that it would never happen again. And I knew in my heart that I just wasn't working out as a lesbian. I was too clumsy and knuckly.

Not that she didn't walk with me the hot summer streets of noon, and not that she didn't teach me, and not that she didn't give me something, just a tiny sustaining something, of her great aura.

I believe it was that same day, in the beer garden on Kastanienallee, that she turned the camera on me, there beneath the chestnut trees in full leaf, and I was shy of the lens and awkward but she told me what to do.

'You don't look at it,' she said. 'You look through it.'

I have the photograph still and it is sacred to me. On the wooden bench between us, in the amber of a stein glass, she is reflected, with her camera raised. She is there, blurrily, and it's just a shade, but it is all that I have left of her.

IX

The end came sharply. I woke one morning to find Silvija packing her stuff. That holdall of hers had seen plenty. I tried to sound casual but there was boy-fear in my tone.

'So this is it?' I croaked.

'You knew it was coming,' she said.

The studio had had its time, she said. She was going to stay with a girlfriend in Kreuzberg. It was time that I stood on my own two feet.

'You need to go find your own life, Patrick,' she said.

'Yeah and you need to go to a fucking doctor!'

I was so angry to be cast aside and I was lost in the city

366

without her. I became depressed. I stayed with some other people for a while, in Mitte – artists, of course – but they all by contrast with Silvija seemed to be acting parts, and I have forgotten all their names. I knew that the sweet days of the summer had passed and it was time to fly away. Reluctantly, she came to the station on the morning I was to leave for the airport. She hugged me on the platform but so awkwardly; she fled instantly from the hug. She said she would email and that I could phone but six years have passed and never once did she reply to an email, never once did she answer her phone, and after a few months, the line was dead.

Which signifies nothing, necessarily, because Silvija changed phones all the time. And anyway I must believe that she is out there, somewhere among the dreaming cities of Europe, maybe in Trieste, or in Zagreb, or in Belgrade again. I must believe that she is out there, still beautiful, foul-mouthed and inviolate.

JEAN-PHILIPPE TOUSSAINT

From

TELEVISION

Translated by Jordan Stump

I QUIT WATCHING television. I gave it up cold turkey, once and for all, never to watch another show, not even sports. I stopped a little more than six months ago, in late July, just after the end of the Tour de France. I'd quietly watched the delayed broadcast of the Tour's last stage in my Berlin apartment, like everyone else – the Champs-Élysées stage, ending in a tremendous sprint won by the Uzbek Abdujaparov – and then I stood up and turned off the set. I can clearly picture myself at that moment, the very simple gesture I made, my arm fluidly extending as it had a thousand times before, my finger on the button, the picture imploding and disappearing from the screen. It was over. I never watched television again.

The TV set is still sitting in the living room, dark and forsaken. I haven't touched it since. I'm sure it still works. I could find out with a touch of the button. It's a standard model, sitting on a lacquered wooden stand made up of two elements, a shelf and a pedestal, the pedestal in the form of a thin black book, upright and open, like a silent reproach. The screen is an indefinable color, dark and uninviting, I wouldn't call it green, and very slightly convex. On one side a little compartment houses the various controls. An antenna sprouts from the top, its two stems making a V, a bit like the twin antennae of a crayfish, and offering the same sort of handle for anyone who might want to pick it up and drop it into a pot of boiling water to rid himself of it even more completely.

I spent the summer alone in Berlin. Delon, whom I live with, went off to Italy on vacation with the two children, my son and the not-yet-born baby we were expecting – a little girl, in my opinion. I assumed it was a little girl because the gynecologist couldn't find a male member on the sonogram (and when there's no male member, it's often a little girl, I'd explained).

Not that television ever held an especially important place in my life. No. On average, I watched maybe two hours a day (maybe less, but I'd rather err on the side of generosity, and not try to puff myself up with a virtuously low estimate). Apart from major sporting events, which I always watched with pleasure, and of course the news and the occasional election-night special, I never watched much of anything on television. As a matter of principle and pleasure, I never watched movies on television, for instance (just as I don't read books in Braille). For that matter, although I never tried it, I was always quite sure I could give up watching television anytime, just like that, without suffering in the least, without the slightest ill effect – in short, that there was no way I could be considered dependent.

And yet, over the previous few months, I'd noticed a slight deterioration in my day-to-day habits. I spent most afternoons at home, unshaved, dressed in a wonderfully comfortable old wool sweater, watching television for three or four hours at a stretch, half-reclining on the couch, taking it easy, a little like a cat in its bed, my feet bare, my hand cradling my privates. Just being myself, in other words. Thus, this year, unlike years past, I followed the French Tennis Open on television from beginning to end. At first it was only a match here and there, but then, with the quarterfinals, I began to take a real interest in the outcome, or so I explained to Delon to justify my long inactive afternoons in front of the set. Most of these afternoons I was alone in the apartment, but sometimes the cleaning woman was there too, ironing my shirts beside me in the living room, mute with contained indignation. On the worst days, the broadcasts started at noon and didn't end until after night-fall. I emerged from those sessions nauseous and numbed, my mind empty, my legs limp, my eyes bleary. I went off and took a shower, letting the warm water pour over my face for many minutes. I was wiped out for the rest of the evening, and, however reluctant I was to admit it, there was no getting around the fact that, ever since I'd very gradually begun to turn forty years old, I was no longer physically up to five sets of tennis.

Apart from that I did nothing. By doing nothing, I mean doing nothing impulsive or mechanical, nothing dictated by habit or laziness. By doing nothing, I mean doing only the essential, thinking, reading, listening to music, making love, going for walks, going to the pool, gathering mushrooms. Doing nothing, contrary to what people rather simplisti-cally imagine, is a thing that requires method and discipline, concentration, an open mind. I swim five-hundred meters every day nowadays, at a rate of two kilometers per hour, a leisurely pace I admit, equaling exactly twenty pool-lengths every fifteen minutes, which is to say eighty pool-lengths in an hour. But high performance isn't my goal. I swim slowly, like an old woman (albeit without the bathing-cap), my mind ideally empty, focused on my body and its movement, carefully observing my motions and their timing, my mouth half-open as I exhale, blowing a spray of little lapping bub-bles over the surface. Afloat in the blue-tinged pool, my limbs surrounded by limpid water, I slowly reach forward and push the water behind me with long strokes, my knees drawing level with my hips; then, as my arms slowly extend

373

once more, my legs simultaneously push the water behind them in one coordinated and synchronized movement. In the end, I rank swimming very highly among the pleasures that life has to offer us, having in the past somewhat under-estimated it and placed it rather far behind physical love, which was until now my favorite activity, apart from think-ing, of course. I do in fact very much like making love (on more than one account), and, without going into my own personal style in that domain, which is in any case closer to the sensual quietude of a leisurely breast-stroke pool length than to the surging, swaggering outburst of a four-hundred meter butterfly race, I will say above all that making love brings me an immense inner equilibrium, and that, the embrace at an end, as I lie dreamily on my back on the soft sheets, savoring the simple companionship of the moment, I find myself in an irrepressible good mood, which appears on my face as a slight, unexpected smile, and something gleaming in my eye, something light-hearted and knowing. And it turns out that swimming brings me the same sort of satisfaction, that same bodily plenitude, slowly spreading to the mind, like a wave, little by little, giving birth to a smile.

And so I realized, busy as I was doing nothing, that I no longer had time to watch television.

Television offers the spectacle not of reality, although it has all the appearances of reality (on a smaller scale, I would say – I don't know if you've ever watched television), but rather of its representation. It is true that television's apparently neutral representation of reality, in color and in two dimensions, seems at first glance more trustworthy, authentic, and credible than the more refined and much more indirect sort of representation painters use to create an image of reality in their works; but when artists represent reality, they do so in order to take in the outside world and grasp its essence, while television, if it represents reality, does so in and of itself, unintentionally you might say, through sheer technical determinism, or incontinence. But the fact that television offers a familiar and immediately recognizable image of reality does not mean that its images and reality can be considered equivalent. Unless you believe that reality has to resemble its representation in order to be real, there's no reason to see a Renaissance master's portrait of a young man as any less faithful a vision of reality than the apparently incontestable video image of an anchorman, world-famous in his own country, reading the news on a TV screen.

A Renaissance painting's illusion of reality, rooted in colors and pigments, in oils and brushstrokes, in delicate retouches with the brush or even the finger, or a simple smearing of the slightly damp linseed oil paste with the side of the thumb, the illusion that you have before you something living, flesh or hair, fabric or drapery, that you stand before a complex, human person, with his flaws and weaknesses, someone with a history, with his own nobility, his sensitivity, his gaze – just how many square millimeters of paint does it take to create the force of that gaze, looking down through the centuries? – is by its nature fundamentally different from the illusion offered by television when it represents reality, the purely mechanical result of an uninhabited technology.

I'd decided to spend the summer alone in Berlin to devote myself to my study of Titian Vecellio. For several years now I'd been planning a vast essay on the relationship between political power and the arts. Little by little, my focus had narrowed to sixteenth-century Italy, and more particularly to Titian Vecellio and Emperor Charles V; in the end, I'd chosen the apocryphal story of the paintbrush – according to which Charles V bent down in Titian's studio to pick up a paintbrush that had slipped from the painter's hands – as my monograph's emblematic center and the source of its title, *The Paintbrush*. I'd begun a sabbatical from my university post at the start of the year, so I could concentrate on my writing. Meanwhile, having learned of a private foundation in Berlin with a mission to aid researchers of my stripe, I'd applied for a grant. I put together a file with a detailed description of my project, carefully emphasizing that my research would absolutely require a visit to Augsburg, where Charles V had resided from 1530 until I no longer know what year (oh, dates), and where, most significantly, Titian had painted several of the finest portraits of Charles V, the large equestrian portrait now in the Prado, for instance, as well as the seated Charles V in Munich's Alte Pinakothek, his face pale and sad, a glove in his hand. It goes without saying that a stay in Augsburg might have been extraordinarily fruitful and profitable for my work, but at the same time I was perfectly prepared to concede that this project on Titian Vecellio wasn't really as specifically German as I'd sought to suggest in the skillfully-crafted little essay attached to my grant application, and that at bottom it was no more difficult, for example, to travel to Augsburg from Paris than from Berlin. Munich would have been ideal. In the end, though, I got the grant (which goes to show), and the three of us went off to Germany. At the beginning of July, Delon left for a vacation in Italy with the two children, one in her hand, the other in her stomach (eminently practical when you're always loaded down with an insane number of suitcases and handbags, as she is), and I'd accompanied the three of them to the airport. My job was to carry the tickets. I can clearly see myself in the great hall, heading toward the massive departures board, tickets in hand, looking up, comparing the one to the other with an uncertain air. Then I came back to Delon, who was waiting beside her baggage cart, and said – I don't know if every word I spoke during this stay in Berlin will be reported so faithfully here – 'Gate 28.' 'Are you sure?' Delon asked. A nagging little doubt suddenly crept into my mind. 'Gate 28, yes' (I'd gone back to check again). We kissed at some length before going our separate ways, and I bid them farewell by the check-in counter at gate 28. I gently passed my hand over my son's head and under my Delon's sweater, tenderly touching her stomach, and I watched them step through the simple little triumphal arch of the metal detector. 'Good-bye, good-bye,' my son signified with a wave of his hand (and now I wanted to cry: that's just like me).

Back home again, I did some straightening up, carefully tidying my study in preparation for the work to come (I was planning to launch into my writing very early the next morning). I began by clearing off the tall black bookshelf, where a great many papers had accumulated since my arrival in Berlin: mail and bills, assorted calling cards, various unclassified documents related to my work, some coins and old concert tickets, and a great stack of newspaper clippings in French and German that I'd been saving to read later, in tranquillity. I must have carefully cut all these articles out, one after another, as the days went by; I can well imagine myself clipping away, sitting at my desk, then standing to go and put them on a shelf with the others, to be thrown away at some later date, if not to be read at some point. Once I'd completely emptied the armoire, I began to sort through my clippings, sitting cross-legged on the floor of my study, the distended sleeves of my old wool sweater pushed up to the elbows. With a large plastic trash bag lying open nearby, I took the articles one by one from the piles around me and began to skim through them a little, naturally, as one does (sometimes, in my archival zeal, I even went so far as to stand up and get a pen from my desk to annotate a paragraph, or underline a sentence, or date a clipping), then tossed them into the bag, preserving only a few particularly interesting specimens, rigorously selected, for later perusal; with delighted anticipatory relish, I went and laid these on the nightstand in my bedroom once I'd finished my tidying. Then I quickly swept up, opened the balcony door to air out my study, went and gave the rugs a good shake in the open air, and got rid of the briefcase and portfolio that were sitting on top of my bed. With these various preliminaries completed, I set my alarm clock to 6:45, and, checking one last time to be sure that everything in the apartment was in order, that everything was ready in my study, my desk neat, a ream of blank paper beside the computer, my books and notes properly arranged and ready for use, I very gently closed the study door, made my way to the living room, sat down on the couch, and turned on the television.

Some time before, as if caught up in some sordid intox-ication, I'd taken to turning on the TV in the evening and watching everything there was to see, my mind perfectly empty, never choosing any particular program, simply watching everything that came my way, the movement, the glimmering lights, the variety. At the time I didn't quite realize just what was happening to me, but looking back, I see that short-lived period of overindulgence as a classic forerunner of the radical decision that was to come, as if, to make a clean break, you first had to go through such a phase of excessive consumption. In the meantime, I spent hours every evening motionless before the screen, my gaze fixed, bathed in the ever-shifting light of the scene changes, gradually submerged by the flood of images illuminating my face, the long parade of images blindly addressed to every-one at once and no one in particular, each channel being

378

only another strand in the vast web of electromagnetic waves daily crashing down over the world. Powerless to react, I nevertheless understood full well that I was debasing myself in these long sessions before the screen, unable to drop the remote, mechanically and frenetically changing channels in a quest for sordid and immediate pleasures, swept up in that vain inertia, that insatiable spiral, searching for ever more vileness, still more sadness.

Everywhere it was the same undifferentiated images, without margins or titles, without explanation, raw, incomprehensible, noisy and bright, ugly, sad, aggressive and jovial, syncopated, all equivalent, it was stereotypical American series, it was music videos, it was songs in English, it was game shows, it was documentaries, it was film scenes removed from their context, excerpted, it was excerpts, it was a snatch of song, it was lively, the audience clapping along in time, it was politicians sitting around a table, it was a roundtable, it was the circus, it was acrobatics, it was a game show, it was joy, unbelieving stunned laughter, hugs and tears, it was a new car being won live and in color, lips trembling with emotion, it was documentaries, it was World War II, it was a funeral march, it was columns of German prisoners trudging along a roadside, it was the liberation of the death camps, it was piles of bones on the ground, it was in all languages and on more than thirty-two channels, it was in German, it was mostly in German, everywhere it was violence and gunshots, it was bodies lying in the street, it was news, it was floods, it was football, it was game shows, it was a host with his papers before him, it was a spinning wheel that everyone in the studio was watching with heads raised, nine, it was nine, it was applause, it was commercials, it was variety shows, it was debates, it was animals, it was a man rowing in the studio, an athlete rowing and the hosts looking on with anxious expressions, sitting at a round table, a chronometer superimposed over the picture, it was images of war, the sound and framing oddly uneven, as if filmed on the fly, the picture shaking, the cameraman must have been running too, it was people running down a street and someone shooting at them, it was a woman falling, it was a woman who'd been hit, a woman of about fifty lying on the sidewalk, her slightly shabby gray coat gaping half open, her stocking torn, she'd been wounded in the thigh and she was crying out, simply crying out, screaming simple cries of horror because her thigh had been ripped open, it was the cries of that woman in pain, she was calling for help, it wasn't fiction, two or three men came back and lifted her onto the curb, the shots were still coming, it was archival footage, it was news, it was commercials, it was new cars gently snaking along idyllic roads in the light of the setting sun, it was a rock concert, it was series, it was classical music, it was a special news bulletin, it was ski-jumping, the crouching skier pushing off down the ramp, serenely letting himself glide onto the jump and leaving the world behind, motionless in midair, he was flying, he was flying, it was magnificent, that frozen body bending forward, motionless and immutable in midair. It was over. It was over: I turned off the television and lay still on the couch.

One of the principal characteristics of a turned-on television is that it artificially keeps us in a state of continual alertness, bombarding us with an endless stream of signals, all sorts of little stimuli, visual and aural, whose goal is to arouse our attention and keep our minds watchful. Provoked by these signals, the mind gathers its forces to think, but the television has already moved on to something else, to whatever comes next, new stimuli, new signals, just as strident as the ones before; soon, refusing to be held in this vigilant state by the television's unending stream of deceptive signals, recalling the disappointments of the previous moments and no doubt eager not to be fooled again, the mind begins to anticipate the true nature of the signals it is receiving, and so, rather than once again mustering its forces for reflection, it relaxes them, releases them, and lets itself drift over the tide of images set before it. Thus, as if anesthetized from having been so little stimulated even as it has been so incessantly appealed to, the human mind remains essentially passive before a television screen. Increasingly indifferent to the images it receives, it soon ceases to react at all when new signals are sent its way, knowing that to react would only mean once again falling prey to television's deceptions. Because television is not only fluid, never leaving our thoughts time to blossom in its perpetual race forward; it's also impermeable, in that it forbids any exchange of wealth between our minds and its matter.

At the beginning of the week, as I was finally preparing to launch into my study of Titian Vecellio and Charles V, my upstairs neighbors, Uwe and Inge Drescher (which we might loosely translate into French as Guy and Luce Perreire), came knocking at my door. They were going to leave for vacation the next day, and they were wondering if I might be willing to look after their plants in their absence. You can imagine my consternation. They suggested I come up for coffee later that same day so they could go over my tasks and give me the necessary particulars. After lunch, I climbed the stairs to their apartment. Receiving me somewhat coldly, they silently offered me a seat at their round dining-room table, not yet cleared, still laden with dirty plates and a blue enamel casserole full of half-desiccated cold pasta, inextricably tangled and glued together. Uwe Drescher (Guy) disappeared for a moment, then returned from the kitchen with a pot of boiling water. Having doled out two spoonfuls of instant coffee for each of us, he cautiously filled the cups with boiling water and began to lay out my plant-watching duties, the volume and frequency of the watering, the technique to be applied, the sort of water to be used; just to be sure that everything was quite clear, he reached into his pocket and pulled out a small sheet of paper, folded in four, which he'd drawn up for my use. He casually slid it across the table in my direction, and I looked it over distractedly, drumming my fingers on the tabletop. It was a plant-by-plant summary of my tasks, briefly recapitulating the various watering frequencies and any special requirements I should be aware of. I wordlessly folded the sheet and put it away in my pocket. Uwe gave me a pleased smile, took a sip of coffee, and invited me on a tour of the apartment to see the plants. Slowly we strolled from one room to the next, Uwe leading the way, very tall and bespectacled, smiling a gratified smile, distinguished and enigmatic, one hand rustling in his trouser pocket, jingling his change (maybe he was going to give me a little something), and Inge beside me in her clingy little dress, very much the mistress of the house, occasionally pausing before a plant for an informal introduction, notifying the plant in German that I would be looking after it for the summer (I'm always a little surprised to meet a plant that speaks German). Reserved as I am, I scarcely said hello, limiting myself to a simple, discreet half-blink in the plant's direction, my cup of coffee in my hand. We entered Uwe's study, a study in every way comparable to my own one floor below, with the same French doors and the same little balcony, onto which Uwe suggested the three of us venture for a moment. It was a bit cool outside, and a light wind was blowing. I stood with my elbows on the railing, my mind elsewhere. Paying virtually no attention now to Uwe's botanical explanations (head down, I was absentmindedly dropping pebbles on the passers-by in the street), I cast only a polite little glance at the fertile, dark soil he was showing me, running his marveling finger the length of the planter, in which, here and there, one could indeed make out several little daisy tots. Standing next to me, Uwe pointed an experienced, loving finger toward each newborn seedling, and I nodded slowly and sadly, vaguely hunched over the soil. We returned to his study, and, as my gaze lingered on the various files piled on his desk next to his computer and printer, Uwe drew my attention to an old rubber tree on the mantelpiece, with lovely, dense, dark leaves, indifferent and taciturn as an old Chinaman, which only half listened in as Uwe informed me of its needs, above all that it preferred a light misting to a copious dowsing (which is entirely understandable on the part of an old Chinaman). On the floor sat a begonia with a fragile stalk, and now it was Inge, taking over for her husband, who asked me to be so kind as to perform a very gentle resurfacing of its topsoil in two weeks or so, which means simply scraping away the old dirt around the stalk and replacing it with a good light mixture, of which I would find a five-liter bag in the hall closet, but I wasn't to worry, it was all written down on the sheet. Furthermore, Inge would be grateful, she added, familiarly taking my arm to lead me out of the room, if, during the resurfacing, I wouldn't mind poking a bamboo chopstick into the pot a few times, so as to make aeration holes in the peat. Yes, of course, I said, aeration holes in the peat (she could count on me), and she gave my forearm a little squeeze of anticipatory gratitude, discreet but ardent. In the front hallway, as the Dreschers stood waiting side by side at their bedroom door, I lingered dreamily before a small painting hung on the wall, briefly studying it, my coffee cup in my hand, wondering what it was supposed to depict (an aularch, shall we say). Rejoining the Dreschers, I walked ahead of them into the bedroom, continuing onward for a few indecisive steps, distractedly pushing aside the limp branch of a plumbago that drooped from a macrame hanger, then finally coming to a halt in the middle of the room, glancing toward the Dreschers' large double bed. I went and sat down. Sitting on the Dreschers' bed, I slowly stirred the contents of my cup, withdrew the little spoon, and sucked it dry. With a perfectly serene gaze I made a slow circular sweep of the room, and for a moment I looked up to consider the plumbago. I took a small sip of coffee and set the cup back onto its saucer. You know, life. The Dreschers stood before me, slightly uncomfortable to be with me here in their bedroom; finally they sat down as well, Uwe on the edge of a wooden table, affecting a casual attitude, his right hand still in his trouser pocket, his carefree left hand caressing a gardenia leaf with controlled agitation, and Inge beside me on the bed, slightly stiff, discreetly tugging at the hem of her dress to protect her upper thighs from my supposed Jesuitical prurience, or at least to shield them from the several prudishly covetous glances I must surely be casting their way, then finally standing up to show me her most precious possession, a fern, a magnificent fern, it's true, moist and spreading, and as she fingered it lovingly she confessed that it was fragile and delicate, and that it would be best to prepare it gently for my coming, lest it take fright when I reappeared all alone to give it a sprinkle. I stood up and forced myself to caress a few fern leaves as well, using the knobby thing on my key-ring. The Dreschers appreciated that, I think. In the entryway, as I was leaving, they handed me a copy of their key.

The first time I went up to the Dreschers' after they'd left for vacation (to water and have a little chat with their plants, as requested) was that day in late July when I stopped watching television. After dinner, I'd gone into the living room and stretched out on the couch with my newspaper, very determined not to turn on the TV. With the dark set before me, I calmly read the paper in the dimly-lit living room, secluded in a little pool of slanting light from the halogen reading lamp I'd turned on beside me (the warm, golden glow skimmed neatly over the top of my head, ringing my bald pate with a most attractive duckling-like down). It was obviously not for the purpose of pointless self-mortification that I'd sat down directly facing the set; rather, I wanted to test my capacity for resistance in the very presence of the object of temptation, so that I could turn on the TV at any moment if it turned out my will wasn't up to the challenge. In times past, I frequently didn't watch television when I found myself alone in the evening, and simply did something else, reading or listening to music for example, to remain in the realm of decency; this evening, though, television had taken on a disproportionate importance for me simply because I'd made the decision to stop watching it, and, although it pained me to admit it, television now completely occupied my thoughts. But I pretended otherwise. I opened my newspaper, and, with a nice little cushion nestled behind my nape, quietly read the TV listings in front of the silent set.

I hadn't once thought of the Dreschers' plants since their departure, now some three weeks past (they'd set off at more or less the same time as the Tour de France), and it was only that evening, as I lolled in the living room in my pajamas before going to bed, that I happened onto their list of instructions. I reread it pensively and, troubled by a certain remorse, concerned in spite of myself for the welfare of the plants they'd left in my care, I decided to go up and pay them a little post-prandial visit. Climbing the dark stairs to the Dreschers' in my pajamas (the lights in the stairway weren't working), I met a rather odd character coming downstairs on tiptoe, carrying a white leather gym bag that looked unusually heavy. In the darkness, I thought I glimpsed several stereo components and some silverware hastily stuffed inside it. I stopped in the middle of the flight, my hand on the banister, and watched him continue down the stairs. He picked up his pace. I stood motionless, my watering can in my hand (I'd brought my own, a big galvanized-tin one). The stranger furtively looked over his shoulder and gave me a quick glance before disappearing. Our relationship ended there (he could be in prison by now for all I know). Arriving on the third-floor landing, I bent over the lock and turned the key, cautiously pushing open the Dreschers' door. I was feeling a little uneasy. I fumbled for the light switch in the entryway and took a few steps down the hall. There wasn't a sound to be heard in the Dreschers' apartment. I noiselessly entered Uwe's study, silent and deserted in the semi-darkness. There was no one in the room, notwithstanding the rubber tree, ever faithful to itself on the mantelpiece, mute, aged, smooth, Chinese. Its tranquillity soothed me, and I sat down on Uwe's desk chair to collect myself. I stood up, my watering can in my hand, opened the French doors, and went out onto the balcony for a breath of night air. But no sooner had I set foot on the balcony than I threw myself back against the wall and froze. Do you know what was happening? Glancing down into the street below, I'd caught sight of the evil-doer I'd met on the stairway a few moments before, now engaged in a hushed discussion with one of his accomplices (a woman, or a man in a wig), who was helping him stow the gym bag in the back of a stolen van. I was witness to a burglary, just my luck. I stood there motionless on the balcony in my pajamas, holding my breath, my watering can in my hand. The streets of this residential neighborhood were soundless at that hour; listening closely, I managed, thanks to my good knowledge of German, of German language and culture I might even say (I'd undertaken a serious study of German since my move to Berlin), to make out a few snatches of their conversation. 'What sort of guy?' the woman was asking. 'He was bald,' said the other one, 'a bald guy in pajamas.' He glanced up toward the building. 'With a watering can,' he added. 'A bald guy in pajamas with a watering can,' the woman said, and she began to laugh uncontrollably, a bald man in pajamas with a watering can on the stairway, it was just too hilarious. 'And he thought you were stealing something,' she managed to add before succumbing to another fit of laughter. She was laughing so hard that she nearly collapsed onto the sidewalk, but at the last moment she clutched at the man's arm and saved herself. 'Yeah, you should have seen the look on his face,' he said, and began to laugh with her. Everyone in the street was laughing now – it felt like another country. Standing on the balcony in my pajamas, my watering can in my hand, even I found myself caught up in the general merriment, and I repressed an irritated little smile.

A few minutes later I was in the Dreschers' kitchen, wrapped in a dressing gown (I'd hastily thrown a dressing gown over my pajamas, a large plaid one of Uwe's, with wide, flared, satin-stitch embroidered sleeves), filling my watering can from the faucet, forearms bared, trying not to dampen my feet. I turned off the tap, let the last droplets dribble into the can, as you do after a pee – the Dreschers' faucet was fitted with one of those limp rubber foreskins whose flexibility lets the housewife aim the stream wherever she wants it – and then, having completed this operation, straining to hoist my tin watering can, now heavy with several liters of water, I set out into the apartment clutching the can in my right hand like a suitcase. Reaching the entryway, I delved into my pocket for the list the Dreschers had left me and reread it distractedly. Good Lord, how am I supposed to wade through all this botanical German? And where do I begin? Here's the complete text of the list, which might help to illustrate my perplexity. Kitchen windowsill: Parsley and basil seedlings. Everyday (insofar as possible). Kitchen: Small pot of thyme. Twice a week. Entryway: Yucca. Once a week. Study: Ficus elastica (Misting is welcome. Little care required). Begonia (Never dampen the leaves. No misting. Resurfacing essential, every two weeks: change the soil, turn it over all around the root). Balcony: Daisy seedlings. Every day (insofar as possible). Bedroom: Gardenia (Never dampen the leaves. Polishing is welcome. Water twice a week). Fern (Considerable care required: twice a day if very hot; once a day if not. No polishing). Hibiscus (Little care required). Plumbago (Twice a week). This was followed by two blank lines, and then an intimidating little nota-bene in a feminine hand, large, enthusiastic, not unpiquant. N.B. Plants love music! OK. I folded the sheet, slipped it pensively into the breast pocket of my pajamas. What on earth was I going to sing for them?

Arriving in Uwe's study, I was pleased to find the rubber plant still on the mantelpiece. I should say that I'd taken a shine to that silent plant, with its large oval green leaves, like ears, their surface so smooth that they might have been painted with lacquer. I liked the impassive melancholy exuded by that rubber plant, its Sphinx-like quality, its calm, its detachment, what you might call its fundamental indifference to its environment. If it could talk, it would yawn: such would be its revelation, its only comment on the world around it. Not even a reproach. I advanced into the room, the watering can in my hand, paying no further attention to the rubber plant. It had earned my esteem. I imagine it was grateful for my discretion. I merely gave it a thoughtful glance as I entered, just from the corner of my eye, and then I quickly looked away. I've always liked these modest friendships, all tact and quiet reserve, all silence and inexcitability. Which is exactly how this was: it was almost as if I weren't there at all. I blotted my forehead. All this trouble I was going to. I squatted down next to the watering can, pushing my dressing-gown sleeve up to the elbow, dipped in my hands, and stood up to let the water drizzle from the improvised sprinkler of my fingers, showering the leaves with a thousand whirling droplets. I repeated this operation two or three times, bending over the watering can and wiggling my fingers in the water for a moment (out of pure lasciviousness, pure lasciviousness), before withdrawing them to bless the rubber plant from a distance, one last time, with a quick, careless aspersion.

Sitting in the Dreschers' bedroom, my chores at an end, I granted myself a short break on the bed with the watering can at my feet (the Dreschers' bed had become my general headquarters for this operation). The room sat silent and orderly around me, the Dreschers having taken care to leave nothing lying around on the chairs when they left for vacation. Behind the door, Inge's négligée hung on a nail, light and filmy, ideal for a brutal crumpling in a clenched hand; at its feet sat a pair of slippers, not so sexy, pale blue, more inhibited. The few green plants in this room appeared to have been abandoned since the beginning of summer, as if left to their own devices, their leaves withered, yellowed, dusty, crazed in spots. The fern was a pitiful sight, limp in its pot, drooping down over the rim in a sad parody of a weeping willow, its leaves drained, its epidermis wrinkled. It must have suffered more in the heat than the others. I took out the Dreschers' list to reread what was said of this fern. Considerable care required (ah yes, considerable care, just what I was saying), Twice a day, if very hot; if not, once a day. In other words, I'd fallen far short of the mark. Nevertheless, I began to fear, without moving from my spot (this was all pure conjecture, most pleasant to indulge in on the Dreschers' bed), that, if I watered the fern too copiously now, it might wilt good and proper. In the end, hoping to spare it too great a thermic jolt, I went into the kitchen and filled an old basin with warm water; then, back in the bedroom, removing the pot from its shelf, I set it to soak for the night so that the plant might return to life at its own speed, by a slow, progressive infiltration of the moisture, by osmosis and capillarity, and so recover the vigor and splendor of times past. I'd gone and sat down on the Dreschers' bed again, and now I was gazing dubiously at the fern marinating in its lukewarm bath. To think: here I was in Berlin, after ten o'clock in the evening, sitting in my pajamas on the upstairs neighbors' bed worrying about a fern. Before heading downstairs, I took off Uwe's dressing gown and hung it next to Inge's négligée behind the door (the dressing gown had a bit of an odor to it, in spite of everything; I then sniffed at Inge's négligée and there it was again, that same little odor you always find on other people's nightclothes, warm and slightly sour). I turned out the light and stood in the doorway for a moment, looking at the fern in its basin in the dark, a handful of leaves strewn languidly over the carpet. I gently closed the bedroom door and left the Dreschers' apartment, and I started down the stairs, my watering can in my hand, enjoying the sense of a job well done.

Arriving home, I went and turned off the little halogen lamp I'd left on in the living room and, feeling my way through the darkness, I walked toward the window. It was pitch dark outside, and I could just make out the straight, even line of the nearby roofs in the night. A few televisions were still on here and there in the windows of the buildings across the street, bathing the living rooms in a sort of milky glow. Every ten seconds or so, in two quick steps, with each change of scene in the program being screened, this glow disappeared and was replaced by another cone of light, which immediately flooded the available space. I watched the lights shifting and changing together, or, if not together, at least in successive, synchronous bursts, presumably corresponding to the various shows they were watching in the various apartments before me, and this vision gave me that same painful sense of multiplicity and uniformity as the sight of thousands of flashbulbs going off in a stadium during an important sporting event. I went on looking outside, standing there in my pajamas at the window, and I didn't know if I should interpret what then happened as a sign from destiny, a small gesture of personal encouragement that the heavens had decided to offer me as a reward for abandoning the secular joys of television, but, at that very moment, in one of the windows of the tall modern apartment building directly across the way, on the fourth floor to be precise, a young woman appeared in her apartment, stark naked. This envoy from the heavens (I recognized her immediately, she was a student I'd already seen two or three times around the neighborhood) was entirely nude, and delectable in every way. She made me think of some creature painted by Cranach, Venus or Lucretia, that same svelte form, fragile, almost helicoidal, breasts as venial as minor sins and next to no hair on her pubis, just a frail blonde lock, a bit tousled and unkempt at the most intimate spot. Apparently she was looking for her pajamas, or what took the place of pajamas, a sailor's t-shirt with blue and white horizontal stripes, which at last she found and lazily pulled on before picking up a bottle of mineral water from a table and slowly walking away from the window, her bottom bare under her striped t-shirt, giving me plenty of time to observe the undulating progression of what was then my most beloved element of her decor, framed in the glowing screen of that window in the night, until at last she disappeared and turned off the light. The heavens had signed off for the evening.

JENNY ERPENBECK

From

GO, WENT, GONE

Translated by Susan Bernofsky

2

ONE THURSDAY IN late August, ten men gather in front of Berlin's Town Hall. According to news reports, they've decided to stop eating. Three days later they decide to stop drinking too. Their skin is black. They speak English, French, Italian, as well as other languages that no one here understands. What do these men want? They are asking for work. They want to support themselves by working. They want to remain in Germany. Who are you, they're asked by police officers and various city employees who've been called in. We won't say, the men reply. But you have to say, they're told, otherwise how do we know whether the law applies to you and you're allowed to stay here and work? We won't say who we are, the men say. If you were in our shoes, the others respond, would you take in a guest you don't know? The men say nothing. We have to verify that you're truly in need of assistance. The men say nothing. You might be criminals, we have to check. They say nothing. Or just freeloaders. The men are silent. We're running short ourselves, the others say, there are rules here, and you have to abide by them if you want to stay. And finally they say: You can't blackmail us. But the men with dark skin don't say who they are. They don't eat, they don't drink, they don't say who they are. They simply are. The silence of these men who would rather die than reveal their identity unites with the waiting of all these others who want their questions answered to produce a great silence in the middle of the square called

Alexanderplatz in Berlin. Despite the fact that Alexander-platz is always very loud because of the traffic noise and the excavation site beside the new subway station.

Why is it that Richard, walking past all these black and white people sitting and standing that afternoon, doesn't hear this silence?

He's thinking of Rzeszów.

A friend of his, an archaeologist, told him about discoveries made during the tunneling operation at Alexanderplatz and invited him to visit the excavation site. He has time enough on his hands, and swimming in the lake isn't an option, because of this man. His friend explained that there used to be an extensive system of cellars all around Town Hall. Subterranean vaults that housed a marketplace during the Middle Ages. While people waited for a hearing, an appointment, a ruling, they would go shopping, much as they do today. Fish, cheese, wine – everything that keeps better chilled – was sold in these catacombs.

Just like in Rzeszów.

As a student in the 1960s, Richard would sometimes sit on the edge of the Neptune Fountain between two lectures, his trouser legs rolled up, his feet in the water, book in his lap. Even then, unbeknownst to him, these hollow spaces were there beneath him, only a few yards of earth separating them from his feet.

Several years ago, back when his wife was still alive, the two of them had visited the Polish town of Rzeszów on one of their vacations – a town with an elaborate system of tunnels running beneath it, dating from the Middle Ages. Like a second town, invisible to the casual observer, this labyrinth had grown beneath the earth, a mirror image of the houses visible aboveground. The cellar of every house gave access to this public marketplace that was lit only by torches. And when there was a war up above, the residents of the town would retreat underground. Later, in the time of fascism, Jews took refuge here until the Nazis hit on the idea of filling the subterranean passageways with smoke.

Rzeszów.

But the rubble-filled vaults beneath Berlin's Town Hall escaped detection even by the Nazis, who contented themselves with flooding the subway tunnels in the final days of the war. Probably to drown their own people who had fled underground, taking refuge from the Allies' air raids. *There you go again, cutting off your nose to spite your face.*

Have any of the men collapsed yet? asks a young woman holding a microphone, behind her a colossus has a camera on his shoulder. No, one of the policemen says. Are they being force-fed? So far, no, the policeman says, see for yourself. Have any of them been sent to the hospital? I think one was yesterday before my shift, another man in uniform says. Could you tell me which hospital? No, we're not allowed to say. But then I can't place my story. That's too bad, the first policeman says, I'm afraid there's nothing we can do about that. The young woman says: If nothing special happens, I can't make a story out of it. Sure, makes sense, the policeman says. No one will want to run it. The other officer says: There might be some action later today, maybe in the evening. The young woman: All I have left is an hour, tops. There has to be time for editing. Makes sense, the man in uniform says and grins.

Richard doesn't glance over at Town Hall two hours later either when he's walking again past the train station, he's looking at the big fountain on the left, its various terraces arranged like a staircase leading up to the base of the TV tower. Built during Socialist times and bubbling over with water summer after summer, it was the perfect spot for happy children to test their mettle, balancing their way across the stone rows separating the fountain's pools as their laughing, proud parents looked on, and both children and parents alike would now and then gaze up at the tower's silvery sphere, enjoying the vertigo: It's falling! It's falling right on top of us! Three hundred sixty-five meters to its tip, measuring out the days of an entire year, a father says, and: No, it's not falling, it just looks that way, a mother says to her dripping children. A father tells his children – but only if they really want to hear it – the story of the construction worker who fell from the very top of the tower as it was being built, but because it's so tall, it took the man a very long time to fall to the bottom, and meanwhile the people who lived in the buildings down below were able to drag mattresses outside while the worker was still falling, an entire huge pile of mattresses while he fell and fell, and the pile was finished just in time for the worker to arrive at the end of his fall, and he landed as softly as the princess and the pea in the fairy tale and got right back to his feet without a scratch on him. The children delight in this miracle that saved the worker, and now they're ready to go back to playing. At the Alexanderplatz fountain, summer after summer, humankind appeared to be in fine fettle and content – the sort of condition generally promised only for the future, for that distant age of utter contentment known as *Communism* that mankind would eventually make its way to via a sort of staircase of progress leading into dazzling, astonishing heights, a state to be achieved in the next hundred, two hundred, or at the very most three hundred years.

But then, defying all expectations, the East German

government that had commissioned this fountain suddenly disappeared after a mere forty years of existence along with all its promises for the future, leaving behind the staircase-shaped fountain to bubble away on its own, and bubble it did, summer after summer, reaching to dazzling, astonishing heights while adventurous children continued to balance their way across, admired by their laughing, proud parents. What can a picture like this that's lost its story tell us? What vision are these happy people advertising now? Has time come to a standstill? Is there anything left to wish for?

The men who would rather die than say who they are have been joined by sympathizers. A young girl has sat down cross-legged on the ground next to one of the dark-skinned men and is conversing with him in a low voice, nodding now and then, rolling herself a cigarette. A young man is arguing with the policemen: It's not as if they're living here, he says, and the policeman replies: Well, that wouldn't be permitted. Exactly, the young man says. The black men are crouching or lying on the ground, some of them have spread out sleeping bags to lie on, others a blanket, others nothing at all. They're using a camping table to prop up a sign. The sign leaning against it is a large piece of cardboard painted white, on which black letters spell out in English: *We become visible*. Beneath this, in smaller green letters, someone has written the German translation with a marker. Was it the young man or the girl? If the dark-skinned men were to glance in Richard's direction at just this moment, all they would see is his back making a beeline for the train station, he is dressed in a blazer despite the heat, and now he vanishes among all the other people, some of whom are in a hurry and know exactly where they're going, while others meander, holding maps, they're here to see 'Alex,' the center of that part of Berlin long known as the 'Russian zone' and still often referred to as the 'Eastern zone' in jest. If these silent men were then to raise their eyes, they would behold – as a backdrop to the bustle of the square and elevated one floor above – the windows of the Fitness Center, located beside the tower's plinth under an extravagantly pleated canopy. Behind the windows they would see people on bicycles and people running, bicycling and running toward the enormous windows hour after hour, as if trying to ride or run across to Town Hall as quickly as possible, either to join them, the men with dark skin, or to approach the policemen to declare their solidarity with one or the other side, even if it would mean bursting through the windows to fly or leap the last bit of the way. But obviously both the bicycles and the treadmills are firmly mounted in place, and those exercising on them exert themselves without any forward progress. It's quite possible that these fitness-minded individuals can observe everything happening on Alexanderplatz in front of them, but they probably wouldn't be able to read, say, the words on the sign – for that, they're too far away.

3

For dinner, Richard makes open-face sandwiches with cheese and ham, with a salad on the side. The cheese was on sale today (at the store now invariably referred to by the West German designation *Supermarkt* – it was a *Kaufhalle* back in Socialist times). It was almost past its sell-by date. He doesn't have to scrimp, his pension covers all his needs, but why pay more than necessary? He slices onions for the salad – he's been slicing onions all his life, but just recently he saw in a cookbook the best way to hold the onion to keep it from sliding out from under the knife, there's an ideal form for everything, not just in matters of work and art, but also for the most mundane, ordinary things. When it comes down to it, he thinks, we probably spend our entire lives just trying to attain this form. And when you've finally achieved it in a few different areas, you get wiped off the planet. In any case, he no longer feels the need to prove anything to anyone with the skills he's mastered, not that there's anyone left to prove anything to. His wife no longer sees what he does. His lover wouldn't have been the least bit interested in the art of slicing onions. He's the only one left who can feel pleased when he masters or understands something. He is pleased. And this pleasure has no objective. This is the first advantage of living alone: vanity proves to be superfluous baggage. And the second: there's no one to disrupt your routine. Frying cubes of stale bread to make croutons for salad, wrapping the string around the teabag to squeeze out the liquid when you remove it from the pot, bending the long stems of the rosebushes down to the ground in winter and covering them with earth – and so forth. The pleasure he takes in having everything in its proper place, accounted for, well-husbanded so that nothing is wasted, the pleasure he takes in achievements that don't hinder others in their own attempts to achieve: all this, as he sees it, boils down to pleasure taken in a routine, a sense of order that he doesn't have to establish but only find, an order that lies outside him and for this reason connects him to everything that grows, flies, and glides, while at the same time it separates him from certain people – but this he doesn't mind.

Back when his lover started to make fun of him and got more frequently annoyed when he corrected her, he still hadn't been able to let go of certain fixed ways of doing things that seemed to him absolutely appropriate. He and his wife had almost always been in agreement, at least about things like this. At the end of the war, she'd been shot in the legs, a German girl strafed by German planes as she fled the Russian tanks. If her brother hadn't dragged her out of the street, she certainly wouldn't have survived. So his wife had learned at the age of three that everything you can't size up properly is potentially lethal. He himself had been an infant when his family left Silesia and resettled in Germany. In the tumult of their departure, he almost got separated from his mother; he would have been left behind outright if it hadn't been for a Russian soldier, who, amid the press of people on the station platform, handed him to his mother through the train's window over the heads of many other resettlers. This was a story his mother told him so many times that eventually it seemed to him he remembered it himself. The *mayhem of war* was what she called it. His father had no doubt engendered mayhem of his own as a soldier on the front lines in Norway and Russia. How many children did his father – himself little more than a child in those days – separate from their parents? Or hand to their parents at the last possible moment? Two years passed before the former soldier found his family again – they'd meanwhile settled in Berlin – and saw his son for the first time. The Red Cross missing-persons announcements kept coming over the radio for another few years, but meanwhile his father sat once more beside his mother on the sofa, enjoying a piece of 'bee sting' cake with coffee made from real coffee beans, and the infant who'd almost gone astray amid the mayhem was now a schoolboy. The boy could never ask his father about the war. Leave him be, his mother said, shaking her head, waving him away, leave your father alone. His father would just sit there in silence. What would have become of the infant if the train had pulled out of the station two minutes earlier? What would have become of the girl – later Richard's wife – if her brother hadn't pulled her out of the street? In any case, there never would have been a wedding joining an orphan boy to a dead girl. *Do not disturb my circles*, Archimedes (tracing geometric figures in the sand with a finger) is said to have exhorted the Roman soldier who then fatally stabbed him. You can never count on freedom from mayhem – Richard and his wife had always agreed on this. No doubt that's why she understood so much better than his young lover what he was after in his constant search for what was right and proper. (She'd also had a drinking problem. But that was another story.)

He sits down and turns on the TV, the evening news has various local and regional items to report on: a bank robbery, the airport workers' strike, gas prices rising again, and at Alexanderplatz a group of ten men – refugees apparently – have begun a hunger strike, one of them collapsed and was taken to a hospital. At Alexanderplatz? The cameras show a man on a stretcher being slid into an ambulance. Right where Richard passed by this afternoon? A young journalist speaks into a microphone as several figures crouch or lie on the ground behind her, the camera picks up a camping table with a cardboard sign on top: *We become visible*, with the German translation written in smaller, green letters. Why didn't he see the demonstration? His first slice of bread had cheese on top, now comes the second slice, with ham. This isn't the first time he's felt ashamed to be eating dinner in front of a TV screen displaying the bodies of people felled by gunfire or killed by earthquakes or plane crashes, someone's shoe left behind after a suicide bombing, or plastic-wrapped corpses lying side by side in a mass grave during an epidemic.

Today, too, he feels ashamed, but goes on eating as usual. As a child he learned the meaning of adversity. But that doesn't mean he has to starve himself just because a desperate man has begun a hunger strike. Or so he tells himself. His going hungry would do nothing to help one of these striking men. And if that man were living in circumstances as favorable as Richard's, he would surely be sitting down to dinner now, just like him. Even today, at his advanced age, Richard is still working to cast off his mother's Protestant inheritance: remorse as a default position. But she hadn't known about the camps. At least that's what she said. He wonders what once, before the age of Luther, filled that region of the soul now colonized by the guilty conscience. A certain numbness has become indispensable since Luther nailed his theses to the door of the church – a form of self-defense, probably. He sticks his fork in the amply filled salad bowl, telling himself it would be a logical fallacy to just stop eating one day out of solidarity with this or that poor, desperate person some- where in the world. He'd still be trapped in his cage of free agency, imprisoned by the luxury of free choice. For him, refusing to eat would be just as capricious as gluttony. . . . The onions in the salad taste good. Fresh onions. And the men still refuse to give their names, the young woman is just saying. She appears concerned about the hunger strikers, she is convincing in her concern. Is this concerned tone of voice something journalists now formally study? And who's to say if the footage of that man on the stretcher is really from Alex- anderplatz? *Summa* was the name given in the Middle Ages to the universal reference books in which a map of Madrid looked exactly like a map of Nuremberg or Paris – the map simply bore witness to the fact that the names Madrid and Paris belonged to different cities. Today, things were perhaps not terribly different. Hadn't he seen figures being carried off on stretchers in countless news reports in all sorts of different catastrophes around the world? Did it even matter whether these images flashing past, in tenths of seconds, really shared a time and place with the horrors that gave rise to the reports? Could an image stand as proof? And should it? What stories lay behind all the random images constantly placed before us? Or was it no longer a matter of storytelling? Today alone, six people died in swimming accidents in the greater Berlin area, the newscaster says in conclusion, a *tragic record*, and now it's time for the weather. Six people just like that man still at the bottom of the lake. *We become visible.* Why didn't Richard see these men at Alexanderplatz?

4

At night Richard gets up to pee and then can't fall back asleep again, as has started to happen these past few months. He lies there in the dark, watching his thoughts as they stray around. He thinks of the man lying at the bottom of the lake, down where the lake is cold, even in summer. He thinks of his empty office. The young woman with the microphone. Back when he was able to sleep through the night, a night had felt like a reprieve, but it hasn't felt like that in a long time now. Everything keeps going on and on, not even stopping in the dark.

The next day he mows the lawn, then opens a can of pea soup for lunch, then he rinses out the can and makes coffee. His head hurts, so he takes an aspirin. Headache. Stomach-ache. *Umach steak.* He and his lover liked to jokingly mix up words. Or else pronounce typographical errors. In this way, *old* became *odl*, *short* became *shotr*, and so on. Why didn't he see the men? *We become visible.* Ha.

Richard takes the prose translation of the *Odyssey* from the bookshelf and reads his favorite part, chapter 11.

Later he drives to the garden supply center to have his lawnmower blade sharpened.

In the evening, he makes open-face sandwiches and salad and calls his friend Peter, the archaeologist, who tells him about the bulldozer at the edge of the pit at Alexanderplatz that suddenly wound up with a modernist statue in its bucket. From the Nazi exhibition *Degenerate Art*, he says. Just imagine. Maybe the offices of the Third Reich's Chamber of Culture took a hit in an air raid, and their cache of forbidden treasures tumbled down into the Middle Ages, as it were. Absolutely incredible, Richard says, and his friend replies: the earth is full of wonders. Richard thinks – but doesn't say – that the earth is more like a garbage heap containing all the ages of history, age after age there in the dark, and all the people of all these ages, their mouths stopped up with dirt, an endless copulation but no womb fertile, and progress is only when the creatures walking the earth know nothing of all these things.

The next day it rains, so Richard stays home and finally clears away that pile of old newspapers.

He pays a few bills by telephone, then writes out a shopping list for later.

2 lb. onions
2x lettuce
½ loaf white bread
½ loaf dark rye
1 butter
cheese, cold cuts?
3x soup (pea or lentil)

noodles
tomatoes

———————————————

16mm screws
varnish
2 hooks

After lunch he lies down for twenty minutes. The blanket he covers himself with – genuine camelhair – was a Christmas present from his wife many years ago.

He decides to wait for a sunnier day to start unpacking the boxes in the basement.

The student whose manuscript, 'Levels of Meaning in Ovid's *Metamorphoses*,' he'd packed in one of the boxes sometimes dozed through his seminar, hiding her face behind her hands. But the paper she'd submitted had been perfectly fine.

By afternoon, the rain is down to a slight drizzle, so he gets in his car and drives to the supermarket – the one that used to be a *Kaufhalle*. Tomorrow is Sunday, he mustn't forget anything. Then he drives to the garden center for the last few items. The store smells of fertilizer, wood shavings, and paint; they also have maggots to use as fishing bait, diving masks, and eggs fresh from the village.

Diving masks.

The local and regional news hour that evening includes a brief report: the refugees on hunger strike have been removed from Alexanderplatz. The demonstration is over.

What a shame, he thinks. He'd liked the notion of making oneself visible by publicly refusing to say who one is. Odysseus had called himself Nobody to escape from the Cyclops's cave. Who put out your eye, the other giants ask the blind Cyclops from outside. Nobody, the Cyclops bellows. Who's

hurting you? Nobody! Odysseus, whose false name – one
that cancels him out – the Cyclops keeps shrieking, clings to
the belly of a ram and in this way slips out of the man-eating
monster's cave undetected.

The placard with the inscription *We become visible* is probably in some trash can now, or – if it's too big to fit – lying
on the ground, sodden with rain.

5

During the next two weeks, Richard sees to the new door
for the shed, he has the flue in the fireplace repaired, he
transplants the peonies, varnishes the boat's oars, deals with
all the unopened mail that's piled up over the course of the
summer; he goes once to physical therapy and three times
to the movies. Every morning, he reads the newspaper over
breakfast as always. Every morning he drinks tea – Earl Grey
with milk and sugar – and eats one piece of bread with honey
and one with cheese (sometimes with a slice of cucumber)
but only on Sundays does he add a soft-boiled egg. He can
take his time every day now, but he still only wants an egg
on Sundays. The way he's used to it. It's a novelty to be able
to linger over his tea as long as he likes, and so he now reads
certain articles all the way through that he might once have
skimmed. He'd really like to know what's become of the
ten men from Alexanderplatz, but he doesn't see anything
about that. He reads that off the coast of the Italian island
of Lampedusa, sixty-four of three hundred twenty-nine
refugees drowned when their boat capsized, including some
from Ghana, Sierra Leone, and Niger. He reads that somewhere over Nigeria a man from Burkina Faso fell from a
height of ten thousand feet after stowing away in an aircraft's

landing gear, he reads about a school in Kreuzberg that's been occupied by a group of black Africans for months, reads about Oranienplatz, where refugees have apparently been living in tents for a year now. Where exactly is Burkina Faso? The American vice president recently referred to Africa as a country, even though – as the article about this faux pas pointed out – there are fifty-four African countries. Fifty-four? He had no idea. What is the capital of Ghana? Of Sierra Leone? Or Niger? Some of his first-year students had been unable to recite even the first four lines of the *Odyssey* in Greek. During his own studies, that would have been unthinkable. He gets up and takes out his atlas. The capital of Ghana is Accra, the capital of Sierra Leone is Freetown, the capital of Niger Niamey. Had he ever known the names of these cities? Burkina Faso is a country to the west of Niger. And Niger? In the Department of German, just a few doors down the hall from him at the university, there had often been students from Mozambique and Angola in the 1970s, mechanical engineering or agriculture majors who were also learning German from his colleagues. Cooperation with these partner nations ceased when German Socialism came to an end. Was it because of these students that he'd purchased the book *Negerliteratur*? He can't remember, but he still knows exactly where to find it on his bookshelf, books are willing to wait, he says whenever visitors ask if he's read all the books on his shelves. . . . The capital of Mozambique is Maputo, the capital of Angola is Luanda. He shuts the atlas and goes to the other room, to the shelf with *Negerliteratur*. 'Negro' is a word no one would say now, but back then people printed it on book jackets. When was that? During Richard's postwar childhood, his mother had often read to him at his request from the book *Hatschi Bratschi's Hot-Air Balloon* that she'd found in a suitcase in the rubble of Berlin.

Cannibal mama's in a rush,
Supper will bring such joy.
Grab him, won't you, hurry up!
Shouts the cannibal boy.

He'd particularly liked the pictures of the little cannibal boy with the bones from his last meal stuck crosswise into his hair. His mother must have given the book away at some point, and later, when he asked a bookseller about it as an adult, he learned that while the book still existed, it had been reprinted in a new politically correct edition featuring an Africa devoid of cannibals, and the original version could be found only in rare book shops at astronomical prices. Here too the prohibition had served only to make the prohibited item more desirable. The workings of causality are indirect, not direct, he thinks, as he's had occasion to think so many times in recent years. But the book *Negerliteratur* is still exactly where it's always been on the shelf, waiting for him. Indeed, the title dates from 1951. He opens the book and reads a few lines. *The earth is round and completely surrounded by swamp. Behind the swamp lies the land of the bush spirits. Under the earth there is only more earth. What comes after that, no one knows.*

6

By the time Richard finally finds the former school in Berlin's Kreuzberg district, it's already dusk. There are no lights illuminating the old schoolyard, so the black figures walking toward him can scarcely be distinguished from the night air. The stairwell stinks. The walls are covered with graffiti. On the second floor, he looks through an open doorway right into the men's bathroom, he goes inside to see what a men's bathroom looks like here: three of the four booths have been sealed up with red-and-white tape. The other side of the room is empty, maybe that's where the showers used to be. The pipes have been removed, all that's left are the tiles and a hideous stench. He goes out again. Not a person to be seen, black or white. There's only a handwritten note on the wall reading *Auditorium*, with an arrow pointing up. Now he can hear voices, too, coming from upstairs. Probably everyone's at the assembly already. He's a bit late. He got lost on the way from the S-Bahn station because he still doesn't know his way around West Berlin. *The Berlin Senate invites local residents and refugees to participate in a general discussion of recent events in the auditorium of the occupied school in Kreuzberg*, he read in the newspaper. So what's he doing here? He doesn't live in the neighborhood, and he's not a refugee either. Is the only freedom the fall of the Berlin wall brought him the freedom to go places he's afraid of?

The auditorium is full of people, they stand and sit on the floor, on chairs and tables. The refugees' mattresses have been pushed to the sides of the room, a few tents have been set up in the middle, firmly anchored on the herringbone parquet. What counts as outside, as inside? The former stage of the auditorium is also covered with mattresses, squeezed in tightly side by side, the theater curtain hangs between white Corinthian columns, it's been raised, revealing pallets, blankets, sheets, bags, and shoes. Richard thinks he sees isolated figures lying under the blankets asleep, but he isn't sure.

I've studied now . . .

People are just taking turns introducing themselves, saying their names, and all of this is being translated twice.

411

Richard has attended many assemblies in the course of his lifetime, but never one like this.

Ich heisse, ich komme aus, ich bin hier, weil.

My name is, I'm from, I'm here because.

Je m'appelle, je suis de, je suis ici.

A good seventy people say who they are. *I've studied now Philosophy and Jurisprudence, Medicine – and even, alas! Theology – from end to end with labor keen.* The auditorium has an ornamental plaster ceiling with a chandelier in the middle, and dark paneling on the walls. Not so long ago, this was a high school.

Aus Mali, Äthiopien, Senegal. Aus Berlin.

From Mali, Ethiopia, Senegal. From Berlin.

Du Mali, de l'Éthiopie, du Sénégal. De Berlin.

A few jackets and t-shirts hang from the crossbars of the windows. Have they been hung up to dry? Where do they do laundry in this former school? Not so long ago, speeches were being made on this stage, and pieces played on the piano, newly admitted students were welcomed, and vale-dictorians honored. Plays were performed, the curtain was drawn aside to reveal Goethe's Faust seated at his desk. *And see that nothing can be known! That knowledge cuts me to the bone.* It's really true – even during this meeting, there are people lying under some of the blankets, asleep.

Aus Niger. Aus Ghana. Aus Serbien. Aus Berlin.

From Niger. From Ghana. From Serbia. From Berlin.

Du Niger. Du Ghana. De la Serbie. De Berlin.

Will they send him away for not being a local resident? He doesn't want to say who he is, or why he's here. Especially since he isn't sure himself. The few white people present include Kreuzberg neighbors, members of refugee-aid organizations, relief workers, and members of an initiative to turn the school into a cultural center, there are representatives from the district office, and the youth-services staff. There's a journalist, but she's asked to leave because the meeting isn't meant to be open to the general public. Among the many black people in attendance are some who have been living here in the school for eight months. Some have been living here for six months, and some have been living here for two. The refugees here state their names and say where they're from, unlike those at Alexanderplatz, but despite their willingness to do so, this doesn't seem to solve the problem. The capital of Ghana is Accra, the capital of Sierra Leone is Freetown, the capital of Niger Niamey.

No, Richard doesn't want to say his name.

Just as he's thinking this, an earsplitting bang is heard suddenly coming from the stairwell, something like an explosion that immediately eradicates all thinking, leaving behind only instinct. Instinctually, the relief worker knows: they are on the third floor. The man from Ghana knows the door to the other stairwell is locked. The neighbor: Don't they know there are white people here? Another neighbor asks herself, what'll happen to my son? Many of the refugees think: So in the end I just came here to die. Even Richard knows something: This is it.

But then all who've been covering their ears, including Richard, take their hands down, and they're still breathing, and now they start thinking again, and they think: So it wasn't a bomb. And they think again: But it could have easily been one.

But just at this moment when they're about to quickly sweep away all the fears they had – or that had them – just at this moment, the lights suddenly go out, and for a few seconds all the people in the room are black. What's going on? What's the idea? several people murmur in the room.

Good Lord, someone says. Then the light comes back on.

As if the past two minutes hadn't yet produced a sufficient quantity of unforeseen occurrences, the moment it's light again one of the Africans suddenly starts screaming and waving his arms around, cursing and hurling a pillow across the room, followed by a blanket. What's wrong? What's gotten into him? Is he in shock? No, someone says. What's happened is that during the explosion or the darkness that followed, someone stole his laptop from under his pillow. What's a refugee doing with a laptop? the neighbor thinks. He must be one of the men who sell drugs in the park around the corner, thinks the woman from down the block. The idea of private property doesn't work if all a person possesses is a blanket and pillow, thinks Richard, who for reasons unclear even to himself has made his way here from the suburbs. He walks past the screaming man, past the others who are trying to calm him down, he leaves behind the tumult and the auditorium in which the meeting hasn't really even started yet, and goes into the stairwell, which is still filled with swirling clouds from the firecrackers set off by some Berlin provocateur wanting to take a stand against the administration of the district office, or some youngster with dark skin who has nothing better to do than scare people to death, or a neo-fascist who hates the refugees and their sympathizers, or else some poor refugee who wanted to steal a laptop from some other poor refugee in a moment of panic.

Richard goes down the stairs, which are difficult to see because of all the smoke, and walks past the brightly lit but empty men's bathroom, down to the ground floor. If he weren't walking so slowly, for fear of missing his footing on the stairs, one might think he was fleeing.

7

It's lovely when everything smells of leaves in autumn, wet leaves that press into the earth and stick to the soles of your shoes. Unlocking the garden gate, filling his lungs with the dark air – this is what Richard's late-night homecomings have looked like for twenty years now. It's been autumn in this garden for twenty years. For twenty years it's smelled like this, and he's unlocked the garden gate in just this way and locked it again behind him. Time here is like a vast country to which one can return home season after season. Unlike many of his neighbors, Richard hasn't placed motion detectors in the trees to light his way when he passes among the trunks to go inside. Sometimes the moon is shining, but he doesn't mind when it's pitch black like tonight; then each step he takes belongs more to the forest than to him, and a state of wakefulness replaces seeing. Darkness – even the domesticated darkness of a garden – briefly turns a human being into a vulnerable animal. Then he remembers the man who even now, gently swaying, floats somewhere out there at the bottom of the lake.

Was he cowardly just now in Kreuzberg? Probably. Here in the garden it always seemed to him that his faint sense of fear bound him more closely to this place. Here in the garden, he was never afraid of the fear he felt. In the city, things are different. . . . His friends make fun of him because he still refuses to drive into the city center. Now that the Wall is gone, he no longer knows his way around. Now that the Wall is gone, the city is twice as big and has changed so much that he often doesn't recognize the intersections. Once he'd known all the city's bombed-out gaps, first with rubble, then without. Later still there might be a sausage stand, or

Christmas trees for sale, or often nothing at all. But recently all these gaps have been filled with buildings, corner lots built up again, firewalls no longer visible. As a child, before the Wall went up, he sold blueberries (having picked them himself) at the West Berlin train station Gesundbrunnen so he could buy his first glossy ball. Glossy rubber balls existed only in the West. When he saw the Gesundbrunnen station for the first time after the fall of the Wall, the tracks leading east were completely overgrown with tall grass, the platforms covered with birch trees swaying in the wind. If he'd been a city planner, he'd have left it just like that in memory of the divided city, and to symbolize the ephemeral nature of all things built by human hands, and maybe just because a stand of birch trees on a train-station platform is beautiful.

Richard pours himself a glass of whiskey and turns on the TV. There are several talk shows, an old Western, news programs, a film with an Alpine setting, animal films, action films, quiz shows, science fiction, and crime dramas. He turns off the sound and goes over to his desk. While behind him a female police detective rattles a basement doorknob, he glances through some papers lying on his desk: insurance policies, telephone contracts, the invoice from the auto-repair workshop. He didn't want to say his name at the assembly just now, but why not? An assembly at which seventy people introduce themselves one after the other – how utterly absurd. Even now, at his desk, he shakes his head at the thought, while the detective behind him speaks with a teenage girl crouching in a corner in tears. Saying his name, it appeared to him, would have been a sort of confession – at the very least he'd have been confessing his presence at that gathering. But how is it anyone's business he was there? He isn't trying to help anyone, he doesn't live near the school, and he wasn't sent by the Senate. He just wants to watch and be left in peace while he's watching. He isn't a part of a group, his interest is his own, it belongs only to him and he is completely dispassionate. If he hadn't been so cool-headed all his professional life, he wouldn't have understood so much. Probably the attempt to find out who was there in the auditorium had something to do with the state of war that had overtaken the building. But what does a name tell you? A person who wants to lie can always lie. You have to know a lot more than just the name, otherwise there's no point. Richard gets up, goes over to the sofa, and sits in front of the silent TV for a moment with his last sip of whiskey. A young man has grabbed an older one by the collar and is shoving him against a wall, both are screaming at each other, then the young man lets go again, the other one leaves, and the young man shouts something after him. Then he sees the detective's office with its glass walls, blinds, coffee cups, papers . . .

8

At breakfast, Richard has Earl Grey with milk and sugar, accompanied by a slice of bread with honey and another with cheese. On the radio, Bach's *Goldberg Variations* are playing. Years ago, Richard gave a lecture on the topic 'Language as a System of Signs.' Words as signs for things. Language as a skin. But words remained words all the same. They were never the thing itself. You had to know a lot more than just the name, otherwise there was no point. What makes a surface a surface? What separates a surface from what lies below it, what separates it from the air? As a child, Richard used to push the skin around on his hot milk

– a repulsive skin that had been milk just a moment before. What's a name made of? Sound? But not even that if it's written and not spoken. Maybe that's why he loves to listen to Bach: there are no surfaces, just crisscrossing storylines. Crossing here, crossing there, moment after moment, and all these crossings join together to make something that in Bach's world is called music. Each moment is like slicing into a piece of meat, into the thing itself. This year he'll reserve himself a ticket for the *Christmas Oratorio* in the cathedral again. For the first time since his wife's death. He clears his plate, shakes the crumbs into the garbage can, then takes his coat and slips into the brown shoes that are his most comfortable pair – never brown in town, they say, but no matter. If you fall off a galloping horse, they say, you should get right back in the saddle and keep going, otherwise the fear creeps into your bones forever. Fear is what he felt yesterday in the occupied school. So: stove off, lights off, keys, subway pass.

Walking across Oranienplatz in broad daylight is easier than paying a nocturnal visit to a godforsaken school. Not long after the fall of the Wall, Richard went to Kreuzberg with his wife for the first time. They'd gotten into the habit of walking in one of the city's Western districts every Sunday. (The evening before, they'd read up on the neighborhood in a guidebook, and then on Sunday morning they'd take their stroll.) Huguenot refugees were the original settlers in the streets surrounding Oranienplatz – lots of gardeners among them, apparently – long before Kreuzberg was part of the city proper. And then Lenné planned out the shape of the square the century before last, back when there'd still been a canal here, the square forming its banks, with a bridge where the street is now. Later Richard showed his lover this square, explaining to her who Lenné was, there was a good bookstore around the corner, a repertory cinema, and a lovely café.

Now the square looks like a construction site: a landscape of tents, wooden shacks, and tarps: white, blue, and green. He sits down on a park bench, looks around, and listens to what's being said. No one here asks his name. What does he see? What does he hear? He sees banners and propped-up signs with hand-painted slogans. He sees black men and white sympathizers, the refugees are wearing freshly laundered pants, colorful jackets, and striped shirts, light-colored sweatshirts with vivid lettering – where do you do laundry on an occupied square? One of them is wearing gold-colored sneakers. Could he be Hermes? The sympathizers have white skin, but their clothing is black and torn, their pants, their t-shirts, and sweaters. The sympathizers are young and pale, they dye their hair with henna, they refuse to believe that the world is an idyllic place and want everything to change, for which reason they put rings through their lips, ears, and noses. The refugees, on the other hand, are trying to gain admittance to this world that appears to them convincingly idyllic. Here on the square, these two forms of wishing and hoping cross paths, there's an overlap between them, but this silent observer doubts that the overlap is large.

Before Richard moved to the outskirts with his wife, they'd lived in an apartment, a mere two hundred yards as the crow flies from West Berlin. And they lived there almost as peacefully as they later lived in the countryside. The Wall had turned their street into a cul-de-sac where children roller-skated. Then in 1990 the Wall was cleared away piece by piece, and each time a new crossing point was opened, a crowd of emotional West Berliners punctually gathered, eager to bid a warm welcome to their brothers and sisters from the East. One morning, he himself became the object of these tearful welcomes: the East Berliner who'd lived on this street that had been cut in half for twenty-nine years, crossing over on his way to freedom. But he hadn't been on his way to freedom that morning, he was only trying to get to the University, punctually taking advantage of the S-Bahn station at the western end of his newly opened street. Unemotional and in a hurry, he'd used his elbows to fight his way through this weeping crowd – one of the disappointed liberators shouted an insult at his back – but for the very first time, Richard got to school in under twenty minutes.

Just a year ago, the park bench he's now sitting on was just a perfectly normal bench in a Kreuzberg park. People out for walks would sit down here to rest their legs and relax. In the 1920s, the canal that had existed here in Lenné's time was filled in by the city government because it stank so badly. Is the water still flowing down there somewhere among the grains of sand?

In any case, no one sits here these days out of a desire to relax. If Richard doesn't get right back up again, it's only because he isn't here for recreational purposes. The ordinary activity of sitting on a park bench has lost its ordinariness because of the refugees camping on the grass behind the benches. Berliners who've known since Lenné's time how to comport themselves in this park while seated on a bench are no longer certain: there's no old lady feeding the sparrows, no mother rocking her baby carriage gently back and forth, no student reading, no trio of drinkers conducting their morning meeting, no office worker eating his midday snack, no lovers holding hands. 'The Transformation of Sitting' might be a good title for an essay. Richard remains seated, remaining in spite of. Whenever an 'in spite of' occurs, in his experience, things get interesting. 'The Birth of In Spite Of' would make a good title for an essay too.

The only person with white skin who seems to be just as much at home in this square as the refugees is a rawboned woman in her early forties. She's just showing a Turkish man where he can leave the flatbreads he's brought as a contribution. Somewhat later she accepts a bicycle from a man with a beard, passing it on to one of the refugees, and both watch the refugee as he happily pedals off. He's got shrapnel in his lung, by the way, she says, and the bearded man nods. Libya, she says, he nods, then both are silent for a moment. The man says, I guess I'll be on my way. A young woman with a microphone in her hand approaches.

I'm not doing any interviews just now, the rawboned woman says.

But it's important that the Berliners—

Maybe you've heard that negotiations are underway for winter lodgings.

That's why I'm here, the interviewer says.

Has he already started looking like a bum, is that why the two women seem unfazed that he's sitting here just a few feet away from them, listening?

Then you might also know that the Senate's only offering eighteen euros a night per man from now until April.

Yes, I've—

Well, the rawboned woman says, the only one who's willing to offer housing to these men is already asking for twice as much. So if you write in your newspaper that there are rats here and only four toilets left, and sometimes nothing warm to eat for three days, and if you write that last winter tents collapsed under the weight of the snow, then I promise

421

you: the only person who'll be happy about your article is this investor.

Oh, the young woman says, I see. She lowers her microphone.

Once again Richard thinks – as so often in recent years – that the effects of a person's actions are almost always impossible to predict and often prove to be the exact opposite of what the person originally intended. And if the same principle holds true in this case, he thinks, it's possibly because the Berlin Senate's negotiations with the refugees all have to do with borders, and a border is a place where, at least in mathematics, signs often change their value. No wonder, he thinks, the word *dealings* refers not just to actions but also business and trade.

Now not switching on her microphone, the young interviewer asks the rawboned woman:

What do the men do here all day long if they're not allowed to work?

Nothing, the woman says. And as she turns away, she adds: When doing nothing gets to be too much for them, we organize a demonstration.

I understand, the interviewer says, nodding, and now the rawboned woman walks away.

Then she packs up her microphone again, still standing in front of the bench he's sitting on with her back to him, not noticing that all this time she's had a silent observer. Meanwhile the rawboned woman walks over to the open tent that appears to be the kitchen, pausing on the way to pick up a wooden signboard that's fallen over and ripped a hole in a tent nearby.

Richard sees one black man walking over to another and shaking his hand in greeting. He sees a group of five men

422

standing together talking, one of them is on the phone. He sees the man who was given the bicycle riding in a circle around the square, sometimes even weaving riskily among others on the gravel paths. He sees three of the refugees in an open tent sitting behind a table, in front of them a cardboard box labeled 'Donations.' He sees an older man sitting alone on the back of a bench – there's something wrong with his eye – and a man with a blue tattoo on his face thumping another on the shoulder in parting. He sees one man chatting with a female sympathizer, and another in a tent with an open flap, he's sitting on a cot, typing something into a phone. There's someone lying on the next cot, but only the feet are visible. He sees two men having an argument in a language incomprehensible to him, when one of them raises his voice and shoves the other away with a hand to his chest, making him stumble backward, the man on the bicycle has to swerve to avoid them. He sees the rawboned woman speaking with a man in the kitchen holding a cooking pot, and he sees the elegant corner building that furnishes the backdrop for all of this, probably dating back to around the period when there was still a canal where he is sitting. It looks like a former department store, but now there's a bank on the ground floor. Back when there was a canal here, Germany still had colonies. The word *Kolonialwaren* was still visible in weathered script on some East Berlin facades as recently as twenty years ago, until the West started renovating everything, including the last vestiges of these ancient grocer's shops with their imported wares. *Kolonialwaren* and WWII bullet holes might adorn the very same storefront. (The dusty shop window of such a building – its tenants evicted to prepare for renovation – might also display a Socialist cardboard sign reading *Obst Gemüse Speisekartoffeln* (*OGS*) to advertise the 'fruit, vegetables, and potatoes' that gave East German greengrocers their acronym.) You can still find 'German East Africa' on the globe in his study. The paper covering the sphere is peeling a little over the Mariana Trench, but the globe is still nice to look at. Richard has no idea what German East Africa is called today. He wonders whether, back when there was still a canal right where he's sitting now, slaves were sold at that department store. Might black servants have carried the sacks of coal up to the fifth-floor apartments of Lenné's contemporaries? The idea makes him grin. An old man sitting alone on a park bench grinning to himself might raise eyebrows. Anyhow, what's he waiting for? Does he really think that after a year of these men camping out on this square, something unforeseen might happen today of all days, just when he's decided to come visiting from the suburbs? Nothing happens, and after two and a half hours he starts to feel chilly, so he gets up from the bench and goes home.

Often when he was starting a new project, he didn't know what was driving him, as if his thoughts had developed an independent life and a will of their own, as if they were merely waiting for him to finally think them, as if an investigation he was about to begin already existed before he had started working on it, and the path leading through everything he knew and saw, everything he encountered and experienced, already lay there waiting for him to venture down it. And probably that's just how it was, given that you could only ever find what was already there. Because everything is always already there. In the afternoon, he rakes leaves for the first time. In the evening, the newscaster says it's just a matter of time before a solution is found for the untenable situation of the refugees on Oranienplatz. Richard's heard sentences like this many instances before, referring to all

424

sorts of untenable situations. Other things too – the leaves becoming earth again, the drowned man washing up on shore or dissolving in the lake – are basically just a matter of time. But what does that mean? He doesn't even know yet if time exists for the purpose of making various layers and paths overlap, or if it's to keep things separate – maybe the newscaster knows. Richard feels irritated without knowing why. Later, already lying in bed, he remembers something the rawboned woman said: When doing nothing gets to be too much for them, we organize a demonstration. And suddenly he knows why he spent two hours today sitting on Oranienplatz. It's something he already knew back in August when he first heard about the hunger strikers – the men who refused to give their names – and he knew it when he walked into the black schoolyard yesterday, but only now, in this moment, does he know it fully. Speaking about the actual nature of time is something he can probably do best in conversation with those who have fallen out of it. Or been locked up in it, if you prefer. Next to him, on the half of the bed still covered with the bedspread – the half where his wife used to sleep – lie a few of his sweaters, slacks, and shirts that he's worn over the last few days and hasn't yet cleared away.

ACKNOWLEDGMENTS

CHLOE ARIDJIS: Chapter 1 from *Book of Clouds*, published by Black Cat Books, a division of Grove/Atlantic, and Chatto and Windus, a division of Penguin Random House. Copyright © 2009 by Chloe Aridjis.

KEVIN BARRY: 'Berlin Arkonaplatz – My Lesbian Summer' from *Dark Lies the Island*, Vintage Books (UK), first published in 2012 by Jonathan Cape. Graywolf Press, 2013.

THOMAS BRUSSIG: Extract from 'Tape 5', section of *Heroes Like Us* (Harvill Press). Translated by John Brownjohn. Reprinted with permission from Farrar, Straus & Giroux. Copyright © Verlag Volk und Welt GmbH. Orginally published 1995.

LEN DEIGHTON: Chapter 5 from *Funeral in Berlin* (HarperCollins), copyright © by Pluriform Publishing c/o Jonathan Clowes Limited. Originally published 1964.

ALFRED DÖBLIN: *Berlin Alexanderplatz*, excerpt from Chapter 2, translated by Michael Hofmann, Penguin Random House UK (Penguin Classics, 2018). New York Review of Books, 2018. Originally published in 1929 by S. Fischer Verlag, Berlin.

JENNY ERPENBECK: Extract (pp. 10–38) from *Go, Went, Gone*, translated by Susan Bernofsky (Portobello Books, Granta, 2017; New Directions, 2017). Originally published by Albrecht Knaus Verlag, Munich, Random House Group, 2015.

HANS FALLADA: Chapters 13–14 from *Alone in Berlin*, translated by Michael Hofmann (Penguin Modern Classics). Penguin Random House UK and Melville House Publishing, New York (as *Every Man Dies Alone*), 2009. Original copyright © Aufbau-Verlagsgruppe, Berlin. First published 1947.

THEODOR FONTANE: Chapter 23 from *Effi Briest*, Oxford World's Classics, Oxford University Press. Translation copyright © Mike Mitchell 2015. Editorial material copyright © Ritchie Robertson 2015. Reproduced with permission of the Licensor through PLSclear. First published in 1895.

GÜNTER GRASS: 'The Diving Duck' from *Too Far Afield*, translated by Krishna Winston. Translation copyright © by Harcourt Inc, 2000. Faber & Faber Limited. *Ein weites Feld* © Steidl Verlag. Originally published in 1995.

ERNST HAFFNER: *Blood Brothers*, Chapter 12. Translated by Michael Hofmann. Harvill Secker, London; Other Press, New York, 2015. Originally published by B. Cassirer, Berlin, 1932 and republished in 2013 by Metrolit, Berlin.

CHRISTOPHER ISHERWOOD: 'A Berlin Diary: 1932–3' from *Goodbye to Berlin*, copyright © Christopher Isherwood 1939. First published by the Hogarth Press, 1939; Vintage Books (UK), 1998. New Directions Publishing Corporation, 2012.

WLADIMIR KAMINER: 'Business Camouflage', translated by Michael Hulse, from *Russian Disco*, Ebury Press (Penguin Random House Group), 2002. Originally published in 2000 by Wilhelm Goldmann Verlag, Munich.

ERICH KÄSTNER: From *Going to the Dogs*, Chapter 1. Copyright © Atrium Verlag, Zürich. Reprinted with permission. Translation by Cyrus Brooks, A. M. Heath Literary Agency. Originally published 1931.

IRMGARD KEUN: Extract from Chapter 2 (pp. 55–70) of *The Artificial Silk Girl*, translated by Kathie von Ankum, Other Press, New York, 2002. First published 1932.

IAN McEWAN: Chapter 4 from *The Innocent* (1990). Vintage Books UK, 1998. Rogers Coleridge & White Limited. Georges Borchardt Inc.

VLADIMIR NABOKOV: Chapter 2 of *King, Queen, Knave* (1968). Penguin Random House Inc. The Wylie Agency.

HEINZ REIN: Prologue from *Finale Berlin* (Penguin Books). First published 1947. Translation copyright © 2019 by Shaun Whiteside. Reprinted with permission.

PETER SCHNEIDER: Chapter 1 from *The Wall Jumper* translated by Leigh Hafrey (Penguin Modern Classics). Originally published 1982. Copyright © Hermann Luchterhand Verlag / Rowohlt Verlag Gmbh. Translation copyright © 1983 by Random House Inc.

UWE TIMM: 'The Reichstag, Wrapped' from *Midsummer Night*, translated by Peter Tegel, published by New Directions Publishing Corporation (1998). Originally published by Verlag Kiepenhauer & Witsch, Cologne, 1996.

JEAN-PHILLIPE TOUSSAINT: Extract from *Television* (pp. 1–24), translated by Jordan Stump, Dalkey Archive Press, 2004. Originally published as *La Télévision* by Les Editions de Minuit, 1997. Reprinted with permission. Georges Borchardt Inc.

ROBERT WALSER: 'The Little Berliner' (1909), translated by Harriet Watts, from *The Selected Stories of Robert Walser*, Farrar, Straus & Giroux, 1982 and Vintage Books, UK, 1983.

CHRISTA WOLF: Chapters 26 and 27 from *They Divided the Sky*, translated by Luise von Flotow, University of Ottawa Press, 2013. First published in 1963, *Der geteilte Himmel*, copyright Suhrkamp Verlag, Berlin.

THOMAS WOLFE: 'The Dark Messiah', Chapter 38 of *You Can't Go Home Again*, published by Harper & Row, 1940. The Estate of Thomas Wolfe, c/o McIntosh and Otis, Inc.